Puritan

By David Hingley

Birthright
Puritan

Puritan

DAVID HINGLEY

Allison & Busby Limited
12 Fitzroy Mews
London W1T 6DW
allisonandbusby.com

First published in Great Britain by Allison & Busby in 2017.

Copyright © 2017 by DAVID HINGLEY

A CIP catalogue record for this book is available from
the British Library.

First Edition

ISBN 978-0-7490-2028-6

Typeset in 11.75/16.75 pt Adobe Garamond Pro by
Allison & Busby Ltd.

The paper used for this Allison & Busby publication
has been produced from trees that have been legally sourced
from well-managed and credibly certified forests.

Printed and bound by
CPI Group (UK) Ltd, Croydon, CR0 4YY

For Mom and Dad,
who nurtured my love of learning

Chapter One

The red blur flew past Mercia's cheek, chill air skimming her face. From atop her nervous horse she looked around, staring at the elm tree quivering beside her. A din of blue and black ascended screeching from its branches; loose leaves fluttered to the earthen ground, settling on top of others now turned a dirty brown from the soil the steady rain was trickling across them.

For a moment she hesitated, but then she shifted in her saddle, her eyes settling on the elm's warped trunk. A slender pole was trembling level with the topknot of her hair, the painted axe head at its end embedded deep in the bark. Still uncertain, her horse pulled up short, taking its lead from the others around it.

As her travelling party reacted to the hatchet, two men rode into place to surround her. Behind, Nathan Keyte, her great friend and perhaps now her lover, not losing his grip on the boy riding with him: her son. In front, Nicholas Wildmoor, her manservant, positioning himself between her horse and the forest, his youthful green eyes the colour of the leaves on their branches as they waited for their annual fall.

A rustling in the bushes – a murmuring – a collective intake of breath. The men in her group – they were all men, besides her – drew firearms, pointing them towards the woods. Mercia took her own pistol from the belt around her dress, specially tailored down the middle so she could ride the rough forest paths more easily. Nathan had insisted on it, as she had on the pistol: she had to protect her son in case of attack.

A barely dressed man stepped onto the forest trail, the anger on his face apparent. The muscles of his bare abdomen hardened above his deerskin breechclout as he clenched a wooden spear adorned with feathers and colourful beads. His many bracelets of white and blue wampum jangled against its tip.

'*Nummayaôntam!*' he cried.

One of Mercia's group signalled to the rest to keep still. After a fashion they complied, although their fingers continued to twitch on their pistols. She glanced left and right; the men's faces were grim, but they held back. Then the man who had signalled turned to the Indian on the path.

'*Tawhìtch musquaw . . . naméan?*' he said, stumbling over the syllables in his broad English accent. '*Wutti . . . neapum . . . mushâuta!*'

'What did you say?' his nearest companion whispered, his thumb stroking the arming mechanism of his loaded doglock.

'I asked him why he was angry, to let us pass.' The man nodded at his friend's gun. 'Best put that down.'

His companion scoffed, not lowering his pistol. 'Can these heathens not learn English?'

The Indian advanced. 'We speak English much better than you do our words. But we know the tongue you prefer is that of death.' Reaching into the fur pouch tied onto his belt, he pulled out a knife, stained with blood; in front of Mercia, Nathan tensed, but the Indian merely threw the weapon to the ground. 'You know this blade, I think.'

The interpreter jumped from his horse to pick up the knife. 'No,' he blinked, turning it in his hands. 'I do not.'

'Then perhaps you will know this.' He let out a screech, a shrill sound more of a bird of the forest than of a man. A ragged object flew from the undergrowth, crashing on the dirty track near to Nathan's horse.

Mercia peered round to be repulsed by a severed head, the pale skin of an Englishman turning grey amidst sunken cheeks. The blood at the neck was black and congealed. She looked away, nauseous, involuntarily thinking of her father.

'Savage dog!' The interpreter's companion pulled his trigger, but his fury impaired his aim; the bullet went wide, ploughing instead into the bushes. A high-pitched voice screamed out in pain, a boy tumbling from his hiding place, clutching his shoulder. Of a sudden a mass of angry men, their shining bodies covered in grease, stormed onto the trail. Nicholas hugged his horse closer to Mercia's, but then another, sombrely dressed man in their party rode forward, turning aside a young follower who had been shielding him just as Nathan and Nicholas had been protecting her.

'*Aquétuck!*' he shouted at their assailants, holding up a wrinkled hand, and then to his own men: 'Stop!' He halted his horse in front of the Indian who had spoken, raising his hands in a gesture of peace, all the while exposed to being hacked down where he sat. The Indian stared up at him a moment, breathing steadily, before curtly nodding and barking orders to his own men. Grumbling, they lowered their hatchets and guns, glaring at their leader in their bloodlust, but obeying his instructions nonetheless.

'Powwow Winthrop,' said the Indian. 'For you I will listen.' He narrowed his eyes. 'But only as it is you.'

'*Cowauôntam.*' Winthrop bowed in his saddle. 'Your wisdom is strong, *sachem.*' His eyes flicked to the severed head. 'Now, let us talk.'

The road to New England should have been well worn after several years' use, but the track was tortuous as it weaved through the dim forest. The deep ruts were causing trouble even for horses accustomed to the colonial wilderness, and the recent rain was making the grooves slippery, the going becoming slower still. As Mercia made her way into a river valley, the water running swiftly below, Nicholas's horse skidded in the mud behind, knocking its head into the flank of her mount. But she kept her balance, soon reaching the narrow river that blocked their path.

While she was waiting her turn to ford the stuttering stream – the men liked her to go in the middle; they thought she needed the protection – Winthrop fell in alongside her.

'Do not mind the men,' he said. 'After that excitement they are anxious for home.'

Mercia nodded. 'I can understand that, Governor.'

Winthrop smiled, his face creasing under his broad-brimmed hat. 'You tire of America already, Mrs Blakewood?'

'Why, no.' She looked up at the trees, the elms by now familiar from their three-day ride. 'Surprise encounters aside, it is . . . invigorating. So unlike home. But home will always be home.'

'I too once thought of England as home,' he mused, fiddling with the reins of his horse. 'But that was above thirty years ago. Now home could never be anywhere but here. I am more pleased than you know that you accepted my invitation to visit us.' He lifted his rein with a gloved hand, pointing towards the riverbank. 'It appears you are next.'

'Careful!' Beckoning her approach, one of the party was shouting louder than he needed: the river was not roaring and there was no wind to steal his words. ''Tis a narrow crossing, but the rains have made it swift. Will you manage to ford it?'

'Will I manage?' she muttered. 'Narrow is right. 'Tis no more than the breadth of this horse.'

Pulling her hood around her, she made sure her grip was tight and sped towards the riverbank. Without stopping she leapt her horse across; its back hooves splashed into water on the other side, but its front legs found muddy land and it pulled itself up to stop beside Nathan who had forded immediately before her.

He shook his head and smiled. 'Always the hard way with you.'

She shrugged. 'Hardly a difficult jump.'

'Well done, Mamma!' Astride Nathan's horse, her son beamed up at her, joy across his young face. 'Can I try?'

Pleased at his approval, she laughed. 'No, Daniel. There will be plenty of chance to ride horses while we are here, but no leaping rivers. And— oh!' She looked behind as she heard a loud thud. Nicholas had made the same jump she had.

'See what you have started,' said Nathan.

'I don't know,' said Nicholas. 'An Indian ambush, and now a river jump. Who says the New World is dull?'

'I have not found it so,' she agreed.

'No.' Nathan calmed his anxious horse. 'But let us hope it is duller in Connecticut than it was in New York.'

Not many miles beyond the river, they emerged from the forest to pass through the town of New Haven, its nine squares of houses laid out around a central green, but they did not stop. As they were passing a white-boarded house set apart on the outskirts of town, she thought she saw Winthrop give her a hasty glance before looking up at the first-floor windows and quickly away. Following his gaze she was too late to see whoever had been peering out, but she thought she had seen two silhouettes. And then a blurred figure returned, only to vanish as she inclined her head, wondering who was watching.

It was a similar story in the main part of the small town, although here most stayed standing at their windows or doors, happy to be seen. Many wore angry grimaces, one woman even hissing as Winthrop passed beneath. He turned his serious face to look up at her; she narrowed her eyes but kept silent, and the party moved on, leaving the town behind.

'Seems like trouble,' said Nathan, back in the forest.

Winthrop manoeuvred his horse alongside them. 'We – that is my brothers and sisters in Connecticut – are in the process of welcoming New Haven into our fold. But as you see, some of the townsfolk would prefer to remain apart.'

Mercia raised an eyebrow. 'But you think differently, Governor?'

'Let us just say I do not think they will have much choice.' He sighed.

'Now the King's brother has taken New Amsterdam and renamed it for himself, they find themselves caught between his new lands and ours.' He raised an eyebrow of his own. 'I would hope they would prefer to join their fellow New Englanders than risk being absorbed by the royal advance.'

Nathan steadied his horse on the bumpy track. 'I take it you have little confidence the Duke will keep to the lands he was granted?'

'Already he has claimed Long Island. We have our charter, but still, our boundaries are somewhat porous. With the Dutch as our neighbours we managed, but with the Duke of York, well – you have met him, I believe.'

Mercia blew out her cheeks. 'Indeed I have.'

He glanced at her askance. 'What did you think?'

'He was not happy when the King gave Nathan and I permission to sail here with his fleet. I do not know.' She played with her reins. 'He did not seem to care much for women. But he has a prize in New York.'

Winthrop nodded. ''Tis where it is sited, at the mouth of Hudson's river. I do not think my cousins in Massachusetts Bay would care to hear me say so, Mrs Blakewood, but one day I think New York could grow greater than Boston itself. And if that happens – well. I want New Haven with us, and not with him.'

They rode a few minutes in quiet, listening to the strange bird calls trilling in the close-packed trees. The gnarled trunks were covered in beard-like moss, the air around them clear and fresh. Away from the town, Mercia felt a renewed shiver of apprehension after the morning's incident, although she knew she was safe in the company of the governor.

She cleared the lump from her throat. 'Nobody wants to speak of the Indians,' she said. 'But you seem to have an understanding with them, Governor. What did you and the – *sachem* is it? – talk of?'

Winthrop nodded sadly. 'If you think the Duke is a problem, then the

Indians are no less difficult. Not in themselves, you understand, for they are a people of no small nobility. But there are those among both them and us who are not so keen to live in harmony. Many would sooner wage war than have peace.'

'We hear tales back in England,' said Nathan. 'In the coffee houses and the pamphlets. Probably most of it is untrue, but well.' He glanced at Mercia. 'They are not as savage as they say?'

'Any more so than many Europeans?' Winthrop smiled. 'I should say we are all God's children, all behaving in similar ways.'

'What of that head?' said Nicholas, riding just behind them. 'I thought there was going to be a fight back there.'

'That was . . . one of our own miscreants, I am afraid. A man named Atterley who thought he had licence to kill Indians whenever they strayed onto his land. Or what he said was his land.' He sighed. 'It is a difficult line we have to tread here, for the Indians claim they have right to the land, while my fellows seek to buy it, sometimes take it by force. Often there is conflict. That knife the *sachem* showed us was used to kill the tribe's powwow. Their healer.'

'And so they took their vengeance on Atterley,' said Nathan.

'In part. But mostly they think to remind us of our promises, that when one of ours is to blame for a crime then we root out the culprit and punish him. And their powwow was important, a great figure in their heathen devotions. They will not forgive so easily as that.' Winthrop shuddered as a sudden gust of wind rose up. 'My task is to delay that reckoning such that it never occurs.'

Nathan shook his head. 'Even here, in this place of beauty, there is strife.'

'Indeed our ways of life oft times resemble those in England. Think of the recent wars you had, family against family, Royalist against Parliamentarian.' He pulled at his white neck collar. 'But let us not dwell on such miseries. We will soon be in Hartford. I should rather you look around and enjoy the ride.'

Mercia was glad to accept the suggestion, interested as she was in the discussion, for as ever the journey fascinated her. Still, it was two bedraggled days more before they came to the end of their road. The final stretch took them along the Connecticut River for which Winthrop's colony was named, and she was entranced by the majesty of the watercourse as it ambled amidst the cultivated fields of the townships that had sprung up along its banks. The few people who were travelling the road, or fishing in the river, doffed their hats to the governor as they passed by; she was impressed as he hailed them in return, seeming to know most of their names.

By the time they arrived in Hartford the sun had replaced the rain, domesticated pigs grunting their porcine welcome to the travellers who had crossed the ocean just a fortnight before. The principal town of Connecticut colony, Hartford was of a decent size, larger than New Haven but likewise centred on a well-kept green, its two-storey houses enjoying elongated plots set back from the few roads. As in the countryside, the townsfolk bowed to Winthrop in respect, then stared with interest at his unknown companions. Mercia had decided to forego the mourning clothes she had worn for the last six months for her father, but choice was limited, and she was still only wearing a simple grey dress. But she felt like a fine lady as she resisted the temptation to wave.

Then a commotion rang out, a portly man hurtling from a nearby doorway. Wheezing, he ran up to Winthrop, patting his horse's flanks as though signalling him to stop.

'Governor,' he cried. He paused to catch his breath, resting his palms on his corpulent thighs. 'I am glad you are returned.'

Winthrop reined in his horse, peering down from under his hat. 'Were matters that complex in my absence, Peter?' He tutted. 'Speak, man. What is it?'

''Tis Meltwater.' The man looked up, his red cheeks paling. 'Their minister. He's been found!'

14

Winthrop looked skywards. 'Thank the Lord,' he began. 'I was beginning to fear—'

'No.' The frantic man cut him off. 'It is to be feared.'

Winthrop frowned. 'Well?'

'He has been found in the river, Governor.' The man swallowed. 'Found dead. He has drowned.'

Chapter Two

'I am sorry.' Winthrop entered his small dining room, skirting the candlelit table where Mercia and Nathan were already seated. A middle-aged servant pulled out a splendid oaken chair at its head. 'That was not the welcome to Hartford I had hoped for.'

She waited for him to sit. 'We should be sorry for the poor minister. Such a terrible accident.'

'Yes,' said Winthrop, unfolding his napkin. 'Very . . . peculiar.' Mercia inclined her head, curious at his tone, but he merely smiled. 'Shall we eat? My wife will join us shortly, when the food has been prepared to her liking. In the meantime, she wants you to start with this soup.'

On cue, the servant strode to the door, cutting off Nathan's unasked question as he beckoned in a smartly dressed maid. Setting down Winthrop's bowl and glass of ale first, her eyes flicked to Nathan as she placed the other two settings and left, the servant following close behind to pull shut the door.

'This looks delicious.' Mercia took in the thick broth before her, crammed with vegetables and chunks of meat. 'What is it?'

'Merely a potage, made with spices and beef.' Winthrop picked up his spoon. 'We thought you might be hungry.'

'You are right there.' Nathan inhaled deeply. 'Mace, and – cinnamon? It smells wonderful.'

Winthrop's face creased in delight. 'Then please, enjoy.'

The diners fell silent as they slurped on their soup. When next Mercia looked up, she caught Winthrop looking at her with an inquisitive air.

'I do not mean to stare,' he said, 'but – you look so like your father. I had noticed it in New York, of course, but only now you are sitting at a table like this, in a room such as this, has the resemblance seemed so striking.'

'Let us be thankful the resemblance does not extend to his nose,' joked Nathan, breaking off a chunk of bread. Across the table, Mercia gave the air a playful swipe.

Despite his words, Winthrop was still staring. 'It is not merely his appearance you have inherited, I believe.'

'It is . . . about the only thing I have inherited, Governor.'

His face saddened. 'Again, I am sorry. I did not think.'

'Do not be.' She gave him a forgiving smile. 'There is hope.'

'More than hope,' said Nathan. 'The King has to help now.'

'Then let us hope. And Governor, do not worry over your choice of words. I was being facetious.'

Winthrop relaxed his perturbed countenance. 'In truth I was rather poorly attempting to render you a compliment. What I mean to say, is that you have proven you have your father's intelligence likewise.'

She felt herself reddening. 'Thank you. That gratifies me more than any comment about appearance.'

Winthrop nodded; there was something behind it, she thought, a decision taken. So she was not surprised when the governor pushed back his chair and stood, waving Nathan back into his seat as he rose from his own.

'I merely wish to fetch something. Please, I will not be long.'

Mercia arched a questioning eyebrow as Winthrop left the room, but Nathan shrugged and fell back to eating his soup. She toyed with her own bowl, tracing patterns with her spoon as she thought about her father, a still unconquered sadness fighting her hunger for dominance. Then she felt a hand on her own; with no one else in the room, Nathan had reached across to comfort her.

'Do not worry,' he said. 'Everything will turn out well.'

'I hope so, Nat. It is . . . still hard.'

'I know. But I am here to help.'

She smiled, grateful for his presence. Then a confident knock resounded at the door and she pulled her hand from his, turning to look. Expecting the servant, she was surprised when a young man's head appeared round the door, even more so when his inquisitive expression morphed into a frown on catching her eye.

'Is the governor not here?' he said.

'He will be back shortly. Would you care to wait?'

He looked her up and down, his broad-brimmed hat peppered with light rain. 'I do not think so.'

'Who are you talking to?' A tall, brown-haired woman pushed past. 'Oh, I see. Who are you?'

'Good evening.' Mercia nodded as she stood. 'We are guests of the governor's.'

Nathan rose and bowed. 'Nathan Keyte.'

The woman shook the felt hat she was carrying in greeting. 'You are not from these parts, I take it?'

The young man set his face, staring at the ceiling. 'We do not have time for this, Clemency.'

She rolled her grey eyes. 'As the governor is not here, I think we do. Where are you both from?'

'By God's truth!' Letting out an expletive, the man turned to leave.

'From England,' said Mercia, undeterred.

Clemency frowned. 'Not . . . recently arrived?'

'Why, yes.'

'England?' In the doorway, the man stopped. 'Surely not with the royal fleet?'

18

Nathan folded his arms. 'What of it?'

The man marched into the room, his thin coat as dotted with rain spots as his hat. 'Why are you here?'

'As has been said, we are guests at the governor's invitation.' Nathan drew himself up, tugging at his collar to let the tip of his chest scar peek out through his shirt. 'Who are you?'

'Someone with more right to be here than you do, stranger.' The man kept his gaze constant, clearly unconcerned at the Englishman's superior height and bulk. 'I should take care folk do not misconstrue your reason for being in New England. Unless perhaps they would be right?'

'A welcoming fellow, aren't you?'

'Percy.' Clemency cleared her throat. 'Percy, perhaps we should leave these people be and wait outside?'

The man locked his eyes on Nathan a moment longer, but then he broke off, retreating towards the door. Clemency shook her head, mouthing an apology at Mercia before leaving behind him.

'What was that about?' said Nathan, staring at the now empty doorway.

'I do not know.' Mercia shook her head. 'I thought you were about to start a fight there.'

'With that whelp?' He breathed out, relaxing his shoulders. 'Besides, I don't think the governor would appreciate blood on his table.'

'Well, whoever he was, he did not like the idea we came with the fleet.'

'I suppose why would he? People here are bound to be uneasy now the Duke of York's soldiers are roaming the old Dutch lands to their west. The Duke has no love for New England and you can bet they know it.' He sighed, rubbing at his neck. 'But that does not excuse incivility to you.'

'Indeed it does not.' Winthrop came back through the doorway, clutching a piece of paper. 'I am sorry about Mr Lavington. I have told him I will talk with him later – after my dinner with you.' He smiled, the simple act dissipating the tension Mercia realised had filled the room. 'Now,' he continued, 'shall we resume our conversation? And please, do not think all New Englanders are as impatient as our friend there.'

Mercia eased herself into her chair. 'We were musing he might be concerned at the Duke's takeover of New York.'

'Indeed he might, Mrs Blakewood. But let us discuss something of greater interest.' He leant across the table to pass her the paper. 'Tell me. What does the Blakewood mind make of this?'

Pushing aside her bowl and napkin, she studied the ragged parchment. The edges were tattered and dark, as though they had been soaked. Scrawled across the paper, in ink that had run somewhat, ran an unintelligible sequence of letters:

RNLENRDFRXSHI O

She looked up. 'A puzzle?'

He inclined his head. 'Assuredly that. It was found in the pockets of George Mason, the minister from Meltwater who drowned. I wondered what you thought of it?'

She ran her eyes over the letters. 'Not much. It reminds me of the ciphers my father would employ when he was writing something he wanted kept secret.'

Winthrop leapt up. 'Precisely what I thought. This is a code, but in heaven's name I cannot fathom it or think why Mason would be carrying such a note. He was a simple man, by all accounts, devoted to his scripture, not to matters that would require such riddles as these. Peculiar, as I said before.'

She stared again at the strange sequence, her curiosity firmly piqued. 'You have tried substitution, or a Caesar cipher, of course?'

Winthrop fairly beamed. 'Briefly. But to no avail.'

Nathan peered over her shoulder. 'A Caesar cipher?'

'A method of encryption,' she said, still looking at the paper. 'Said to

20

have been used by Julius Caesar himself. It moves each letter forward in the alphabet by a set amount.' She twisted her head to look up at him. 'For instance, if the Caesar cipher is two, then the letter A would be written in code as C. B would be written as D, and C as E, and so on.'

'And if the cipher were three, then A would become D, and B would be E?'

'That is right. But it does not apply here, apparently.'

'No,' sighed Winthrop. 'I am not sure if that space between the I and the O is significant, but I cannot see how.' He looked at her. 'It does not remind you of anything your father would have used?'

She shook her head. 'I am afraid not. But he only ever used such codes in two cases, as far as I know. When he was writing of a secret matter to his fellows in army or government, and when he was indulging his scientific interests. Not that he would ever share such knowledge with me.'

'A pity.' Winthrop was almost bouncing on his old heels. 'But I think I hear someone coming, no doubt my wife.' He retook his seat. 'We can talk more of this another time.'

Hearing footsteps approach, Mercia turned to the door. A smiling woman soon entered, her simple black dress fronted by a sharp white apron. Although not young, her face sported fewer creases than Winthrop's: Mercia guessed she would be around fifty years of age.

'Good evening, everyone,' she said. 'I am delighted you are able to stay with us.'

Winthrop beamed with pleasure. 'Mrs Blakewood, Mr Keyte, this is my wife Elizabeth.'

Elizabeth glanced at the paper on the table. 'Discussing your theories again, John?'

He held out his hands. 'They seem to find it interesting.'

'I am glad.' She gave a mock sigh. 'But perhaps – not at the table.'

'You are right. Mrs Blakewood, if you could . . .' He waited for her to pass him the paper. 'Thank you.'

Elizabeth took her seat. 'Did you like the soup?'

'Very much,' said Mercia, as Nathan rushed to agree. 'You had some yourself, I hope?'

'In the kitchen. In a New England home we have to help out. Even the governor's wife.' The door creaked open, an unseen person's arm holding it ajar while the two servants entered with food and fresh ale. 'Now, we usually eat earlier, but you have had a long journey. Try this rabbit. We have fried it in breadcrumbs specially.'

The clattering of forks and knives betrayed the guests' hunger. Nathan sliced into his meat with enthusiasm; Mercia took efforts to be more decorous as she relished the delicious gravy, but she enjoyed the meal all the same.

'So tell me, Mrs Blakewood,' said Elizabeth. 'How fares England of late?' She leant into the table. 'And how fares it for we women? John has been back many times since we came here, but I have not returned since I arrived in, oh, '35.'

Mercia considered her reply. 'I suppose most women are hopeful we will no longer turn to war to solve our differences. War with ourselves, that is. The King seems secure enough on his throne now to prevent another such conflict. But I should say that women are carrying on much as before.' She smiled. 'The head of the household, in other words.'

'A woman with opinions,' said Elizabeth. 'No wonder John admires your courage.'

Mercia blushed. 'I am flattered.'

'As well you should be. After all, you are dining with the most esteemed man in all of Connecticut. This year he was elected governor for the seventh time.'

Winthrop tutted. 'Come now.'

'My husband is too modest. He has done much to improve our lives here, as well as our relations with England. There was little love for us there when I left.' She looked down at the table. 'Even when Cromwell was in power, he did not seem to care much for us. And now, there is a

King who must despise us. Tell me.' She glanced up again. 'Do you think we are safe?'

'We women?'

'We . . . Americans. We who sailed the ocean to be free to worship Christ.'

'Oh.' The ringlets of her hair bobbed as she shook her head. 'In truth I do not know. It is for men like your husband to decide that.'

'Then I am sure we will be well protected.' Elizabeth smiled, regaining her spirits. 'What with the Indians and the Dutch, I suppose one's own countrymen are easy to handle.'

'I think I prefer the Indians,' said Winthrop. 'Less . . . duplicitous.'

Elizabeth took a sip of her ale. 'Enough of this. John has not had time to tell me what brought you to New York.'

'Elizabeth—' he began.

'No.' Mercia straightened her napkin. 'It is well to talk of it. I came to America to restore my family home.'

Elizabeth rested her chin in her palm. 'John knew your father, I think.'

'We met from time to time,' he agreed. 'Whenever I was in England. We shared an affection, Mercia, for those scientific interests you mentioned just now.'

Mercia raised a surprised eyebrow. 'I did not know you were so close.'

'Not close, particularly, but we corresponded. He liked to be informed of developments.'

A happy image of her father working in his study came to her mind, but she could see her hostess's eager face. She turned back to Elizabeth. 'In short, then. You will know that the King's father amassed a great collection of art.'

'Ah, the first Charles.' Elizabeth shook her head. 'Now there is a man who mistrusted us. So many sailed here in the '30s because of him.' She puffed out her cheeks. 'The Great Migration.'

'It meant you avoided the war.' Mercia closed her eyes for a moment in remembrance, thinking as she often did of the family, of the friends, she had lost. 'But my story.' She took a deep breath. 'When the troubles with Parliament began, and the old King moved his capital to Oxford, you may recall how he took his favourite paintings with him. Then long after, when Cromwell was in power, those same paintings were stolen. As his advisor, my father was appointed to investigate, but he found no trace.' Her throat drying, she sipped at her ale. 'The years went by and the monarchy returned, the old King's son now on the throne. Anyone who had been close to Cromwell was in danger. My father kept to himself, but earlier this year he was arrested.'

Elizabeth reached out a hand. 'I was very sad to hear what happened. From what John has said, he was a good man.'

'A clever man too.' She rubbed at a knot in the table. 'Before his . . . execution . . . he shared his knowledge of the paintings with me, hoping if I could locate them somehow, I might regain favour with the King.' She looked up. 'Father may have been on Cromwell's side but he was a practical man above all. He knew my uncle would seize our family's manor house when he died. He reasoned the King could help me win it back.'

'So Mercia being Mercia, she began to investigate,' continued Nathan. 'The paintings led us here, to America, and Mercia uncovered who had stolen them.'

She nodded. 'The King was desperate to get his father's art back. He advanced his invasion of Dutch America so we could sail here with his fleet to retrieve it. We succeeded at no small cost. But I have met my side of the bargain. Now it is for him to be true to his own word.'

'He will,' smiled Nathan. 'Or King or no, he will answer to me.'

After supper, the two women left the room, leaving Winthrop to converse with Nathan over a case of rum he had acquired in New York. Entering what Mercia supposed was a parlour, a rustling from a fireside chair made her catch her breath: the exact same sound had preceded the end of that troubled Manhattan night from which she had barely managed to escape. But the woman who rose from the chair was nothing to do with the events of that place. Mercia hurried to hide her discomfort behind a querying smile, waiting to be formally introduced.

'Mrs Carter.' A tone of surprise – irritation perhaps – studded Elizabeth's words. 'I did not know you had stayed. The servants should have told me.'

It was the same brown-haired woman from before, her pale face burning in the light of the flames. 'No, Elizabeth, I knew you had company. I was happy to wait.'

'As ever you are a forgiving guest.' Elizabeth turned to Mercia. 'Mrs Blakewood, this is Clemency Carter. And this is Mercia Blakewood, the daughter of one of John's old acquaintances.'

'Mrs Blakewood.' Clemency gave a tiny bow. 'It is pleasing to meet you more properly. Although I have already heard something of you from your manservant, Nicholas. He was quite charming. Such . . . startling eyes.' She shook her head. 'I apologise for earlier. Percy can be a little eager.'

'Thank you.' Mercia noticed Elizabeth frowning at Clemency's words. 'The governor and his wife have been kind enough to allow us to stay while we visit Connecticut.'

Clemency smiled. 'That man I saw is your husband?'

'A friend. I have a son, but I am widowed.'

'Then we have something in common already. I lost my husband too.'

Elizabeth reached down to stoke the fire with a poker; embers whirled into the room and up the chimney. 'Well, you are very welcome here, Mrs Blakewood. 'Tis a blessing to have a child in the house once more.' She pulled herself up, a supporting hand on her lower back. 'Is all well in Meltwater, Clemency?'

She blew out through pursed lips. 'As well as can be. Standfast and Renatus are vying to be minister now.'

'That was expected.' Elizabeth straightened her back. 'You rode down with Standfast, I take it?'

She nodded. 'Yesterday. He wanted to be the one to bring the news, but Percy and I had planned to come in any case.'

'John only heard of George's death this afternoon. It has shocked him somewhat.'

'I was with him at the time,' said Mercia. 'You are from Meltwater also, Mrs Carter?'

Clemency waved a hand. 'Call me Clemency. And yes, it was we sorry three who brought the news of Mason's death here. There was rather a commotion when he was found in the river.' She grasped the back of a leather-bound seat. 'But enough of sadness. Shall we sit?'

As they settled into chairs Mercia looked around the compact parlour. Nothing like as plush as the sitting room even in her own small cottage at home, let alone the manor house she hoped to reclaim, the room was still fresh and pleasant. A dresser in the corner was stocked with fruits and plate, the dark walls lending the room a comfortable, wintery feel.

'Clemency is one of John's many women,' Elizabeth was explaining. Mercia sat back, confused, and the older woman reddened. 'I mean one of the women who distribute his medicines.'

'Oh.' Mercia relieved the awkwardness with a laugh. 'This is to do with the governor's scientific work?' She inched her chair closer to the fire. 'He seemed most enthusiastic about it earlier.'

Elizabeth shook her head. 'Too enthusiastic, at times.'

'He is the best physician in the whole of New England,' said Clemency, straightening her green bodice. 'Whatever he does with those minerals he takes from the ground, they have a marvellous effect on the sick. They cannot be expected to cure everyone, but by God's truth they are better than anything else we have. I hand them out in Meltwater, as many other women do in their own towns.'

Intrigued, Mercia leant forwards. 'Tell me more.'

Clemency smiled. 'For a stranger, you are a curious woman. I like that.'

'Please, if I am to call you Clemency, you must call me Mercia.'

'That is an unusual name.' She pursed her lips. 'The ancient kingdom?'

'Yes.' Mercia tilted her head, surprised at Clemency's knowledge.

'The realm of the Anglo-Saxons. My father was so enthralled by them he named his own daughter after one of their places. But I think he found the name a beautiful one too.'

'Indeed it is. It is a mystery of a name with a story to tell, a whole people behind it. Unlike some of our English names here, which merely hide a person's true nature behind a trait wished on them by their parents.'

'Clemency,' admonished Elizabeth.

'You do not suffer it.' Clemency leant back in her chair, her arms draped down the sides. 'John and Elizabeth, both strong names. Come to Meltwater, Mercia. We have some choice names there. Like mine, indeed. Clearly my parents wished me to have a clement character. But you will find there is more to me than that.'

'Yet all names are merely translations,' persisted Elizabeth. 'My own is from the Hebrew tongue, for instance. It means God is my oath.'

'Yes, and it will not be long before someone here calls their daughter God-is-my-oath Jameson or whatever. There is no magic in calling your child by a literal English name.'

'Many people around you would disagree. They think it makes the truth plainer to God.'

'Then I am glad I am not many people.' She held out a hand. 'Consider what a marvel your name is, deriving from *El* meaning God, and *sheba*, which means oath. But then see how *sheba* also means perfection, as well as the number seven, and so 'tis a masterpiece of a name, alluding to the perfection of God in creating his world in seven days.'

'I am impressed.' Mercia found herself warming to the woman. 'I did not know that.'

Clemency raised an eyebrow. 'You see, names that contain mysteries are much more interesting. But here I am in the minority.' She edged her chair closer. 'I am glad to meet you, Mercia Blakewood. I think we will get along very well.'

Chapter Three

Mercia slept well that night, tucked in a comfortable bed covered in thick linen, revelling in the pleasurable warmth of the newly laundered bedclothes. It was a welcome change after the five-day journey from New York, dozing in starts in makeshift tents under the open sky, even if she had enjoyed gazing at the stars with Winthrop, listening to his tales of the constellations. So she awoke the following morning refreshed, invigorated by the now familiar sound of New England birdsong as the American sunlight swept into her cosy room. In the distance, a muffled bell sounded out the hour: seven o' clock, time to rise.

She was eager to get ready, for Clemency had said she would return early to the house, and she was anxious not to miss her. Throwing on one of the three dresses she had brought, a brown woollen skirt split down the front to reveal a black petticoat – she could still follow the fashions, even out here – she descended to find Nathan perched on a table edge, sipping a mug of milk.

She looked around. 'Is Mrs Carter not here? She was to meet with Winthrop.'

'Good morning to you, too. Who is Mrs Carter?'

'The woman we saw last night, with that rude man.' She glanced through the window into the backyard: the plot of land stretched on for a long way. 'Has she been and gone?'

'I don't know. But the governor asked me to tell you he was in his workshop.' He took another sip of his drink. 'What shall we do today?'

'Take Daniel to look around the town, I think.' She pointed to Nathan's mug. 'Is there more of that?'

'In the pitcher. 'Tis still warm.' Nodding towards a white jug on the table, he set down his mug and filled another. Passing it over, his fingertips brushed against hers. 'You are sure that is all you want to do?'

She took the mug from him. 'What do you mean?'

He laughed. 'You know what. Something about a code?'

'Oh, that.' She took a quick sip; the milk was thick and full of flavour. 'I had not thought about it.'

He grinned. 'Of course not.'

Draining her mug, she went to wake Daniel and made sure he ate, leaving him to talk with Nathan about his latest interest, the trees of New England – a fascinating subject until discussed to the exclusion of all else. Wondering what his young mind would fixate on next – native animals was a safe bet – she pulled a thin shawl around her neck and stepped out into the garden. She knew Winthrop had his workshop halfway down from the house; she betted she would find Clemency there too, assembling the medicines she was to take back to Meltwater.

It was a bright day, the still-green leaves shining in the sun under a patchy blue sky, wispy clouds sauntering from east to west. She stopped a while to take in her surroundings, the governor's house behind, two others to either side of much smaller proportions, but all three the same two-storey height. She inhaled deeply: the air smelt fresh and untainted, the light scent of verdant grass tingling her nostrils. The smell of pine penetrated her being: it was as though she could taste it. For a moment she closed her eyes, soothing her spirit.

Opening her eyes once more, she squinted momentarily in the sunlight before continuing down the winding path. A large single-storey outbuilding sat to her left, smoke pouring from its stone-clad chimney. She caressed the rough wood of its door, clearly recently made. Everything here felt new, she thought, full of promise and hope, less crowded and complex than life back home.

Working the latch, she pushed open the door and entered, closing it behind her to keep in the warmth of the fire. Enough light came in through the two windows to see that the whole structure comprised one large room. Taking care not to knock over the several glass vials stacked across the floor, she approached the far side where two darkened figures were hunched over a bench. As she drew near she brushed against a conical bottle; it vibrated as it turned round on the spot, emitting a low sound that made the figures look up.

'Mrs Blakewood,' said Winthrop. Beside him Clemency widened her eyes in greeting. 'Come closer, please. Now, if only Elizabeth were here I should feel as if I were poor Paris, unable to choose between you.'

'See how he tests us?' Clemency looked over his head and winked. 'We debated the story of Paris last month, how he was forced to choose the fairest goddess.'

Mercia played along. 'But which of the goddesses would we each be?'

Winthrop sucked in through his teeth. 'I should say Elizabeth for Hera, Clemency for Aphrodite, and you, Mrs Blakewood, would be Athena.'

'Indeed? And Governor, Mercia will suffice.'

'I am honoured.' He turned to Clemency. 'You know the first time I saw Mrs—Mercia, she was a baby in a cradle?'

'Back in England?'

He nodded. 'I had gone to her father's house to discuss matters of philosophy, and, well – this.' He held out his hands towards his workshop.

Clemency put hers on her hips. 'And why does she get to be Athena?'

Winthrop tutted. 'Because, Clemency, she is wise and intelligent and you are more controlled by your passions.'

Clemency laughed, a deep sound of happiness that made Mercia smile too. 'I can be wise.' She looked at Mercia. 'Not that some of our menfolk would believe a woman so capable.'

'My father always thought a woman had a certain place.' Winthrop ran his finger down a table of sorts, avoiding their gaze. Glancing over his shoulder, Mercia was intrigued by a strange symbol dotted across the page that seemed somehow familiar. 'And I agree with—no, wait a moment, I have not finished.' He held up a quietening finger as the two women began to protest. 'I believe everyone has unique responsibilities in God's world. Where my father and I differ is I do not see such rigid distinctions. And yet clearly a woman's mind is better suited to some tasks as a man's is to others.'

'Hmm.' Clemency pursed her lips. 'To needlework and child-rearing, no doubt.'

'To other things as well.' Winthrop held up a box and shook it. 'Like medicine. You are a great doctress, Clemency.'

'Is that one of your mixtures?' Mercia leant in. 'May I see?'

'Of course.' He untied the red ribbon that was keeping the small box closed and opened the lid, revealing a fine white powder within. 'This is antimony. More specifically, ceruse of antimony. It causes the body to perspire and so drive out fever.'

She frowned. 'Is not antimony poisonous?'

'Yes, until an alchemist removes the impurities and makes it the exact opposite. It is a discovery such as this that excited your father so, as it excites me.' He closed the box and turned to Clemency. 'You know the dose?'

'He always asks this,' she sighed. 'Although I have administered it a hundred times.' She smiled at Winthrop. 'Yes. One grain only as it is for a child.'

Mercia looked up. 'A child is sick?'

Clemency nodded. 'Praise-God Davison. Who deserves treatment in spite of his ridiculous name.' At her side, Winthrop shook his head. 'Now, Mercia,' she continued. 'I must attend to other errands, but I

31

would like to see you again before I leave. Praise-God is sick but not in mortal danger.' She began tying on her bonnet. 'Will you meet me this evening?'

'I would like that.'

'Then I will see you later. Governor, if I may call on Mrs Blakewood at sunset, I will leave the antimony with you until then.'

'I will put it with the other varieties and the saltpetre. I will give you extra to see Meltwater through the winter. You said you had antimony of copper enough?'

'Most definitely.' She paused. 'And do not be concerned over – the other matter. It is in hand.'

Winthrop's eyes flicked to Mercia and away again. 'Very good.'

Clemency gave a slight bow and left, sending a cold draught whipping around the laboratory as she opened and closed the door. A wind had sprung up since Mercia had come in; some of the glass jars nearest the door jangled.

'Perhaps a storm is brewing,' said Winthrop.

'It was fine weather when I was in the garden just now.' She looked around the room, wondering what Clemency had meant about the other matter, but even more entranced by what she could see. 'You described yourself just now as an alchemist. Is all this concerned with such endeavours?'

He beamed. 'Indeed. I am proud to help the people with the discoveries I have found.'

'So many vials and parchments. I never knew alchemy was so involved.'

'Perhaps you thought it was all fools on a quest to turn lead into gold?' He arched a grey eyebrow. 'Did you think your father a fool?'

'My father was the cleverest man I knew.' She paused, saddened as the last image she had of him, standing grey but proud on the scaffold at Tower Hill, filled her mind; she shook the picture aside and concentrated on Winthrop, a man of roughly the same age. 'How well did you know him? Did you discuss this?'

'Matters like this.' Winthrop folded his arms, leaning against the fireplace. 'The last time was two years ago, when I was securing Connecticut's new charter from the King.' He smiled. 'When I was not flattering the royal ego, I managed to visit friends across England. Sir Rowland was one of them.'

'But you did not come to Halescott.'

'No, we met in Oxford, not long after I was elected to the Royal Society.' He scoffed. 'They want me to be their colonial expert, to send them intricate details of America's wilds. Well maybe I will, but I will not tell them anything that will hurt my people. I know the King's brother is no friend to New England.'

'But my father—'

Winthrop bowed. 'I am sorry. Your father was a curious man. He wanted to know things, to understand the world. Cromwell must have valued his council.'

'I think so.' She looked again about her. 'How involved was he in your work? I had no idea.'

He wandered to one of his overflowing shelves. 'He was never one of the principal actors, but he was certainly interested.' Taking a well-worn book from the shelf he placed it on the bench, opening it at a page near the front. 'Take a look.'

''Tis a letter.' She peered at the page. 'In my father's hand!' She looked up at Winthrop, amazed. 'But it is in some sort of code.' She read the first word, or rather scanned it, for it was impossible to take it in:

JFDRJNCWWRBLZDTIYVGSPUOAIHCRBYICDHPBFHOY

She frowned. 'I cannot make anything out.'

'This volume is full of correspondence I have pasted in, all from alchemical practitioners across Europe and the New World. As we are dealing with God's secrets, we must write to each other in code so the Devil cannot use our work to his own ends.'

'I see.' She leafed through a few pages of notes. On many the same strange familiar symbol she had already seen was repeated. 'I confess I know little of alchemy, Governor, but I do seem to recognise this mark here.'

'Ah.' He smiled. 'Do you recall its name?'

She pondered a moment, examining again the symbol, a crowned circle with a dot at its centre, the circle perched on a cross that nestled between two mounds.

'Yes,' she said eventually. 'I think I might.' She screwed up her forehead, thinking back to her childhood. 'From one or two of my father's books, among those he told me not to read.'

Winthrop laughed. 'But which you looked at nonetheless.'

'Of course. Although at that age I did not understand most of his library, the religious treatises and philosophical works. But I do remember this symbol. It was so . . . captivating.' She tapped on a large depiction. 'It is a *monas*.'

'A *monas hieroglyphica*, to be exact. It is the very symbol of creation.' Animated, Winthrop leapt to another workbench, taking up a paper and quill and beckoning her to watch. 'The circle represents the heavens,' he said, scrawling on the paper, 'and the dot is the Earth.' He jabbed a dot at the circle's centre. 'And this, is the moon.' He intersected the top of the circle with an upside-down arch.

She glanced at the *monas* in the workbook. 'What of the cross?'

He sketched an elongated cross beneath the circle. 'The cross is quite naturally the cross of our Lord. But its four lines also represent the four elements of air, fire, water and earth.'

'And the flourishes at the bottom?'

Winthrop finished by adding two adjoining semicircles, one each side of the bottom point of the cross; they had the appearance of two small hills. 'This is the symbol we use for Aries, the first constellation of the zodiac.'

'A most mysterious depiction.'

He looked at her. 'Can you see anything else in the *monas*?'

'I . . . do not think so.'

'I suppose your father would not have taught you the signs of the metals.'

She pursed her lips. 'I suppose not. Although . . . is not gold represented as a circle?'

'Very good.' Winthrop seemed impressed. 'And silver is depicted as a crescent, like here at the top; copper is the circle and cross combined, and so on. If you look at the *monas* from different angles, you will see all the metals within it. And so also the signs of the planets, for their signs and those of the metals correspond.' He looked up, his elderly eyes shining. 'The *monas* is a perfect symbol of creation and alchemy.'

She shook her head. 'And you devised this yourself?'

'Oh no.' Winthrop smiled. 'It is a century old. But we alchemists are still searching for the hidden meanings of God's world.' He held up the box of antimony. 'The Lord has allowed me to discover some morsels of use. I have found that minerals in the earth can have wonderful recuperative powers for the sick. But I have not been deemed worthy enough to uncover the two ultimate prizes, alas.'

'And what are they?'

'Why, the philosopher's stone, and the alkahest.' He rested his hands on the table, entwining his thin fingers. 'The first will allow us to refine base metals into the purest gold and silver.'

'So that is part of it.'

'Indeed, but the aim is not merely to gain profit, even if so doing will help us support ourselves in our endeavours.' He sighed. 'Of course there are many who do seek financial gain through the stone. But then the second of the prizes, the alkahest, is of universal good, for it is the ultimate elixir. Once discovered, the alkahest will cure all sickness, and nobody will be infirm or die of illness again.'

She stared at him. 'You believe that is possible?'

'Oh yes.' Winthrop was earnest. 'One day we will uncover these wonders. Adam knew them before his fall from Eden, but God hid them until the time shall come for us to reveal them anew. Indeed it is said that the Second Coming of Christ will be preceded by a time of great discovery. The Book of Daniel makes clear that at the time of the end, many shall run to and fro, and knowledge shall be increased.' He turned back to his workbook. 'That letter of your father's.' He flicked through the pages to find the correct spot. 'It was the alkahest that encouraged him the most. Here, he reports meeting a man who claimed its discovery. But his next said the man was a charlatan, an all too common occurrence.'

She looked again at the unintelligible page. 'How do you decipher it?'

Winthrop smiled; on a separate piece of paper he wrote down the first jumble of letters beside another much smaller sequence: *NCUYNB*.

'This would be your Christian name in the same code. Let me know when you have worked it out.'

She raised an eyebrow. 'You wish to see if I am worthy myself?'

'A simple riddle, that is all.' He inclined his head. 'Have you thought further about the code found on Meltwater's minister?'

'Oh, a little.' Scraps of parchment in her bedroom would argue otherwise; they were full of attempts at interpreting what the code might mean. 'Have you?'

'Yes, but I am no closer to understanding it. John Lavington, Meltwater's magistrate, is an alchemist. It may be the minister was simply carrying some workings of his.'

'Lavington?' She blinked, trying to recall where she had heard the name before. 'Oh yes. That man from last night was named Lavington.'

'That was John Lavington's son, Perseverance. He and Clemency came from Meltwater together, on some business of theirs.' He cleared his throat. 'But never mind that.'

Mercia waited for him to elaborate, but he remained silent, busying himself with his notebook. 'Another alchemist,' she said at last.

Winthrop laughed. 'We are everywhere. Indeed there is another young man in Hartford now with similar interests. Amery Oldfield. Lavington has appointed him to be Meltwater's very first schoolmaster.'

'The town is that new?'

'Four years old, and on the edge of our lands. I only gave Lavington permission to found it as he wanted to search the frontier for God's secrets.' He scratched his cheek. 'That, and to stop Massachusetts from sneaking round us from the north by claiming that territory for their own.' He smiled. 'Well, Mercia. I will write to John myself to see if he knows anything further. I do not think the constable there has much respect for him, otherwise the code paper would still be in his hands instead of mine, but I have more faith.' Without setting a hand on her back, he held his arm behind her and shepherded her across the room. 'Now stop talking to this old man and go and see Hartford. Take a look at what we have accomplished. I am sure you will find it good.'

Feeling buoyant, Mercia fetched Daniel and Nathan and set off into Hartford, indulging her son by letting him skip a little way in front. But the trio did not get far before a commotion near the house arrested their attention and she called Daniel back to her side. A wild-eyed man was balancing on a picket fence, shouting down at a small crowd. His physical dexterity was impressive, his words less so.

'We must be ready!' he cried. 'The Second Coming is nearly upon us!'

'Yes, yes,' sighed an elderly woman in his audience. 'So you keep saying. But when will it come?'

'Do not mock,' he shrilled. 'The Lord will appear when He is ready. He will descend from heaven and judge us. Each of us!' He looked around him. 'And you, lady, He will judge most of all! See, she has come, and He will find her wanting!'

Mercia shook her head, feeling pity for the old woman who had incurred the speaker's wrath. But then she looked up at the preacher and took an involuntary step back, for he was not pointing his shaking hand at his audience, but at her.

'You bring calamity to this land,' he cried. 'Over the ocean you have come, and like the ancient Flood that destroyed all things, the waters you travelled will surely destroy us now.' His whole body began to shake in rage. 'Leave us, Mercia Blakewood, for you bring naught but death!'

Chapter Four

Nathan strode to the fence; with one arm he pulled the thin preacher to the ground. The young man stumbled but Nathan yanked him upright.

'I should strike you where you stand. What do you mean by speaking so foully to strangers?'

The preacher threw back his head, the mole on his neck jutting against the stiff white collar of his shirt. 'I mean that your woman should take care what she does. She is in danger for her soul and will imperil us all.'

'The only one in danger here is you.' Nathan gripped the man's shoulder and twisted him round. 'By God's wounds! How do you know who she is?'

Recovering her wits, Mercia looked down at her son. 'Don't mind what he said, Danny. There are strange people everywhere. But will you run back into the governor's house a moment while I calm Uncle Nathan?'

Nodding, Daniel ran back inside. When she was sure he was safely in the house, she turned back round, her calm expression gone. The preacher was staring defiantly at Nathan in silence, the small crowd eagerly looking on.

'Answer the question,' she said, marching towards him. 'How do you know me?'

The preacher inclined his head. 'The Lord reveals all to me who are hounded by Satan.'

Usually she did not heed such pronouncements, but a chill came over her at his words. 'What do you mean?'

He looked at her as though she were a child. 'Through witchcraft he seeks to divert God's path. England is the home of the Devil. Many come thence to corrupt us.'

Nathan gripped him more firmly. 'How do you know her?'

'That is probably my fault.' A well-dressed young man stepped forward through the crowd, a sheaf of wavy blonde hair just visible under his broad-brimmed hat. 'As is his demeanour towards you. I told him people not of these parts were staying at the governor's house.'

'And you are?' said Mercia.

The man bowed. 'Amery Oldfield, lately of Boston and now resident of Connecticut.' He chuckled two bursts of a nervous laugh. 'I know Clemency Carter.' He turned to the preacher. 'As I know this man, Standfast Edwards. He has been waiting to get a look at you.'

She frowned. 'Why?'

'Well.' Amery inclined his head, a bashful smile on his face. 'Clemency told me she had met you, and I mentioned it to Standfast when I met him.' He glanced at the preacher. 'And as usual, he has jumped to the suspicion that anyone new here is tainted by the Devil until they prove otherwise.'

'There is much sin around, Amery,' said Standfast, still in Nathan's grip. 'It falls to those whom the Lord trusts to find it out.'

'And you do a marvellous job. But you have been wrong before and I am sure you are wrong about these people.'

Standfast hesitated. 'The Devil does seek to hide the truth. I suppose you may be right.' He looked at Mercia. 'This is a land of hidden sin, Mrs Blakewood, of men who claim to be one thing but are something

40

quite else. You will have to show yourself worthy if you want to receive God's blessing.'

'I think I have proved myself enough recently.' She sighed. 'Nathan, let him go. There is no harm done.'

Nathan's expression remained bleak, but he released his grip and straightened Standfast's crumpled jacket, pulling hard on the cloth. 'See that you learn manners in future.' He jerked his head to one side. 'Now go.' Standfast looked at him in fearless challenge, then wandered away, followed by the now bored crowd.

Amery watched him go. 'We knew each other when we were children. He was never so devout back then, but as he grew older he decided he was one of the most saintly of we saints. But there are others, I think, more saintly.'

'He should take care,' said Nathan. 'Do many around here think as he does?'

'There are many devout people in New England, if that is what you ask.' Amery looked at him sharply. 'Are you with the godly, my brother?'

Nathan folded his arms. 'I believe in spreading the Lord's word through English.'

'So do the Anglicans. But yes, New England remains the land of we saints. There are those who worry that the arrival of the royal fleet will spell the end of us, but I hope we can live with each other.' A gust of wind fled past and he drew tight his coat. 'Well, good cheer, my friends. Send kind word of us to England.'

Touching his hat, he strolled away.

The rest of the day passed merrily in touring the town and its surroundings. Mercia was surprised by its complexity; although small, she had not thought to see a place so developed in the middle of Connecticut. But then, she thought, it was much bigger than Halescott, the village where she lived back in England. Daniel had certainly enjoyed himself, still playing outside with two boys he had met during the day,

41

ecstatic to have new friends after so many long weeks at sea.

By the time they returned to Winthrop's house she was worn out with the walking; removing her heavy boots gave her such pleasure that she remained in her chair for a full five minutes, enjoying the sensation of lightness in her legs. After another delicious dinner she felt deeply satisfied, and retiring to the parlour she eagerly waited for Clemency to return in the hope of good conversation. She smiled as the door opened behind her, but then her face clouded as she turned, for a different person entirely had appeared in the doorway, a grandly dressed man in a sweeping fur coat, an uncertain smile on his face.

'Mercia,' he said. 'I hope I am not intruding on your solitude.'

'Sir William.' She rose from her seat. 'I did not expect to see you in Hartford.'

Sir William Calde, one of the noblemen she had sailed with on the King's invasion fleet, entered the room. Removing his ostrich-feathered hat with his left hand he kept his right behind his back. 'I am here on the King's business,' he said, more confident now. 'His commissioners want a report on Connecticut before they make their personal survey of New England.' His cheek twitched. 'And I wanted to see how you were faring.'

Mercia ran a hand through her hair; realising the gesture could be interpreted in quite different ways, she quickly lowered it to her side.

'I am quite well, Sir William. But I thought you would still be in New York? Are matters there not proceeding as planned?'

'Indeed they are. Now we are turning our attention to the New England colonies, but you need not trouble yourself with such tiresome concerns.' He pulled an extravagant bouquet of red and yellow flowers from behind his back. 'For you, to brighten your spirits.'

She smiled out of indulgence, setting the flowers on the table by the fire. 'Thank you. I will put them in water later.' She sucked in her top lip. 'Does the governor know you are here?'

Sir William nodded. 'His good wife told me where I could find you.'

'How kind of her.'

He paused a moment. 'It is good to see you, Mercia.' His gaze lingered on her face, her neck, her chest; she glanced away and he laughed, nervous again. 'But I know you must be tired. I merely wanted to let you know I would be in Hartford for a few days.' He hesitated. 'Winthrop tells me you have spent the day in the town. Perhaps you would join me soon to show me what you have seen?'

She inclined her head. 'Perhaps.'

'Then I shall look forward to it.' His face faltered slightly. 'We were never able to talk after what happened in New York. I know you must have suffered.'

Mercia glanced at the flames in the fire. 'You have suffered yourself, Sir William. I think of Lady Calde a lot, in my dreams.'

'As do I.' He sighed. 'I think perhaps if I had acted sooner, some of those deaths could have been prevented.'

'Perhaps. But then, perhaps I should never have come.'

'You came to regain your manor house.'

'True.' She looked up at him, trying to calculate his motives. 'But in the meantime, I am enjoying my respite here.'

He smiled. 'Well then, enough of this. I am keeping a lady waiting who wishes to come in. Winthrop has found me ample lodgings nearby. I shall see you soon.' Bowing, he replaced his hat and strode from the room, bestowing her with one last, long glance. His expression seemed boyish, almost pleading; Mercia wondered what was really going through the great man's mind.

She did not spend long in thought. Seconds later, Clemency entered the room in a deep scarlet dress; or rather she danced in, as though she were breezing through the air.

'Two questions,' she said. 'Is that impressive man a friend of yours, and should Nathan be as jealous of him as he clearly is?'

Mercia laughed, regaining her spirits. 'No, and no.'

'Still, you seem out of sorts. But I have an idea to change that. If you are willing, I could take you somewhere where life always seems happy.'

'Is there such a place?'

'Oh yes. Your manservant has already discovered it. He seemed to think you would enjoy it too.' She backed towards the door. 'Will you join me?'

Mercia was about to refuse, when a peculiar feeling came over her – a feeling of . . . what was it? Friendship? 'Yes.' She clasped together her hands. 'If Nicholas is involved I can guess what sort of place it is. But Daniel is abed, and Sir William has irked me, so yes. Why not?'

Expecting to be led to the tavern two streets down from the governor's house, when Clemency turned towards the stables instead, Mercia frowned. 'Are we not going to—?'

'Samson's place?' Clemency scoffed. 'I think not. They enforce the law there. Nothing worth drinking and no more than thirty minutes in the place at a time.' She lowered her voice. 'The penalty for being so close to the governor's residence.' She led a horse from a ramshackle stall. 'No, I am taking you somewhere far more exciting.'

Mercia looked back in the direction they had come. 'Did you not see Elizabeth in the house? Where does she think we are going?'

Clemency shrugged. 'I told her I was taking you to visit a friend of mine. She seemed pleased you were showing such an interest in her town.'

'Clemency!'

'Clemency nothing.' She mounted her horse, sitting aside. 'Now, there is a horse for you in that stable there. Are you coming?'

She paused. 'What about Nathan?'

'Nathan thinks it would do you good to have female company tonight.'

Mercia laughed. 'Then who am I to say no?'

They rode out of town for about two miles. Although it was dark, the moon gave some light and the road was straight, if rutted. Clemency rode quickly but Mercia was more than a match, racing alongside her through the night. Soon a black building loomed at the side of the road, no lights shining within. Slowing her horse, Clemency dismounted, beckoning Mercia to follow her round the back. They tied their horses at a long bar where several others were already pawing the ground or nuzzling oats.

'Where are we?' whispered Mercia.

'You will see.' Clemency walked to a door in the side of the house, her boots thudding on the earthen courtyard. She adjusted her hat and knocked, four short taps followed by three longer ones. The door inched open and the women were ushered inside, the young man who had let them enter retaking his seat atop a barrel, sipping at a tankard of what smelt like rum.

Clemency led the way down a narrow passage, halting at a thick door through which the muted sounds of conversation and laughter could be heard. Pushing it open, she stood aside for Mercia to enter, bowing in imitation of a courtier of old. They passed through into an intimate room where several other people turned to look at the new entrants. Mercia felt herself reddening, but Clemency strode forward unabashed.

'Two glasses of sack, Hugh, and no excuses like last time. I know you have the good stuff, I saw it being delivered myself!' To a drunken roar of approval she took a seat at a round table, waving Mercia over to join her. At the other end of the room Nicholas was sitting with two strange men, a collection of empty tankards cluttering their larger bench. Grinning, he raised another mug, calling out a greeting. She nodded, more curtly than she intended, and he broke off his gaze.

'Those eyes,' said Clemency, fixing Mercia with an inquisitive look as she brushed out the back of her dress.

Removing her hood, Mercia fiddled with her topknot. 'I had not noticed.'

'Of course not.'

'He is my manservant.'

'Lucky you.'

Lightly embarrassed, Mercia was glad when the proprietor came over with the drinks.

'Who's this?' he asked.

'This, Hugh, is my new friend. She has come all the way from England.'

'From England?' He glanced sideways at Mercia. 'Well, Clemency, as you say, your friend.'

Clemency shook her head as he walked back to his seat. 'I am sorry about him. But suspicion seems to be a common trait round here at present.'

Mercia pulled her chair closer to the table. 'But not with you?'

'Shall we say I am more willing to trust people until they prove themselves otherwise?' She ran her finger round the rim of her glass. 'With many it is the other way around.'

'Indeed.' Mercia took a sip of her sack and winced. 'That has a powerful taste.'

'Good, isn't it?' Clemency took a longer sip of her own. 'Hugh gets it from a merchant friend in Boston.'

Mercia took another drink, rolling it around her palate. 'Yes,' she said. 'Nutty and sweet, as it should be.' She set down the glass. 'Talking of mistrust, I met Standfast Edwards this morning.'

'So I heard. There is one who mistrusts by default, especially anything concerning heathen England.' She smiled. 'Mercia, you will tell me why you are here when you are ready to, but not now. I sense it is not an easy tale, and tonight I want you to enjoy your life.' She called over to Hugh. 'Two more!'

'But I have hardly touched the first.'

'No matter. We may as well order them across.'

Mercia looked at Clemency, not knowing how she should feel about this forward woman she had only just met, who had brought her to a hidden, no doubt illegal, drinking den. But then Clemency smiled, her face a picture of genuine friendship, and she knew. She picked up her glass.

'To New England,' she pronounced.

'To New England.' Clemency chinked her glass against Mercia's. 'So who was the man in the coat? Careful!'

Mercia set down her now drained glass. 'That was Sir William Calde. He . . . well, I shouldn't say.'

Clemency sidled closer. 'Now you have to.'

She sighed. 'He . . . has an interest in me.'

'Does he?' She wiggled closer still. 'He seems rich.'

'No doubt he is.' She waited as Hugh brought the second round, then leant in. 'He wants me to be his mistress.' She jerked up her head. 'By the Lord. Now he is widowed, dare he think even wife, perhaps?'

'The scandal!' Clemency grinned. 'What does Nathan think?'

'Nathan knows I will never agree. It was my uncle's idea. But he did not count on my fighting it.'

'We women have to fight sometimes, do we not?'

Mercia took up her second drink. 'That we do.'

'And Nathan. Are you two . . . ?'

She fidgeted in her seat. 'In truth I do not know. It is . . . complicated. We have been friends for many years.'

'Only friends?'

Mercia shrugged. 'I had always suspected there might be something. But I never really allowed myself to think it. My husband was his friend, you see, and his wife was mine.'

'But now they are—'

'Dead.' Mercia looked up. 'Both.'

Clemency nodded, a momentary sadness flitting across her face. 'What does your boy think?'

She smiled. 'He adores Nathan.'

'Well, then. That is that.'

'I do not—'

'And what of him?' Clemency interrupted before she could finish. She

47

jerked her head at Nicholas, who was showing the two engrossed men beside him a trick with a pack of cards.

Mercia glanced over. ''Tis as I said. He is my manservant.'

'But there is some tension there, I think, that goes beyond mistress and servant.'

She blew out her cheeks. 'You spoke of trust just now. Let us just say he needs to regain mine.'

Clemency nodded thoughtfully. 'Another drink?'

Half an hour and three sacks later the two women were rolling in conversation.

'Such a shame you have to go back home tomorrow,' said Mercia. 'We are getting along so well.' She frowned, for Clemency was staring. 'What is it?'

'Oh, nothing.' She inclined her head. 'I was just wondering, that you might want to, with your family having been . . .' She glanced away. 'I probably should not.'

'What of my family? Has Elizabeth been talking?'

'A little.' She sighed. 'But I should not ask. Not at all. No, do not worry.'

'Come, what?'

'Just an errand I have to help with.' She raised an eyebrow. 'Nothing that need concern the great Mercia Blakewood, voyager of the cruel Atlantic depths!'

She gave up her questioning. 'You make it sound like crossing the seas was a unique endeavour. All the people here will have sailed the ocean.'

'I never have.'

'Their parents, then.'

She nodded. 'Mine came in the '30s, like the governor. A shame my father never lived to see all that we have built. Or that I never had children of my own to continue building it. But. . . forget the past.' She looked up at Mercia, a sudden brightness in her eyes. 'I have a wonderful idea. You are here now, and you can see our present.'

48

'What do you mean?'

Her emerging smile grew to a grin. 'Come to Meltwater. All of you. You will be bored staying with the governor for too long.'

'To Meltwater?' Mercia felt the sack rising to her head. 'I cannot.'

'Why?'

She slouched in her seat. 'I cannot think why.' Then up straight. 'Because it is a long journey.'

'By God, woman, you have come thousands of miles!'

'I am well travelled.'

'You are well drunk.' Clemency put her hand on Mercia's shoulder. 'You want to see New England, understand its spirit? Well, you will not find that in Hartford. Meltwater is at the edge of our lands, it is the real New England, people forging their lives in the most beautiful of places. Stay with the governor for a couple more days, then ride out to us. The road is – well, rotten – but 'tis an obvious route, and with Nathan and Nicholas you will be perfectly safe.'

Mercia stared at her. 'Where would we stay?'

'I only have a small cottage, I fear, but I will find you lodgings easily enough.' She rested her chin on her hands. 'Come for a few days. You will enjoy it.'

Mercia considered. She had intended to stay in Hartford for at most a week before returning to New York to await a ship to England, but now Sir William had appeared in the town the thought of staying there had considerably soured. But it was either the drink or the companionship, most likely both, that made her certain. 'Yes!' she cried. 'Nicholas! Get ready!'

'For what?' he called across. 'Do you need me?'

'I need you to take me to Meltwater,' she slurred. 'We will leave the day after tomorrow!'

It was fortunate the horses were sober, for the three riders were not. Relying on their steeds they returned to the governor's house around

49

eleven. Clemency bade them goodnight as they left the horses at the stable; Nicholas helped Mercia into the hall and up the stairs before retreating to his shared quarters elsewhere in the house.

As she was opening her door a chink of light falling through another grew brighter. A silhouette lit by a candle stepped onto the landing.

'Mercia?' the figure whispered. 'Is that you?'

'Yes, Nathan.'

'Are you well?'

'Yes, Nathan.'

'Where have you been?'

'Yes, Nathan.'

He sniffed the air. 'Have you been drinking?'

She giggled.

'Get in your room.' He took her by the elbow and eased her through her door; immediately, she collapsed onto the bed.

'Nathan,' she said. 'Let's go to Meltwater.'

'To Meltwater?'

'That's what I said!' She rolled her hands in her sheets. 'Clemency asked us.'

'Mrs Carter.' He tutted, setting his candle on a rickety table. 'I think that woman is—'

'No.' She sat up. 'Whatever you were going to say, don't. That woman, as you put it, is the first woman I have met in a very long time I feel I can talk to.' She stood up, indignant in her drunkenness. 'How long is it since I have had a friend?' She scowled as Nathan looked away. 'I do not mean you, Nathan, I mean a female friend, someone to talk to about all those things that bore you.' She smiled. 'We are going back to England soon. In all likelihood I will never see her again, and we can go back to caring for your farmland and fighting my uncle and stopping Daniel's grandparents from trying to steal him away. But this week, let's do something different. You're interested in New England, aren't you, how the people live? Then let's find out.' She looked at him coyly. 'Come,

Nathan. You say you care for me, well then give me this. Please. Give me this.'

'An impassioned speech.' He reached out his hand. 'I do care for you. Always.'

She looked at him. 'Stay with me tonight.'

'Mercia, I don't think—'

'I don't mean that. Just, lie next to me. Sleep.'

He bit his lip. 'What if the governor finds out?'

'You sound like a timid boy. I don't think it will be the worst he has dealt with.' She flopped back on the bed. 'I do not have the strength to take off these clothes anyway. It will be the least indecent sleeping together in history.'

'Well, if you are sure . . .'

She grunted.

'And I am not a timid boy.' He pulled at the bottom of his nightshirt. 'Do you mind? 'Tis so hot tonight.'

She turned on her side to get comfortable, waving a dismissive hand, not caring either way in her insobriety. Her eyes drooping, she heard him laugh, felt him lean over to blow out the candle, smelt his skin as he threw off his shirt. She rested her hand on his chest, feeling the roughness of his scar, feeling safe. But when he stretched out his own arm to pull her close, she was already in blissful sleep.

Chapter Five

The hammer in her head thumped her into fragile consciousness. Tired from constant waking in the night, she slowly opened her eyes, pushing stray ringlets from her forehead and cursing as she realised her curling papers were absent: she had forgotten to put them in to keep the style set. Then a change of speed: she darted up straight, remembering she had invited Nathan to stay, but when her sight came into focus she saw he was no longer there.

What time is it, she wondered, noticing the stream of bright light rushing in through the window, and then: I wish that pounding would cease, it is harming my head. She rubbed her temples, trying to count the number of sacks she had drunk, until the banging renewed itself, seemingly stronger. Dragging herself halfway alert, she realised the knocking was not coming from within, but from the bedroom door.

She pulled the linen sheets around her. 'What is it?'

''Tis only me,' came Nathan's chirpy voice. 'The morning is passing. The governor's wife was wondering whether you were ill.'

'You can come in.'

He opened the door a crack, a broad grin on his face. 'Are you ill?'

'No.' She coughed, feeling the pulses reverberating through her head. 'It was only a couple of drinks.'

'I see. But you have been so long abed you have missed Clemency.'

'What?' A strange, sad feeling came over her at the news; she would have liked to have seen Clemency that morning, perhaps commiserate over the repercussions of the night. 'How was she?'

'She was fine,' said Nathan. 'No headache at all, so she said.'

'Why am I not surprised?' She shook her head and straightaway regretted it. 'Did she say anything about meeting later, before she leaves for home?'

'Ah.' Nathan sucked in through his teeth. 'I am afraid she has had to return already.'

The unexpected sadness deepened. 'Why?'

'That sick child. His mother sent a message that he has worsened. It came last night but was only delivered this morning. Clemency was furious, but she made sure to call in here to let you know.'

Mercia nodded; the slight movement made her queasy. 'Then of course she should go. I know how I would feel were Daniel ill: the boy's mother will need her.'

'But don't worry. She repeated her invitation to visit Meltwater to me.' He paused. 'You are sure you would like to go?'

'Oh yes.' Of a sudden she felt more cheerful. 'I think it would be pleasant.'

'Very well.' His merriment unabashed, he looked her dishevelled form up and down. 'But I would get up now, lest Mrs Winthrop send in her husband with one of his remedies.'

She blew out her aching cheeks. 'Nat, that might be a good idea.'

The rest of the day passed slowly as Mercia restored her strength and her wits. Finally confessing her bad head to Winthrop, he prescribed her a small amount of a red powder he called rubila, and whether through the power of the mineral or through the passing of time, by evening she was back to her more healthy self, vowing not to touch American sack again. She had been worried she would offend him by suggesting she might leave to visit Meltwater, but his enthusiasm surprised her.

'Yes, you should go.' A whimsical look came over his face, bathed in orange from the crackling firelight. 'You will see the real America, what it was like thirty years ago when we arrived. My, it was a struggle then, even for me, the governor's own son.' He smiled. 'I have travelled to Meltwater but twice myself. It is a most intriguing town.' He arched his fingers. 'But I would caution against mentioning you came to America for the King. Like in all New England, the people there can be mistrustful of his royal motives.'

She scratched her neck. 'I came to America for my son, Governor. Acting for the King was a necessity to that end.'

'I know that, but others are quick to judge. I merely say be careful, that is all.' He pursed his lips. 'I do wonder, though – and I am merely thinking out loud – whether you should take your son.'

Mercia pulled herself closer to the fire. 'Why do you say that?'

'There is no particular reason. But I doubt the lodgings will be as comfortable as they are here, and he does seem quite settled. If you wished it he could stay with us. I know how Elizabeth would like it.'

She looked into the flames. 'In truth, it has been worrying me today, with that sick child Clemency is treating. And he has met some other boys here already. I think he would prefer to stay with them than to traipse off with his mother.' She smiled. 'He is a boy. He tires of travelling.'

'Well, the offer is there if you need it.' Winthrop's left eyebrow twitched. 'It is good for a parent to have time on her own – or with a friend.'

She blinked: how loudly had she and Nathan been talking last night? But he immediately changed the subject, studying her from over his arched fingertips in that way of his she knew by now meant he had something to ask.

'Now. Did you solve that riddle I set you?'

'Ah. I suspected you might ask.' She delved into her pockets, withdrawing the paper he had given her. 'Indeed I have.'

He inclined his head. 'And?'

She pointed at the code word for her name he had scrawled on the paper: *NCUYNB*.

'It is a variation on the Caesar cipher. For the first letter, you go one back in the alphabet. For the second, you go two forward. Then 'tis three back from the third, four forward from the fourth, and five back from the fifth. Then you start again. M-E-R-C-I-A.' She tapped at the longer word alongside the other. 'And so this phrase my father wrote reads: I have met a man who has knowledge of the alkahest.'

Winthrop clapped his hands together. 'Very good.'

She smiled, pleased at his approval. 'It was not hard.'

'Maybe not.' He paused. 'But your ability might find outlet in another puzzle. That found on the Meltwater minister. I did not want to speak of it to Clemency or Percy Lavington, for they are . . . occupied. But if you are travelling that way, I wonder if you would mind speaking with the magistrate on my behalf?'

She felt a surge of pride. 'You wish me to act for you?'

'You are clearly your father's daughter, Mercia. I have no doubt in your curiosity and your intellect.'

She tried to hide the broad grin emerging on her face. 'So the puzzle you set me . . . it was a test, after all.'

Winthrop tutted. 'A challenge, more like. Besides, how could I have known then you would be going to Meltwater?'

'That is true, but would you have mentioned the minister again if I had failed your challenge?'

He smiled, batting away the question with a wave of his hand. 'Mercia, I ask this because I have great confidence in you: that, and that alone.' He reached into his pockets. 'Here is the code from the minister's jacket. Please, take it with you. I would dearly like to know what it means.'

She reached for the proffered note. 'Then I am honoured. I am happy to be your proxy, you know that.' She hesitated. 'But I wonder – if I can help with this matter, perhaps I can help with another also.'

He waited. 'Go on.'

'Several times now I have heard you or Clemency talk of some mysterious business. It may not be my place to know, but if there is any way I can assist now she has had to return early, I would be glad to do so.'

Again the arched fingertips. 'A difficult business indeed. A shame I know nothing of it.' He studied her face, and then he winked. 'But as you ask, I did, shall we say – overhear – Clemency wondering whether you would like to help. Whether you would like to meet with him, at least.'

'Him? This is about a man?'

Winthrop smiled. 'Are not most strange affairs to do with men, or women come to that?' He leant in towards her. 'As for this man, I am sure he would like to meet with you.'

She waited with Nathan on the corner of the street. It was a warm night for the time of year, so she did not feel the need to wrap up in her hood, all the better as it afforded her a clearer view of the darkened streets.

'How long has it been?' she asked.

'Again,' he sighed. 'About ten minutes. Be patient.'

'I am patient.' She tapped her foot.

'Mercia.'

She scowled, but made herself still. 'What do you think about Daniel?'

'What about him?'

'Winthrop thinks I should leave him here when we go to Meltwater.'

'That might be for the best, Mercia. There are no sick children here, and with this new matter – I am still not sure you should be involving yourself in it at all.'

'Are you not?' She laughed. 'Well, let us see what happens this evening, and then I will decide. But it has been a while since he had someone to play with, and when I asked him he seemed more than happy—wait.' A whinnying came through the air up ahead. 'Is this who we're expecting?'

A large silhouette emerged from the darkness, making them stand back. As the vague shape coalesced into a horse and rider, the animal was manoeuvred alongside them, and the rider jumped down.

'Mrs Blakewood,' he said. 'Mr Keyte. I am pleased to meet you again.' He led the horse to a bar on the side of the road, tying it fast. 'I must admit, I had no idea you were so in the governor's favour. Or that of our mutual friend.'

'Mr Oldfield,' acknowledged Mercia. 'If the governor esteems us, the regard we hold for him is even more pronounced.'

Amery Oldfield, the soon-to-be Meltwater schoolmaster, let out a quiet chuckle. 'Of course, I do not know you myself – and Percy will be most displeased when he learns I have gone along with this – but our friend is so looking forward to seeing you again.'

'As we are to seeing him,' said Nathan. 'You will take us there?'

Amery nodded. 'The route will be a circuitous one, but do not be alarmed. It is necessary in case we are pursued.' He lowered his voice. 'I am concerned I am being watched. Follow me a little way behind, and if you are asked, say you are taking the night air.'

Without waiting for a response he set off, drawing his cloak around him in spite of the warmth. In truth he could not walk far before he disappeared from sight, so almost immediately they were forced to set off in pursuit. They did not pass many people as they walked, but some townsfolk were abroad, discernible in the light of torches: another couple walking out; a hunched figure carrying a basket; a tall man standing against a fence, his square head turning to follow them as they passed.

'He was not jesting,' said Nathan after several minutes walking. 'I think we have—yes! There is his horse. We are back at the corner where we met.'

Now Amery took a different path, striking out more quickly towards the edge of town. He passed through a gate, marching along the wall that marked the town boundary, before turning back in through a different entry, walking right, then left, then exiting through a third gate. This time he headed straight, walking a small distance into the fields until a lonely edifice came into view, seemingly abandoned: unlike most of the houses they had passed in the town, there were no candles at these windows.

'Here,' a voice murmured from behind a tree. 'Step in here.'

They did as the voice bade them, melting into the darkness; anyone on the road would need to have been looking right at them to notice.

'Are we here?' whispered Mercia.

'Yes.' Amery was looking over her shoulders. 'Good. I do not think we have been followed.'

Creeping towards the house, they stepped over a low fence and stole quietly through long grass to reach a recess in the rear wall; in the moonlight, Mercia could just make out a low cellar door at its base. Amery eased open the heavy hatch and held it for her to enter, but Nathan tapped her on the shoulder and went in first. She shook her head but let him, following immediately behind.

Feeling for purchase, she found herself descending a narrow set of wooden stairs, a strong earthen smell coming from all around. Behind, a soft thud signalled Amery had pulled the door shut. The space was now totally dark; she had to feel carefully so as not to fall down, but a few steps later her left ankle jarred as she came to the unexpected foot of the stairs. Holding onto Nathan's shoulder she shuffled a little way forward on what sounded like a cobbled floor. A short way off, a faint orange glow emanated from a spot to her right.

'The spirit of England lives on in her new namesake,' called Amery, making her jump. 'But the pines here are sweeter than the oaks of Kent.'

A pause, and then a familiar voice spoke from the darkness. 'Well remembered. Now I expect you should all like some light?'

Briefly the orange glow intensified before seeming to split in two, the brighter portion moving up and to the left. Its unexpected strength hurt Mercia's eyes, but once she had adjusted she looked across to see an illuminated figure in a man's doublet, his shadow cast on the wall behind. A small alcove in the wall was seemingly aflame, no doubt a fire at which the man had lit his torch.

'Mercia Blakewood,' he said, passing the torch to Amery and coming forward, his arms outstretched. 'I did not think to see you again so soon, but the meeting is most welcome.'

She put her hands in his, squeezing hard. 'Indeed, Mr Dixwell. Or should I be calling you Davids still?'

He laughed, keeping hold of her hands. 'Davids is the name I shall still go by in these parts, so I suppose tonight we had better stick to that.' He looked over her shoulder. 'And you, Mr Keyte. It is good to see you as well.'

Nathan stepped forward, a broad beam on his face. 'The pleasure is mine, sir. Thank you again for what you did in New York.'

'I shall never get used to calling it that.' He smiled, releasing Mercia's fingertips. 'But I doubt I shall be returning there, so what matter?' He turned to Amery. 'You are satisfied with the integrity of these people, as I said you would be?'

'Clemency and the governor are, and so I am too.' Amery looked at her askance. 'You must forgive the secrecy, Mrs Blakewood. But you understand, I hope.'

'I think so.' She nodded slowly. 'You and the others are a group helping men like Mr Davids hide away. I know of such societies in England and in Europe. It is natural one should exist here too.'

Amery's face was all seriousness. 'Clemency, Percy and I, we are part of such a group. We seek to help those men who must flee the King's wrath. Those men who sat in trial on his royal father to keep the peace – those same men who must now hide away or be killed.'

'You speak of men, Mr Oldfield,' said Nathan. 'There are more here than Mr Davids alone?'

'Perhaps,' said Amery, looking away. 'But it is best not to say too much.' He switched the torch between his hands. 'Let us just say that the

King may be restored in London, but he is not so welcome here. Many folk offer help and sustenance.' He turned to Mercia, looking on with interest. 'And you, Mrs Blakewood? What think you of the King?'

She glanced at Nathan. 'He is the King, Mr Oldfield. There is little one can say about that.'

'Yet he executed your father.'

She narrowed her eyes at his bluntness. 'He was misled into that. It is a bitter thing to accept, but I would be unjust to afford him all the blame.'

'Yet do not think so softly on the King,' said Davids. 'He has executed many of my fellows, and will have no remorse executing me if he gets the chance.' He raised an eyebrow. 'I am – what are they calling us in London now? – a regicide! One of those terrible judges who ordered his father's execution.' He spoke with drama, but Mercia could hear the worry in his words. 'It was fifteen years ago, at the end of a cruel civil war, but the King's memory is fierce. There is no mercy for us.'

'Perhaps one day,' said Nathan, 'you will be able to go back.'

Davids shook his head. 'The King will not rest until we are all on the scaffolds of Tyburn, hanged, drawn and quartered in his vengeful retribution.' He rubbed at his forehead. 'I am a regicide, Mr Keyte. I fled to America for safe haven, and now New York is denied me I must come here.' He glanced at Amery. 'I am grateful for your help, my friend. But I would rather give myself up than place others in danger for my sake.'

'We gladly give you our help,' said Mercia. 'You did not shy from aiding us when we needed it. Do not hold back from requesting what you need now.'

Davids frowned at Amery, the torchlight accentuating the creases in his forehead. 'You have not even asked her?'

'I have not yet had the chance.' He swapped hands again, causing Davids' shadow to waver on the wall. 'You see, Mrs Blakewood, we intend to take him to Meltwater. With the arrival of the royal fleet, the larger towns like Hartford and New Haven are no longer safe. We hope to hide him there for a short time before moving him further north.'

'And as we are now going ourselves, you wondered if we could help?'

He nodded. 'It was meant to be Clemency and I, but she decided she had to leave.' He looked between her and Davids. 'You seem to know each other already, so I do not see any harm can come of it.'

Davids bit his lip. 'Amery, I am still not sure. I came to Hartford as I knew I could seek out your group, but I did not think to involve Mercia.' He looked at her. 'If you are found out, you will be in grave jeopardy. You have a son, do you not?'

'Yes. But there is such a thing as honour, Mr Davids. Danny can remain with the governor.'

'Wait.' Nathan folded his arms. 'If we agree to this, I need your assurances that Mercia will be protected.'

'I understand your concern,' said Amery, 'but there will be no reason to suspect us. We are all riding to Meltwater in any case, me to take up my position, you to visit Clemency. We will put our belongings in a cart and hide Mr Davids with them. Percy will meet us as we near the town.'

Davids frowned. 'Does Percy know about this?'

'Not . . . as such.'

'You mean no. Will he approve Mercia's involvement?'

'He has little choice. Clemency and I are satisfied, if you are. Otherwise it will be me alone, and one man could raise suspicion with such a large cart.' He turned to Mercia. 'But Clemency was anxious that I say her invitation stands whatever you decide. There is no expectation on you of any kind.'

Mercia looked at Nathan. 'We have decided. We are going to help.'

Davids held up a hand. 'One thing more before I consent. What of Thorpe? You said he was in Hartford.'

Nathan's head jerked up. 'What is this?'

'Thorpe is—hold this, will you?' Amery passed the torch to Nathan and shook out his aching hand. 'He lives in Meltwater, a keen supporter of the King. I do not know why, but he is in Hartford tonight.' He chuckled his double laugh. 'But do not worry. Although the governor knows nothing. . . he does seem to have arranged a meeting with Thorpe at about the time I was hoping to leave in the morning.'

'The cunning fox.' Nathan shook his head. 'Very well. If Mercia is happy, so am I.'

Davids bowed. 'My friends, I am humbled by your kindness. Let us then hope our little intrigue works.'

Chapter Six

A lazy beam of sunlight sundered into five dust-strewn rays as it played its way through the branches of the tall Connecticut trees. Riding through the forest, Mercia stopped at a bend in the track to look back at her party: Nathan riding close behind; Nicholas steering the horse that was pulling their cart; Amery Oldfield keeping a steady eye on the bundle of covered belongings from the rear. They had been three hours on the road, and although the weather was good, the mood in the group was tense.

Having agreed to help Davids, there was no longer any question Daniel would have to stay behind; she had felt a mixture of melancholy and guilt as she watched him wave her off, but before she was out of sight he had returned to his friends, his mother already forgotten. Picking Davids up had taken her mind off it: while her company had paused at the side of the road as if to rest, Amery had fetched the regicide from his hideout, the group keeping close watch as he crept into the cart to be enveloped in a mass of blankets.

It was around thirty miles to Meltwater, so Winthrop said; they had started at first light with hope of arriving by mid afternoon. The road was now dry, the earth hard for the horses' hooves, but the ruts were deep in places, formed after the previous rains. She pitied Davids, surely feeling each jolt as the cart stuttered along the track. Nicholas was continually pausing his horse, allowing it to gather its strength to drag the heavy cart onwards.

They were rounding a bend when the sound of distant hooves floated into Mercia's hearing. She stopped, listening, signalling to Nathan to do the same. The sounds were coming from behind, and were growing in volume, the individual clops following each other in quick succession. Whoever was on the horse was approaching fast.

'Side of the road,' ordered Nathan. 'Wait in the shade of these trees. Let me see who is coming.'

'Hopefully just another traveller,' said Amery.

'Hopefully.' Nathan watched as Nicholas reined in his horse and stopped the cart. 'But let us be safe. Winthrop said not many people travel this road.'

The oncoming rider seemed now nearly at the bend. Of a sudden a horse burst into view, the rider bending low over his mount. Remarking the stationary group, he reined in, slowing quickly. Too quickly, for the horse stopped too suddenly for him to control: it was only the straps holding him down that prevented him vaulting over its neck and onto the hard earth.

'Here you are,' he managed to shout. 'I have pursued you all the way from Hartford!'

'Pursued us?' Aware of a sharp intake of breath from Amery, Mercia trotted to the other side of the rider's horse, drawing his attention from the cart. 'We were not expecting anyone to travel with us.'

The rider stared, stroking the brown sash he was wearing over his jacket. 'Really, Mrs – Blakewood, is it? Sir William must have informed you of me? Perhaps Governor Winthrop?'

The lightest of shrugs. 'Sir William has mentioned nothing.'

In truth she had spoken with the nobleman only briefly that morning, telling him more from courtesy than anything that she was leaving town. He had seemed disappointed, even irked, but she was too preoccupied with her impending task to take much notice.

'What?' The rider seemed genuinely surprised. 'Didn't mention my special commission from the King himself? I spoke of it with Governor Winthrop this morning, although of course you will have left by then.' He coughed. 'Still, he said nothing about your departure. It fell to Sir William to inform me you were headed the same way.' He looked at her over his horse's swinging head. 'And in somewhat of a hurry.'

Nathan rode forwards, positioning himself alongside her. 'Be that as it may, you have still not said who you are.' Briefly, he shot Mercia a glance; she saw he suspected as well as she did who the man must be.

The rider rummaged in his saddlebag, withdrawing a rolled parchment and handing it over. There was a steady gleam in his eyes, his head too straight in the air. A cold twinge began to form in Mercia's stomach.

'Read this,' he said.

His eyes fixed on the man, Nathan unrolled the parchment before looking down to read. 'I see. This is Richard Thorpe. He has been appointed an agent of the King's commissioners in New York. This is his authority; it has the seal of Governor Nicolls himself.'

The cold twinge grew stronger. She blinked, resisting the urge to look at the cart. 'Does it say anything further?'

He scanned the parchment. 'It says he is to – hell's teeth, this writing is difficult to read – take advantage, is that? – of any opportunities . . . presented to him to survey the lands of New England . . . and so on . . . for the purpose of expediting the mission of the King's commissioners in understanding their American lands' – he looked up – 'and in uncovering the King's enemies in so acting.'

'Let me see that.' Amery came forward to take the parchment, adding his mount to the equine barrier now formed in front of Thorpe. When he had finished reading, he looked up. 'Mr Thorpe, my name is Amery Oldfield. I am to be the new schoolmaster in Meltwater. I have heard of you by reputation, but I did not realise you were acting on behalf of the King now.'

'Yes.' Thorpe's stern expression relaxed. 'I rode to New York as soon as I heard of the fleet's arrival. I wanted to offer my services to the King's commissioners. I have the time, and well, I have the inclination.'

Mercia put on a smile. 'Your dedication does you credit, Mr Thorpe, but we have a long way to go.' She shunted closer to Nathan, opening a side gap she hoped Thorpe would ride on through. But he simply stared.

'Why are you going to Meltwater?'

She steadied her horse. 'To see a friend.'

'And why are you travelling with this man?' he said, looking at Amery.

'Because it is convenient, that is all. We met in Hartford and are now riding together.'

'A pleasant grouping, then.' Drawing a thin finger across his square jaw, Thorpe leant up in his saddle, trying to peer into the cart. 'Perhaps I will ride with you. Meltwater is my home. I am physician and surgeon there.'

'Thank you,' said Amery, attempting his two-tone laugh, 'but surely we will slow you. Do you not need to inform the magistrate of your commission as soon as possible?'

'Indeed.' Thorpe kicked his right foot from its stirrup. 'But I shall need to observe the terms of that commission first.'

'Meaning what?' said Nathan. Unlike the other two, he seemed perfectly composed; a result of his soldiering past, perhaps.

Thorpe jumped from his horse. 'I journeyed to Hartford from New York with Sir William.' He looked up at Mercia. 'Then this morning, as I was taking my leave before intending to ride for home, he seemed agitated. He said you had been in town, but that you were leaving sooner than he had expected.' Straightening his sash, he began to walk around the horses. 'I was surprised, for I had thought if you were going to Meltwater, you would have been told I was in Hartford and would welcome the company. But you left without me. Quickly. And heading to visit a woman who has been known to indulge in certain . . . illegal activities. So while I am sure nothing will be untoward, I fear I am required to examine your cart.' He grunted. 'I owe it to my horse, which I pushed hard to catch you up.'

'Mr Thorpe.' Mercia's stomach was now churning. 'Where I ride and whom I visit is really none of your concern. And as you see fit to mention him, Sir William is an acquaintance of mine. If we could get back on our way, it would be much the better for all of us.'

'Mrs Blakewood.' Thorpe wagged his finger at the parchment Amery was still holding. 'If you read that thoroughly, you will see I have orders to check all who use the highways. The Duke is anxious nothing eludes him.' Clear of the horses, his eyes rested on the cart. 'So I must ask what you are carrying with you.'

'Mr Thorpe, these are friends of Governor Winthrop.' Amery's voice was grim. 'He would not be happy at this treatment.'

'Alas, that matters not.' Thorpe sniffed. 'Particularly given Mrs Blakewood's . . . family.'

Nathan set his face. 'Have a care how you speak – Mr Thorpe.'

Thorpe sighed. 'I am trying to be delicate, Mr . . . whoever you are – but if I must spell it out, I will. Her father was executed for treason. Now she is here in America. My commission demands that I search anyone I feel I should.' He stepped towards the cart. 'I am going to do just that.'

Mercia closed her eyes, feeling sick. She had intended to help Davids; would her very presence now be the reason he was discovered? She made herself look at the cart, her hands clenching her reins. But then she frowned, surprised to see Nicholas dismounted from his horse and barring Thorpe's way.

'Out of my way,' ordered Thorpe.

Nicholas did not move. 'Ask nicely.'

'I beg your—who is this man?'

'He is my manservant,' she said.

'Then tell him to stand aside.'

'Why, so you can go through a lady's garments?' Nicholas folded his arms. 'I would be a poor manservant if I let that insult go unchallenged.'

Visibly irked, Thorpe tugged at his sash. 'Show me what is in the cart, or I shall assuredly report your insolence.'

Nicholas stared him down for several seconds. Then he smiled, taking a pace to his side.

'If you insist.'

Shaking his head, Thorpe brushed past to set his hand on the side of the cart. Scarcely breathing, Mercia saw Amery, calmer than she, move his hand to his side; looking askance, she watched as he pushed back his cloak, revealing a pistol wedged in his belt.

'Now, let me see,' muttered Thorpe.

Slowly, Amery gripped the handle of his gun. As Thorpe reached into the cart, he began to ease it from his belt. Mercia held herself ready, her whole body on alert as Thorpe threw back the blankets, and then – she stifled a gasp.

Where Davids had been hidden, nobody was there.

She looked at Nicholas, battling to prevent a deep frown of puzzlement from breaking across her face, but he remained impassive. Amery withdrew his hand, covering his pistol once more with his cloak. Nathan merely held still his horse.

'Well, then.' His inspection complete, Thorpe's cocksure demeanour had fled. 'You understand I am merely following instructions. It is part of my new role.'

Recovering her composure, she cleared her tight throat. 'I suggest you be more careful whom you inspect in future, Mr Thorpe. You may have the right but you do not have to use it.' She pursed her lips. 'Now I shall have to ensure my belongings remain in order.'

Thorpe stared. 'You cannot think I have—'

She jumped from her horse, sending up dust from the dry earth. 'I can think what I like. Please, I am embarrassed enough. I would like to check, and to do so undisturbed.' She glanced at Amery. 'Besides, given this – misunderstanding – perhaps you should more properly explain your

68

commission to Mr Oldfield here, so he can better know what to expect.'

'Yes.' Amery nodded, tugging on his reins. 'Shall we ride ahead, Mr Thorpe?'

Thorpe swallowed, his unsure eyes darting in all directions. 'I suppose that would be wise.' Remounting his horse, he kicked at its flanks. 'Very well. Get your cart in order, and then back on the road. Meanwhile, Oldfield – you come with me.'

Unseen by Thorpe, Amery widened his eyes at Mercia before falling in beside him. As soon as the pair were a safe distance ahead, she rounded on Nicholas.

'By God's truth, man. What is going on?'

He held up his hands. 'No need to be angry. All I did was get off my horse and help Davids from the cart. I knew Thorpe would pay me no heed while he was talking to you. That sort of princock never does.'

'But what if he had seen?' she pursued, still agitated from their near escape.

He shrugged. 'He didn't. You had him fair well surrounded.'

'Nicholas, I—' About to rebuke him for taking such a risk, she stopped in surprise as Nathan burst out laughing.

'Well done,' he said, fair shaking in the saddle in his mirth.

His unexpected reaction broke the tension. She found herself smiling too, although she did not know why.

'Yes, well done,' came a voice from the wood. Brushing leaves from his jacket, Davids emerged in their midst. 'Thank you, Wildmoor. I think you just saved my life.'

'He saved Thorpe's,' she said, a powerful relief now racing through her body. 'Amery had a gun.' She looked up at Nathan. 'And I think he would have used it.'

'Amery?' Davids smiled. 'All he talks of is alchemy and books. But that was good thinking, Wildmoor.' He put a hand on the cart, raising his left leg to clamber in. 'Back to my comfortable lodgings, I suppose.'

A short time after restarting, Amery dropped back to join them, but Thorpe continued to ride ahead, whether preferring his solitude or through haughty aloofness Mercia could not tell. But she was thankful, for it kept him from the cart, its human contraband once more hidden within.

As the afternoon progressed she felt the tension return, worrying ever more frequently whether they would be unmasked. Every stretch of road, every bend seemed to take forever, but they had no more encounters, Thorpe gradually passing from sight. After some time, longer to her than in reality, she supposed, the trees began to thin, a purl of smoke appearing above the canopy. A log blocking the road was the marker for them to release Davids into the woods; her heart thumped as she saw Thorpe waiting before it, but he merely ordered them to move the flaking trunk before leaping over and continuing on. She said goodbye to Davids with a proud sense of fulfilled duty: in turn, he gripped her hands in gratitude before disappearing into the trees where Amery said Percy Lavington would be waiting.

Their task complete, and the log heaved away, the mood in the group changed to cheerful relief. Soon the trees gave way to open meadows where a number of people were scything corn, the unfamiliar crop surrounded by numerous orange heads of a large, grooved vegetable Amery called a pumpkin. As they approached, the workers broke from their tools, staring at the new arrivals; Mercia smiled down, receiving uncertain greetings in return. And then a wooden palisade appeared before them, curving away left and right. Beyond, the smoke rose now more clearly, filling the air with the promise of homes and people.

'Meltwater,' said Mercia. 'At last!'

Riding alongside, Nathan was leaning forward in his saddle. 'I cannot wait to see what they have accomplished.' His eyes seemed to glint. 'Such fearlessness to live out here.'

Away to their left rose a small, flat-topped hill, a half-finished structure sitting atop, before the road ducked down to avoid a tiny plot of gravestones, finally ending at an open gate in the south section of the palisade. A severed head was nailed above the narrow opening, the spear and arrow beside it suggesting their former owner's provenance had been Indian. So, considered Mercia, thinking of the heads of traitors that were displayed on London Bridge, some things are very much the same in America as they are in England.

Leaving Nathan and Nicholas to look after the cart and horses, she entered the town with Amery. A wide main street led directly in front, meeting the encircling palisade at its far end, although the gate on that side was currently closed. A shout to their right drew her attention; Thorpe, who had entered the town before them, was waving his letter of authority at a sturdy-looking man, a number of townsfolk looking on.

'I ask you again,' he was saying. 'Where is Mr Lavington?'

'And I ask you,' returned the other, 'to pass that parchment down here.' He stood with arm outstretched, waiting.

'My business is not with you, Constable.'

The burly man kept his gloved arm straight. 'Thorpe, did you see that festering head on the gate?'

Thorpe peered down. 'Of course.'

'Well, it was I cut it clean off that thieving brute's shoulders while you were away and nailed it there. Your surgeon's knife is not the only sharp blade here.' He tightened his fingers against the hilt of the rapier that was hanging at his side. 'Now pass me that letter, lest you want your own head to join it.'

Some of the townsfolk laughed, making Thorpe's jaw clench, but he leant over his horse to pass down the parchment. The constable snatched it from his fingertips and read quickly, his eyes speeding from left to right. As he read, Mercia felt a bright presence beside her; she looked round to see Clemency smiling, the breeze fluttering her light-red dress. Feeling conscious of her own dusty brown outfit, she brushed at her sleeves and returned the smile.

'You came, then,' said Clemency. 'I was not certain you would.'

Mercia beamed at her new friend. 'Of course I have. How could I not?'

Clemency lowered her voice. 'I feared you might think I was using

71

you for . . . the other matter. But I am so glad you are here.' She nodded towards Thorpe. 'He was on the road with you?'

'Yes.' Not wanting to alarm her, Mercia feigned nonchalance. 'But most everything went as it should.'

By now the constable had finished his perusal of the document. Without looking up, he clicked his fingers and a wide-eyed boy ran forward.

'Take this to Mr Lavington,' he ordered. 'Now.'

'That is for me to do,' objected Thorpe.

'Go!' The constable handed the boy the paper, sending him on his way with a swipe to the head. Ignoring Thorpe, he instead marched across to Mercia. 'Now,' he said. 'Who are you?'

'You know who she is, Godsgift,' said Clemency. 'She is the friend I talked of. Mercia Blakewood, the daughter of one of Oliver Cromwell's old aides.'

The constable grunted dismissively. 'Much good he ever did.'

'And this is Amery Oldfield, our new schoolmaster.'

Amery bowed. 'Constable. It is a pleasure to be greeted by you.'

Another grunt. 'Save your flatteries for the magistrate.' He sniffed. 'Very well, Mrs Carter, I will leave you to vouch for these people.' He pulled the bottom of his jacket down tight and pivoted on his well-worn boot heel, striding away.

'Wait,' shouted Thorpe. 'Now you have read my authority I insist you acknowledge it!'

'Insist all you like.' The constable carried on, not turning his head. 'I make the laws here, Thorpe. Not the King, and certainly not you, for all you preen in that foolish sash.'

As Thorpe blustered on his horse, Clemency laughed. 'Welcome to Meltwater, my friends. Don't mind Godsgift. He is quite the old soldier. I would say he is harmless but' – she glanced back towards the gate, where the iron spike that was securing the severed head was sticking through – 'he is not.'

'It is of no matter. We are just pleased to be here. The journey was long.' Mercia looked at Thorpe's back as he rode off down the street.

72

'If I had known he would arrive with you, I would never have put you in such danger.' Clemency bit her lip. 'But I hope you understand why I had to leave.'

'Of course. How is the child now?'

'Better, I hope. And thank the Lord you are both here safe.' She turned to Amery. 'When I returned, I could barely restrain Percy from setting out for Hartford in my stead.'

Amery sighed. 'Percy needs to trust us better.' He bowed at Mercia. 'Thank you again, Mrs Blakewood, for your help. You will excuse me while I pay my respects to Percy's father.'

'Yes, you go,' laughed Clemency. 'Mr Lavington will not like to be kept waiting.' She winked at Mercia. 'Come. I will take you to secure your lodgings.'

Amery gone, Mercia returned outside the palisade for Nathan and Nicholas, leading them in through the gate. Deprived of their prior entertainment, the townsfolk turned their attention to the new arrivals, eyeing them with undisguised curiosity. Feeling lightly embarrassed, Mercia looked instead at the town as she walked after Clemency. Smaller than New Haven or Hartford, she could only make out two streets: the thoroughfare she was walking, running south to north, and another intersecting it at a crossroads up ahead, where a small rectangular building sat shorn of adornments.

'Our meeting house,' said Clemency as they turned right at its steps. 'In other words, our church.' She drew to a halt, setting her hand on a white fence post. 'Where is Daniel, by the way?'

'I left him with the governor. After today, I am glad I did.'

'As long as he is well, that is the important thing.' She swung off the post. 'Now, we need to go in here before we do anything else.'

Mercia looked up at a wooden-slatted building slightly larger than the others surrounding it. 'This is our lodgings?'

'No.' Clemency smiled. 'This is Old Humility's place of gathering for the Elect.'

73

'The Elect?' said Nicholas.

'And anyone else who wants to use it. The Elect is what we – Puritans – call those among us who are chosen by God to be saved. A reward denied more and more of us as the years go on, it seems.' She edged towards the building. 'This is supposedly a tavern, Mercia, but 'tis nothing like where we went the other night, so do not expect much.'

Pushing open the white door, she led them into a dim, sparse room, about as remote from an English tavern as Mercia could envisage. There was no noise, no bustle, no stickiness to the floor, no serving hatch either, just a number of tables and benches, not many of them occupied. In the corner, an older, corpulent man rose from a chair altogether too small for his weight.

'The inaptly named Humility Thomas,' whispered Clemency. 'The tavern keeper.'

Wiping his hands on his apron, the man ambled across. 'So this will be the English folk,' he said. 'And near right when you thought they would come.' He looked at Clemency. 'I always said you were a clever one.'

Clemency rolled her eyes and had begun to retort when the other men in the tavern leapt from their seats. Three ran for Nathan, forcing him against the wall as another two grappled with Nicholas. Both struggled but were caught off guard, trapped in a strong grip.

'What on earth?' said Clemency.

'Sit down.' Humility peered at Mercia. 'You too, my lady. Now, you had best answer my questions in a way I find pleasing, or we shall see who fights better, Americans or English.' He licked his lips. 'And from the look of it, I don't think your boys stand much chance.'

74

Chapter Seven

'My God,' growled Nicholas. 'This is worse than the Anchor back home. I thought you lot were meant to be holy.'

'Let them go.' Mercia took a seat, undeterred by the men posturing about her. 'You do not know me, for if you did you would know I have been in worse situations than this.' She looked down, straightening her dress with deliberate palm strokes. 'Which means neither I nor my companions are scared of your threats.'

Humility stared a moment, before throwing back his head and descending into guttural laughter. 'A feisty one you have here, Clemency. I see why you have an acquaintance.'

'There is no need for this,' said Clemency. 'What do you think is going to happen?'

'That is what I am trying to find out, perhaps prevent.' Humility called to his friends. 'Vic, show those two to a seat.'

The man he called Vic grabbed Nathan with a muscled arm and thrust him towards a chair, or rather he tried to, for no sooner was he released than Nathan slammed him against the wall in his place. Immediately the other townsmen seized him by the shoulders.

'By God's truth!' Clemency stared at Humility. 'Tell your dogs to be silent.'

'Nathan, Nicholas, come and sit,' ordered Mercia. 'Perhaps talking will solve these people's problems more readily than fighting.'

Gradually the five combatants broke off, but nobody sat. 'I think we should stay standing,' said Nathan.

Nicholas nodded. 'Too right.'

She sighed. 'As you wish.'

'And you, Victory, Fearing,' said Clemency. 'Come now. What grievance do you have with these folk?'

'That depends why they are here,' said Vic, his lightly pockmarked face sharp with distrust. 'Perhaps they would enlighten us?'

'They are here because I invited them. That is all.'

He peered into her eyes. 'And how do you know this? Trust?'

'That is not fair. I do trust these people.' She glanced at Mercia. 'This woman, at least, and she speaks for the rest.'

Mercia inclined her head. 'Are you always so welcoming to strangers?'

A younger, dark-haired man, one of the duo who had tackled Nicholas, emerged from the back of the group. His eyelashes were long, accentuating his handsome aspect.

'When you live on the edge of God's creation you learn to question others' motives,' he said.

'Kit.' Clemency sighed. 'Surely someone not long come from England should not treat others with such suspicion.'

Kit shrugged his slender shoulders. 'There were those who did not trust me when I arrived. I do not hold it against them.'

The man Clemency had called Fearing folded his arms. 'Perhaps you have come to take news of us back to your masters in New York.'

Mercia studied him; after Humility he seemed the eldest, his tanned face worn with creases. 'So that is what worries you. You think we are here to spy for the Duke. I assure you we are not.'

'And yet Percy says you arrived in America with the King's own fleet. Then you appear in Meltwater close behind Richard Thorpe.' He looked at Humility. 'He has gone to see Lavington. We will have to get him to tell us what they spoke of.'

'Good luck.' Humility lowered himself into a seat. 'Now answer Vic's question, Mrs Blakewood. We are keen to hear your response.'

'Very well. It is a long story, but if you are prepared to listen, I will tell it.'

Taking in her audience, Mercia began her tale, heeding Winthrop's advice by talking of the King and his brother as little as possible. As she spoke, some of the men sat, leaning towards her so as better to hear. They nodded; they winced; they glanced away; and when she had finished, only the breeze rattling in the windows could be heard. 'So you see,' she concluded, 'I am here because I am fighting for my son and for myself. I came to Meltwater as I understood you would share something of the same spirit.' She looked around the room. 'Was I mistaken?'

A brief silence. Then Kit, who had stayed standing, bowed his head. 'You were not. I apologise for my actions.'

'As do I,' said Vic. 'We shall judge you by your conduct.' The others remained silent but made no fresh argument.

Humility rose from his chair: it took some seconds. 'Clemency has asked if I will offer you my son's cottage this week.' He reached into his pockets. 'So here is the key to the plate chest. You can stay there for naught, in apology for our rough welcome.' He rubbed the small key on his apron. 'But you must understand – we love our town. The spirit you spoke of, we plough it into the buildings, into the land, our church. We will do what we must to protect it, from the King or from anyone.' His circular eyes drilled into hers. 'Anything at all.'

Mercia took the key. 'I understand. And I am grateful.'

A sudden chill swept into the room as the door fell open, a woman on the threshold removing her woollen hood. She was young, her auburn hair falling over red cheeks, her rough brown jacket contrasting with Clemency's more colourful attire. Her eyes roved the group, resting on Nicholas for a brief moment; he smiled, but she did not respond, continuing her sweep.

'Father,' she said, her eyes stopping on Fearing. 'What are you doing here?'

'Talking with these newcomers, Remembrance, that is all.' Fearing frowned, the furrows around his eyes deepening into grooves. 'I thought I told you to stay at home.'

The young woman's eyes flicked to Mercia. 'These are the people from Hartford?'

'England,' said Fearing. 'Come at Clemency's request for a few days.'

Remembrance nodded; she did not appear particularly interested. Behind her Nicholas was still staring; Mercia noticed Nathan looking too. She could not deny the woman was beautiful, if a little haggard for her age, the signs of an outdoor life clear on her ruddy skin.

'Mother is looking for you,' she said. 'She fears Praise is getting worse.'

Gruff until now, Fearing swallowed. 'Worse?' He turned to Clemency. 'But I thought you said the antim—the medicine would help?'

'I thought it was helping.' Clemency rose from her chair. 'The Governor prescribes it for many such cases of flux as this.' She tightened her jacket. 'Mercia, I must go and see to Praise-God. I am sure now tempers have calmed that someone will show you to your lodgings.'

'Please,' said Mercia. 'Do what you must.'

Clemency followed Fearing through the door. 'I will call on you later. Forgive me – I must go.'

Mercia watched her friend leave the tavern, a shard of anxiety in her chest. She thought of Daniel, and was glad he was safe with Winthrop. Then she looked at Nathan and she could tell what he was thinking, recalling what had happened in his own past. The worry in Remembrance's eyes was unmistakable. Silently, she uttered a prayer as the young woman glanced at Humility and left.

It was Kit who showed them to their cottage. Turning right at the meeting house to take the northern road, it was not far off.

'This is Old Humility's place.' Kit rested his hand on the wooden gate, a number of small grazes fading from his pale skin. 'Or his son's, at least. He lives in New Haven, but he owns this too.' He shook his head. 'Still, it means it is empty, and furnished enough for your needs.' He looked from Mercia to Nathan. 'There are two bedrooms.'

Mercia peered up at a well-kept cottage, wooden clapboard walls beneath a shingled roof. It was simple; she liked it. 'What of Nicholas?'

Kit tugged at a thin cord around his neck. 'I think Clemency was hoping he would share with someone – Amery, I think. He has a cottage next to the new schoolhouse, just down the way.' He glanced at Nicholas. 'As he has no wife, she did not seem to think you would mind.'

'Fine by me. I am used to sharing.' He looked at Mercia. 'Shall I fetch the cart?'

Mercia nodded and he set off back the way they had come. She smiled at Kit. 'You are not long arrived from England, Mr . . . ?'

'West. I have been here about three years now.' He pushed open the gate. 'But Meltwater is still recently founded, so we are all new in a sense. Shall we go in?'

He led them inside the cottage, the door knocker swinging its beaver's tail against the wood as they bent under the lintel to enter. A tiny hall space with the brick end of a fireplace directly in front led onto two rooms to left and right. Indicating the left, Kit ushered them into a cosy sitting room enhanced by a smattering of wooden furniture and a large ironclad hearth.

'This is what we call the best room, the sitting room. It is agreeable?'

'Most certainly.' Mercia looked around the small room in delight. A staircase led up from the back corner. 'The bedrooms are upstairs?'

Kit nodded. 'Two rooms upstairs, and two down. The other room on this floor is the keeping room and can be used as a place to eat or prepare. There are cooking tools within.' He turned to leave. 'And now, if I may, I must return to my sawmill. It will be dark before long.' He bowed, setting his hands together in prayer. 'May God watch over you while you are here.'

She looked out the window. 'I would rather God watch over Praise-God Davison.'

Kit's face twitched. 'It is not for you to tell the Lord what he should do, nor I. We can only ask and hope his angels are watching.'

His words disconcerted her. 'I did not mean to offend.'

'You did not.' He stooped to regain the hall. 'Please, ask if you need anything. Despite what you may think, we are friendly folk.'

Nathan waited for him to leave, then pulled a face. 'A peculiar kind of friendliness.'

'They will get used to us.' Smiling, she busied herself looking around the house, relatively small but more than sufficient for a few nights. The bedrooms were sparsely furnished, just a bed, table and dresser in each, but the view from one bedroom made up for it: if she stood in the right place, she could see over the palisade to the fields and woods beyond.

'You will want this room, then,' Nathan grinned.

'Oh yes.' She turned her head the other way towards the meeting house. 'Ah – Nicholas is here with the cart.'

As the two men unloaded her belongings she reviewed the contents of the keeping room: ironware to cook with, firewood for the hearth. Back in the best room she found the plate chest, then set to work lighting the fire, swearing as she struggled to make the kindling catch. Finally succeeding, she stepped back to take in the burgeoning heat.

'That's everything,' said Nicholas, coming up from behind. 'I'll find out where to leave the cart and then, I suppose, where Amery lives.'

She roused herself from the growing flames; fire was always captivating, somehow. 'That reminds me. Amery said he was going to pay his respects to the town magistrate. I had best do so myself.'

'What – now?' Nathan came into the room, wiping his forehead with a ragged cloth. 'We have only just arrived.'

'Politeness does not wait.' She smiled. 'But you should stay here in case Clemency comes.'

He wound the cloth round the leg of an upturned stool. 'Merely to introduce yourself, eh?'

She scratched at the back of her hand. 'Why else?'

'Winthrop's request about the drowned minister, perhaps?'

'Oh, that.' She pulled her hood around her topknot. 'It has not much crossed my mind!'

An elderly woman sweeping leaves from the meeting house step told her where Lavington lived: it was the largest house in town, halfway between the central crossroads and the southern gate. Leaving Nicholas to hunt for Amery, she ambled in the direction she was shown. A metallic clanging drew her attention to an open gateway: Vic from the tavern was striking with a heavy hammer at an anvil, orange sparks flying in all directions. She paused for a moment to watch, but when he looked up she bowed her head and carried on. A woman in the doorway of the next building bade her good cheer as she passed, and then she came to Lavington's house, much more extensive than the neighbouring dwellings, its chimneys thrusting into the sky. A single-storey addition was visible at the back.

Pushing open another white gate she walked down a short weeded path. A bear's head stared straight out at her, an iron knocker sitting flush in the middle of the front door. She rapped twice, awaiting a response.

Shortly the door swung open. A red-cheeked woman poked her head through the gap, a questioning look on her face.

Mercia put on her best smile. 'My name is Mercia Blakewood. My companions and I are guests in your town – I wonder if I might see the magistrate to offer him my regards?'

The door opened further, revealing the woman's black serving dress. 'He is busy,' she said.

'With Mr Thorpe, perhaps?'

The woman tutted. 'Thorpe was here for all of five minutes.'

'Then could you ask?'

The woman pursed her lips but nodded, disappearing inside. Mercia waited on the step, unwilling to enter until invited. After a minute she looked back at the street. A tall man was staring at her, his arms folded, but when their eyes met he walked on. He looked like Standfast Edwards, she thought, although without the mole on his neck: a relation, perhaps?

Behind her, the serving woman cleared her throat. 'Mr Lavington will receive you. Will you come this way?'

Mercia followed her into an ample hall and through a wainscoted room where an oval table was laid with a fine pewter service. The far side of the room opened to the extension at the back of the house; entering the long space, she saw ranged along the right-hand wall a large bench covered with glassware, rather like Winthrop's equipment but of much more limited scope. A vial of a clear, viscous liquid was bubbling away above a small flame, the condensed drops collecting in a tall cylindrical beaker alongside. On the opposite wall, a series of shelves held rolls of parchment and books, while a grey-haired man was writing at a desk beneath, shaking his quill over a dripping vial of ink. A male servant waited nearby.

'Mrs Mercia Blakewood,' announced the woman.

The man rushed some last scribbles and rose, turning to face his guest. His expression seemed both welcoming and wary, his angular nose nestling between distinctly narrow eyes.

'Mrs Blakewood.' He smiled. 'Welcome to Meltwater. But come, let us talk in more comfortable surroundings. I am sure you cannot be interested in my work.'

'But I am.' She advanced towards the bench. 'What are you doing here?'

'No, I know how all that bores a woman.' With a nod at his man, he draped an elegantly covered arm around her back and steered her into the house. 'Let us go to the parlour and talk there.' He ushered her through the dining room; mildly irritated, she nonetheless allowed herself to be taken away.

'In here.' Lavington shepherded her into a finely decorated room across the hall, its walls papered with green fabric. Beckoning her sit in a blue-cushioned seat, he relaxed into an armchair that could only have been made in Europe: its rich satin upholstery spoke to its maker, an artisan on the continent.

'Mrs Blakewood,' he purred, smoothing the back of his hair. 'Such a delight. Will you take some wine?' He rang a silver handbell on a low table at his side. Within seconds, the female servant reappeared.

'Some of the best wine, Jemima. After all, Mrs Blakewood has come all the way from England.'

'Right away, sir.' The servant glanced at Mercia then stepped from the room, leaving them to engage in platitudes about travel and the weather. Moments later she returned, handing over two diamond-patterned glasses with curving stems.

'Thank you.' Mercia took a sip. 'This is excellent.'

'From France. I knew you would like it.' Lavington leant back in his chair, waving Jemima from the room. His crisp doublet creased as he reclined, exposing the white silk shirt beneath. 'Well then, Mrs Blakewood. What do you think of my town?' He swirled his glass, spilling a red drop unnoticed on his breeches. 'Somewhat different to what you are accustomed to, I expect?'

She held her glass on her lap. 'From what I have seen, it is a remarkable achievement. I understand it was founded but four years ago?'

'I led the people here myself.' He smiled. 'Governor Winthrop – we are close friends, you know – gave me the authority. An important trust, for we are close to the territory of the Dutch.' He looked away a moment. 'The Duke of York's lands now, I suppose.' He hesitated. 'I understand you met Richard on the road. Mr Thorpe. I hate to ask a stranger, but . . . since he was widowed, he does so like to keep things to himself.' He cleared his throat. 'I wonder – did he happen to say anything about this commission of his?'

She roved her eyes over his expectant face. 'Nothing he cannot have told you, I am sure. But people do seem nervous that the Duke's men are near.' She thought of her encounter in the tavern. 'Do you think they have cause?'

For a moment his liveliness faltered. 'Meltwater is mine, Mrs Blakewood, and it will stay that way – whatever Thorpe and his like care to think.' He sipped at his wine and smiled. 'But you are right. Such affairs need not concern you. You are staying as a guest of Mrs Carter, I hear?'

For several minutes they talked about the town, or rather Lavington talked, Mercia nodding at appropriate moments. When finally he paused to take another drink, she grabbed the opportunity to lead the conversation in a different direction.

'I wanted to ask you about a delicate matter,' she said. 'Governor Winthrop and I discussed it briefly.'

He held out a hand. 'Please.'

'It concerns your old minister.' She sighed; it was as well Nathan was not there, or he would have seen through it. 'I was with the governor when he found out the news of his death.'

A cryptic flicker of emotion crossed Lavington's face: annoyance, she thought, maybe sorrow?

'Indeed. A tragedy.'

She ran her finger round the rim of her glass. 'We were told he drowned.' She paused, but received no response. 'I know it has saddened the governor. He would be interested to know more of what happened, I am sure, and as you are close friends . . .'

Lavington set his glass on the table. 'We assume he fell in the river while out walking. There is little more to tell.'

'What of the paper that was found in his pocket? You have tried to read it, I presume?'

He pursed his lips. 'Naturally. But I did not think there was anything to heed. Godsgift asked Standfast to take it to Winthrop – a waste of his time, in my opinion. But the constable does as he pleases.'

'But the code itself,' she pursued. 'The governor wondered if it might not be symbolic of alchemy?'

Lavington sat up straight. 'I have no idea why Mason was carrying that parchment.' He reached up to twist at his left ear. 'He never expressed an interest in such things to me.'

'But you did investigate?'

'Why? The man was found drowned. An accident.'

'Drowned, as you say, but surely when a death like that—'

'Mrs Blakewood.' He laid his palms on the armrests of his chair. 'You will have to forgive me, but these are not really matters we need to discuss. And I am afraid I am a busy man.' He rose to his feet. 'My experiment, and then business to attend to – the latest agreements from the General Assembly and so forth.' He smiled, but it was clearly forced. 'We will meet again, no doubt.'

'I should like that.' She stood up herself, burning to ask more, but aware she had reached the mark. 'It was a pleasure to meet you, Magistrate. I look forward to my few days in your town.'

'A pleasure to meet you likewise.' He reached for his bell. 'Now please, let Jemima show you out.'

Chapter Eight

Leaving the grand house behind, Mercia did what she always did when she had more questions than answers: wander and think. Somehow, the act of walking calmed her, allowing her to focus on the problems at hand. She took a stroll through the small town, ambled outside the palisade, roamed the edge of the forests that opened up before her. It was not long before she reached a narrow river coming out of the woods. In the near distance, a small building straddled the flow: Kit's sawmill, no doubt, its wheel gently turning in the water's steady gait.

She allowed her mind to drift into the air around her, drawing in the sounds of the river and the scents of the pines, watching as the long grass underfoot brushed across her boots and the clouds journeyed across the sunlight overhead. She closed her eyes, breathing deep, the tree pollen tickling her nose. But then she sneezed, her mind drifted back, and she returned towards the palisade.

The pleasant environment was disturbed too soon. Not far from the northern gate, a woman came into view; facing the other way, her red dress nonetheless betrayed her for Clemency. She was clearly annoyed, shaking her head and throwing up her hands, arguing with the man she was blocking from sight, but as she approached, Mercia recognised Percy

Lavington, returned from his task with James Davids. He was talking as furiously as Clemency was waving, although his tone was subdued. Looking over her shoulder, he scoffed.

'And here she is herself!' he said. 'Mrs Blakewood, why don't you join us? Then perhaps you can interfere still more!'

Clemency twisted her neck. 'Hello, Mercia. I apologise for this.'

Mercia glanced at Percy. 'For what?'

'For him. For his ingratitude.'

'Ingratitude?' Percy laughed. 'I am not the one who asked her here. You imperilled the whole errand, Clemency. How can I trust you again?'

Mercia set her face. 'I came here of my own will, Mr Lavington. And I owed Mr Davids a debt. I intended to repay it.'

'What debt?' He waved a dismissive hand. 'All I know is I put a lot of effort into helping – those men – and I will not see them threatened. Do you have any idea what would happen if they were discovered?'

Mercia bridled. 'Of course I do.'

'Then leave these matters to me.' He turned back to Clemency. 'As for you, your tongue is too quick to let secrets slip.'

Clemency gritted her teeth. 'Amery agreed.'

'And he will hear my mind also.' Percy shook his head. 'But he is new to this, and you and I are not.'

She held his gaze an instant, but then she sighed. 'Very well. I am sorry, Percy. But I knew Mercia could help.'

'Let us just hope nobody saw her – help.' He snatched at his hair, long strands of black that snuck out from under his hat. 'Damn this. I have to think. Make plans, in case.' He thrust his finger towards Clemency. 'Leave me be for a while.'

'Is he always so contentious?' said Mercia, as he strode away.

'No. But where all . . . this . . . is concerned, he becomes taken with a harsh spirit.' She blew deeply out. 'I suppose he needs it. It drives him to take the risks he does. He probably gets it from his time in England.'

Mercia looked at the palisade gate. 'England?'

'I thought that would interest you.' She smiled. 'He went all that way to serve in Cromwell's government, but then the King was restored and he had to return. I think the disappointment is why he behaves so fervently with . . . our friends. That, and the mundanity of the everyday tasks of government he is charged with in the town. Counting fence posts, placing boundary stones, and the like.' She shook her head. 'He is not usually as you saw him today. He is an intelligent man, with little of the pomposity of his father. I would not stand it otherwise.' She raised an eyebrow. 'Maybe he needs a wife.'

Mercia laughed. 'Well, perhaps when he has calmed a little, we will be able to talk.'

'I hope so. I am used to his fretting, so it matters not to me.' She took her arm in her own. 'But forget that. We have some time to ourselves. Shall I show you my town?'

By next morning Mercia was already quite at home. Clemency invited her and Nathan for breakfast, Nicholas too, and the quartet made a morning of it. That Nicholas was Mercia's manservant seemed to make no difference to Clemency, for she involved him in her discussions about the town, about America, as much as she involved the others. Come late morning everyone was full on conversation and food; promising to call on Mercia later that afternoon, Clemency bade them farewell so she could set about the errands she had been putting off in consequence of their visit.

While Nathan went to talk with some of the townsfolk – local farming methods, she thought he said – and Nicholas disappeared she knew not where, Mercia kicked off her boots and stretched out in front of the unlit best-room fire, revelling in the lingering smell of woodsmoke that she always enjoyed. After a time she grew restless and she pulled on her cloak to wander the southern way out of town, thinking to investigate the structure she had seen on the hill when they had arrived. As she climbed, the sun lowering in the sky, she thought of Daniel in Hartford, hoping he was well, but confident he would be having a good time.

The structure turned out to be a half-finished fort made of wooden staves planted in the ground. A covered platform above the townward half sheltered a solitary cannon and a mortar besides, the smaller mortar aimed towards the town, while the more useful cannon was pointing at the forest. The open plot had the forlorn air of a halted building site. She sat for a while against the barricade, feeling drowsy in the warm afternoon air from the morning's feasting. After a time she began to doze in starts, never truly falling asleep but not quite awake either.

Finally she roused herself, or rather an unfamiliar animal did: as large as one of Nathan's farm dogs, its black and white face made her jump as it peered from atop the cannon, its striped tail swishing against the ironwork. She laughed at her foolishness and walked back down the hill, shaking herself awake with the freshness of early evening. Slinking through the cottage door she heard movement in the best room and smiled as she saw Nathan, knowing the tale of the strange creature would amuse him. But before she could speak he leapt from his chair.

'What is it?' she asked. 'Did you miss me that much?'

'No. Well, yes – but listen.' He bit his lip. 'It is that boy Clemency was treating.'

The distress in his eyes dispelled her good mood. 'No. Don't tell me—'

'I am afraid so. Clemency came to see you just now, to let you know.' He laid his hands on her shoulders. 'I am sorry. The boy is dead.'

This time she left by the western gate, venturing along the forest's edge although the light was fading. Soon she took a narrow path that rose through the trees, until after a short distance the sound of water began to permeate the air, gentle at first and then growing in strength until her destination came into sight: an extended waterfall, tumbling over cascades of worn-away rocks to whirl on stony outcrops below. The faint path climbed further to a clearing at the top, where a silhouetted figure sat alone on a rock, pulling at the long grass growing up around her.

Clemency raised her head as Mercia drew near, forcing a weak smile. Mercia could tell she was deciding whether she wanted company, but in the end she shuffled right, opening up space alongside.

'Nathan told me where you said you would be.' Mercia looked at her friend. 'I am so sorry.'

'It happens.' Clemency crumbled the ends of a grassy shoot into nothingness. 'But it is hard to lose someone you have been treating, especially a child.'

'You made every effort. You cannot blame yourself.'

'Perhaps.' She sighed, the unhappy sound fading into the water's roar. 'I do not even know why I went to tell you. All I wanted was to come here, to my favourite place, away from people. I did not want to talk to anyone, but I had promised to visit you, and suddenly that promise seemed very important.'

'You wanted something to hold onto.'

'I suppose I did.' A moment of silence when both women stared at the cascades, captivated by the white movement. 'Beautiful, isn't it?'

She sat beside her. 'Very.'

'This is why the town is called Meltwater.' Clemency swivelled to face her. 'When we arrived, in springtime, the ground at the base of these falls and all along the river was flooded from the thawing snow coming from the hills. The meadows further down, near where the town now lies, were so covered in the meltwater it seemed a natural thing to name the settlement for it. A change from the usual borrowing of English town names, at least. Even John Lavington agreed.' She looked away. 'It was one of the children who suggested it, I cannot remember who. We thought it apt that one of our youngest should give our community its name. Hope for the future.' A tear fell down her cheek. 'But this is no use. You have come to see New England and I have brought you this.'

'You have brought me nothing but excitement. Two weeks ago I was fighting for my life. Now I am in a new place, with a new friend.' She took Clemency's hand. 'Thank you.'

90

Clemency wiped away the tear. 'It has been a while since I had a real friend.'

'I said the same to Nathan.'

'I was already a widow when I moved here. What friends I had I left behind, but I wanted a new start. And I never had children. We tried, but I could not . . .' She closed her eyes. 'You are lucky to have Daniel.'

'He is my light.'

'And Nathan?'

'Yes. And Nathan.'

'Yet you feel guilty, I think, that your husband would not approve.'

Mercia withdrew her hand, shifting on the rock. 'Will and Nathan were close friends. It has taken me some time to accept that our own friendship could become different.' She looked again at the waterfall, at the darkening sky, so large. 'Perhaps if we had never come to America, nothing would have changed. You see, even in adversity there are surprises.'

Clemency slapped her palms on the rock. 'You are right. Who knows what will happen? Look at Praise-God, last month a happy child, now with our Lord. And my husband, so strong until a consumption wasted him away. Yes, those of us that still live must live. We owe it to those who do not.'

Mercia reached again for Clemency's hand. 'We can return here tomorrow, if you like. It would be wonderful to see it in full daylight.'

'That would be pleasant.' She smiled. 'I feel a little better now. I know I did what I could. Usually Winthrop's medicines work well, but the poor child must have heard the Lord calling and decided to be with Him.'

The women remained at the waterfall a short while longer, talking about their past, their present, as dusk descended around them, the river flowing over the falls in its eternal struggle with the rocks. Then Clemency rose, leading Mercia down the faint path, and they walked arm in arm to the town.

* * *

Not much hungry, Mercia soon retired and slept through the night, leaving yet again unread the hard-going book on alchemy Winthrop had decided to loan her for her stay; sometimes, she thought wryly, she would do well to appear less keen. She woke refreshed, stretching her arms into the sunlight darting through the small window of her room. Washing her face in water Nicholas had brought in last night from the town well, she pulled on her brown dress and hurried a breakfast of cold meats before heading outdoors with Nathan.

Immediately a gathering at the central crossroads caught her eye. A number of the townsfolk were assembling, Clemency among them, her grey bodice enhanced by its diamond- and dot-patterned stitching. Two men stood much taller than the rest, evidently on some sort of platform. As they drew nearer, she saw one was Standfast Edwards, the accusing preacher they had met in Hartford, while the other was an older man she did not recognise, bunched tips of thick white hair visible under his well-worn hat.

'Mercia, Nathan, good morning.' Clemency waved them across to her place at the back, seemingly recovered in spirits. 'I was coming to call on you. But as you are here – I am not sure if you will find this interesting. Renatus and Standfast are about to tell us why each of them should be our next minister.'

'You choose your own preacher?' asked Mercia.

Clemency nodded. 'When a new town is settled it is usually by a congregation following their minister, as happened here, although Lavington always claims we followed him.' She smiled. 'But whenever there is a vacancy, the congregation picks who they want as replacement. When there is more than one candidate the people assemble to choose.'

'And you all participate?'

'In the hearing, at least.' She raised an eyebrow. 'But today is merely a start, not the choice. So if you would like to listen to two bores debating the Half-Way Covenant then you are in luck. Otherwise I thought a ride into the forest, perhaps further into the hills.'

92

Nathan was looking at the two men with interest. 'Would you mind if we stayed to listen for a while? Just a few minutes.'

'Of course not,' said Mercia, not quite as enthusiastic. Clemency shrugged, indicating the proceedings were about to begin.

'Friends!' John Lavington had pulled himself onto the platform and was declaiming to the crowd, quite the natural. 'It was a sorry day when the Lord took Minister Mason, but in every loss there are beginnings. We all know how Renatus and Standfast wish to learn, through prayer and approbation, if it should be they to receive God's blessing to lead our congregation.' He paused. 'The choice is not mine, nor the General Assembly's, nor the King's' – here a jeer from the crowd; Mercia looked around for Thorpe, but did not see him – 'but it is a duty on us to decide who that man should be.' He lowered his head. 'No doubt as they preach, they will have words of instruction from the death of poor Praise-God Davison.'

The crowd gasped multiple intakes of breath: clearly not everyone had heard the news. As one they turned to scan their surroundings, but neither Fearing nor Remembrance were present, and so continuing their sweep, they fixed on Clemency instead. Quickly she lowered her eyes, but the murmuring died down as the elder candidate, Renatus, began to speak.

'First,' he said in sombre tones, 'I ask that you join me in praying for the soul of our beloved son Praise-God. Like too many he was not suffered to live long among we mortal men, but he is blessed to be received into the Lord's embrace so soon. We grant our child to His love and care, knowing we will see him again when our own time is come.'

Bowing his head, the crowd followed in still and shared quiet, birdsong and the rustling of leaves replacing their whispers. When the prayer was over, he continued:

'Brothers, sisters. You ask why I should be your shepherd. And 'tis well you ask, for the responsibility is great, not least here in the wilds where George Mason led us to the edge of the civilised world, naught but

God's innocent children in the woods beyond.' Beside her, Mercia heard Clemency gently scoff. 'Mark how I said led, friends, for a leader is what we need, to bring the gospel to those innocents, and to ensure our own children are educated in the ways of our Lord.' He paused. 'I can be that leader for you.'

'No matter that those innocents may not want to be converted,' whispered Clemency.

Renatus, head upright, now studied the crowd with searching eyes. 'I know there are many of you,' he pursued, 'who, like me, are discomfited that not all our children are permitted the cleansing of baptism. Should I receive your blessing, I will strive to bring them that right.'

At this, two reactions divided the crowd: for the most part there was nodding, even cheers, but a minority mingled sharp gasps with passion-filled cries: '*Not in Connecticut!*' Wondering what it was about baptism that inflamed the people here, Mercia looked around. At the crowd's edge, she noticed some bystanders giving way to a figure making its way through. As the auburn-haired newcomer pushed deeper in, the people parted in two waves, leaving her way open.

It was Remembrance Davison, the young woman staring straight at Mercia's group. She stood still for a brief moment, then ran screaming towards them. Mercia stepped back, the force of Remembrance's onslaught palpable even at a distance, as though the fury evident on her face could push back the cold air itself. Beside her, Clemency swallowed but stood her ground. In an instant Remembrance was upon them, arresting her quivering hand in impossible proximity to Clemency's throat.

'You killed him!' she cried. 'Little Praise! My little Praise.'

'I tried—' began Clemency, but Remembrance was not listening. She reached inside her black dress to draw a small pouch from her pockets. Tearing off the thin cord she took out a large pinch of powder, in one movement rubbing the white residue across Clemency's cheek.

'Take back your foul medicine, witch.' Smearing another pinch onto Clemency's forehead, she flung the remainder into her face.

'Take it back to whichever devil told you to poison my brother.'

Clemency stepped back. 'It was – one of Governor Winthrop's salves. It has worked before. I do not know why it failed this time.'

'It was not the governor,' screamed Remembrance. 'He knows his art. As you know yours!' She spat a drooling globule of hate into her face. 'Witch!'

Angered, Mercia wriggled from Nathan's loose grasp to stand between them. 'She was trying to help.'

Remembrance broke from Clemency, looking Mercia up and down. 'My brother is dead.' She hissed the words, a deep anger twisting them from her soul. 'What business is this of yours, stranger?'

'I grieve for your brother, as any woman would, stranger or friend. But—'

'How do you know what it is like to lose a brother?'

Personally stung, Mercia recoiled from the words. She looked away and noticed Fearing, Remembrance's father, now at the fore of the staring crowd, but holding back, not intervening. She swallowed, thinking how to respond, but Nathan laid a gentle hand on her shoulder and inched her aside.

'Miss Davison.' He moved to stand in front of Clemency. 'I know what you must be feeling. I lost a young child once. My daughter. She was only two.'

Slowly, Remembrance turned to him.

'There was an accident with her nurse. The woman who was meant to be protecting her caused her death.' His chest rose and fell. 'I blamed that woman for a long time, God forgive me. I wanted her to suffer for it, to lose her own children in place of my beautiful Anne.'

He rubbed at his right eye. Mercia wanted to reach out to him, but she held back.

'But then I realised, with help, that all my hate was achieving was my own damnation.' He glanced at Clemency. 'I have known this woman only a short time. But I can tell she blames herself when the blame is

95

not hers, and that is suffering enough, for it is the blame I realised I was giving myself and which fed my fruitless anger.'

Remembrance looked into Nathan's eyes, seeming to notice him for the first time. A spark of feeling flashed into life in the brown pools; she opened her mouth to speak, but no words emerged.

'Remy, I am sorry,' said Clemency. 'I returned as quickly as I could with the medicine. It grieves me so that it was not enough.'

The spark of feeling dissipated. 'Not enough.' Remembrance glared behind them. 'No. Not one of us ever gave him enough.'

Now Fearing stepped forward, laying a hand on his daughter's shoulder. 'Come, Remy. Let us not waste time with these people. Come back home.'

Remembrance hesitated, the anger rekindling across her face. Then she shook off her father's hand and fled through the hushed assembly.

With Remembrance gone, the crowd's eager attention converged once more on Clemency, unheeding of Renatus as he urged them to understand the young woman's pain. But Clemency's face trembled, and she looked at Mercia, shaking her head. Without a word she pivoted on her boot heels and stole away. Mercia pursued, barely able to maintain the distance between them, still some way behind as Clemency pushed open her cottage door. But she followed her inside, sitting with her friend until she no longer shook, and she could hold up her head as before.

Chapter Nine

Standfast had taken the podium by the time they reappeared. The younger candidate clearly held stricter views, pronouncing how baptism should be reserved for the children of the Elect. A murmur broke out as the crowd saw Clemency return, but she fell silently in at the back, and deprived of an object of interest the townsfolk turned back to the platform soon enough.

Amery had now arrived with Nicholas, frowning as he took in Standfast's speech; Kit was with them too, listening intently. Evidently Nathan had told them of the morning's events; Amery held up his hand at Clemency in greeting, although Kit merely nodded, barely turning to say farewell when the group departed the crowd.

'He is a quiet soul,' said Amery, walking with them down the street. 'Quiet and strong of faith. Sometimes I have thought he should become a minister himself.' He smiled. 'Ever since I met him in Boston, not long after he arrived on these shores.'

Nathan's eyes flashed. 'Boston . . . what is it like?'

'Boston is the greatest city we have, friend, a noisy, busy place of wonder. I studied at our new college there.' Reaching what passed for the town stables, a straw-strewn plot next to the southern gate, Amery stood aside to allow the others to pass in. 'Harvard has the potential to become a great university, far though it is from your own Cambridge, or from Leiden and the like. One day, perhaps, it could become the College of Light itself.'

Running her hand through the mane of a fine-looking chestnut colt, Clemency winked at Mercia. 'The College of Light again, Amery?'

His exuberant expression darkened. 'Do not mock, Clemency. It is a noble ideal.'

Mercia glanced between them. 'What is the College of Light?'

For a moment Amery stared at the ground, but after a short silence he picked up. 'It is to be the Universal College, where all scholars will bring their knowledge so we may better understand God's world.' Of a sudden his eyes shone. 'And where could a more exalted place for that task be found than here, at the frontiers of Eden? Here in this wilderness where His secrets are countless and untold.'

'Amery is a believer in pansophism,' explained Clemency. 'The world's greatest minds pursuing collective wisdom.' She raised an eyebrow at Mercia, carefully so Amery would not see; nonetheless his face saddened once more.

'As are Governor Winthrop and Mr Lavington. What is wrong with wanting to learn how God's world works?'

Effortlessly sliding her boot into a stirrup, she mounted the handsome colt. 'There is nothing wrong in it. I am teasing.'

'Unless in searching for God's secrets you uncover the Devil's too,' said Nathan, jumping onto a horse of his own.

Amery folded his arms. 'You speak of diabolical magic. I have no interest in such an abomination.'

'And yet others might.' Clemency steadied her horse as it shifted left beneath her. 'You heard, Mercia, how Remembrance called me a witch.'

'Yes, though I did not think to heed it.'

'But where is the line to be found between the Devil and the Lord?' Clemency watched as Mercia swung onto a sorrel mare. 'For different people it is at different places. Do not doubt the zeal of some of the folk who live here, or of those in England. What is medicine to the governor, to you and I, is poison to others, whatever good it does.' She smiled. 'You have not yet met my cousin, for Hopewell spends most of his time away from his house, earning his living through trade with the Indians. But perhaps he is right to claim they have more wisdom in these matters than we.' She clicked her tongue and her horse moved off. 'Now enough of this. Amery? Nicholas? You will join us?'

His cheek sucked in, Amery shook his head. Nicholas glanced up at Mercia, his face uncertain; she shrugged, indicating he should do as he pleased.

'No, thank you,' he said. 'I don't want to intrude.'

'You wouldn't be.' Clemency glanced at Mercia. 'But very well. Enjoy your day.'

Leaving the town, the chattering trio rode to the waterfall, delighting in its magnificence before riding further through the forest, following the river for a time. Soon Clemency picked a way up a gently sloping hill until they emerged at a gap in the treeline, the panorama of New England revealed to them in its glory: seemingly endless trees, some of the leaves beginning to redden, but most all shades of green, the blue sky above peppered by lazy clouds. Close by they could see Meltwater ringed by its circular palisade, nestled at the heart of cleared fields where men and women, specks in the corn, were hard at work keeping their community alive.

'That is what we do here,' said Clemency, a great pride in her voice. 'That is home.' She sat up tall on her horse. 'When you go back to England, if go back you must, tell everyone you have seen what America is, and that this is it. A thing of great wonder is being forged here, Mercia, one the people will not surrender lightly, not to a Duke, nor even to a King.'

They stayed for several moments in silence, taking in the view and its meaning. The intense freshness of the pine-tinged September air gladdened their hearts, and Mercia thought, yes, this is a special place, and I am glad I have come. She looked at her friend and felt through her happiness the wonder and the pride; Clemency, seeing her job was done, smiled and pulled her away before she could get enough.

A few metres into the forest Mercia paused her horse and turned back. 'Nathan?' she called. 'Are you coming?'

'Sorry.' He turned and trotted towards her, taking a final, long look back. 'I did not notice you had gone.'

On they continued, enjoying the ride, dodging the trees, finally halting in a clearing bordered by a brook a half-hour's distance from the viewpoint. Dismounting, they sat on a flat, smooth-topped rock with room enough for three, munching on the food Clemency had stashed in her saddlebag.

Breaking off a chunk of bread, she looked keenly at Nathan. 'You seemed taken with the view, my friend.'

'How could I not be?' he smiled. 'It is so . . . beautiful here.'

'Beauty of all sorts in your life.' She chuckled as Mercia's cheeks flushed. 'More ale?'

Eager to avoid further embarrassment, Mercia reached inside her pockets to retrieve a familiar parchment. 'Would you take a look at this?'

Nathan laughed. 'I might have known.'

'Well.' Mercia passed the parchment to Clemency. 'I have yet to deduce its meaning.'

Clemency wiped her lips. 'What is this?'

'A puzzle from the governor.' Sitting in the middle, Mercia shuffled closer, staring at the senseless letters. 'It was found on your old minister when he died.'

'I did not know of this.' Clemency studied the paper. 'But I suppose there is no reason why I should.'

'The constable – Godsgift – he sent it on to Hartford.'

'Did he show Lavington first?'

'It seems so. I introduced myself to your magistrate the other day. He did not seem especially interested, or rather he pretended as much.'

'You have been to his house?' Clemency smiled, letting the paper dangle from her slender fingertips. 'What did you think of his laboratory? Lavington is a pompous ass, but he has a curious mind.'

Mercia raised an eyebrow. 'I was not allowed to see much of his work.'

'You wouldn't have been.' Clemency puffed herself up, affecting a deep and steadied imitative tone. 'You women should not bother yourselves with such endeavours.'

Mercia laughed, doubling up with mirth as she slid off the rock onto the grass, crashing down hard on the earth, yet she barely noticed the bump.

Clemency glanced at Nathan. 'I did not think it so clever as that.'

He looked at Mercia, a large smile on his face. 'No. But she is happy. It is good.'

On the grass Mercia was blowing out her cheeks, her fit of laughter subsiding. She rubbed at her aching sides. 'I am sorry. But you were so accurate.'

'I have had practice.'

Clambering upright she retook her stony seat. 'Now what do you think of this puzzle?'

Clemency inclined her head as she looked at the parchment. 'I do not know. Just a series of letters.' She frowned. 'Although, there might be something.' She shook her head. 'No, well – maybe – I will think on it.'

'On what?'

'I don't know. 'Tis possible I have seen something like this before. In the governor's house perhaps, or in Lavington's, when I was there with Percy.' She passed the parchment back across. 'But I may merely wish to think that in my hope of helping you. All those alchemists' codes are so much confusion.' She smiled. 'Why are you so interested?'

Nathan swallowed a morsel of ham. 'How could she not be? It is a mystery, and if there is one thing Mercia cannot abide it is an unsolved puzzle.'

She swiped the air in front of him. 'I was hoping to help the governor. He has been so kind to me and does not have the time to act on this himself.'

'True indeed.' Clemency pushed herself up. 'I will think some more about it and let you know.' She reached to the ground. 'Now, how about some of this pie?'

The rest of the day was equally pleasant; by the time they returned to the town the sun was already nearing the horizon. Back at the stables, Mercia felt exhilarated.

'I am so pleased you invited us to stay,' she said, looking at Clemency as she jumped from her horse. 'You live in a magnificent place.'

'And yet times can still be difficult.' Clemency patted the colt's flank; it whinnied, apparently as content with the day's relaxation as its rider. 'We do not have half the town dying of hunger as happened years ago, but a misunderstanding with the Indians, a harsh winter – yes, it can still be hard.'

Nathan tied up his horse. 'You have lived in America always?'

She nodded. 'My mother was pregnant with me on the crossing. She and my father sailed with the governor's parents, back at the start. The original settlers, you could say, lest you count Plymouth, or the plantations much further south.'

Mercia straightened her jacket, crumpled from the ride. 'You are proud of it, I can tell.'

'I am.' She scattered a bundle of straw on the earth. 'After my father died, my mother remarried and helped to found Hartford. I still remember the journey even now – how the men drove the cattle and sheep all the way from near Boston, how that dog almost drowned until one of the women pulled him from the river. I have been a Connecticut girl ever since.'

'A fine place for a fine woman,' Mercia joked. 'Would you like to come back to our cottage to rest a while?'

Clemency sighed. 'Alas, I have to be at home tonight. I have some annoying matters to conclude.' For a moment the cheer in her eyes dulled, but then she recovered herself, arching a mischievous eyebrow. 'Besides, I think you two should spend the evening without me. 'Tis not easy to find the time.'

'Do not be foolish.' Mercia shook her head. 'But perhaps it would do us well to get some sleep.' She reached for Clemency's hand. 'I will see you tomorrow, then.'

'Yes.' Clemency smiled. 'Tomorrow.'

Bidding her good night, Mercia strolled with Nathan towards their cottage, greeting the townsfolk they passed with a light heart. Even Standfast Edwards doffed his hat, walking with the man who looked just like him; introducing herself, he turned out to be his younger brother Sil. Then at the meeting house she frowned. Percy Lavington was waiting on the steps, but he surprised her by standing and beckoning her across.

'Can we talk?' he called.

She hesitated, then looked at Nathan. 'Why don't you light the fires?'

Nathan glanced between them. 'You are sure?' he said. When she nodded, he walked away, turning once to stare back at Percy. As he reached the cottage gate, she drew a deep breath.

'I am listening.'

'Please, sit with me.' Percy resumed his perch on the steps; she waited a moment then sat beside him. 'You have had a good day?'

She studied his face. 'I have.'

'I was hoping I would see you.' He looked down. 'I . . . wanted to ask your pardon. I was rude the other day.'

She flicked a loose thread from her sleeve. 'A little.'

'More than a little.' Checking no one was nearby, he lowered his voice to a whisper. 'But Dixwell – Davids, that is – told me you were nearly caught. It made me uneasy.' He brushed back a straggling lock of black hair that was poking from under his hat. 'He says you are a good woman. Brave.'

'He is kind to say so. But he is the brave one.'

'He has led such a life, that is certain. I never met him until now, although I knew of him before, of course.'

A light breeze whipped up, agitating the few leaves at their feet. 'From your time in England?'

A startled flash of annoyance passed his face, but it vanished as quickly as it arrived. 'I suppose Clemency told you that.'

'She said you served Cromwell in some way. My father too was part of his government.'

He widened his eyes. 'Your father?'

'Sir Rowland Goodridge.'

'Oh.' He leapt to his feet. 'I . . . I had no idea.'

She smiled. 'You did not give me much chance to tell you.'

'No.' He scratched at his cheek, the broad brim of his hat bobbing in the wind. 'Then I met your father once, although we barely spoke. And I heard . . . what happened to him this spring.' He wrung his hands. 'Tyranny once more. When Cromwell died, why could not the people see they were better without a King?'

It was a discussion she had heard many times before. 'Another war was threatening, Mr Lavington—'

'Percy, please.'

'—and the people could not stand it. The King offered stability.'

'A high price.' He sighed. 'Yes, I served Cromwell. My father advised I should learn the art of ruling from the best.' He blew out his cheeks. 'It was over all too soon. Now I fight the fight here in my own way.' He reached out a gloved hand to help her up. 'Well. I have said what I wanted to say. I regret my earlier discourtesy.' He released her fingers and bowed. 'I hope we can talk again while you are here.'

'As do I.' She gave him a curt nod. 'Good evening, Percy. Sleep well.'

Mercia eased herself from bed early the next morning, full of confidence and joy. Despite the hour, children were already playing scotch-hoppers in the street below, and she thought of her own son, optimistic she could

104

come through the trials and provide for him. As she dressed herself, wishing her maidservant Bethany was there to help fasten the laces at the back of her dress, her mind turned to Nathan, wondering whether now was the time to change the bounds of their relationship to something greater. It would be well, she knew, to discuss such matters with a friend, and for the first time in a long age she felt she had someone she could confide in, however temporary that might be. Looking out the window at the trees and the picket fences, listening now to the pigs in a neighbouring garden, she found herself thinking – could it not become more permanent? And then again she thought of Daniel, and the manor house in Oxfordshire, and she knew that no, this was for the moment, but it was a moment she would be sure to enjoy.

After a brief breakfast she snatched up her jacket, tying it firmly round her bodice. In good humour she ruffled Nathan's hair, flashing him a broad smile; he looked up from the table and grinned, his brown eyes staring into hers. Waving him farewell she picked up a basket that was lying in the corner, intending to ask Clemency where she could secure supplies in the town, hoping she would have time to walk with her to buy them.

Skirting the meeting house she saw Amery chatting animatedly with Percy; just behind them Humility Thomas followed her with his eyes, doffing his hat, before he turned back to Vic and another man to resume their conversation, Lavington's manservant she thought. With a light gait she swept along the western road to Clemency's cottage, swinging open the small white gate to walk up to the house.

Tapping on the front door she pushed it ajar, calling out as she entered, 'Clemency, 'tis only me, are you in?' When there was no response she passed into the hall, shutting the door behind her. It was dark; she waited for her eyes to adjust to the lower light before looking through the doorway of the keeping room – there was nobody there – and next into the sitting area, but again, there was no sign of her friend.

At the foot of the staircase she called up, receiving no answer. Setting one foot on the bottom step she climbed with a deliberately heavy tread, accentuating the creaks so that Clemency would hear her ascent.

'Clemency?' she called again. 'Are you up there?'

There was still no response. Mercia frowned: it was too late for Clemency to be abed. Perhaps she was out – or maybe ill. She quickened her step, pausing on the upstairs landing, uncertain which of the two doors led to Clemency's bedroom. She tried the door on her left, but there was no one inside, not even a bed. She set her hand on the second door, rapping on the rough brown wood with her other fist, the basket slipping down to her elbow.

'Hello?' she said.

She pushed on the door. It fell open, revealing the darkened room behind. Mercia peered in, not wanting to embarrass Clemency if she were indeed still in bed, but there was a large object hanging in her way and she had to move past it to—

She screamed. The basket fell to the floor.

Clemency was in her bedroom, but she was not in her bed.

She was hanging from the ceiling, a thick and vicious rope desecrating her proud neck. Gently, she swung around, a terrible groaning noise coming from the straining beam above. For a moment she wavered, her lower lip hanging open as though appealing to her friend for help. But she could not call out, could never beseech aid again. All the wondrous life had fled from her eyes; the twisted rope caught, swinging her limp body away.

Chapter Ten

Nothing moved. Not the tree branches outside the window, not the dust in the slender rays of light. There was only Clemency, only the rope. Mercia stood immobile as lost seconds sped by, and then her right boot walked forward of its own will – she did not control it – then her other leg, then boot, then leg, until she was standing beneath her friend, her new, invigorating friend, listening for breath, listening for heartbeat, but to no avail: consciously, unconsciously, terribly, Mercia knew Clemency was dead.

She stood alone, feeling the coldness of Clemency's hands, the soft material of Clemency's dress – the same she had been wearing the day before – until her mind snapped back into the awful reality of that September Connecticut morning. She ran from the room, down the stairs, through the red front door and the small white gate, stumbling into the street, running for the central crossroads, falling in amongst the people, Humility, Percy, Sil now too, all staring at this mad woman, this peculiar stranger who could not get her words out, who was hoarse, whispering, mute, until in a torment of rage and despair she cried:

'Clemency!'

And she pointed down the street to the small white gate. 'She is . . . she is dead! She is hanged!'

Then the truth overwhelmed her and she collapsed on her knees, stricken by the terror and the loss.

There was a sensation in her left hand, she was sure of it. Gradually she focused on the feeling: yes, she could feel it, something familiar, something warm. She lowered her gaze to see a hand encompassing her own, and then she raised her eyes, slowly, to a face she knew, Nathan, looking at her in great concern. His familiarity brought all around him into focus, and she awoke from her waking sleep to see the sitting room in their cottage, Nicholas standing against the fireside, looking down in shared anxiety.

'Mercia,' said Nathan. 'Mercia, my God. How are you feeling?'

She shook her head. A deep, wrenching hollowness burst into her chest; she had to push the torrent back, refuse to accept it, or it would have destroyed her. 'I do not know.' She swallowed. 'I do not feel anything.'

'Why wasn't I there?' Nathan lowered his head, his stubbled face white. 'I am sorry. I should have been there.'

She stared at him blankly. 'How could you have known?' And then her control wavered, and the mixture of violent emotions erupted once more. She gasped, as if struggling for breath. 'Oh God. Clemency!'

Nathan reached over to hug her tight. She accepted the comfort; there was nothing else to do. It helped her regain herself, for now at least: her breathing slowed, but her heart still beat fast in her chest.

'She was my friend, Nat.' She stared past his face into nothingness. 'I never have friends. But she was.' She sniffed. 'She was.'

He stroked down her arm. 'I know.'

She half closed her eyes, blinking away the moisture, and her blurred vision coalesced on Nicholas: like Nathan, there was something consoling in his presence, something of home, but there was utter futility in the reassurance. Her mind kept drifting to Clemency, but as soon as she thought of the dreadful scene in the cottage she forced it away. To avoid the mental confrontation, she searched for some other thought, some other place. Anything but that rope, please God.

'I remember being in the street, at the meeting house.' She fixed on the green of Nicholas's eyes. Yes, that was better. 'But getting here – I recall nothing of that.'

Nathan leant back, rubbing her hands in his own. 'I heard a commotion in the street, people running past the window. I came outside and found you on your knees. You had your hands out in prayer. We could not prise them apart.'

'I do not remember.'

'No. I stayed with you while Nicholas ran up with Amery. They went after the other men into the—'

Her jaw began to shake; she tried to focus on Nicholas again, but tears were welling up and she could barely see him.

'Did you—?' With one hand she scratched at the tears. 'Did you see?'

His eyes swam wide with sorrow. 'She is lying down now. Amery and Vic have made her comfortable. She is warm, and covered.' He bit his lip. 'Oh, Mercia. I am so sorry.'

A faint and impossible ray of hope struck her. 'She is not . . . alive, somehow?'

Gently, he shook his head. 'I'm afraid . . . no.'

A chill passed through her. She gulped in deep breaths, forcing herself to master her emotions. A moment passed – a moment, or for ever? – but when the chill had settled, nestling beside her heart, her tears had vanished and a hardness had set in. Suddenly all around was in sharp clarity.

'Do not be sorry for me.' She straightened herself in her chair, withdrawing from Nathan's touch. 'Be sorry for Clemency, by God, but do not be sorry for me. Neither of you.' Her eyes burnt. 'Nor for the demon who has done this. For I promise that he will suffer for what he has done.'

Nathan reached to stroke her hair. 'Mercia, I know you are upset, but you cannot know if—'

'Upset?' She thrust his hand aside. 'Someone has killed my friend. Killed her, do you hear? And you say I am upset?'

A knock sounded at the door but she barely remarked it, closing her eyes as she once again struggled to retain her control, refusing to acknowledge the pain. In the distance – was it far off? – she heard Nathan clear his throat. Footsteps – Nicholas – strode past, the walker's boots heavy on the echoing floor. When she opened her eyes, Amery and Percy were standing behind Nathan. How they had appeared she could not say, and nor did she care.

'Mrs Blakewood.' Amery's face was ashen pale, his hat tilted askew. 'We wanted to see how you were. At the crossroads you were quite unwell.'

She took deep breaths: in, out, in, out. Next to Amery, Percy was staring, shuffling from side to side, sucking at his lip. ''Tis not me you should be concerned with,' she said. 'Rather you should find whoever did this.'

'Did this?' Amery glanced at Percy. 'Then you think—?'

'Of course I think.' She rose to her feet to stand beside the fireplace, her eyes fixed in front. 'What else could it be? Can you, who claim to know Clemency, believe a woman like that capable of her own murder?'

In the corner of her vision Percy pulled at his fingers. 'But what you are suggesting—'

'I suggest nothing. I state it as a truth. Somebody killed Clemency and left her – hanging like a slaughtered pig ready for the butcher!' She screwed up her hands. 'Someone killed her, and I swear before God and you all that I will not leave this place until I find out who.' She banged her fist against the wall; Amery stepped back although Percy kept his place, tilting his head as he took in her fury with undisguised interest. 'And when I do,' she continued, 'I will see that bastard hang if I must do it myself.'

Nathan put a hand on her shoulder, but she shook it off. 'Mercia,' he said. 'Please. Come back and sit.'

'I will not sit.' The calmness she had tried to foster fled as her fingers trembled. 'I will have no more deaths. No more! How many people died on our voyage here, Nathan? How many in New York? And now here, where I was beginning to find peace!' She took a sudden deep breath. 'Here, where I had found a good and dear friend.' As quickly as the anger had risen it fell away again, and tears came to her eyes. 'No.' She rubbed at her watering eyelids. 'No! There will be no peace, not for anyone until I find this devil out!'

A moment's silence. Amery scratched at his cheek.

'What do you intend to do?' he said.

'Think. I need to think.' She ran a hand through her hair. 'Speak to the constable, to Mr Lavington. Make sure something is done.'

'And you will.' Nathan tried another hand on her arm; this time she did not throw it off. 'But Mercia, for now, will you rest?' He looked into her eyes: his were deep, full of her own heartbreak. 'Please. For me?'

Finally, she gave in. 'You are right. I am so tired.' She fell back into her chair, snatching at her temples as she became aware of a fierce headache spreading down her face. 'I need to rest.'

But rest was elusive. Acknowledging her tiredness had opened a chink in the armour of her mind, and she could hold back the awful image no more. All she could see was Clemency and the rope, Clemency hanging, Clemency alone. She sat in the rigid seat, oblivious to the men's pity, crying silent, unseen sobs.

'She was a witch.'

Mercia stared at the constable. He was reclining on a high stool, his booted feet dirtying the narrow window ledge in his sitting room, looking out at the town. The cottage was centrally located on one of the choicest plots: it had ample land.

'How can you say that?' Disgusted, she shook her head.

He sighed, lowering one leg at a time before brushing down his breeches and standing, his back against the window.

'Mrs . . . Blakewood, isn't it?' He folded his arms. 'I should ask how you can say she was not.'

Mercia blinked. 'Well, Constable, aside from avowing that witches do not exist, it would seem evident Mrs Carter was not. She helped people, for one. At least she tried to.'

'What folk think in England and what folk think here are different things.' Godsgift scowled. 'You cannot make assumptions. Least of all a woman, a stranger to this town.'

'I mean no offence. All I am asking is what you propose to do about finding who did this.' She sucked in her cheeks. 'You have been obstructive since I came through your door.'

'I do not have to tell you what I plan to do.'

She held up her hands in exasperation. 'Then what about last night? You walk a patrol each evening for some length of time. I have seen you myself. Was there anyone else in the streets?'

For an instant, his eyes darted to the floor. 'I say again, this is not your concern.'

'Very well. I will go to Hartford to speak with the governor. He is a friend of my family, but of course you knew that.'

She had no idea whether he did. Still, she was prepared to venture any tactic, even name-dropping. But he only narrowed his eyes.

'Do not think to threaten me, Mrs Blakewood.' He glanced at his rapier, stored on a splintering shelf half way up the wall. 'I do not stand to be toyed with.'

A swift rap on the door cut off her response. She turned to see John Lavington coming in, the constable's maid peering from the hall until the magistrate shut the door on her curiosity. Seeing Mercia he paused, recovering himself with an unsteady smile.

'Mrs Blakewood. I did not know – is Godsgift behind you?'

She moved to one side. 'Please.'

He brushed past. 'Thank you. I—such a tragedy. I am overcome.'

'I hope not so overcome you will be as incredulous as he is.'

He frowned. 'Godsgift?'

The constable shrugged. 'Mrs Blakewood was leaving.'

The edges of her lips curved into a slow smile of her own. 'I was leaving, and now I am not. Perhaps Mr Lavington will be of more help.'

Godsgift growled, pushing himself from the wall with a heavy boot. 'The magistrate and I are more than capable of seeing to one of our own. We do not need any meddling woman who arrived with the King's own fleet to harry us.'

'The King's fleet be damned. All I care for is bringing a killer to justice.'

Taking his time, Lavington removed his silk gloves. 'You seem to be speaking of murder, Mrs Blakewood. When none has taken place.'

She stared. 'I suppose you are about to tell me that Clemency, a woman full of life, who but yesterday spoke to me with such pride of what this town has accomplished – that woman would take her own life?'

'It is possible.' Lavington set down his gloves. 'Probable, even. Think, Mrs Blakewood. Clemency was distraught about Praise-God's passing. And you do not know her, in spite of the friendship you have clearly convinced yourself that you formed.'

Her chest rose in indignation. 'Convinced?'

'Clemency Carter was a troubled woman. Troublesome. She was a widow, childless, living alone. Despite her . . . appearances . . . it was hard for her here.'

'She did not seem to find it so.'

'She spoke out on issues she should not have been concerned with, matters of government and conduct that—'

'Why? Because she was a woman?'

He sighed. 'What I am trying to say is that the matter is not so simple as you imply.'

'Suicide is a sin, Magistrate. Clemency knew that.'

'Sin was not anything Clemency ever let bother her,' scoffed Godsgift. 'She was not the most saintly woman.'

'Indeed not,' agreed Lavington. 'And now really, Mrs Blakewood, I should like to talk with my constable here.' He inclined his head. 'Alone?'

She looked between the two men, uncertain how she should react. Then Godsgift raised his left hand, jerking a dirty finger towards the door. She stared at his dismissive gesture, the chipped fingernails, the scratched back of his hand, before turning away to grab hold of the door, thinking to slam it as she left. But she stayed herself from the childish act. Instead she eased the door shut and walked out into the dark.

Back in her lodgings she could no longer restrain her contempt. She paced around the tiny sitting room, circling the small table at its centre.

'He is an arsworm.' Her pacing increased. 'An incompetent fool.'

'Who is?' said Nathan, glancing at Nicholas.

'Both of them. The constable and the magistrate. They are both inept.' She looked up. 'Or duplicitous. Someone in this town is a murderer. Why not one of them?'

Nathan put himself in her way, forcing her to stop. Laying his hands on her shoulders he looked into her eyes.

'Mercia, I think we should leave.'

His abrupt words caught her off guard. 'I do not . . . earlier you agreed we should stay.'

'I know. But I have thought about this.' He lowered his hands to take hers in a light grip. 'I do not think you should become involved.'

'But—'

'Listen.' He gripped more firmly, stroking her palm with his thumb. 'I think you should go to Winthrop and tell him your suspicions, and then let Nicholas and me take you back to New York. We can wait for the next ship to return home. There is still your manor house, after all.'

'He is right, Mercia,' said Nicholas. 'The only thing that matters is you.'

'What?' Mercia pulled her hands away, looking over Nathan's shoulder. 'Since when were the two of you in such agreement?' She nodded as Nicholas glanced down. 'I see. The menfolk joining together to protect the delicate woman, is it?' Her jaw clenched. 'What men were there to help Clemency? Not one! And now I am to allow men like Lavington to take charge?' She let out a bitter laugh. 'All he cares for is the reputation of his precious town. For that is all it is with him, I can tell. Justice means nothing, magistrate or no.'

'Then it is the same here as in London,' said Nathan, his voice calm and steady. 'But Mercia, this need not be your concern.' His pleading eyes softened. 'I am sorry this has happened. You know I am. But you have suffered enough lately. Please. Think of yourself.'

Mercia stared at him, at Nicholas, at the space by the fire where Clemency had brushed away a cobweb the day after their arrival, come to make sure they had settled in. It was strange: a shadow seemed to hang there still.

'No.' She walked to the window. 'Clemency gave me something. She gave me friendship. And I will not abandon her now.' She looked out onto the damp street, longing to see Clemency stroll past, but knowing now she never would. The unfairness was overwhelming; as much for herself as for her friend, she had to make sense of the loss, somehow. She rested her palm on the cold wall. 'You both leave if you want. I am going to stay.'

Chapter Eleven

She could not leave. She had come to New England hoping for peace and instead she had found death. But no – it was death that had found her. It had pursued her, that awful spectre, that feared tyrant of time not even the most favoured of God's children could defeat. No matter that death welcomed you to God; it swooped its unsharpened talons low too often, taking too many innocents too soon, as she and all the scarred souls who had survived the bitterness of the civil wars could lament. But lately, death seemed to relish those around Mercia most eagerly. Her husband. Her father.

Clemency Carter.

And those it did not take, upon whom perhaps it should have feasted? She knew enough of those, the crowded brigade that she, a mortal, had no right to judge, but whom she turned from all the same. Who was it could decide when a life was at its end? Who was worthy of making that choice? God certainly, but surely no man or woman had the right to destroy a fellow life, to cause the pain and the grief for those still living. It was a forbidden step, and anyone taking it had to be revenged upon. Clemency had left no children, no husband, but for that brief, happy time, she had known Mercia. And Mercia, her friend still, her revenger for ever: Mercia would not leave.

If death was following her, taunting her, it was her task to turn around to face it, however repugnant its countenance, to stand in its way and to say no more. But – it? Was death, that infernal betrayer, that constant certainty, more a man, more a woman indeed? Mercia did not much care. She could not defeat death, but she could expose its agent, the murderer who had taken Clemency from her world.

It was the day after the evil event. Mercia had awoken with a black pit in her stomach of an intensity she had not experienced since the days following her father's execution. She felt bare, as though she should be taking out her mourning dress, but the well-worn garment was in a trunk in New York and Clemency had not been family. Nor did she think her friend would have appreciated the gesture, so she was content to stay in the browns and greys she was wearing in semi-mourning still for her father. Aching within yet resolute, it was now afternoon; she leant a sleeved arm against the best-room wall, listening to Nathan, yet not really caring he was there.

'I still think we should leave,' he was protesting. 'I know. You want to stay awhile yet. But we are bound by when ships depart New York for England. Before we set out for Connecticut, Governor Nicolls there told me the *Elias* would be returning home soon. We need to be on it.'

She looked at him unblinking. 'I will stay here as long as it takes.'

He sighed, a gentle lament, but she could divine his thoughts. 'Mercia,' he said kindly, 'if we miss that ship, we may be trapped in America all winter.'

'It will not come to that. Meltwater is not London. If one of the townsfolk killed Clemency, it should be an easy matter to find them out.'

'Yes, but small towns are also close towns. As soon as you ask questions, people will fall silent.'

'They already are.' She tugged at a ringlet of her hair; despite everything, she had still combed the ends and set the style, the familiarity of the regular act a needed reassurance. 'When I went into the street before, nobody would dare speak with me.' She rubbed at her forearm. 'Well, almost nobody. Amery told me what people have been saying, although they say little to him too. It seems they agree with Lavington, that Clemency took her own life out of guilt for the boy's death.' Her face set. 'These same people who claim to have known her for years. That, or they pretend she was some kind of witch, because she knew something of medicine, because she tried to help people.' She chewed on her knuckles, digging her fingernails into her flesh.

'Mercia.' He hesitated. 'Is it not just possible that she did—'

'No.' She threw down her hand. 'Do not even speak it. Clemency Carter did not kill herself. Even forgetting she knew it would have damned her soul, it was simply not possible. I spoke with her at the waterfall after the boy's death. She felt a deep guilt, yes, but she was not about to destroy herself.' She began to pace the room. 'You know as well as I do that she was murdered.' She stopped and looked at him. 'If nobody here is courageous enough to face that truth, then I shall have to furnish them with proof. Maybe Clemency's cousin can help.'

Nathan frowned. 'The trader? I recall Clemency mentioning he was out of town, but – what was his name?'

'Hopewell Quayle. Amery says Lavington sent a rider to fetch him back, but she could not find him. I shall have to wait until he returns of his own accord, every two weeks or so, it seems.' She sighed. 'In the meantime, maybe Nicholas will have better luck convincing Amery to do more to aid us.'

A sharp rap sounded on the front door, followed by three gentler taps. 'Speak of the devil,' said Nathan, rising to answer. But the man he showed into the sitting room was neither Nicholas, nor Amery.

'Mr West,' said Mercia. 'This is a surprise.'

Kit West entered the room, giving a slight bow as he removed his spruce hat. 'Mrs Blakewood,' he said, his English accent evident. 'Am I interrupting?'

'We are just talking.' She looked at Kit, taking in his simple outfit:

smart for a sawyer, she thought, his white shirt crisp and his black breeches tidy, if speckled with sawdust.

'I hear you have been asking questions,' he pursued.

Nathan folded his arms. 'What of it?'

Kit played with the hat in his hand. 'Nothing.' He turned slightly. 'Perhaps I should come back.'

'No.' Mercia glanced at Nathan. 'You wanted to see me, Mr West, so you may as well speak.'

Kit paused a moment, then turned back to face her, the freckles on his cheeks reminiscent of the dust in his dark hair. 'I came to say – I mean, I wanted to say, I regret no one here is heeding you. I knew Clemency. She did not take her own life.' He frowned, speaking more clearly. 'To do so would have been to abandon her own soul to the Devil. Clemency was many things, many of them not liked in these parts, but . . . I wanted you to know that.'

Mercia latched onto his words like a babe in arms to its mother. 'It is a relief to hear someone say so. I was worrying nobody would care to acknowledge the truth.'

'The truth can be hard for people, at times.' Kit tugged at the cord round his neck. 'I was talking with Percy before. He explained how distraught you were. I thought I should speak with you myself.' His cheeks tautened, flattening the corners of his mouth. 'There are those of us who will not run from the truth.'

She could feel her pulse quicken. 'So you will help?'

'In whatever way pleases God, Mrs Blakewood. You should not suffer when others do not.'

'Save your pity.' She closed her eyes, embarrassed at her brusqueness. 'I am sorry.'

Nathan laid a hand on her shoulder. 'Do you know who might have done this, Mr West?'

'Kit. Or Christ-carry, but most folk call me Kit.' He shook his head. 'And I cannot say, although one thing I will say, Mr Keyte.'

Nathan smiled. 'Nathan.'

'Nathan, then.' He nodded. 'Do not mistake how strongly people care for this town, new though it may be. Myself included. It comes from being on the edge of God's lands, from the calling we have to be here.'

Mercia looked up. 'Strongly enough to be a reason to kill?'

'Surely anything is a reason, if someone believes it well enough.'

'That is true. But then someone had savage reason indeed.' She waited for him to say more, but he stood against the wall in silence. 'Were you a sawyer back in England, Kit?'

'I was to enter the law, if you can believe it. But instead I sailed to America. I could have remained in Boston, I suppose, but I preferred to come here, to the wilderness.'

'That calling you mentioned?' Behind Kit, she could see Nathan nodding, as if in understanding.

His eyes seemed to light up. 'I wanted to live where I could use my hands. It feels – cleaner. More at ease with the land. Does that make sense to you?'

'I think so.' She studied his keen expression. 'Your family, are they in America also?'

'Still in England. What is left of them.'

'They are Puritan folk?'

'No.' He shuffled his feet. ''Tis one reason I was eager to leave.'

'But your name?' In the corner, Nathan raised a cautioning eyebrow. She knew he would seek to dissuade her from delving into the personal matters of a man she barely knew. But she needed to learn about the people of the town, and she would do so whenever she could.

'Christ-carry?' His earnest face took on a serious air. 'When I arrived here, I had the Boston minister baptise me again, in the river. A cleansing, if you like, from the sins of the past. The water is so pure here, don't you think? So clear.' He shook his head, as if drawing himself from some reverie. 'So now I am Christ-carry, to make my heart plainer to the Lord. To show how I carry His Son's spirit with me always.'

She nodded, thinking. 'Is everyone in Meltwater so devout, Kit?'

'As much as we can be. I strive to be as faithful as the Lord wishes. But no, not everyone believes as they should.' He looked at her. 'You are asking about Clemency?'

'I am asking about anyone.'

'She had detractors, of course. People did not approve of the way she sometimes lived.' He frowned. 'You think this could be a private matter? That the man who killed her could have borne some grudge?'

'Perhaps.' She paused. 'You said man.'

'Evidently.' Kit held out his hands; his fingers were long, like his eyelashes, and pale. 'Whether conscious or insensible, she had to be forced into the noose. It had to be someone with strength.'

The pit of sorrow returned at his cavalier words. 'So not an old man either.'

'Old or young, here it makes no difference. Men need strength to survive, Mrs Blakewood, and wits, however many their years. 'Tis hard here, friends. We must struggle that we may live.'

Another silence fell. Nathan stepped towards the hall. 'Mercia has had a difficult ordeal, Kit. Thank you for coming, but would you mind . . . ?'

Mercia turned her head, her eyes widening in annoyance. She opened her mouth to respond, but Kit cut off her riposte.

'Of course.' He replaced his hat. 'I have said what I came to say. We should speak again when you are feeling better. That is – if you intend to stay.'

'I want to,' she said. 'But there is no need for you to leave if—'

'No, Nathan is right. I should let you rest.'

He bowed, passing into the hall as Nathan opened the front door. The two men gave each other a cursory nod before Kit stepped out. A cold draught blew into the cottage as Nathan pushed the door back shut.

Drawing close her jacket, Mercia followed Kit a half-hour later to brave the chilly streets. Irritated at Nathan's protectiveness, they had spoken

121

little since the sawyer had left, but her pique was giving her the push she needed to face a task she had been dreading.

She was not walking far, but she felt everyone staring as she passed, and she knew what they thought, that she, a stranger, had no business to interfere with the town now that Clemency, the woman who had invited her in, was no more: it was for the town, not for Mercia, to decide how to respond. But she continued unabashed, for so far their response had been shameful. Perhaps, indeed, a stranger was what they needed.

Her breathing quickened as she reached the white gate of Clemency's cottage. She could tell the watching eyes were still on her as she laid a hand on the rough wood, but she did not pause. Approaching the familiar red door she was surprised how she could push it open without panic. She called inside lest anyone was within, but it seemed the house was deserted.

She closed the door, shutting herself in with the memory of her lost friend. She was unsure what she hoped to find, did not even know if the constable had already searched, but she knew it was the right place to come. And yet – not right. The rooms screamed with emptiness, torn by an unnatural void deep with missing presence. Clemency had been too vital a character to slip away unchallenged by the world, and so the house, and the world, had noticed. Walking through the cottage was like walking through an aberration. The air was cold, the humble furniture at odds with the vibrancy of Clemency's life.

She took a deep breath, steadying herself. Nothing mattered but this, as though a barrier had descended that she would not shatter until justice was released into the hall, into the kitchen, into the travesty that was the bedroom. She forced herself to search for anything that might help, but there was little to find. Clemency's clothes: the yellows, the blues, no longer to grace the town. Clemency's provisions: the hidden bottle of rum. Clemency's medicines for all the ailments she would no longer treat, the antimony of ceruse that had failed Praise-God Davison and perhaps failed Clemency herself.

In a small chest covered in a thin layer of dust, Mercia found a pile of letters that she made herself read. Sitting cross-legged on the wooden floor, she felt uneasy scanning her friend's correspondence, but she supposed Clemency would not mind. As she read, she began to sense the room warming, as if Clemency herself had entered and was reading behind her, cheering the dim house with her wit and her smile. But when Mercia turned round, Clemency was not there, the longed-for resurrection a fallacy.

The most recent letters were from Clemency's cousin, Hopewell Quayle, in which he wrote of the things she knew must have delighted her: the Indians he had met on his travels, the makeshift tents he had constructed with their help. Underneath these was a well-thumbed, yellowing letter, scrawled in a scratchy hand by Clemency's mother in Hartford, long since dead. Mercia paused her reading, thinking of Clemency being welcomed into heaven, her parents helping her now as they would have done when she was their child, sad to see her too soon, but happy to be reunited. That was some comfort at least, the same she tried to give herself when she thought of seeing her own father and husband once more.

Breaking from her musings she returned to the letters, one from Winthrop about a new mineral he had discovered, and then another from—quickly she set down the paper, turning away her face. But then she chided herself for her prudishness, and continued to read. The letter was from a man, imbued with passion; not in terms of love or endearment, but intensely sexual, describing acts the writer clearly wanted Clemency to enjoy with him. Feeling slightly ashamed for reading, Mercia wondered that Clemency could have stood to read such unadorned sentiments. Surely she had never indulged in these . . . proposals? And yet here was another letter in the same hand, not describing acts that had happened, but acts this man wanted to happen. Even assuming Clemency had never agreed, the letters were still here, not burnt, not discarded, proof of a man's coarse desires, proof, perhaps, that Clemency did not feel threatened by them at least. Who the man was, was unclear – there was no signature, not even an initial, but the references to where he was writing were apparent enough: the man lived here, in Meltwater.

There were four more such letters, all on a similar theme. Mercia thrust them in her pockets, unwilling for the townsfolk to discover them to be used as further proof against Clemency's character. She herself was disturbed enough, but that barrier she had thrown up was still there: the letters changed nothing, save that here perhaps was a motive for murder, a crime of savage longing, of jagged desire.

She pulled herself up to finish her search of the cottage. Although each object spoke of Clemency's life, nothing seemed pertinent to the hanging. A mirror Clemency would have studied her reflection in; a cup she would have sipped ale from; a shawl she would have warmed herself at night with – all these things were simple, belying the majesty of the woman, and unhelpful in understanding her end. Wanting to be thorough, Mercia exited the red door and passed round to the backyard, ignoring the stares of John Lavington who was watching from the street, no doubt alerted to her presence and come to check for himself, but he made no move to follow.

Running her hand along the uneven stone of the cottage's exterior wall, she winced as a sharp point dug into her flesh, drawing a pinprick of red. She sucked on her finger as she came into the pretty backyard, well-groomed plants dotted about an impressive twelve-foot tree a little set back from the house. Too tall to have been planted recently, it must have been in place well before the settlers arrived. What was it witnessing here? Mercia thought. The beginning of a new way of life, a new future? Or was Clemency's end an indication of what was to come if the colonies failed to take, if America refused to countenance the settlers' promise?

She wandered the neat garden, but as in the house she found little. Not that she expected it; maybe, she pondered, her hand resting on the bark of the tree, she should—

'She was a good woman.'

124

Mercia broke from her contemplations and turned to face the house. An unfamiliar woman was leaning against the back wall, her bare, toned arms folded across her full chest. Her skin was darker than the pallor of most of the English, and in contrast to Mercia's strict bodice her own covering was loose and of a warm fur.

The stranger pushed off from the wall and approached. 'She was a kind woman. She tried to understand our ways.'

Mercia looked the newcomer up and down; she was about mid twenties, she thought, and confident, holding her bearing erect. Her straight hair was lush and intensely black.

'Did you know her?'

The woman nodded. 'We exchanged goods. Sometimes we talked. She was interested in our medicines. And she had a kind heart.'

'Yes.' Mercia felt a dull sadness. 'She did.'

'Susanna.' The woman pointed to herself. 'That is my name. The name you English have given me, at least.' She held out her hand. 'I never know what I am supposed to do with your customs, but I think this is what the men do.' She jiggled her hand up and down. 'Shake hands – is that it?'

Mercia took the woman's hand. 'They do like to do that.'

Susanna inclined her head, looking into Mercia's eyes as though scrutinising her purpose; the black wells were intelligent, Mercia thought, full of curiosity. 'I have not seen you before,' she said finally. 'Were you Clemency's friend?'

A shiver ran through Mercia's soul. 'I was, but . . . do you know what has happened?'

Susanna's face clouded. 'I do. It is . . . horrific.' She frowned. 'Is that the word?'

'It is one word. You speak English well.'

'It is my role in the tribe. I speak with your people and take the news back to mine.'

'An interpreter.' Mercia was impressed. 'What is your real name, then?'

125

Susanna cocked her head. 'You wish to know?'

'I would.'

She seemed surprised. 'Then it is Sooleawa. It means silver. But it is not a Christian name, and so I must be Susanna here.' She looked behind her. 'I come as often as I am allowed, or asked. Standfast – he is my friend – he told me about Clemency. I came to look.'

Mercia folded her arms. 'For what?'

'For nothing. For her spirit. Because I wanted to be here.' She looked up at the house. 'Because I knew her.'

'Yes.' Mercia followed her gaze to the bedroom window. 'I understand.'

'I was bringing her herbs, from upriver. She uses them in some way.' Sooleawa lowered her gaze. 'I don't know who will be interested now.'

A cough from towards the house made Mercia look over. John Lavington was crossing the yard with Humility Thomas, but then he paused, hovering back, while Humility hobbled towards them.

'Mrs Blakewood,' he said, ignoring Sooleawa completely. 'Why are you here?'

She glanced at the magistrate. 'If Mr Lavington wishes to address me, he can do so himself.'

Humility grunted. 'Forget Lavington. Your business is with me.' Despite his words, he looked back at the magistrate, who nodded. 'You have no right being here. You barely knew Clemency and this is a private house.'

Mercia bridled. 'Clemency was my friend. I was here at her invitation, and as nobody—'

'Exactly what I came to say.' He thrust his tongue out in his cheek. 'Now Clemency is gone, there is no reason for you to remain. I must ask you to leave my son's cottage and go from the town.'

Mercia stared at him. In truth she had been expecting this, but the stark manner of his words appalled her. 'Mr Thomas, I know I am staying in the house at your kind indulgence, but if nobody has need of it I would like to help the town solve this.'

He blinked. 'Solve what?'

'You cannot—why, Clemency's death, of course.'

The hefty man rested a large arm around her shoulders, drawing her out of Sooleawa's earshot. When they were a little distance off, he lowered his voice.

'She took her own life. There is nothing to solve. Unless, of course, she was engaged in some devilish magic that went wrong.' He leant in still closer. 'And if that happens to be so, then nobody would thank you for raising it, not least when the King's commissioners are so near. Now, leave well alone and go.'

An anger rose. 'I cannot believe you would put the town's repute above finding the truth!' She jerked her head at Lavington. 'Him, yes, but surely you want to understand? For Clemency's sake, if for nothing else!'

'A cart will arrive in an hour to take you and your menfolk to Hartford. Go and make ready.' He jabbed a podgy finger at her chest. 'This is our town, Mrs Blakewood, not yours. 'Tis past time for you to depart.'

Chapter Twelve

'So that's it?' Nicholas wrung his hands in irritation. 'You're just going to leave, do as they say?'

'I do not see that we have much choice.' Leaning against the sitting room doorway, Nathan folded his arms. 'We have nowhere to stay.'

'We could . . . stay with Amery.'

'How? His cottage is barely large enough for the two of you. Where would Mercia sleep? We have to face facts – this is not our town.'

'But—'

'He is right, Nicholas.' Standing at the window, Mercia had been listening to them argue. She watched as a horse and cart pulled up in the street. 'We are not welcome here.'

'What does that mat—'

'Nicholas, that is enough.' Mercia turned to face them. 'Nathan, the cart is here. Would you load my trunk?'

Nicholas swallowed. 'Now I cannot even—'

She quietened him with a keen glance. 'Nathan, please.'

'Of course.' Nathan lifted the battered trunk from in front of the fireplace and hauled it outside. She watched him push it into the cart, the driver offering no assistance. Then she looked again at Nicholas.

'Of course I am not giving this up.' She sucked in her lips. 'Once we have returned to Hartford, I shall want you to accompany me on a journey. But not a word to Nathan. He will object, and then he will want to come, but I want him to stay with Daniel.'

Nicholas smiled. 'Now that is more like it. Where are we going?'

She picked at a loose thread on her dress. 'Upriver, Nicholas. We are going to find the Indians.'

Several rainy hours later they trundled into Hartford, returning once more to Winthrop's home. As they unloaded the cart Daniel rushed out to meet them, and for an instant she forgot her pain as she hugged his thin frame, but when Nathan scooped him up with a broad smile the breaking of contact allowed the tragedy back in, and not even her son could now dispel it. Still, it was a happy hour that she spent in the damp garden outside the governor's workshop, listening to Daniel talk of his friends and the fun things he had done. Later, she sat with Winthrop in his parlour, sitting in silence as he digested the awful news. Too distraught to join them, Elizabeth had already retired. Mercia herself was in no mood for sleep.

'I agree with you.' Winthrop sat by the fireplace, his fingertips arched against his chin. 'Clemency would not have killed herself.' He studied the dancing flames. 'The suggestion is abhorrent.'

'Can you not do something?' said Mercia, her tone blunt.

Winthrop looked at her; the fire was casting his shadow on the stone floor behind him, rendering his presence still larger than normal.

'I can write to Lavington and Godsgift Brown, but the governorship holds little real power beyond influence and ceremony. And Lavington is a magistrate, the principal authority in the north-west.' He sighed. 'I put him there. Still, I would ride to Meltwater tomorrow, much good it would do, had I not received word that the King's commissioners want to meet with me next week, and I needs must prepare. We would do better to convince the townsfolk to act.'

Mercia nodded. 'I think some of the younger amongst them may be questioning their elders' story.'

'What of Lavington's son, or Amery Oldfield?' His elbow on the arm of his chair, Winthrop rubbed at his temples. 'They . . . knew Clemency, of course.'

The tacit admission that he knew the trio had worked together did not escape her. 'They seem . . . concerned, although we did not have much occasion to speak before Lavington had me removed.' She bit her top lip. 'May I ask a question?'

'By all means.'

'Forgive me, but – the antimony of ceruse you prescribed for the child.' She hesitated. 'There is no chance it could have been poisonous, or the wrong dose?'

Winthrop shook his head. 'I know all my medicines intimately, Mercia, and I cannot believe Clemency made an error in her administration.'

'Then no one should have cause to think her negligent.'

'Such as the Davison family?' He intertwined his fingers. 'I cannot see them stooping to such awful revenge – not that I much know them. But I cannot think why anyone would wish to harm Clemency.'

Mercia's jaw twitched as she thought of the passionate letters she had found, but she kept that information silent. 'No. And I know you will need to keep somewhat distant from this.'

He shifted in his chair. 'It is not that I do not want—'

'There is no need to explain.' Emboldened by events, Mercia waved a dismissive hand: the norms of social conduct held little meaning at present, even with a man of Winthrop's status. 'I understand the delicacies of men in your position, Governor. My father was in government, after all. But with your permission, I would like to stay in Connecticut to investigate.'

Winthrop roved her face. 'Do you think yourself well enough? Finding anyone – like that – would be difficult, but a woman who was becoming your friend . . . I do not want you to feel obligated in any way.' His forehead creased in sorrow. 'Not when I invited you here to find respite and peace.'

'Governor, somebody must do something. If the townsfolk will not, and you cannot, then it must be me.'

His voice dropped to a whisper against the crackling flames. 'I just wish it were not so.' Then he pulled himself up straight. 'You are welcome here as long as you wish, and Daniel will be cared for as long as needs be. I can do that for you, at least. If there is anything more I can do from here, I pledge to do it.' He reached out a hand, arresting it halfway. 'I want you to know you are not alone in your sorrow, Mercia. Clemency was very dear to me.'

The concern in his gaze was reassuring, somehow. 'I know.' She gave him a weak smile. 'But sorrow must wait. First we must discover the truth.'

It felt uncomfortable, keeping her designs from Nathan. She flicked her eyes away when he smiled goodnight to her that evening, knowing that when he awoke it would be to discover she had taken Nicholas and gone. She knew he would think to come after her, but she had not told even Winthrop her precise intentions. Keeping her secret from her son was worse, but he might let slip if he knew. Not that Nathan would have prevented her – she would not have allowed it – but there would have been an argument, a galling insistence that she think of herself. No, Nicholas was the right companion for this task. And part of her, conversely, wanted to protect Nathan from any dangers the road might entail.

It was still dark when she led a horse from the stable, a light brown mare that snorted its derision at the early hour. They rode briskly, wrapped in warm riding cloaks borrowed from Winthrop against the chill of the dawn air. Nicholas went in front, scouting the landscape for trouble: she allowed herself that concession to safety, at least.

They took the familiar road to Meltwater: north out of Hartford, then west. They kept up their pace on the thankfully deserted road, but it was several hours before they came near the town. When they approached within a few miles they slowed their horses to a trot, listening intently lest anyone was riding east: a good precaution when Standfast Edwards raced past, but they heard his approach and darted into the woods before he could see them. Resuming their ride, a track came into view on the right, a narrow trail she knew bypassed the town and headed north. They took it, urging their steeds through the thickets of trees, their leaves as russet now as green, the encroaching hand of autumn shaking the first brittle husks from their branches.

'How much further from here?' asked Nicholas.

Now ahead, she steered her horse around an elm blocking the middle of the path. 'Clemency talked of it once, when we were out riding. She said it was not far.'

'Are you sure they will talk to us?'

She twisted round in the saddle. 'Are you nervous? I do not think it will be the same as when we met the smugglers in London.'

He gripped his reins and trotted alongside. 'Of course not. I wasn't nervous then, either.'

'Of course not.'

Soon the path faded to almost nothing, but a clear line of cut-back undergrowth guided them forwards. Minutes later the path reappeared, a pencil-thin sliver of earth that gradually widened. As they progressed, their surroundings seemed to brighten, ever more light falling through the thinning trees. She eased her horse onwards until the path broadened out and finally left the forest altogether. Now in full daylight, a wide space of unwooded land filled the openness before them. Smoke was rising from an encampment of tents beyond the far edge of the field.

'See,' she said. 'Not far.'

The large space was partially harvested, the nearer half towering with crops, tall corn plants bobbing about in the light breeze as beanstalks slithered up their slender height. Around the corn, the tops of by now familiar pumpkins protruded through the ground. A number of Indians sat at the edge of the crop. As they got closer, Mercia realised they were all women. She spurred on her horse to where two of the labourers were taking a rest.

'What cheer, *nétop?*' she said, addressing the women with a phrase Winthrop had suggested she use.

The younger of the two stared up and frowned. She glanced at her companion, a middle-aged woman with a tightly creased face, possibly her mother, Mercia thought, for they had a common appearance.

'*Awaùn ewò?*' said the girl.

The elder woman set down her basket of yellow corn and looked the newcomers up and down. '*Asco wequassunnúmmis,*' she said. '*Askuttaaquompsìn?*'

Nicholas looked at Mercia in confusion. The woman repeated her words, this time more slowly. Keeping her gaze on the Indians, Mercia leant over the horse to take a thin book from her saddlebag. She flicked to the first section and glanced down at the page. Then she smiled at the woman, making a circular motion with her wrist. 'Could you please – again?'

The woman repeated herself still slower.

'Ah.' Mercia looked up from her book. 'She says good morrow. I think. And then – how are you?'

'Another phrase book?' said Nicholas.

'That is right, like the Dutch one I made for New York. Except this is more useful, by a man called' – she looked at the cover – 'Roger Williams, of Providence. He calls it a key, so that we may speak with the Indians.' She looked again at the book; she had skimmed its contents in preparation, but she had not had chance to retain much. She turned back to the stares of the Indian women, still wondering who she was, no doubt.

'*Asnpaumpmaûntam,*' she tried slowly, her eyes on the book.

Accentuating each syllable, she did her best to pronounce the strange word, but the girl still laughed. The elder woman waved an admonishing hand and signalled at Mercia to continue.

'*Neèn*,' Mercia said, pointing a vigorous finger at herself. 'Mercia Blakewood.'

'*Túnna cowâum?*' The woman bent forward. 'Where you come? Meltwater?'

Mercia shook her head. '*Acâwmuck notéshem.*' She had no idea if she was pronouncing the phrase even the slightest bit correctly. 'Over the water.' She turned the page, flicking to a word she had highlighted and practised. '*Acawmenóakit.*'

'What did you say?' muttered Nicholas, barely keeping his horse from nuzzling at the corn.

'That we have come from England – *Acawmenóakit* – although here it says the word means "the land on the other side".'

'Interesting. What should—?'

He broke off as the two women let out a sudden wailing of an uncomfortably high pitch. Mercia's face fell – had she done something wrong? Her stomach went cold when another woman in the field took up the call, followed by another, and another, and then a similar howling broke out from inside the encampment itself until it seemed as though the whole village was screaming.

'Perhaps we should go,' said Nicholas. 'Before anything bad happens.'

'Maybe you are right.' She was on the verge of turning her horse when a figure sped from the settlement, running barefoot towards them. Mercia squinted to see better who it was and felt a surge of relief.

'Wait. 'Tis Susanna. Sooleawa.'

'That woman you met?' he said, putting himself between Mercia and the encampment. 'Still, be ready to leave if we need to.'

Her hands on the reins, Mercia watched Sooleawa approach. Exactly as she reached them, the wailing stopped.

'What cheer, Sooleawa?' Still uncertain, she affected a smile.

'What cheer, *nétop.*' Sooleawa laid her hands on her fur-covered hips. 'What are you doing here?'

Mercia pulled up her pawing horse. 'I came to find you, to talk.'

'Oh.' Sooleawa's face softened. 'Then, please. You are welcome.'

'Thank you.' Relieved, Mercia jumped to the grassy ground. 'And now I am here, I was hoping you could help me find someone else.'

'Hopewell Quayle.' Mercia took a polite sip of the beverage Sooleawa offered as they sat inside a small, bare tent covered in rough sheets of bark. 'I need to find Hopewell Quayle.'

Sooleawa prodded at a burning fire; the smoke blackened and rose through the round hole above. 'He is still away from Meltwater?'

'He was not there when we left. Unless someone has ridden to him since, I fear he remains ignorant about Clemency. And I need his assistance.'

'Mr Lavington is not helpful?'

'He has sent me away.' She paused. 'Clemency was killed, I know it. But I need to be there to find out why. Mr Quayle may be able to help with that. I understand he has dealings with your people. Maybe someone here will know where he is.'

Sooleawa drew a line on the ground with her stick. 'There is a place of change – a boundary, I think you say – behind which even in the same place, at the same time, people exist on different sides. I think here, you are on one side' – she teased a single dot into the earth on the left of the line – 'and the rest of the town is on the other.' She jabbed multiple dots on the right. 'You are one, and they are many. What do you hope to achieve?'

'May I?' Mercia gestured at the stick. 'I am not alone.' Taking it, she twisted another three dots on the left of the line. 'This is my friend Nathan, and this is Nicholas. This is Governor Winthrop. And this' – she set a fifth dot alongside the other four – 'is you, if you will help me.'

Sooleawa considered. 'And Hopewell?'

135

'This.' She placed a dot on the line. 'I do not yet know, but I must find out. And then, perhaps, the line will vanish altogether, and we will all be on the same side.' She scrubbed out the line with the stick.

'Except the killer.'

'Indeed.' Mercia drew a new, smaller line, separating one of the dots from all the others. 'And then he will be alone in the place of change, set apart from the rest.'

'You are wise, Mrs Blakewood.' Sooleawa rose. 'I, too, will find out.'

Under the watchful gaze of two bare-chested Indian men, Mercia waited with Nicholas in a much larger, oblong tent, about seventy feet across. The structure comprised a series of pairs of amply sized trees bent to meet in the middle, the subsequent frame covered in a diversity of woven mats. At each end an opening led outside, the hides that acted as doors pushed up in the fine weather. Around the tent's edges, a number of narrow platforms were strewn with animal skins and baskets.

One of the watchers was well built; despite herself, Mercia found it difficult not to look, the attractive man's demeanour alien yet familiar. Nicholas sat upright, holding himself taut as if ready to leap up. She looked at him, thankful for his presence and discretion, and she found herself absent of all the uncertainties she had held for him. Did it mean she had forgiven him his former betrayal? Perhaps. But he would have to acquit himself some more for her to be truly sure.

A rustling to the right indicated Sooleawa's return. She was accompanied by two others: an older man, dressed more resplendently than any of the Indians Mercia had yet seen, outstretched eagle wings tied to his back; and a young man, his body decorated with markings, his black eyes alert. Holding a spear, he stared down at Nicholas, the pride in his gaze clear enough.

'Sooleawa has told me you are looking for Hopewell,' said the elder. 'I

136

know what has happened in Meltwater. It is sad their medicine woman suffered the ultimate fate, but we too have suffered deaths lately, and nothing has been done.'

Mercia stifled a gasp. Beneath the decoration it was the same chief who had ambushed Winthrop's party on their way to Hartford from New York, the same who had thrown the head of the Englishman at Nathan's feet. Now towering in front of her, he turned to face them. 'My powwow too is dead. Where is my promised revenge?'

Mercia made to push herself up, but the *sachem* thrust out a tattooed palm.

'Stay where you are, woman of the English!' He turned to Nicholas. 'What say you, *nétop*, if friend you are?'

Nicholas rose, dusting down his breeches. 'I say nothing. This woman, as you call her, is my lady. You must speak with her.'

The younger man growled. 'Take care with your tongue, friend.' He spoke jerkily, spitting the last word with contempt. 'Do you not respect our *sachem*?'

'I respect him – friend. But you.' Nicholas smiled. 'Perhaps that is different.'

The warrior looked at Sooleawa. 'Different?'

Sooleawa shrugged, although it was evident she had understood, as had the chief, who pondered a moment, then turned to Mercia.

'Very well.' He sat on a bear hide, indicating that she join him. 'Your servant says you are his chief. And powwow Winthrop must be yours, for I saw you riding with him when first and last we met.'

Mercia edged across. 'I recall our encounter.'

'Then you recall what happened. We are not afraid of the English. We seek vengeance for those who have been killed, as is our custom. And we will get it.'

A slight tremble of anxiety struck as she realised what she had done in wandering alone into the Indian encampment with just Nicholas for protection. But she had been in difficult situations before, and she knew how the Indians were renowned for their courtesy: at least, Roger Williams's *Key* professed as much.

'I understand.' She did not know whether to call the man sir, *sachem*, chief, or something else. But if she had erred in choosing no title he did not frown. 'If not vengeance, I too seek answers to the death of a friend. A friend to your people, if she did not lie, and I know Clemency would not.'

The chief brought his face close to her own. She could smell the unfamiliar food on his breath, but she did not move away. She recognised the roving eyes: it was the same look she had received many times on this journey, from many men, all querying her intent and her worth.

'What is your name?' he finally asked.

'Mercia. Mercia Blakewood.'

'I do not know this name. Mercia. What does it mean?'

'It is a recognition of our heritage, *sachem*. An understanding that the present must stem from the past.'

He held his gaze on her, the corners of his thin mouth creasing into a narrow smile. Then he jerked up his head and stood, signalling to the younger man to approach.

'I have heard enough. Take her away.'

Nicholas and Sooleawa both made to come forward, but the *sachem* kept them silent with a glance.

'To Hopewell. We will take her away to Hopewell.' He laughed at Mercia's surprised face. 'You thought we would not help? That I would question you for hours, demand some tribute?'

'I . . . did not know what to think.' She rose in her turn. 'Thank you.'

'So, Mercia Blakewood. I will help you with your search.' He nodded at his warrior. 'My *pniese* here will lead you. Hopewell is not far. Then once you are back with your people, you will ask them to help me in my search.' He stared at her, his expression impassive. 'For we both want vengeance, do we not?'

'I seek justice. It is different.'

138

The eagle wings quivered as the *sachem* turned to leave. 'So says your head.' He walked towards the opening, peering back from over the deep brown feathers. 'But your spirit. What says that?'

His aquiline presence swept from the tent as she found she could give no response.

Chapter Thirteen

'I thought that chief, *sachem*, whatever – I thought his tribe was miles away?' said Nicholas, as they followed the dour young Indian on horseback. 'Didn't he ambush us south of Hartford?'

'Not much south.' Mercia was not really listening, thinking of the *sachem*'s words about vengeance. It was justice she wanted, wasn't it? 'But Winthrop showed me a chart of the tribal boundaries. This tribe, the Wappingers I think he said, have territory all around this area, some of it now in the land the Duke of York claims. And they move around with the seasons, they do not stay put as we do.'

Up ahead their guide grunted. Mercia looked at Nicholas, who shrugged.

'Hey,' he shouted. 'Anything the matter?'

The Indian turned in his saddle, not slowing his horse. 'You know where you are, English?'

'Yes,' said Nicholas. 'In America.'

He laughed. 'So you call it. You name it for one of your great *sachems*, yes? But to us, this is not America.'

'What do you call it then, *nétop*?'

The Indian's black eyes stared into Nicholas's green. 'I call it home.'

140

'Hmm.' Nicholas jutted out his chin. 'Good answer.' Despite his approval, he continued to hold the guide's stare, but the Indian merely smirked and turned back to face front.

'Nicholas,' whispered Mercia. 'Do not provoke him.'

'Don't worry. I've seen enough of his type before. Indian or Londoner they're all the same, puffing themselves up like a prize cock at the fights.'

'I wonder.' She stared over the guide's head into the distance. 'If London were destroyed, and England sent into ruin, would we survive as these people can? We talk of morals in Europe, of manners, but who is to say where true nobility lies?' Nicholas threw her a glance and she sighed. 'I know. But we came close to ruin not long ago, did we not? The war reduced many a proud man to stealing and begging. Where went our nobility then?'

He bobbed up and down in his saddle. 'There was never much nobility where I grew up, not before the war, not after it.' He grinned. 'But plenty of stealing and begging.'

'No doubt.'

'You saw for yourself not long back.'

'I suppose I did. But there are many things I have seen of late I never thought to witness.'

They fell silent as they followed their taciturn guide through the unfamiliar landscape – unfamiliar, and yet more recognisable each day. Until Clemency's death, Mercia had found she was enjoying America more and more, but ever since that day it had seemed forever tainted, despite the broad spaces, the pine-infused wisps of cool breeze. And yet there was something in the surroundings now, a comforting lack of definition, an ethereal quality that spoke to heaven as much as to the Earth, that rekindled her affection; and she found, surprisingly, that it was not incompatible with the pain of Clemency's death, for Clemency had loved this country and had wanted Mercia to love it too.

Two hours passed before the horse took a sharp twist to the left, rousing Mercia from her distracted thoughts, but she was too strong a rider to let the unexpected movement make her fall. She looked up to see a thin line of grey smoke rising in the near distance, a faint indicator of humanity in the midst of the virgin wilderness.

Up ahead their guide had stopped, waiting for them on a flat outcrop of silver-grey rock. As she drew up beside him he pointed towards the smoke.

'Hopewell,' he said, and then resumed his course once more.

'Do you think he doesn't like us?' said Nicholas, urging his horse to follow.

'He does not seem to. But how do we know how he has been treated by the English?' She steadied herself as her horse leapt a fallen trunk. 'Clemency told me that some of our compatriots, like that constable back in Meltwater, would sooner hold dominion over these people than live peacefully side by side with them.'

'Just as the King and his brother would hold dominion over the colonists.'

'A wry observation, Nicholas.'

'And here's another. How do we know how the English have been treated by him? While we're still in the woods, we had best stay mindful of that.'

She looked at him askance. 'When did you become so cautious?'

He laughed. 'I don't rate my chances if I return to Nathan without you.'

'No.' She allowed herself a smile. 'Neither do I.'

'Oh.' He peered at her. 'Thanks!'

The twirling smoke disappeared behind a thicket of pine trees, their sweet scent tantalising Mercia's nose as their guide led them on, coming out in a hidden clearing at the bottom of a rise. A tent was pitched to one side of a gentle brook, its deerskin door flapping lightly against the sheets of bark covering the wooden frame. The smoke they had seen was drifting up from a fire on the other side of the clearing, where a man was sitting atop a roped-up pile of logs. He stood at their approach, setting aside the artefact he had been whittling with his knife. He was stocky in build, although whether from his physique or through the furs he was wearing, it was impossible at a distance to tell.

He held up his free hand in greeting. 'What cheer, *nétop*?' he called to the guide.

'What cheer,' returned the Indian, ignoring his charges as he trotted across the space. Mercia and Nicholas followed, keeping a short distance behind.

The man took a swig from a flask propped up against the pile. 'Want some of this, *nétop*?'

The Indian smiled. He reached down for the flask, the sunlight glinting off the animal grease caking his muscled arms. 'Thanks.'

'Good, no?' He watched the guide shake the last brown drops into his mouth. 'Who are your friends? I never saw them before.'

The Indian shrugged, throwing back the drained flask. A faint smell of rum permeated the air. 'Don't know. Sooleawa said to bring them to you.'

Mercia dismounted. Brushing down her dress, she turned to the Englishman. He was unshaven, his unruly beard in keeping with the messiness of his hair. 'You are Hopewell Quayle?'

The man twirled his knife in his fingertips. 'Delighted. And you are?'

She ignored his deft display. 'I am Mercia Blakewood, recently arrived from England, visiting at the governor's invitation.' Her proud speech faltered. 'I have come to . . . have you seen anyone from Meltwater in the last day or two?'

Hopewell laughed. 'Don't tell me you've come to live there.'

'Please – have you spoken with anyone?'

'Not for days. Look, Mrs Blakewood, I don't wish to seem unwelcoming, but why have you come?'

The smell of the smoke seemed very intense. 'I have some bad news, Mr Quayle. About your cousin, Clemency.'

He frowned. 'Bad news?'

She tried to continue, but of a sudden she was choked with emotion. An unexpected lump blocked her throat, making it hard for her to breathe.

'Mrs Blakewood?' Hopewell leant forward. 'What is the matter?'

She coughed from her stomach, forcing herself to regain her composure. Nicholas hastily dismounted his horse. 'I am sorry,' she said. 'But the news is the worst.' She found she could not look him in the eye. 'Your cousin is dead.'

The knife he had been twirling stopped still. 'Dead?' He looked at the Indian. 'But I was with her not three weeks since. She was in perfect health. Has there been an accident?'

'No.' Mercia drew in a long breath. How did you tell anyone a relative had been killed? Her thoughts flashed to Nathan bringing her the news of her husband's death. Perhaps in the way he had spoken then: quickly, and to the point.

She focused again on Hopewell. 'She has been murdered.'

'Murdered?' Again, he repeated her word, but this time his face contorted into a deeply furrowed field, his knuckles whitening on the sheath of his knife. 'What are you saying?'

She made herself look. 'I do not know. But it was I who found her.' Now she had begun, the words poured forth. 'The townsfolk are saying it was suicide, but I know it was not, she was too alive, I know she was murdered.' Nicholas put a hand on her shoulder; a light, respectful touch, removed straight away, but it helped to calm her. Behind, the tent door was flapping in the breeze. 'She was hanged.'

For a moment Hopewell held her gaze. Then he turned away and flung his knife at the nearest tree. A piece of bark fell off, but the knifepoint held fast.

'I do not believe it.' He stood unmoving, clenching his fists, as if deciding how to react. Then he punched the one hand into the other. 'Who are you to bring me such devilish news?'

'Her friend. I was her friend.'

'And you?' he rasped at Nicholas.

'What she says is the truth. Clemency asked us to Meltwater. Now she is dead.'

Hopewell turned to the Indian. 'What do you know of this? Of Clemency?'

'Nothing,' he replied. 'What Sooleawa said. Clemency died, maybe killed.'

'Sooleawa knew?' His face flushed red. 'And she did not think to ride to me?'

The Indian frowned. 'She is not your—'

'No.' Eyes darting, he gestured for Mercia to follow him across the clearing. 'Sit with me, Mrs Blakewood. I think you had best tell me what you know.'

When she had finished, Hopewell remained silent, running his tongue across his teeth. Finally he spoke.

'You are right. She would not have killed herself.' His eyes narrowed. 'I cannot believe that pompous . . . princock—'

'Lavington?' said Nicholas.

'As I said, that princock – I cannot believe he thinks it is suicide.'

'I am not sure he does.' Mercia shifted her position on the uncomfortable log. 'I think he worries most for the standing of his town.'

'Oh yes, the noble magistrate lording it over us all.' The trader was seething. 'As if he cares for anything but his own glory! What he cares about, Mrs Blakewood, is finding that absurd philosopher's stone, so that the intellects of Europe will think he is one of them!' He shook his head. 'Was that boy of his in town when you were there?'

'Percy?' She inclined her head. 'Why?'

'I don't know.' Hopewell pulled at a loose chunk of bark. 'Because he has a mind where his father sometimes does not. Maybe he would see sense. But Godsgift – he brooks no incompetence. Why does he shun the truth?'

'I was hoping you could tell me.'

He looked at the chittering brook. 'He is a taciturn creature, Mrs Blakewood, living inside a mercenary mind. Leave it to him and he would wipe out the Indians with one sweep of his vicious hand. As for Clemency, I'm sure you know that half the town thought she was a witch? And yet when any of them were sick, they came to her soon enough to seek her help.' He scoffed. 'The damn hypocrites. Why do you think I spend so much time on my own, or with our friends, the Indians?' He jerked his head at their guide. 'Lavington and his ilk talk of our civilising them, making them like us, as if it were a marvellous gift. But I say we could learn more from how these people live their lives, how they work with nature instead of seeking to master it. But of course, we English know better.'

'Mr Quayle.' Impatient to return to the matter at hand, Mercia gripped his arm. It had the desired effect: he broke from his rant and listened. 'I only knew Clemency a short time, but she lit something in me, something good. I want to bring her justice. Will you help me return to the town?'

Hopewell's angry face dissolved into a lopsided smile. 'By the Lord, Mrs Blakewood, there is more of courage in you than in any of them downriver. You wish to go to Meltwater, then I will take you. Lavington may be magistrate, but he cannot do exactly as he likes. I have my own house and you are welcome to it.'

A great relief broke out inside her – relief, and uncertainty. 'Mr Quayle, thank you.'

He looked at the dimming sky. 'But we cannot ride now. You will have to stay in my tent here for the night.'

She coughed. 'Mr Quayle, I do not—'

He laughed, a guttural roar of out-of-place mirth. 'I shall sleep under

146

the stars, as can my friend and your man. But tomorrow we ride to Meltwater.' He reached behind the log pile to retrieve another flask. 'I cannot wait to see the look on John Lavington's face.'

They rode back to Meltwater late the following morning. She had hoped to leave sooner, but when at dawn she emerged from the tent, Hopewell had already vanished into the woods with his Indian friend, hunting for beavers so he said, although he returned with little. Still, it meant she could spend a peaceful few hours in the open air, walking along the brook to its source.

After devouring a quick dish of something Hopewell called *samp* – corn swirling in milk, as far as she could tell – they set off, making good time as they journeyed to the encampment, leaving their guide to return to his people. No sign of Sooleawa, Hopewell conversed briefly with the *sachem* before leading them on, choosing a different, less obvious path then the route they had taken before. As Meltwater came into sight, he grinned profusely.

'My, my.' He drew up his horse, its front hooves skidding into the air. 'This should be amusing.'

With a raised eyebrow at Nicholas, Mercia followed through the northern gate. Just inside the palisade, a townsman was standing on watch where none had been posted before. Hopewell called out a greeting, making plain the others were with him. The man glanced across, his mouth falling half open on seeing who had returned, the comical action making Nicholas stifle a laugh.

Hopewell continued to the central crossroads, taking a turn around the intersection to shout loud salutations to everyone in earshot. His brashness was irritating, jarring with Mercia's nerves, but there was little she could do to save herself the embarrassment. Near the steps of the meeting house, Fearing Davison stared at them before walking briskly away.

His performance over, Hopewell signalled for Mercia to follow him along the eastern street. Passing the tavern, he halted outside a small cottage three quarters of the way down.

'This,' he said, 'is mine. You can stay for as long as you like. I shall not need it.'

'You are leaving town already?' An unwanted tension clawed at her chest. 'Even with your permission, I fear we may be hounded out.' She looked at him. 'Did our entrance have to be so obvious?'

He smiled. 'I told you, I want to make clear to Lavington he cannot do just as he pleases. And no, I will wait in Meltwater a while, then I shall go to Hartford on some usual business.'

'But where will you stay?' She cast an eye over the house, constructed in the same style as the cottage belonging to Humility Thomas's son; other than subtle differences in craftsmanship, the dwellings could have been the same.

'At Clemency's cottage.' He sighed as her face fell. 'Look. The only way you can be in Meltwater is to use my house, and so I must sleep elsewhere.' He shrugged. 'She was my cousin. As I see it, there is nobody else to take ownership of her house, save her brother, and he is not even in America. I will look after it until Renton ever comes back, which he will not, and so I will keep it. I shall certainly stay there for the next few days.'

She shivered as the sun went in. 'I did not know she had a brother.'

'Well,' Hopewell leapt to the ground, 'there will be much about her – about all the town – that you don't know.'

Of course he was right. A few spots of rain dropped from the quickly darkening sky. 'Will it not be – discomfiting? To sleep in the house where she was . . . ?'

'Oh, no. That won't bother me at all.' He put his hand on the gate and the top hinge fell loose. 'You can tell I don't come back much. Let me help you tidy and I'll be out of your way.' He turned to Nicholas. 'By the time I come out, Lavington will have heard you are back in town. I wager you five beads of wampum he will storm round here within the hour, rain or no.'

Nicholas grinned from atop his horse. 'I thought you Puritan lot hated gambling.'

'They do.' Hopewell raised an eyebrow. 'I don't. Now, will you wager?'

He stretched out his hand as the torrent began. 'Oh yes.'

Chapter Fourteen

As Mercia suspected, Hopewell won the bet – and convincingly. Not twenty minutes after their arrival, she was balancing one-footed on a rickety stool, stretching on tiptoe to clean a strand of silky thread from the top corner of the cluttered kitchen area, when a loud rap resounded from the entrance passage behind. Moments later the front door thumped against the interior wall.

'Quayle!' Even in the keeping room, Lavington's outrage made itself felt. 'Where are you?'

Mercia froze on the stool, swaying as though she were a statue of Cupid in a country garden back home, one hand in front and the other behind where the boy-god's chubby fingers would be clutching his bow. As much as she was not afraid of Lavington, and wanted to charm him to her side if she could, she did not want to be the first to speak with him today. Holding her breath, she waited for Hopewell to respond.

'Who is it?' the trader called from upstairs. 'I have just this hour returned from upriver. Who is it come to greet me home?'

'Quayle!' roared Lavington. 'Come down here now!'

Her outstretched leg aching, Mercia bent to set her foot quietly on the floor. Moments later a wooden groaning from above signalled movement.

'Mr Lavington.' The stairs creaked, Hopewell's voice less muffled now. 'What a delight.'

Lavington was in no mood for games. 'Quayle, what do you mean by bringing those people into my town?'

The creaking stopped as Hopewell reached the ground floor. 'Your town? I thought we all had equal share in its success or failure, was that not what you said when we arrived?'

'Yet I am magistrate. I think that gives me some authority, or it should.'

Footsteps clunked as the men passed into the sitting room. Mercia crept into the hall, daring to peek round the doorpost, but her hand brushed against a patch of sticky grime and she yanked it away without thinking. Hopewell's eyes flicked up towards the movement; she ducked back, but too late.

'So there you are, Mrs Blakewood.' Lavington whipped round to face her. 'You may as well show yourself.'

She took a deep breath and came into the open. 'Mr Lavington.'

He held her innocent gaze. 'It will do you no good, returning here.'

'I do not intend it to do me good. Doing myself good was never the issue.'

'You understand my meaning. You were told to leave town. Why have you returned?'

On Lavington's other side, Hopewell scratched at his beard. 'Mrs Blakewood was concerned that I should know of Clemency's death. She had the courtesy to seek me out. I am curious, John, why nobody from the village would be bothered to do so themselves?'

The magistrate threw up an irritated hand. 'How could we find you out? You are always so well hidden.'

'You merely have to ask the right people.'

'Bah. You would have returned sooner or later.'

'Indeed.' Hopewell's face was set, his facade of mischief gone. 'By which time Clemency would be long buried. I take it she has been laid to rest?'

'Yesterday, in the plot outside the eastern gate. But that is not the point of this discussion.'

'There is no point to this discussion. Mrs Blakewood believes my cousin was killed, and so I have invited her to stay while we search for answers. I will sleep at Clemency's house.'

Lavington reddened, pointing a rigid finger. 'Quayle, I promise that if you—'

'Hold, sir. There is naught you can do. Besides, she is in Connecticut at the invitation of the governor himself, that man with whom you claim to hold the deepest affinity.' He raised a provocative eyebrow. 'Now, I would be obliged if you would allow me to continue to prepare the house for my guests.'

Lavington bestowed a look of total contempt on the trader, before turning to Mercia, his narrow eyes blazing.

'I will allow you here only because of that acquaintance with the governor. Any trouble, any disturbance, and I will use the law to remove you. I will not allow Mrs Carter's death to be sullied unnecessarily.' He thrust on his hat. 'Good day.'

'Pleasant man,' said Nicholas, stepping from the staircase as Lavington slammed shut the front door.

'He is an idiot,' said Hopewell. 'And with the King's fleet arrived in New England, he is a scared one. He fears Meltwater will be absorbed into the Duke of York's new lands to our west. Do not be worried. He is lashing out.'

'They buried her.' Mercia was looking at the floor. 'I should have liked to have been there. They knew that.'

Hopewell put a hand on her shoulder. 'They did not know you were coming back.'

'I suppose not.' She sighed. 'Still, I shall be able to visit the grave now.' She shrugged off his hand and walked to the window. 'Is that true, what you said about Lavington being afraid of the Duke's ambitions? You are well informed for a man who spends his time out of town.'

'It is not so surprising. The Indians learn everything, and more quickly than the Englishman. I am never far from news.'

She nodded, looking out onto the muddy street where a few shallow puddles were reflecting the emergent sun. 'Thank you for your words just now.'

He grunted. 'There are difficult times ahead, Mrs Blakewood. I would not thank me yet.'

There was no sense in deferring it. Throwing back her hood so everyone could see her courage, she walked into the fresh afternoon light. Courageous, yet not stupid: Nicholas was at her side.

'Good evening.' The shower over, people were back on the streets: she nodded at Renatus Fox as she passed the would-be minister, his white hair flopping from under his battered hat; a similar greeting she bestowed on the Edwards brothers, and then a squat, middle-aged man, who introduced himself as Seaborn Adams, walking arm in arm with a woman of around his age. The men returned her greetings, politely she thought, although Seaborn's companion merely held her gaze. She was surprised, for she had anticipated a purely hostile return. At the central crossroads, Percy Lavington was talking with Amery on the meeting house steps. Amery leapt up to greet them, although Percy remained sitting, observing from his wet vantage point.

'Hopewell said you were back.' He shook Nicholas's hand with relish. 'It is good to see you again, both of you.' He lowered his voice. 'I spoke with Kit, while you were gone. He said he had talked with you. I did not even know you had left until it was too late.' He hesitated. 'I have spent much time in thought since. And . . . I think you are right. About Clemency. I assume that is why you have returned?'

She studied his face; his blue eyes seemed earnest, genuine. 'Thank you, Amery. What say the rest of you? Are the other townsfolk as convinced?'

He glanced around him. 'Unless Mr Lavington changes his

153

mind . . . some of them just want it forgotten, you can tell. But at the funeral yesterday, the uneasiness was obvious.' He fixed her with a pitying look. 'Renatus conducted the ceremony. He said some beautiful words.'

An uncalled-for tear came to her eye. 'At least she is at rest now.'

'Do not let your absence trouble you. Percy, too, was out of town.' He leant closer in. 'Overseeing arrangements for our friend Dixwell to—'

'Don't mention that here!' Silent until now, Percy jumped to his feet. 'Anyone could be listening.'

'Who?' Nicholas looked around. 'There is nobody in the street.'

A quick burst of annoyance flashed across Percy's face. 'That is irrelevant.' Then he sighed. 'Mrs Blakewood, I am speaking rashly again. I am . . . anxious, that is all.'

She gave him a reassuring smile, although in truth the force of his words had alarmed her. 'Do not be concerned, Percy. We are all upset. Or we should be.'

'Thank you.' He bit his lip. 'I should leave you to your conversation.'

He walked away, leaving the others to stand for a time in silence. Then a bird flew overhead, its song brightening the air, waking them from their individual thoughts.

'Poor Percy,' said Amery. 'He does get so nervous about—but as he says, we should not talk about it.' He turned to Nicholas. 'Where are you staying now? You are welcome to my spare bedroom again if you wish.'

Nicholas smiled. 'I'd been wondering where I was going to sleep.'

'Oh, Nicholas, I am sorry.' Mercia shook her head. 'I had not thought. Could you? Nathan will need the other room at Hopewell's cottage. If he wants to return, that is.'

'He will. That would be helpful, Amery.'

'Then I shall see you later.' He bowed, setting a hand on his tilted hat just in time to prevent it from falling. 'In the meantime, be careful.' His eyes flicked up. 'There are those here who would sooner ignore what is in front of them than seek the truth.'

Mercia watched his departing back. 'Oh, friend. You have no need to warn me of that.' She looked across at the window of the tavern, where Humility Thomas had appeared beside his wife, her frilled sleeves folded, the frowning expression on his pudgy face oozing with mistrust.

'Well, there we are,' said Mercia, choosing to ignore Humility's disdain. 'Our first success. Amery thinks as we do.'

'And Percy?'

She blew out her cheeks. 'He was . . . clearly listening. And he did not argue differently.'

Nicholas laughed. 'I always did prefer the optimistic point of view. Shall we press on?'

Deliberately avoiding the western road where Clemency's cottage stood, Mercia took them south, pausing outside Vic Smith's forge where the muscular blacksmith was once more at his anvil. He looked up and his eyes met hers, but aside from a slight double-take he made no other sign he much cared, merely returning to his work.

Passing outside the southern gate, the unfinished fort rising on the hill above them, she nodded towards a solitary figure tramping his way through the field, the town's cattle herd lowing as he traversed the muddy space. 'I suppose we do need to talk to everyone,' she mumbled. 'Even him.' She nudged Nicholas. 'Look, 'tis Thorpe.'

'What's he been doing out here in the rain?' He scoffed. 'Still wearing that coxcomb's sash.'

Walking in their direction, Thorpe raised his eyes as he heard them approach. Unlike Vic, his reaction was violent. He stopped up short, jerking back his head and yanking at his cloak.

'By God's truth!' He stared at her. 'You were ordered to leave!'

'Good afternoon to you also, Mr Thorpe. We left, and now we are back.'

'Of all the impertinent—'

'Mr Quayle has invited us.'

155

'That reprobate. I should have guessed.' He dodged to one side, making to continue on his way. 'Well, I doubt you will be here long.'

Nicholas sidestepped into his path. 'Hold a moment. My mistress would like to speak with you.'

Thorpe shook his head. 'Yet again, this servant is barring my way. You should discipline him with stricter force.'

'Nevertheless, I should like a minute of your time. I did not have the chance to speak with you before.' She tried a smile. 'You are, I think, an intelligent man. A physician moreover. Perhaps we could discuss what you thought of Clemency's—'

'Suicide?' He sniffed. 'I should say she is being tortured in hell for it. Wouldn't you?'

She recoiled, stung by his bluntness. 'There is no . . . I only want—'

'Madam, I have nothing I need say to you.' Slipping past Nicholas, he pulled his cloak tighter, covering his sash. 'So if you have finished disturbing my evening, I shall return to my work.'

Part unwilling, part incredulous, Mercia let him go. 'Well, Nicholas. Not so successful that time, would you say?'

Hopewell waylaid them as they returned through the gate, inviting them to share in a convivial supper, for they had not eaten since their journey from his camp. Not relishing the prospect of dining in Clemency's house, Mercia asked him to bring his provisions to her lodgings – his own cottage, after all – even offering to cook. As darkness fell, he appeared at the door, handing over a colourful platter of vegetables and corn, following Nicholas into the sitting room to help him light the reluctant fire.

She chopped and boiled, stirring a thickening potage above the keeping-room fire, wishing her maidservant Bethany was there in her place, for she had the ability to conjure up nectar from the most mundane of morsels. But soon the food was hot, and she carried it out in a large iron pot.

She ladled out two servings at the sitting-room table, a chipped wooden bowl for herself, a larger trencher for Nicholas and Hopewell to share. Standing back, she looked on the seated men as if daring them to criticise her efforts. Nicholas looked at the sorry mush, hesitating just an instant before he picked up his spoon to scoop a portion into his mouth. He swallowed, eventually. Hopewell did not seem to mind the lack of taste. Mercia herself was simply embarrassed.

'Do you want a cook while you're here?' Hopewell asked. 'Remy Davison prepares an excellent repast, when that father of hers lets her out of the house.' He looked up. 'Not that this isn't – but perhaps you don't want to worry about—'

She took her seat. 'I appreciate your thoughtfulness, Mr Quayle. I will manage.'

'As you wish.' He winked at Nicholas. 'You got that wampum for me yet?'

'I will have.' Nicholas grinned. 'I'll have to find someone to win it off, but I always pay my debts.'

'As any good man should. Now I just need Amery to pay up.'

Nicholas leant over his soup. 'Amery plays?'

'Not as such. But last time I was in town, I convinced him that a wager could encourage his alchemical endeavours.' He laughed. 'He was to have made some useful discovery by the time I returned, but I seem to be back too soon, for I spoke with him earlier, and he has not.'

Mercia forced down a spoonful of potage. 'I thought Amery was new to Meltwater?'

'To live, yes, but he has been here before.' Hopewell ripped off a chunk of bread; the dense loaf still looked more appetising than the mush. 'He knows Percy, of course, and Kit, as he did Clemency, and he has always corresponded with Lavington.' A crumb of bread dropped from his beard to the table. 'About time that one found a wife. 'Tis not natural for a young man to be so interested in books.'

Nicholas set down his spoon, the trencher still mostly full. 'He seems harmless.'

'Many folk do.' He looked at Mercia. 'Did you speak with any of my fellow Precisians this evening?'

She raised an eyebrow. 'I did not think to hear that word here. In England, 'tis mostly a term of abuse.'

'Precisians, Puritans, Hot Protestants, the Elect . . . there are no end of terms to choose from.'

'I suppose not.' She smiled. 'Yes, I have spoken with a few of your fellow – townsfolk. But mostly platitudes, no real discussion.' She chewed at her lip. 'We talked with the Edwards brothers briefly. They are close?'

'Standfast and Silence? Both self-righteous do-goods, if you ask me. There's something odd about Standfast in particular. But maybe I don't like him because he spends so much time trying to make the Indians like us, instead of finding ways we can work with the beliefs they already have.'

'He is a missionary?'

'Of a sort. His brother is less zealous, but godly all the same. Fierce, though. A good fighter, and loyal.' He laughed. 'I reckon he drowned George Mason so his brother could have a try for the job. But Renatus will beat him to it.'

She looked at him. 'You are joking, I take it?'

He took a sudden interest in his soup. 'Just an expression, Mrs Blakewood. But it isn't them you need to worry about.' He shovelled the potage into his mouth. 'As I always say,' he garbled, 'I am not one for clattermouths, but our blacksmith, you should watch him. Him and Fearing Davison.'

'Why?'

'Too quiet.' He slurped at the soup. 'Both of them. And Fearing . . . I don't think he treats his family too well. Not that I know, but . . . I hear things. As everyone does.'

'I see.' She glanced at Nicholas. 'Anything else?'

Hopewell waggled his spoon in the air. 'Godsgift Brown. He hates the Indians. Loathes them, the Lord knows why. Another one that could have done with taking a bride. Never know why he didn't.'

'Were you never married yourself?'

'Once.' His cheerful demeanour wavered. 'She has been in the cemetery since the month after we arrived. With my baby boy.'

She reached across a hand. 'Forgive me. I should not have brought it up.'

'Don't be.' He shrugged. 'She was pregnant when we followed the old minister here, and then – she died in childbirth. I . . . find it hard to spend much time in the town now. Not like Thorpe, who can't bear to leave his wife's grave. But enough of that.' He smiled. 'Sarah Thomas – there's a clattermouth for you. Remy Davison, the exact opposite. Aside from being a good cook, she is an angel.'

'And the prettiest woman in town,' said Nicholas. 'But that would count for nothing, of course.'

'Until Mrs Blakewood arrived, that is,' joked Hopewell.

She joined in the newfound reverie. 'Oh come, I hardly think—'

A sharp rap at the door cut her off. Nicholas fairly jumped to his feet. 'I'll see who it is.'

As he opened the door a chill wind flew in, but there was no one there. He stepped outside, looking around.

'Who's there?' he called. Still no response, she heard his footsteps walk out a little further. 'Ah – no use hiding.' And then: 'Hey, come back!'

She scuttled to the door, holding onto the jamb as she poked her head into the cool evening air. She leant forward, trying to see, but the clouds were obscuring the moonlight, and her eyes struggled to adjust.

'Nicholas?' Hopewell pushed past. 'What is it?' He ran forward, his silhouette soon merging into the darkness. 'Back in the house, Mrs Blakewood,' came his voice. 'I'm not certain what's—God's truth!'

As Hopewell sped away, Mercia's vision finally caught up with the night. She could see neither of the men, but directly outside the door sprawled a strange, uneven mass that had not been there before. She

159

crouched down to touch it, frowning as she ran her hand over the ridges in the soft material. Curious, she picked it up; the object was grey, mostly, but dirty in parts, a garment of some kind, patterned with a series of small diamonds and dots, just like the bodice Clemency . . .

Of a sudden she knew what she was holding. She gasped for air, unable to breathe.

Chapter Fifteen

She leapt back, throwing down the appalling garment, reaching behind to feel the supportive firmness of the wooden door. She swallowed, feeling sick, the sound of chirping crickets thrumming all around her. But a shout from the street forced her to look up, and she turned to see Hopewell hurrying back.

'There was someone in the road,' he said. 'Nicholas is chasing – what is it? Your face is pale.'

Unable to look, she pointed at the ground. He crouched, the cloth of his breeches creasing loud in the otherwise near-silence; even the crickets seemed to have vanished, but perhaps she just did not hear.

'I don't understand,' he said. 'What is this?'

'A message,' she managed. 'A message for me.'

He turned the garment over in his hands, holding it against the candlelight falling through the sitting-room window. 'A bodice?'

Composing herself, she stood up; now more brightly illuminated, she could tell it was dirty, covered with dark streaks, but the pattern was unmistakable.

''Tis Clemency's bodice,' she said. 'The one she was wearing when . . . I found her.'

'Clemency's? How do you know?'

'She was wearing it the day before. It is . . . carved in my memory.'

His fist tightened around the stained material. 'Who would do this?'

The sound of footsteps thudded low in the street. She looked into the blackness as Nicholas appeared from the gloom.

'Gone,' he said. 'He threw a rock at me and ran. He could have hidden anywhere.'

'I saw you running,' said Hopewell. 'I came to help, but—'

'Too late now.'

'Did you see his face?'

'No. He was wearing a hood of some sort.'

'And you are sure it was a man?' said Mercia.

'I think so.'

'But you are not certain.'

'Well, I don't think he – whoever it was – was wearing a dress.'

She teased the bodice from Hopewell's grasp and led them inside. Calmer now, she pushed the trencher and bowl aside to lay it on the sitting-room table, feeling the coldness of the cloth, the ridges in the lace. But handling the garment brought back an intense memory, and she had to take a moment's pause. She closed her eyes, striving to remember Clemency as the woman in the illicit tavern, or the woman in the clearing that overlooked the town. Anything but the woman in the rope.

Hopewell cleared his throat. 'Do you want me to take this away?'

She breathed steadily, in and out. 'I think that would be best. I do not know why this has been left precisely, but I can guess. Someone wants to scare me, or play a sick jest.'

He folded the bodice and pushed it away. 'Try not to let it worry you.'

'If I find who did this,' said Nicholas, 'it is not Mercia who will have to worry.'

Hopewell clapped him on the shoulder. 'I doubt whoever left it will be back tonight. But I think it might be better if you stayed, nonetheless.' He turned to Mercia. 'Mrs Blakewood, this is a foul act indeed, but try to get some sleep. I should leave you to rest.'

Mercia rubbed her tired eyes. Now Hopewell had mentioned it, she realised how weary she was. 'Will you be safe walking home, with . . . all this?'

He set his broad-brimmed hat across his brow. 'I am often abroad at night. And I have my knife.' He patted the side of his breeches, where a sharp dagger hung from his belt. 'In case of animal attack.'

She looked at the blade. 'Still, be careful.'

'Whoever he is, he will be abed by now. As we all need to be.' He turned towards the door, the bodice crunched up in his fist. 'Now goodnight, and sleep well, both.'

Despite Amery's offer to Nicholas of his spare room, she had already decided to ask him to sleep in the cottage: until Nathan returned they agreed it would be better she did not stay alone, especially with malicious deliveries after dark. But the night passed peacefully, in the real world at least. In her dreams she walked with Clemency, the dead woman calling to her from the eaves of a golden wood, beseeching her to take her sullied bodice and hide it.

The smell of nutmeg teased her awake. She dressed to find Nicholas hunched over the kitchen fire, stirring a pot of milk. He looked over his shoulder and smiled.

'It is remarkable here, you know.' He agitated his spoon. 'So far from anywhere, and yet still they manage to survive. Different to back home, mind. For all its noise and filth, London's the town for me.' He took out the spoon to taste the milk, gingerly touching it with the tip of his tongue. 'A bit hot,' he winced.

'It is a rare life they are building.' She took a seat. 'And I would love to be able to share it with them. But not now. All that has changed.'

'I hope it won't change this place for ever. Here.' He poured some of the milk into a mug. 'It will cool quickly.'

'Thank you.' She sipped at the thick liquid; the heat snatched at her tongue, but she bore it. Somehow she liked the pain: it made her feel more alive.

'After I went to bed, I remembered that letter to Nathan I wanted to write. I was tired, so the script is not the neatest, but you recall how Standfast Edwards said he was riding to Hartford this morning? Do you think 'tis too late to catch him?'

'Not if he leaves the same time we saw him the other day.' Nicholas set down the spoon. 'You want me to ask him to take the letter to Winthrop's house?'

'Please. I left it on the shelf in the other room. As long as Standfast delivers it, Nathan will be here tomorrow evening, hopefully with our belongings.'

He nodded, snatching up the letter from the best room and sprinting off without a coat. She followed him out the door, leaning against the front wall of the house with the hot mug of milk in her ungloved hands. It was a fine morning, early, the air fresh and pure, crisp as only dawn air can be. The sound of the town awakening rang out around her; not far off, she could tell Vic was already at his anvil, the regular chiming of his hammer striking away at his work. A pig grunted in the dusty street in front of the house, wandering down the road from who knew where. She breathed in deeply: the scent of America, of newness. Would that Clemency were there to share it.

She looked up from her reverie to see a shawled figure coming down the street from the meeting house. Reaching the gate to the cottage the figure hesitated, but eventually she made up her mind. She opened the gate, casting back her gaping hood with a rough tug, exposing her auburn hair.

'Good morrow, Miss Davison,' said Mercia. Seeing Remembrance brought back memories of the callousness with which the young woman had treated Clemency at the ministerial gathering. But she had just lost her brother: Mercia was mindful of that. 'How do you fare this day?'

'Good morrow, Mrs Blakewood. I . . . was not sure you would be awake so early.'

164

'I do not sleep well, of late.'

'No.' Remembrance kept her eyes averted. 'I—'

She looked at her pallid face over the steaming rim of her mug. Remembrance's aspect was so forlorn she could not help feeling pity.

'What is the matter?' she said.

'I wanted to see how you were faring. It cannot be easy, returning here.'

'It is not. But I had to come back.'

'I know.' A steady pause. 'I regret what I said – before. To Clemency. I did not mean . . . I did not want to bring the Lord's wrath on her. I was angry.'

'And your father?' She stooped to set the mug on the ground. 'Is he still angry?'

'Father says little. I . . . just wanted to come.' She looked up, her eyes darting this way and that, never quite settling on Mercia's face. 'Is Mr Keyte with you?'

'Nathan?' She frowned. 'Not yet. Why?'

At last Remembrance met her gaze; in her eyes glowed a trace of the same defiance she had shown when assaulting Clemency. 'I merely wondered. I was hoping to talk with him. He seemed to . . . understand things.'

Mercia folded her arms. 'You will have to wait. I do not know when he will be back.'

'But it will be soon?'

'I hope so.'

Remembrance pulled up her hood. 'Truly, I am sorry about Clemency. I am sure you must blame me, but . . . I hope now I can make amends.'

'When her killer is discovered, then we can talk of amends.'

The young woman stared. 'Then it is true you think she was—' She cut herself off. 'I should get back to father. He will be wondering where I am.' She shuffled towards the street. 'Farewell.'

* * *

That afternoon she visited Clemency's grave, laying a yellow bunch of wild flowers on the light brown plot. There was no headstone yet, the death too recent and sudden. But she knelt at its side, her hands clasped in prayer, asking God's kindness, and begging to receive guidance on the answers she sought.

'Clemency,' she said, once she had finished her prayers. 'I am sorry. I wish I could have been there, to stop this from happening. I wish . . . I had insisted you stayed with us that night.'

And then she felt Clemency rise from her heart, smiling as she had the day before her death, and at least, Mercia knew, she had been happy then. But she did not speak today, content just to sit, as Mercia wept her tears until the sadness fell away, a hollow ache carving into her soul. Then Clemency returned to her heart, and another presence arrived, this one real and human.

'Mercia,' said Nicholas, crouching beside her. 'You have been here for hours. Do you want to come back now?'

She looked up and gave him a sad smile. 'Hours?'

He nodded. 'At least two.'

She took a deep breath, pulling herself to her feet, holding onto his shoulder as her legs strained to regain their feeling.

'I needed to be here.' She looked at the ground, at the shallow indentation where she had been sitting in the grass. 'If I could not be at the funeral, then I had to be with her today.'

'I know.' He looked into her eyes. 'Do you want to eat?'

'I ate earlier.' She looked up; the sun was setting, but she had not noticed the change in light. 'I am not hungry now.'

'That was breakfast.' He tilted his head. 'I think you should have food.'

'Perhaps.' She breathed in the light dampness of the pines and the birches in the forest around her, the ashes and the elms. And she thought again of Clemency, about the pleasure she had taken in the beauty of this land.

'Can we go to the waterfall a moment? I would just like . . . more than

166

this grave, I think that is where I should be, to say goodbye. It was her favourite place.'

He smiled. 'Lead the way.'

She took him through the meadow, skirting the palisade, aiming for the forest at the settlement's western edge. Not far from Kit's sawmill, she found the rising path, and although the greyness of evening was nearly upon them, she climbed without pause, stepping over roots and rocks as she took in the crescendo of the waterfall's descent, finally emerging into the clearing near its top. But then she halted, for she and Nicholas were not alone.

On the edge of the clearing, sitting on the same rock where she had comforted Clemency the day of Praise-God Davison's death, Percy Lavington was talking with Silence Edwards, a small fire burning at their feet. The weak flames cast a subdued orange glow on the rocks, the slight crackling no match for the steady flow of water cascading over the lip of the falls behind them. As she came into the circular space, the two raised their heads, breaking from their conversation.

'Mrs Blakewood,' acknowledged Percy. 'Welcome. What are you doing here?'

She tried to hide her disappointment. 'Clemency said it was her favourite place, and well – I merely wanted to come.' She turned back towards the path. 'But I can do so another time.'

'No.' Silence hastily jumped from his perch; more thickset than his brother, he was still dextrous. 'I think we have finished now.'

'But the fire?'

'Not long lit,' said Percy. 'We did not mean to stay much longer in any case.' He turned to his companion. 'You are certain about . . . ?'

Silence nodded. 'Of course.'

'Well, then. A fine night, Mrs Blakewood.'

'Calm, at least. And please, you can call me Mercia.'

He touched the brim of his hat. 'You know Sil, of course. Would you . . . like to share the warmth?'

Not much in the mood for conversation, she shook her head. 'Do not worry, Percy. I am happy to come back.'

He leapt to his feet. 'If you wish a moment's reflection, then do please stay. We can show Nicholas further down the falls, along this path here, if he has an interest.'

Nicholas stepped forward. 'I think you would like that, Mercia. We won't be long.'

'Ten minutes,' said Sil, reaching down for his own, brown, hat; like the green jacket he was wearing, his attire was less formal than most she had seen in the town, a thin sort of bracelet circling his wrist. 'Then it will be getting dark.'

She made to protest, but Percy beckoned to Nicholas, leading him and Silence down a hidden path that ran the course of the waterfall's long cascades. The three men gone, she walked alone to the smooth platform before her and sat, feeling the caress of the fire. She fell to thinking of Clemency, the time passing again unnoticed as she enjoyed the same evening views her friend must have known; and she realised, then, that not even here, in this beautiful glade, could she truly say goodbye.

The darkness deepening, she was lost in her contemplations when a call startled her from her thoughts.

'Do you feel better now?' asked Percy, returned from their exploration.

She looked up and smiled. 'I do.'

'Shall I take you back?' said Nicholas. 'The light is going.'

She rose to her feet. 'And you, Percy? Sil? You will come with us?'

'You go on,' said Sil. 'We will put out this fire and follow soon after.'

'We can wait.'

Percy shook his head. 'The path back to town can be awkward in the dark. Best for you to go. We can finish up here.'

'Very well.' She looked between the two in gratitude. 'Thank you, both, for your understanding.'

As Sil crouched by the fire, Percy accompanied them to the head of the path. Glancing back, he gave Mercia a wry smile.

'I know my father does not much care for your being here, but that does not mean you and I cannot discuss . . . what has happened.' He looked at the sky; stars had begun to appear, their pinpricks of white glinting on the horizon. 'But perhaps not tonight.'

His words enthused her. 'That would be welcome.'

'Although . . . I do wonder one thing. Forgive me, but – why are you still here, in Meltwater? Coming back after my father made you leave . . . it was brave. But you do not need to suffer with us. You could return to England whenever you wished.'

She looked down the path into the fast encroaching gloom. 'I could. But I would leave part of me behind if I abandoned Clemency now. She was a friend, when so many others in my life have not been.'

He nodded slowly. 'I doubted her when she trusted you. I am sorry for it. She did not know you long, but she spoke of you with great affection.' He looked her up and down, a little longer perhaps than proper. But then he bowed, bade her good night, and she turned away from the falls.

She followed Nicholas down the forest trail, taking note as he pointed out obstacles in the path. She managed not to trip, for the most part, only once sucking in through her teeth as she went over on her ankle, but she righted herself in time. Soon they came out into the meadow between the forest and the town, the blackness of night now upon them.

Out in the open, she relaxed her concentration. 'I want to thank you, too, Nicholas. For giving me that time alone.'

'You needed it. Watch this stone here.'

She stepped over the lonely rock. 'Did they say anything?'

'Percy and Sil?' He laughed. 'Very little. They took me halfway down the falls and up again. Talked a little of the town, I suppose.'

'Nothing about Clemency?'

'No. And . . .'

She frowned. 'What?'

'I just think . . . for all Percy's talk, I'm not sure I'd trust him yet.

169

I mean, what was he doing out here with that Silence?'

'Probably just talking, Nicholas. As you said, this is not London. There are few places to go to be—' She broke off as a movement in the near distance caught her attention. 'Nicholas, what is that?'

'What is what?'

'That!' She stopped dead, pointing towards the town's northern gate. 'Is it a bear?' A shock of fear coursed through her body. ''Tis rearing up!'

Nicholas ventured forward. Outside the gate a large black figure was lurching left and right, just about lit up in the moonlight.

'I don't think 'tis a bear, if bears in these parts are like those in the Southwark pits.' He craned his neck. 'Stay here. I think 'tis a man, but let me be sure.'

She let him move on a slight way in front, then followed regardless.

'Mercia.'

'Just . . . keep moving.'

As they approached, the figure came into focus. Closer up, she could tell it was clothed. 'It must be one of the townsfolk wandering abroad at night,' she whispered, feeling foolish. 'Keep back, Nicholas. We do not want them to see us.'

'I think – I'm not sure – is he in trouble? Look how he's wobbling about.'

'You are right. Damn.' She followed him forward again. Now almost on the dark figure, she could see he was clutching at something in his hands.

'He definitely doesn't seem well,' said Nicholas.

The man lurched over, hitting the earth. His hat fell to the ground, revealing his bearded cheeks.

'Shit.' Nicholas dashed forward. 'I think 'tis Hopewell.'

'Is that a bottle he is holding?' She raced behind Nicholas to come alongside the prostrate man. 'He is drunk, isn't he?' At their feet, Hopewell began to roll on the ground, groaning and grabbing at the long object in his hands.

Nicholas crouched down. 'Are you well, friend? What's the matter?' He jumped back as Hopewell began to convulse. 'By God's truth, Mercia, he is starting to shake.' He turned round. 'Mercia?'

But Mercia was not listening. She was staring at Hopewell's hands, at the bottle she had assumed he was holding. Suddenly she threw her head to the side and was violently sick.

'Mercia! What is—fuck!' Nicholas recoiled as he saw what had made her so ill. He turned away, retching himself.

She recovered enough to turn back to Hopewell's writhing figure. She wiped her mouth and spoke in a trembling voice: a simple, heartfelt phrase.

'But he is still alive.'

'Yes.' Nicholas looked at her, horror in his eyes. 'My God, Mercia. Yes.'

'And there is nothing we can do.' Despairing, she looked at Hopewell's shaking body, his constant moans betraying the agony he must have been feeling. 'Nicholas! What can we do?'

'Help!' Nicholas shouted as loud as he was able, his strident voice booming around the night. 'Help!'

For a time Mercia took up his chorus, but then she dared to look back at Hopewell and her cries fell silent. His trembling hands were overrun, covered in a thick fluid that could only have been blood, a gurgling noise stemming from his throat. For it was no bottle of rum that the trader was holding, but a more sinister thing entirely, a throbbing, viscous mass pouring from a deep gash in his clothes, draining from the savage rip in his flesh she knew must be lying beneath.

He was holding his own entrails in his quivering hands, fast on the way to death.

Chapter Sixteen

From behind, the sound of heavy boots came thudding on dry earth. Percy and Sil rushed up, alerted by the cries for help. With Nicholas they carried Hopewell into the town, but by the time they rested him once more on the ground, he was mercifully dead, blood dribbling from his mouth as it continued to trickle from his stomach.

'Who did this?' Percy looked up at Mercia, his mouth open in apparent shock. 'Did you see?'

'No.' Feeling utterly sick, she forced herself to speak. 'We only saw Hopewell, staggering towards the gate.' She looked at Nicholas, unbelieving. 'We thought he was drunk.'

Nicholas made to wipe his brow, but stopped abruptly, the stench of Hopewell's entrails covering his fingers. 'Oh God,' he cried, flinging bits of stomach to the ground.

'The alarm!' Sil whipped round. 'Percy, the alarm!'

'God, yes, I—' Percy ran back to the gate, reaching up to grab at a hidden object, shaking it back and forth. A loud bell rang out across the town.

'Alarm!' Percy cried. 'Alarm! Everybody out!'

'Alarm!' Sil took up his call. 'Alarm!' Now Nicholas and Mercia joined them. 'Alarm!' The quartet's cries drowned out the bell, Mercia's shouts alone louder than she thought possible. 'Alarm!'

Dogs began to bark, cows to grunt, pigs rummaging around the gardens squealed, adding their mammalian chorus. And now candles began to move inside windows, doors squeaked open, people poured into the streets. An eerie procession of candlelit townsfolk wavered outside the gates of their houses, looking towards the alarm call, straining to see. Some carried weapons in their free hands, perhaps assuming the town was under attack.

Finally – or quickly, Mercia could not tell – some of the men made their way towards the gate, encircling her group, drawing in appalled gasps as they caught sight of the macabre spectacle at their feet.

'God protect us!'

'Who could have—?'

'Fetch the constable!'

'I am already here.'

The crowd stepped aside to let Godsgift Brown through their midst. The burly constable crouched over the corpse, no trace of emotion on his face.

'He is dead.'

'Of course he is dead!' Percy loomed above him, hands on his hips. 'What are you going to do?'

Godsgift scratched at his cheek. 'This was an Indian.'

'What?'

'An Indian, I say. One of the bastards must have killed him.' He looked impassively at the bloody entrails. 'With one of those axes of theirs.'

Percy looked down, incredulous. 'Why? Of all of us, he was the best liked among them.'

'You know as well as I do how they are quick to turn. Perhaps the rum he insisted on giving them addled their heads.' He stood, stroking his chin. 'You found him?'

'Yes – I mean, no – Mrs Blakewood did, and Wildmoor.'

173

Godsgift turned to face her. 'So yet more death since you have returned.'

Mercia recoiled, physically stung. 'We must discover who did this.'

He licked his bottom lip. 'Did you find him here?'

She shook her head. 'He was walking – lurching – towards the gate. He must have been attacked nearby, and not long before we saw him, with . . . these wounds.'

Godsgift nodded, addressing the crowd. 'I need a group of men to come with me to search.' Every man in the circle stepped forward. 'Good. Those of you without arms, go and fetch them, and tell others you see.' He looked at Percy. 'Any Indians nearby will be brought back here and we will have just revenge.' He grabbed the sword hilt at his side. 'No savage does this to an Englishman and lives.'

The men murmured in ready approval, drawing their weapons. Nicholas placed himself in front of Mercia, but she stepped to the side, wanting to see what would occur.

'Wait!' called Sil. 'You cannot merely go and kill whichever Indians you find!'

'Can't I?' snarled Godsgift.

'No.' Another man stepped through the crowd. 'No, Godsgift, you cannot.'

'Lavington.' The constable's hands twitched on his sword hilt, his voice dripping with scorn. 'So what do you propose? That we do nothing?'

Lavington raised himself up, sweeping the open flaps of his hefty cloak to each side. Although Godsgift was stockier, Lavington was taller, and the thickness of his cloak distorted the difference between them. The crowd's eyes swivelled from one to the other, waiting.

'What I propose, Constable, is that we do not leave the town undefended by sending all its men out to search in the darkness for an Indian who may not even be there.'

Godsgift moved his hand from his sword, folding his arms across his puffed-out chest. 'So we do nothing.'

'Did I say that?'

'So far you have said little.'

More people were now joining the group, swearing in horror at the corpse on the ground. They joined the circle around Lavington and Brown, as intrigued as Mercia at the power play taking place in front of them. What Winthrop had said appeared to be true. The constable and the magistrate did not always get on.

'Father.' Percy approached Lavington, his hands red from the dead man's blood. 'Hopewell has been murdered.' He paused. 'The person responsible must still be near. Whether 'tis an Indian or not, the men should at least go and look.' He glanced at Godsgift. 'But 'tis only recently that their powwow was slain, they think by an Englishman. If we kill another now without consulting them first, they will assume the worst kind of treachery and retaliate.'

Lavington peered at his son. 'I believe I implied that?' Then he turned back to Godsgift. 'You may search the fields, but you will not take all the men, and you will not kill. If anyone is out there, I want them brought back here to explain themselves.'

Godsgift stared, his eyes aflame, but then he broke off his gaze to review the men in the circle, ordering those already bearing a weapon to follow him through the gate. Once they had marched out, Lavington removed his thick cloak and knelt by the corpse. He reached his hands close in, but the gore repelled him, holding him back.

'I spoke harshly with him but yesterday afternoon. 'Tis strange the ways God presents His will.' Again he hovered his hands over the body, but again he did not touch. Then he stood, pushing his large frame off the ground. 'Percy, will you take him to my storehouse? Perhaps Stephen can help you.' He gestured at the crowd, waving across the male servant Mercia had seen at his house.

'Let me help,' said Nicholas. 'I am already . . . dirty.'

'No!' Lavington shook his head. 'These two will be enough.'

Nicholas turned to Percy, who nodded. 'Stephen and I can manage.'

He looked at his father. 'But why take him to your yard?'

Lavington rubbed his eyes. 'Percy – just do it. And quickly. We do not want – this – on sight for women and children to see.' He gestured at Amery to trundle over a nearby cart. 'Especially women who are strangers.'

Loading the cart with its gruesome cargo, Percy led his father away into the dark. The rest of the town waited, fired up by Godsgift's certainty and the sight of the ravaged corpse. As their constant murmurs attested, Hopewell might have been a pariah in the town, but death had made him one of them, and they were ready to avenge his loss. No matter, it seemed, that they would not do the same for Clemency, persisting in their belief that she had taken her own life.

The fear running through the group was palpable, leaping from person to person and nestling in their nervous glances, but they seemed incapable of returning to their homes. For her part, Mercia hung back with Nicholas, feeling ill at what she had found. And she began to question, and to wonder, and to think: George Mason, Praise-God Davison, Clemency Carter, Hopewell Quayle. Four deaths, two at least unnatural. Were any of them connected, or was the town merely cursed?

Percy returned from his unwelcome errand, standing beside her with Amery and now Kit, who had run into town from his sawmill after Godsgift's party had left. He comforted her for her discovery as the other townsfolk did not, and she wondered too about Lavington, about why he had insisted Hopewell be taken to his store. She turned to Percy, who was looking out over the gathered crowd.

'Does your father always keep the dead in his yard?'

He frowned. 'Usually the minister would see they are cared for. Perhaps as we don't have one, he thought that duty was his.'

It was logical, she supposed. 'Perhaps. Where is he now?'

'Father? He will come back.' He sighed. 'Each time there is a death here, he feels it, you know. Whatever else, he cares deeply for this town. When someone dies, a small part of himself goes with them.'

She let out a bitter laugh. 'But he did not feel that way with Clemency?'

His face seemed to darken. 'It is not for us to judge how he feels.'

Beside them, Kit broke from his conversation with Amery and Nicholas. 'In the fields,' he said. 'I think I see movement.'

The group tensed, uncertain what to expect. Then Seaborn Adams came in through the gate at the head of Godsgift's party of six. But no. Seven. The hunters had brought quarry: six powerful men dragging a skinny Indian boy, his frailty no match for their brawn. He was young, in his teenage years certainly, in the fire of twenty candles his face full of fear. One of the townsmen, Mercia did not know him, had never seen him, she thought, threw him to the ground, his long black hair strewn across the earth. The people of the town – the women, the men – formed a circle around him, its enclosing menace surer than the firmest earthworks or the sturdiest fence. The boy could not escape.

'What did I say?' said Godsgift, sheathing his rapier. 'An Indian.'

'Wait.' Percy stepped forward. 'You are saying this boy killed Hopewell?'

'We found him right near the town, just at the edge of the field,' said Seaborn. Behind him, the other men nodded their confirmation. All but one: while the rest looked down on the boy, Vic Smith's pockmarked face was turned to the gate.

An eighth figure ran in. Fearing Davison, Remembrance's father, pushed through the onlookers to kneel beside the Indian as though shielding him from their malice.

'What are you doing?' he shouted. 'In God's name, leave him be!'

'Stand aside, Fearing.' Godsgift reached to pull the farmer up, but Fearing thrust away his hand, knocking it back against the constable's holstered pistol.

'Not until you tell me what he has done!'

Mercia looked at the boy. He was a slight youth, his thin frame shivering in the cold night. She leant in to Percy.

'Who is he?'

'One of Fearing's farmhands. A helpful lad.' He raised his voice. 'Godsgift, where is the proof of what you claim?'

Godsgift beckoned to one of the men, who handed him a wooden cup. He turned the vessel over in his hands before throwing it at the Indian's feet.

'There. That cup is Hopewell's. Isn't it, boy?' He kicked the Indian in the stomach; doubled-over, the boy nodded, terrified. 'This bastard was drinking from it.'

'What are you talking about?' said Fearing, the deep creases lengthening across his face.

Godsgift snorted. 'Hopewell has been cut open, Fearing. Killed. And your man there did it.'

Fearing recoiled, staring at his labourer. 'Killed Hopewell?' His head drifted to Godsgift and his jaw seemed to shake. 'I didn't know. I have been inside all evening. I . . . I want no part in this.'

As he continued to babble, he stepped back, merging into the crowd. The Indian, until then looking on his employer as though he were some sort of divinity able to intervene and spare him, cried out in anguish.

Next to Mercia, Percy was laughing. 'Hopewell bartered those cups all over. Many of the Indians have one. This boy most likely traded for it months ago.'

'Who is master here? Us or them?' Godsgift reached to his side, stroking his sword hilt. 'Shall we let the death of one of our own pass unpunished?'

'And what if it is not an Indian at all?'

'Who else could it be?' Removing his hand, Godsgift glanced at Nicholas and Mercia. 'You said these two found him. Are you suggesting they killed him instead?'

'Do not be absurd. By the time they found him he had already been attacked.'

There was something of malice in Godsgift's eyes, something devil-like, making Mercia feel she had to explain herself.

178

'We wished to walk off a late supper,' she said. 'We found Hopewell on our way back into town. Percy arrived immediately afterwards.'

Godsgift smiled, but it was not a gesture of understanding. 'So, Percy. Who else, then, but an Indian? Surely you cannot be accusing one of us? One of your own?'

'Of course he is not,' said John Lavington. Mercia looked across, wondering how long the magistrate had been waiting in the crowd. 'Why would he?'

'Well then,' simmered Godsgift. 'An Indian.'

The townsfolk shuffled and stamped ever closer to the boy, their circle somehow shrinking, the pressure within growing. Percy held his ground, protesting the boy's innocence, but nobody would heed him, not even his father, who stood watching, his restless eyes darting, simply surveying the crowd. The people fidgeted, unable to look each other in the eye, even as they closed the circle still tighter.

Nicholas glanced at Mercia, questioning whether they should act, but she shook her head, hopeful the boy would merely be questioned, even beaten if they must, but ultimately released. She looked at Percy, now silent, his shadow in the candlelight flickering large on the palisade. But now a chant broke out, a sinister hum, and she saw how the Devil was outstretching his hand, dissolving the people's humanity into a primitive creature of savage retribution. The crowd in their mindlessness were calling for vengeance, and all the while Godsgift was standing at their heart, pumping their bloodlust through their veins.

Seaborn grabbed the boy's head, holding him down. Others held his legs, so he could not kick out. The boy whimpered, whinnying, frantic. A terrified stench filled the air.

Mercia turned away, appalled, listening as Nicholas argued with Percy to make them stop. But then she thought, damn this. Damn their warped justice, that allows a woman's death to go unpunished, and the first Indian they find to be accused. She pushed herself forward into the crowd. Closer now, she could see not everyone had been overtaken by madness – Kit had his eyes closed, intoning a prayer, Fearing too, although his lips were unmoving. Vic looked again to the gate, away from the boy. Thorpe stood at the back, newly arrived she thought; certainly, she had not seen him there before.

'Are you not listening to anything that is being said?' she cried. 'You cannot just slaughter an innocent man!' She held onto the crowd's shoulders. 'What if – what if Hopewell was killed for the same reasons as Clemency?'

It was too much for the town to endure. As one they turned on her, pushing her back, ordering her out. At their centre, Godsgift lifted his sword above the trapped boy's chest.

And then another voice raised itself above the din.

'Godsgift Brown, I forbid this! In the name of the Lord, put down your sword!'

The crowd grumbled, unhappy at the intrusion, but the voice had shaken them, and they parted in two lines to allow Renatus Fox in. The old preacher walked slowly towards the constable, Silence Edwards bearing a flickering torch at his side.

'Think on your soul, Godsgift.' Renatus came to a halt in front of him. Not wearing his hat, the moonlight seemed to intensify the whiteness of his hair. 'All of you. God is watching here. Be very certain of what you do.'

Some of the crowd seemed to waver, but others amplified their calls, baying their merciless justice. Godsgift hesitated, looking into the preacher's eyes. Then he lowered his sword, returning it to the carved scabbard at his side.

'Perhaps you are right,' he said. 'Perhaps the sword is not the best way.'

The crowd muttered, the crowd roared. Renatus nodded his encouragement.

'Seaborn,' said Godsgift. 'Move away.'

Seaborn looked up and frowned, but he and his companions did as

Godsgift bade. Still trembling, the boy stayed put. As Mercia breathed out, a woman in the crowd shouted her disgust.

'My soul, Renatus?' Godsgift stared down at the cowering boy. 'You have told me time enough how I lost that long ago. So yes. I am certain.'

He reached for his gun and shot the Indian dead.

Chapter Seventeen

The street was silent, absent of human sounds at least. Birds still whistled, a cat mewled. A dragonfly hummed atop a low picket fence, the heady scent of animal dung behind enticing the walker to move along. Mercia, the walker, approached the meeting house and looked around, a measure of controlled sadness, craning her neck to search out people, but no one was in sight. As far as she could tell, she was alone in the noontime streets. She had stayed most of the morning in bed, thinking through what had happened. It seemed most of the town had done likewise. It had been a late night, last night.

At the meeting house she swallowed, trying to avoid looking towards the bloody memory of the northern gate, but she could never forget that desperate scene. Nauseous, disgusted, she pulled her hood around her face so as better to avoid the physical presence of the place, but the image that scarred her mind betrayed the painful truth: avoidance of this crime was impossible, indeed unpardonable.

Still she turned south, thinking she could see faint movement through the southern gate. As she passed the smithy, finally signs of life: Victory was leaning against the back wall, watching a teenage boy, his apprentice perhaps, running about the yard, but he was not yet at work himself. He looked up as she passed, and as their eyes met he jumped forward from the wall, picking up a hammer and approaching his anvil, beginning to work as though she had startled him into it, turning his cheek to her as the townsfolk had seemed determined to do to the Indian boy last night.

She walked on, and as she drew nearer to the gate, a murmur of human voices grew steadily louder. She passed under the arch to squint in the sunlight at a crowd gathered in the meadow just outside the palisade. It could have been an ordinary town meeting, but no one was arguing or calling their agreement, the mood firmly subdued. She had no particular wish to join them, even be seen by them, but she forced herself, or rather that tenacious part of her that had crossed the Atlantic forced herself, taking dominance as it did ever more over the woman who had been happy watching the daffodils from the window of her Halescott cottage each spring. So she approached the gathering, watching the faces turn towards her one by one. She was startled, for there was none today of the certainty of last night, their ferocity replaced by worry, concern, even guilt. Nobody spoke, but most seemed drawn by the gate, for their eyes continually flicked towards it. She turned to see what was so compelling: nothing, as far as she could tell, but then she looked up, and the bile rose in her gullet, for it was not the gate they were caught by, but the foulness projected above it, nailed to the posts that formed its arch. The head of the Indian boy, staring out, the stump of his neck as black with blood as his hair that flapped black in the growing wind. The boy who was the town's shame, their shared tragedy of last night.

Sickened, she retreated through the gate, hurrying back towards the meeting house. Passing the smithy she again looked in, slowing momentarily, and this time Vic did not turn away. She lowered her head and resumed her walk, but seconds later a shout from behind made her stop: Vic was calling her name.

'Mrs Blakewood.' He stood in the entrance to his yard, the sweat from its heat gathering on his chest. 'Pray, come talk awhile.'

She paused. 'As you wish.'

She entered the smithy. In the cluttered yard, the teenager was dunking hot pliers in a trough of water, the steam hissing and rising, obscuring his young face. Not much younger than the Indian boy, she thought, but she spared him only the briefest of glances, curious to know what Vic wished to discuss.

The smith wiped his brow, patting the tips of his tied-back hair. 'I don't like this, Mrs Blakewood.'

She waited. 'Don't like what?'

'This.' His hand twitching, he grabbed a rusted iron rod that was lying on a workbench beside him. He squeezed it, as though relieving his tension. 'All this.'

Again she waited, but still no more. 'Mr Smith—'

He waved the tool. 'Vic.'

'Vic.' She had her eye on the rod, half expecting him to lash out with it. 'Why have you asked me in?'

He sighed. 'I don't know.' He threw the rod on the bench and looked away. 'Because—' He sucked in through his teeth. 'No. Forget it.'

Warily, she approached, positioning herself in front of his turned away face. 'There must be something.'

'I suppose there must.' He ran his hand through his hair to untie it, letting it fall to cover his hot cheeks. 'Obedience! We need more water. Fetch some from the well.'

True to his name, the boy ran to carry out his task. When he had gone, Vic snatched a ragged shirt from a menacing hook hammered into a post at his side. Pulling it over his chest, he looked Mercia full in the face.

'This town isn't right.'

She inclined her head. 'An accurate observation.'

'Last night – that shouldn't have happened.'

'You think so?'

'That lad was no more guilty of Hopewell's death than you or I.'

'But you said nothing at the time.'

'Still, one more Indian dead doesn't exactly matter, does it?'

'You really believe that?' She frowned. 'I may be new in these parts, but I can see that the Indians belong here as much as we English do. You cannot be blind to that.'

He looked away. 'They attack us, Mrs Blakewood. They steal our things. They peer from behind the trees, chanting the Lord knows what at us. Renatus and Standfast say once they are converted to Christian ways they will become like us, but I don't have their faith.'

She raised an eyebrow. 'You did not ask me in to discuss religion, Vic, or Indian concords.'

'No.' He sighed. ''Tis these deaths. They make me uncomfortable.'

'Not as uncomfortable as Clemency and Hopewell are in their graves.'

His eyes dropped. 'I didn't mean . . . I am sorry they're dead. I wanted to say' – he glanced nervously towards the street – 'that I agree with you. I think they were murdered.' He rubbed at his forehead. 'Both of them.'

A peculiar lightness, inappropriate she knew, fluttered into her chest. 'Why do you say that?'

'I knew Clemency. I know she wouldn't have killed herself. She was too strong.'

'And yet you said nothing after her death, either.'

He shuffled his feet. 'I was deciding what to do.'

'It is taking a long time for you to decide.' Her voice dripped with acerbity. 'And what now?'

'I don't know.' He shrugged. 'I can't just . . . I'm here at Lavington's permission.'

'Meaning what?'

'Meaning I cannot afford to cross him. I would lose my position, Mrs Blakewood. 'Tis evident he does not think these murders are such, and so—'

'And so you do nothing, as you said nothing.'

He growled. 'I am speaking with you.' He held up a hand. 'Just listen.

185

I know Clemency did not kill herself, so she must have been murdered. I do not think Hopewell was killed by that boy, and I begin to wonder whether George Mason was killed too.'

Mercia's head jerked up. 'Your old minister?'

'They say he fell in the river and drowned. But now I am not certain.' His eyes darted about. 'Wait here.'

He walked to a large wooden chest at the back of the yard; even from a distance, Mercia could tell it was well made, the lock on the front gleaming in its newness. Reaching down, he unhooked the clasp and rummaged inside. After some trawling he tugged out a ragged piece of cloth and returned, handing her the fading rag.

'Of course this isn't the paper I found on her, but I thought it was strange, so I wrote it down when I had the chance here alone.'

'Paper? I don't understand.'

Frowning, she looked at the cloth. It was stained with ink marks, letters of the alphabet. Some of the letters had run at the edge and the writing on the coarse fabric was inevitably a mess, but she could tell clearly enough what she was holding. She looked up at the smith open-mouthed.

'But this is exactly like—'

'Yes.' He looked at her. 'Like the note found on Mason. The original is gone, but this is a copy of a piece of parchment I found when I . . . laid her out. I wanted you to see it because . . . perhaps it might help.'

She looked again at the cloth. It bore a simple sequence of letters, different to that found on Mason, but it was the same principle:

BNFOWVPSGGJNB .

'You are telling me a paper with this strange word was placed on Clemency's body?'

'Yes.'

'And you are certain this is an accurate copy? That dot at the end too?'

His forehead creased. 'Yes.'

'By God's wounds!' She stared at him. 'Why could you not have said something before?'

He set his face. 'I'm giving it to you now, aren't I?'

'Who has the original?'

'I cannot say.'

She let out an exasperated sigh. 'Come, Vic! This makes it look as though someone killed them both. Two of your fellow townsfolk. If you know more—'

'I don't.' His jaw twitched. 'And what of Hopewell?' Although they were alone in the yard, he lowered his voice. 'There may have been no message found, but I don't think he was killed by any Indian. Gutting their victims – 'tis not their way.'

'By our Lord, Vic.' Overwrought, she steadied herself against the smithy wall. 'Who is doing this?'

He hesitated. 'Will you stay? Humility cannot order you out this time.'

She looked up, her thoughts a roaring jumble of confusion. 'I want to. Now all the more. But the cottage I am in is not mine.'

'It is not anyone's, now. And Hopewell – he would want you to stay.'

'Perhaps.' A keen gloom was settling in her heart. Was it really possible that three of the townsfolk had been killed by the same person? 'If only I had not brought him back here. He was only in town because I asked for his help.'

Vic shook his head. 'Hopewell had many enemies. He annoyed people, and he enjoyed doing so. You cannot blame yourself. Besides, he was due to return here soon in any case.'

'So I am told. But to stay in his house – how can I?'

'I could tell last night that some others think the same, that these deaths are not so easily explained. We will have to speak up for you. Lavington cannot have everything his way.'

'So poor Hopewell said.' She looked across the yard, the tip of

187

the magistrate's roof visible further down the street. 'Well, then. My discomfort is scant price to pay. I will persevere, as long as I can.'

She returned to her lodgings, struggling to concentrate, barely touching the *msickquatash* Nicholas had procured from one of the townswomen, a dish of boiled corn and beans the settlers had learnt from the Indians. She had always been certain that Clemency was murdered, and now she had proof, evidence besides that linked her death to Mason's, which she had hitherto assumed to be an accident.

But the revelation, crucial as it was, was not the only concern on her mind. Uncertain who to trust, she shut herself into the cottage with Nicholas, staring at the code, comparing it to Mason's, and growing ever more frustrated when she found she was unable to decipher the nonsensical phrase. She was concerned that Lavington could arrive at any moment, seeking to remove her from the town once more, but he did not. As the hours passed, she grew more and more nervous, but not because of the magistrate. She laid the codes to one side, thinking forward to the other confrontation she was expecting any moment.

She got up, standing at the open door. She turned away, pacing the tidied rooms. She walked into the kitchen area, fiddled with the pots and pans, and returned to the sitting-room window, craning her neck to see as far down the road as she could.

'Come and sit,' said Nicholas, patting a stool.

'No, I am well.'

'You will not be if you keep worrying.'

She went to the door, stepped outside a moment, then came back in. 'If he is coming – how long now, do you think?'

He shook his head. 'I don't know. 'Tis several hours' ride, so if he got the letter yesterday and set off at first light – then soon. You told him where to come, and you know he rides fast.'

Another hour passed. She dismissed Nicholas, sensing he was in need of a distraction; that, and because she wanted some time alone. She looked again at the cloth Vic had given her, but she remained too agitated to think, or else to rest. It was not that she was needy, or desperate, but she thought she knew how Nathan was going to react. She wanted to sort out the dispute and move on. With his help, she knew she could bring Clemency's killer to justice. Clemency's – and Hopewell's now too.

Finally, a horse snorted as it was reined in outside. She scurried to the window; sure enough, Nathan was tying his steed to the picket fence. Closing her eyes to calm herself, she waited as his boots pounded their way to the front door, and then a pause – he was waiting to delay the moment, she knew – before a gentle knock on the door. Not a sharp rap, she noticed. Maybe that was good.

'I am here,' she called. Of course she was here, where else would she be? A stupid thing to say. 'Come in.' Another stupid statement. What else would he do?

Nathan pushed open the door and entered. He took off his hat, setting it on a hook in the wall, and turned to face her.

'Hello,' he said.

'Hello.' A greeting – that was good. No immediate descent into argument.

'How have you been?'

'I have managed. Nicholas has been very good.'

A frown. A mistake to mention Nicholas.

'You could have had my help.' He came closer. 'And I meant, how are you feeling?'

She smiled weakly. 'I have felt better. To think, we came here looking for calm before returning home.'

'It could still happen that way.'

'No. It cannot.'

A pause. 'I suppose it can't.'

'I am glad you are here, Nathan. I value you deeply, you know that.'

'Value? Is that all?'

She sighed. 'Let's not . . . for now. There is too much to do first.'

'Is there?' He moved around so she was facing him. 'Look at me, Mercia. What is more important?' She did not reply. 'I have been frantic with worry. I would have ridden after you immediately had I known where you were. But Winthrop said he thought you would be returning to Hartford, as I think you well know, and that he had no idea where you were going in the meantime.'

She looked through the window at his horse. 'On that point he was right. I did not know myself.'

'Then last night that quick-mouthed preacher brings me a letter saying you have come back to Meltwater and want me to follow. And so here I am. I had to let Winthrop pay a driver to cart your belongings. They should be here before long, but I wanted to get here sooner.'

'That was good of him.' She tried to soften her tone. 'I am sorry, Nat. But I thought it best you stayed behind.'

'Why? What can Nicholas do that I cannot?'

She allowed herself a smile. 'Follow my orders.'

'Like I do not.' He looked around the room, fixing on Nicholas's satchel on the floor. 'Is that his?'

'He has been staying here.' She scowled at his dark face. 'As protection. And now you are here he will share again with Amery.' She blew out her cheeks. 'Look, what is done is done. You would have tried to stop me coming back. But I could not give up on this. I cannot give up on it, especially not now.'

'You are too damn stubborn.'

She hesitated. 'There has been another murder.'

'What?' His face turned pale.

'The man I went to meet, Clemency's cousin.' Briefly, she filled him in on the past few days. When she had finished, he looked at her in deep concern.

'Mercia, this is . . . I was going to agree we should stay, but now – two dead, the same two you have had most connection with in the town – you have to leave!'

She stared at him. 'No.'

'Damn it, Mercia, from what you say they may not even be murders. Or at least, nothing other than an Indian killing and a . . .' He trailed off.

'I have said it before. Clemency did not commit suicide. And now I have proof.' She picked up Vic's cloth, unfolding the dirty rag to hold it against the light, waiting for the inevitable reaction.

It took a moment. 'But that is . . . just like the one Winthrop showed us in Hartford.' He looked at her. 'The code on the old minister.'

'Indeed.' She pivoted to face him, letting the cloth dangle at her side. 'It is exactly as I have been saying. Clemency was murdered, and this shows it.'

'Just because—'

'Two people dead, both with a strange message found on their bodies. A rather obvious sign, don't you think?'

He scratched the back of his neck. 'You may be right. But it would mean the minister was murdered as well.'

'Yes, and I wager the same man killed poor Hopewell Quayle.'

'Was a similar code found on him?'

'Not in public. Lavington was very keen for the body to be removed, and without Nicholas's help.' She dropped the cloth on the table. 'Vic would not say, but I suspect he may have given Lavington the code he found on Clemency, and was told to keep quiet. Then last night, Lavington was trying to stop anybody finding one on Hopewell.'

'Why?'

'To protect his town from a scandal, perhaps. Sometimes people refuse to believe the obvious when the truth is too terrible.'

He glanced down at the cloth. 'So what now? Confront him?'

'He will merely continue to dissemble. We need further proof.' She inclined her head. 'Like . . . another code.'

His eyes narrowed. 'You aren't thinking . . . ? No. Don't answer. I know damn well what you're thinking.'

'The body was taken to Lavington's backyard. If the body was there, then any message will have been at the house too. If it is there, we need to find it before he has a chance to destroy it. Assuming he has not already.'

'Mercia, wait.' He held up his hand. 'Just wait. Do you not think, perhaps, this is something you need not be involved in? It is not a game, Mercia, it is a dangerous concern of a dangerous man. You do not need to put yourself in his way.' He folded his arms. 'No. I want you to leave.'

She looked him in the eye, concealing all trace of emotion. 'Nathan, you are not my husband. Even if you were, you could not make me go.'

He stepped back, stung. 'I thought maybe we . . .' He looked away. 'Very well. Forget about us if you want. But do not forget you have a son.'

An unexpected anger suddenly rose, shattering her calm facade. 'My son is my life, Nathan. My life. Why the hell else am I in America at all? But nobody here seems to care for justice, for the truth, for honour, and what in God's name kind of mother would I be, if when he is older I cannot teach him by my own example that those are noble qualities he must teach to those who will follow him, and that it is possible to make a difference in this world if we but try to overcome those who seek to thwart them?'

She stood defiant, breathing hard, her eyes boring into his. But he held her gaze as proudly as she did.

'Very well. We will stay a while longer, if we can. But this time, I will help. Starting with that third code, if it exists.'

She nodded, the emotion still pumping. 'Thank you.'

'I am sorry for my words, but . . . I love you, Mercia. All I want is for you to be safe.'

'I know.' She looked at him kindly, and then away, her thoughts already elsewhere.

Chapter Eighteen

Lavington's house rose up before them, the grandest in the village, occupying the central plot of the southern thoroughfare. The smithy yard was empty as they walked past; Mercia thought she could see Vic leaning against the south gate, watching the few townsfolk still milling in the meadow, their great agitation overshadowing them all.

'What are they doing?' said Nathan, craning his neck to see.

She scoffed. 'Admiring their handiwork.'

She took advantage of the street's emptiness to dart down the side of the property, aiming for the back door that led to the conjoined laboratory she had seen on her previous visit. Peering briefly behind her, she opened the door and stole inside, making sure nobody was there.

'This brings back memories,' whispered Nathan, easing shut the door. The silence inside was eerie, even oppressive.

She grunted. 'Not quite the same as breaking into Halescott Manor.' Nathan sighed and she softened her tone. 'Shall we look around?'

He moved to her left. 'Mercia, this is part of a residence. There will be no dead body here.'

'No, it will be long gone – I hope. But if there was a note on the body, Lavington may have brought that here, where he works.' She moved off, vaguely surprised at how cold she could sound in the face of a man's death, but she shrugged to herself and surveyed the laboratory benches. They were strewn with an unruly mass of parchment and notes.

She took a shallow breath. 'This could take some time.'

Thirty minutes passed. It seemed as though they had scoured only a small percentage of the documents in the laboratory, their haste not aided by the great care they were taking to replace everything as they found it – a corner of a parchment overhanging the edge of a shelf here, a precariously balanced quill pen returned on the same diagonal there. Nor did it speed matters that they were forever pausing to listen for a creak or a call announcing someone's return.

'This will take for ever,' said Nathan, repositioning an inkwell. 'Lavington has more parchment and books than even your father ever had.'

'Father was certainly more methodical.' Mercia stopped, inadvertently drumming the fingers of her left hand on Lavington's wooden desk. 'Let's think about this. If we were Lavington, and wanted to keep something hidden, what would we do with it?'

'A code on a piece of paper? Burn it.'

'That is not helpful.' She sucked in her lip. 'But you may be right.'

Five minutes more of fruitless search passed. She was flicking through a ream of indecipherable alchemical correspondence – Winthrop's handwriting she thought – when she heard a cough.

'Nathan,' she cautioned. 'Keep quiet.'

'Mercia.'

She ignored him, replacing the enigmatic notes and turning to a thick leather-bound volume stuffed with jagged bits of paper.

'Mercia,' he repeated.

Her hand on the tome, she looked up at him and frowned. He gestured with a nod to look behind her. She tensed as she realised they were no longer alone.

'Ah,' she said as she turned. 'This is not . . . I mean, we are not—'

'Nosing around?' Percy Lavington stood before her, his left thumb tucked into the side of his breeches. In his other hand he held a dirty scrap of parchment.

'No.' She hesitated. 'That is, this is not how it appears.'

'Yes, it is. I know exactly what you are doing.' His face impassive, he held up the parchment. 'You are searching for this.'

In Amery Oldfield's cottage, an evening meeting was in session. On one side of the small table sat Mercia and Nicholas, the latter now moved back in with the schoolmaster. On the other, squashed across two chairs, a more local trio: Percy, Amery and Kit. Not having rested since his fast ride from Hartford, Nathan had returned to the room he was taking from Nicholas to change his clothes and to supervise the return of their belongings; he would join them later, but for now, laid out on the rough-hewn table, the quintet was surveying a foreboding set: a blackened piece of parchment, a fraying cloth, a torn paper. On each was scrawled a jumbled message, each different, but each following the same pattern.

Percy laid a finger on the paper. 'This is the sequence that was found in George Mason's pockets,' he said. 'This is what you say Vic Smith copied from Clemency.' He looked at Mercia as his finger hovered over the cloth. 'And this is what I saw my father find on Hopewell, which I retrieved from the fire before it could burn.' The parchment. 'Three messages, and yet no clue as to what they might mean.'

'No.' Mercia studied his intelligent face. Although it had been his idea to convene like this, she was still hesitant. 'But you do concede they show the deaths are linked? That these are murders?'

He raised an eyebrow. 'I always suspected they were.'

She sighed. 'Does no one in this town reveal what they think?'

'Yes, to each other.' He smiled, the surprising gesture disarming her frustration. 'And now to you.'

'Well . . . it is good we all see so. What then shall we do about it?'

'We?' He broke off his gaze. 'I am the magistrate's son, for one, and as neither my father nor most besides we few are convinced we have anything more than an Indian problem—'

'They do not want to be convinced, you mean.' She turned to Amery. 'What say you of this?'

Amery looked at Percy, who gave the slightest nod. 'We merely think – we three – that in a situation as delicate as this, that it is best to keep matters as contained as we can. The smallest number seen to be acting, the rest offering quiet support.'

'I see. Does Lavington have a hold on all of you?'

'My father has nothing to do with this,' scowled Percy. 'But everyone knows you only came back because of Clemency. We think you could play to that, while we help behind. It may trip somebody up.'

'And in the meantime, the glares, the ill will, they all fall on me, on Nicholas. Perhaps the murderer's wrath, even.'

'It will not come to that. In the meantime, Amery and I have argued for your staying in Hopewell's cottage. I will not say father was pleased, but he will not ask you to leave this time.' He glanced askance at Kit, who was absent-mindedly fiddling with the cord around his neck. 'And do not forget, I have . . . other tasks.'

She set her face, well aware what he meant, that he was putting his duty to protect the regicides first, while making clear she needed his support to remain in the town. Yet he knew she would not argue the point in front of Kit: the younger Lavington, it seemed, could be as devious as his father.

'Very well,' she said. 'We will proceed as you suggest.'

Kit was looking at the code on the blackened parchment. 'Speaking of your father, you have not explained something. Why he was burning that in the first place.'

Percy's face clouded over. 'He will have his reasons. The way he acted, yes it was strange, but he will not talk of it. I refuse to doubt my own parent.'

196

Amery shuffled in his seat. 'It will be for the same reason he refuses to acknowledge Clemency's death. He does not want the people to panic.'

Kit made to reply, but a chill wind rushed in as the front door was pushed open and slammed shut. Anticipating Nathan, Mercia rubbed her thin sleeves for warmth as she looked towards the hall. But then she inclined her head, confused, for he was not alone.

Percy frowned. 'Why is she here? This is supposed to be a private meeting.'

'Good evening to you also, Perseverance.' Remembrance Davison threw back her hood and shook out her hair; her cloak was spotted with water, the tips of her wavy auburn ringlets wet with rain. 'I would join you, if I may.'

'We are just talking, Remy.' There was no welcome in his words. 'Nothing that will interest you, I am sure.'

'I see.' Glancing at Mercia, Remembrance shed her cloak and sat down nonetheless. 'You will talk to strangers, but not to me.'

'She wants to help,' said Nathan, brushing the water from his own jacket. 'She knows things that could be of use.'

'To what?'

'To this.' He smiled at Mercia in greeting. 'Her father was the one who found the code on Mason.'

Percy sighed. 'I suppose that is right.'

'And I am not foolish, although I know you think it.' Remembrance held up her head. 'Clemency and Hopewell both dead within days? And cousins? No, I have thought much on this. I want to help. I accused Clemency of witchcraft, when she was trying to be kind.' She looked at Nathan, who nodded in encouragement. 'The morning she was . . . found . . . I followed Vic and Amery as they took her body away.'

Amery turned his head. 'I never noticed. Why?'

'Out of guilt.' She swallowed. 'I felt as if God was judging me for my actions. I could not keep myself away from her.' Briefly, she closed her eyes. 'She looked so peaceful, lying out, just as Praise did. Then after you had gone, Amery, I saw Vic find something in her pockets. Father told me not to mind it, that Mr Lavington would make things right.' Her cheeks reddened, her sorrow vanquished by her visible anger. 'But when Keme was slaughtered last night, just to see someone blamed for Hopewell . . .' She looked at the codes on the table. 'So this is what Vic found, Nathan, as you said?'

Percy rounded on him. 'Who else have you told?'

'Nobody. Just her.'

There was a brief silence. 'Well,' said Amery. 'As Remy is here, I suggest we invite her to stay.'

Percy sucked in his cheek, but then he shrugged. Nathan pulled out the empty stool beside Nicholas, gesturing to Remembrance to sit. Mercia looked between them, wondering how they had come to arrive together, but quickly returned to the matter at hand.

'These messages.' She tapped at the table. 'They were meant to be found. Why?'

Once again, the group studied the strange codes:

RNLENRDFRXSHI O
BNFOWVPSGGJNB .
HDWRVDWMPAQCY †

'A confession?' said Remembrance.

'Perhaps. Or an explanation for his reasons. Hopewell and Clemency were both friendly with the Indians, Hopewell particularly.' She looked at Percy, who was staring at the wall. 'What of the minister, George Mason? Was he?'

He turned back round. 'Not especially. He believed in converting them, of course, but he did not think that meant he had to be their friend.'

'He liked that one Indian well enough,' said Kit.

'I do not think—'

'No.' Mercia held up a hand. 'What do you mean, Kit?'

'I mean,' Kit leant back, 'that he had an eye for that Susanna. The Indian woman Humility says you met.'

'And yet nothing happened,' pressed Percy, fixing Kit with a penetrating stare.

'But he was enamoured with her?' she pursued.

'I'd say so,' said Remembrance. 'Anyone with ears could hear him stumbling over his words at the mere sight of her.'

Kit shook his head. 'The old fool could not contain his lust. He should have kept to administering to the townsfolk, and then maybe he would still be alive.'

Standing over them, Nathan frowned. 'Which means what?'

'Merely that it behoves all men to act as the Lord wishes, Nathan. Preaching men, above all. Mason did not always obey that stricture.'

'I wonder.' Nicholas joined the conversation. 'Hopewell seemed to like his drink well enough. If Mason was lustful, maybe someone in this godly town doesn't like loose behaviour.'

Nathan scratched his chin. 'Then what of Clemency?'

The sexually laden letters shot into Mercia's head, but she was not about to bring them up. ''Tis clear many here think she delved in witchcraft,' she rasped, more forcefully than she intended. Cheeks warming, she tried to soften her tone. 'Perhaps that was the inducement.'

Remembrance closed her eyes. 'I should never have accused—'

'I don't know,' interrupted Amery. 'You are implying someone is passing judgement. And why so violent?'

'Does it matter?' said Nicholas. 'Once we find the bastard we can wring the truth from him then.'

'Of course it matters.' Mercia found herself growing fractious. 'Understanding his reasons may help us save someone else.'

'Then you think like me, that he could kill again.' Percy's voice rose in pitch. 'If he does, it would be a disaster. The town – my father – it could all fall apart.'

Remembrance's face had turned pale. 'Kill again . . . ?'

'Then shouldn't we let everyone know?' Nathan looked at her in concern. 'Warn them?'

'Yes.' Amery arched his fingers. 'Show them these codes too, as proof.'

'And scare the town witless?' Percy shook his head. 'There would be a panic. Right now people hope this is a suicide, an Indian killing. As soon as they start to think the killer could be one of their own, they will begin to turn, accusing one another. I have seen it happen before, in England, when Cromwell's regime was at its end. Simple, terrible fear.'

'And in the meantime the Indians can take the blame,' said Remembrance. 'Why should they?'

'No. We keep this to ourselves.' He looked around the table. 'We are agreed?'

Amery hesitated. 'Percy, are you sure you are not just—?'

'I asked if we were agreed.'

He sighed. 'As you wish.'

'Very well,' said Mercia, as Remembrance nodded her assent. 'This is your town. We will stay silent for now. But sometimes fear is what is needed to make people take notice.'

Percy's head jerked up. 'Perhaps, Mercia. For now, I would sooner hold fear aside.'

'The fear of man bringeth a snare,' observed Kit. 'But who so putteth his trust in the Lord shall be safe.'

'Scripture, Kit?' said Amery.

'You know my views. If we choose to trust in the Lord rather than in our own fallibility, then He may provide us with the answers we seek.'

'Well here's my view,' said Nicholas. ''Tis a plain and simple man we're dealing with here, and whatever his reasons he may already be planning his next attack.' He leant forward in his seat. 'And if we don't act swiftly, some other poor soul could pay a heavy price.'

They did not get much further with their discussion. It proved impossible to decipher the codes, and the meeting broke up, Nicholas's sobering opinion ringing round the room. As she stood, Mercia could not suppress a yawn; she was ready for bed.

'Are you coming?' she asked Nathan.

'In a minute. I want to speak with Remy.'

She raised an eyebrow. 'Remy, is it?'

He returned the gesture. 'Just one minute.'

She watched as Nathan took Remembrance to a corner, but she could not make out their conversation. With Percy and Kit already gone, she chatted with Nicholas and Amery until five minutes later he came back across, asking the schoolmaster to walk Remembrance home and bidding Nicholas goodnight.

'Why didn't you walk her home yourself?' she said as they came out into the street.

He chuckled. 'Because you are more important.'

'Why did you bring her, Nathan? Weren't you going back to change?'

'She was in the street, Mercia. She approached me. And I think she is lonely. She is grieving for her brother and wants to talk with someone about it. Someone who understands.'

'I suppose so, but I find it hard to—wait.' She broke off. 'Who is that?'

'Where?'

'Over there, against the fence. Staring at Amery's house.' Peering through the semi-night, the candlelight from the cottage window behind them offering scant illumination, she cursed under her breath. 'Him again.'

As Percy and Kit must likewise have found, Richard Thorpe held their gaze as they strode down the street, unabashed they had caught him staring. He was shorn of his usual sash, but his smile was just as brazen a replacement. Mercia ignored it, but Nathan shot him a cocksure greeting.

'You don't think he's been listening?' she whispered as they moved out of earshot.

'What, lurking beneath a window, straining to hear at the door?'

'That sort of thing.' She rubbed at her neck; it felt unfathomably stiff. 'But Nicholas thinks we have to be careful of everyone, especially after that bodice was left on my doorstep. I did not want to mention that even to those three in there.'

'For once he is probably right.' Gently, he took her by the arm as they reached the meeting-house steps. 'Here, sit for a moment. 'Tis a calm night.' He reached for her neck. 'Let me.'

As they sat on the cold steps, he eased her hand from her neck, replacing it with his own. He squeezed tenderly, not too hard, but exerting more pressure than she could manage herself. For the briefest of moments, she allowed herself to forget Meltwater, feeling the knots in her neck untie themselves as Nathan caressed his palm across her flesh. But then a grunt brought her back into reality.

'None of that,' said Godsgift Brown, his steely gaze firm as he looked down from the street. His rapier gleamed in the light of the torch burning in the meeting-house sconce. 'This is not England. Folks here get married first.'

'No, Constable.' She waited until he marched off. 'Folks here get killed before they get the chance.'

Chapter Nineteen

A dark silence enveloped Mercia as she lay in bed, reflecting on the evening's meeting. As much as she was pleased that Percy had called the group together, she was disappointed by his seeming detachment, more preoccupied with the regicides than with protecting his own town. But at least they had finally come together, even if none of the town elders were yet on her side. Maybe, at last, they had a chance to avenge Clemency's death, and it was this hope she had to hold onto. For to her, it was still about Clemency, distressed as she was for Hopewell's end. In her prayers, it was Clemency she cried for, and it was for Clemency that she would bring the murderer to a fatal justice.

She turned on her side, musing then on Remembrance – Remy – wondering how the young woman had latched so quickly onto Nathan. In truth she was vexed by her demeanour, unforgiving of her harsh words on the day of Clemency's death. She knew it was juvenile, but such were her thoughts. If only she could talk to someone about it, to laugh away her silliness. Someone like Clemency.

'Did you see her?' she would have asked. 'Fawning after Nathan?'

And Clemency would have grinned. 'Jealousy does not become you.'

In her imagination, Mercia protested. 'I am not jealous.'

'Come now, 'tis clear.' Clemency leant in closer. 'Do you really think Nathan would want a woman ten years his junior when he has you? One he has only just met, when 'tis evident how he longs for you?'

'Do not talk so,' smiled Mercia, enjoying the moment of friendship.

But although she could feel her presence, Clemency was gone; there was no like-minded woman to talk with in the manner of a longed-for friend. Lying alone in bed, it made the pain of her loss still the more acute. And so her need for justice – for vengeance – grew.

Three days passed. Rain came to Meltwater, dripping its depressing tedium from the sodden rooftops, two days and two nights of intermittent downpour, but the droplets were heavy, rebounding off the fences faster and sharper than in England. Obstinate, she tried again to convince Lavington to side with her, but the magistrate would not listen, even when she had approached him with his new schoolmaster after Hopewell's funeral. No harm in it, Amery had said, seeing as he knew of the codes in any case. Just as obstinately, smilingly, Lavington had refused to hear her point of view – she was a stranger, after all, so how could she understand his town? – but as Nathan said, when a proud man such as Lavington has his life's work threatened, perhaps it is easier to ignore the tragedies and hope they go away. As for the constable, she could not yet bring herself to talk with him after what he had done to the Indian boy, a mutually satisfactory notion.

On the third day the clouds parted, revealing a forgotten blue sky. Fed up with her failures, she took a stroll in the muddy streets. She passed Lavington's house, wondering whether to try him again, but deciding against it she passed through the southern gate. Sil was walking with his brother in the meadow, and she realised she had seen neither of them for the previous couple of days. She raised a hand in greeting, but Sil quickly lowered his face, steering Standfast in a different direction.

She sighed, breathing in melancholy from the still-damp air, fresh from another argument with Nathan about the wisdom of her remaining.

She decided to climb the small hill, wondering if she should take a leaf out of Kit's philosophy, and gain inspiration by standing nearer to God. Resisting the gruesome urge to look back at the severed heads on the gate, she pressed onwards, but if she had hoped for solitude she was out of luck. Pulling herself up to the low summit, she was in reach of the half-finished fort when someone ran up behind.

'Mercia!' called a by now familiar voice.

She cursed to herself and turned, forcing a smile. Percy drew alongside her, not at all out of breath in spite of the slope he had climbed: Mercia had felt the burn in her calves well enough.

'Mercia,' he repeated. 'I was with my father. I have chased you from when you passed the house.'

'Oh.' She was nonplussed. 'I had not noticed there was anyone behind me. I have been lost in my thoughts again.'

He nodded. 'We are all deep in thought of late.'

She looked at the town from atop the small hill. From here, she recalled the first time she had ventured up the grassy slope, awakening from her doze to the nonchalant stare of the strange striped animal. Today the sound of gunfire drew her attention to the other side of the town, where beyond the palisade light smoke was rising, a group of tiny men firing off their muskets. One was standing apart from the rest; even at this distance she could see him marching back and forth, waving his rapier in the air.

'I see your constable is drilling the men yet again,' she said dryly.

Percy laughed. 'I should be there.'

'So why aren't you?'

'Would you choose to spend time with Godsgift? Besides, I can get away with it. Being the magistrate's son has to have a few perks.'

'That it must.' She hesitated. 'Percy, why won't your father see sense?'

'Because he is a stubborn old goat who thinks he is always right. But he is also a clever man, a great alchemist and a fine leader, someone who had the courage to found this settlement, here on the edge of our lands with only the forests and the Indians behind. He no longer has my mother, no other children left but me. Would you not be scared if you feared your life's meaning could be lost?' He removed his black cloak, spreading the woollen garment on the damp earth. Dropping to sit on one half, he patted the space beside him. 'Will you join me?'

Thinking it was more that he was joining her, Mercia knelt down, as well as she could in her heavy dress. Feeling awkward, she flipped to a sitting position, trying to avoid getting dirt on the hem, but it brushed in the mud all the same.

'Never mind,' said Percy. 'Take it to Jemima or one of the other women, if you like. Monday – tomorrow – is washday.' He pulled at a wet blade of grass. 'Monday was washday when I was born, it was washday when I left for England nigh ten years since, and it is washday still. They say the first day they came off the *Mayflower* was a Monday, and the first thing the women did was to wash their stinking clothes. And so, like much else in New England, it has followed the same rigid pattern ever since.' He exhaled deeply. 'For people forging a new world out here, there is yet much resistance to change. My father, like many of the townsfolk, is petrified of it. Mostly they are petrified of the Indians, and now the King's fleet has arrived they are petrified of that too, scared he will take their autonomy. On that, at least, they are right. We stand to lose everything if the King has his way.'

Mercia grunted, recalling a recent conversation in Whitehall Palace. 'It is not the King you should be concerned with. It is his brother.'

'The Duke of York.' Percy grimaced. 'Ah yes. We received such noble reports of his scuttling around Europe when I was working in Cromwell's government.' His tone took on a scornful note. 'It does not surprise me that he has named his new conquest after himself. New Amsterdam becomes New York, and New Netherland becomes – surprise! – New York also. But how far north and east does he intend his royal territory to extend? To Hudson's river? To here?' He waved a hand across the landscape. 'To the Bay itself, to Boston?'

206

Mercia thought again of that fateful conversation back in April, when the King had authorised her to join his fleet bound for America. Only five months ago, and half of that aboard ship, yet it seemed much more time had passed.

'I do not think there is much limit to the Duke's ambition. And with the King still without an heir . . .' She let the sentence drop.

'Indeed.' He tugged harder at the grass, pulling out whole clumps. 'But I tell you now, we will not let him take away our lives.' For an instant his eyes seemed to blaze, or was that a reflection of the sun? Then his cheeks softened and he turned to her. 'But enough of that.' He bit his lip. 'I am sorry our acquaintance began sourly.'

'As am I.' She smiled, drawing on his own improved humour. 'You certainly seem more cheerful today.'

He returned the gesture. 'And I am sorry for my demeanour at our meeting the other night. Kit tells me I was a little brusque at times. I have said the same to Remembrance.'

A light breeze drifted over the knoll; as it passed, it seemed to take away some of the antipathy she had felt for him. His apology had sounded sincere.

'Do not worry on it,' she said. 'You—' She looked into the open fort behind her to ensure nobody else was near, lowering her voice all the same. 'You are entrusted with the safeguarding of a wanted man. It cannot be easy, especially with people like Thorpe waiting to pounce.'

He gave her a glance, rising to his feet and searching the fort himself. Apparently satisfied, he sat back down, but there was no harsh rebuke today.

'Not just Thorpe. Maybe not so much here, or in New Haven, but some in other parts would be ready to give him up for scant return.' He looked at her, thinking for a moment, and then nodded. 'Very well. You proved yourself with Dixwell, and I know they would not object, for they have said as much. Why not?'

Intrigued, she sat back. 'Why not what?'

He took a letter from his pocket and handed it across. 'I received this yesterday. It relates to this very matter.'

As she scanned the document a chill broke out inside. 'Percy, I cannot read this. It is in code.'

'It is not the code you are thinking of. Can you translate it?'

'Not without time.'

He smiled. 'I just wondered if you . . . because your father would have understood.'

She looked at him sharply. 'My father?'

'Yes. 'Tis a code from Cromwell's time.' He took back the letter and sidled closer towards her, giving her a meaningful look. 'This has been written by William Goffe himself.'

'Goffe?' Mercia was startled. 'I thought he had vanished? You don't mean to say he is here?'

'You think John Dixwell is the only one of those heroes to have thought to travel to New England, far from the King's soldiers at home? What if I said there were two others here – not just William Goffe, but his father-in-law too, Edward Whalley?'

Her eyes widened. Amery had hinted at other regicides hiding in New England when they had met with Davids – truly Dixwell – in Hartford, but she had never pursued the issue, respectful of the need for silence. 'Goffe and Whalley,' she said, 'both here?'

He tilted his head, an amused expression on his face, a new playfulness as charming as it was unexpected. 'You have seen them already, I am told.'

She shifted her position to face him more fully. 'When?'

'When you came through New Haven with Winthrop. They had heard your party would be passing through, and . . . well. It seems they wanted to spy Sir Rowland Goodridge's daughter for themselves. Apparently you saw them as they peered out.' He frowned. 'It was impetuous of them. Thank the Lord nobody else saw.'

'Goffe and Whalley. I cannot believe it. Men who worked with my

208

father . . .' Leaning closer, she crossed one leg under the other. 'You said you met him yourself once, did you not? When you were in London?'

'Ah, the London times.' Percy went back to pulling at the grass. 'The Cromwell times, when I thought God had been kind and helped us. But those days in England were not meant to last. All too soon after I joined the cause there, the old fox died.'

'You mean Cromwell.'

'I always wonder – what would have happened if he had lived? When his son took over, I hoped things would continue, but of course they could not. Richard Cromwell was weak, nothing like his father.' He scoffed. 'We all know that. The regime collapsed, the King returned, and I decided to come home to America. And now the King has caught up with me.'

'You make it sound like he is hunting you down.'

'He would be if he knew what I was doing. He calls those men regicides, no? 'Tis death to all who help them.' He waved a dismissive hand. 'But I merely meant he has come to America, or at least his soldiers have. As for your father, yes I met him. Briefly, but he bade me good day. If I had known sooner, I would never have spoken so harshly with you when first we met. He was a man of deep honour.' He looked at her. 'He died . . . bravely?'

A gunshot resounded from the training ground, but she barely noticed as she found herself back at Tower Hill, the site of her father's execution. The crowds, the noise, the yearning for death. And then she pushed the memory away.

'Yes. Yes, he did.'

'I wish I could have known him. But towards the end of my time in England there was such confusion, and I was but a clerk of sorts, far too lowly.' He stared into the distance. 'Still, it was more worthy than the tedium I am tasked with in this town.'

She smiled. 'I am sure he would have spoken with you. He was not the haughty type.' A gust flew over the hilltop and she patted down with

209

her topknot, checking it was still in place. 'Does Winthrop know Goffe and Whalley are here?'

Percy laughed. 'Of course he does. As does Governor Leete of New Haven, Governor Endicott of the Bay, and every other person of importance in these colonies. By God's truth, when they first arrived the Bay folk held a party for them.' He traced a circle on the cloak in his evident pride. 'There is a story that a bragging man challenged all-comers to a swordfight, and that Goffe, dressed as a roadsweeper, made a wager with him; of course the braggart accepted, and of course Goffe won, revealing himself onstage to the delight of all.' The laughter in his eyes dulled. 'But then the King's demands for his return came to Boston, and he and Whalley were forced into hiding. They have been living near New Haven for a long while now. But the fleet you arrived on has orders to hunt them out, and New York is too close to New Haven for our liking. It is time to move them into safer territory, far from the Duke's hounds. John Dixwell too, for a time, although he is not so well known in these parts. It may be he can blend in unknown to others, have some sort of life. Maybe Goffe and Whalley can too, if ever we rid ourselves of the King's unwanted yoke.'

She looked around. 'Be careful what you say, Percy. Such talk is seditious.'

He puffed out his chest. 'I care not.' He stood up and smiled, shouting to the wind. 'I care not!' Then he jiggled his letter. 'This is a summons for me to help them move.'

She patted the cloak, uneasy at his sudden bravado. 'Sit back down. What will you do?'

'Bring them to Meltwater, to the same place as Dixwell. It is halfway to their new safe house. I will take them there when I am sure the road is secure.' He retook his space beside her. 'When I went north last week, it was to check on their new accommodation. But you are right about needing to be careful. If I am ever away too long, certain people get suspicious.'

'People like Thorpe, you mean. Or those others you mentioned.'

'Anyone inquisitive, or who cannot stay their mouth.' He raised an eyebrow. 'Why do you think I have never told Kit?'

'He is not one to hold his tongue when he has an opinion, that is certain.'

'No. But do not judge him too harshly for his quick speeches, for he is a good friend, and has suffered deeply in his young life.'

She nodded. 'I think perhaps he wears that suffering from the cord around his neck.' She looked at Percy askance. 'I have often seen him reach for it, as though it is a comfort, or a memory.'

'Perhaps.' Percy glanced down. 'You will have to ask him about it, although he will not tell you. He is a secretive man, spending much time alone in his sawmill, but he joins in the militia, helps out in the fields, and is accepted here now.'

'Only now?'

Percy smiled. 'It takes years to gain acceptance, even by men who came here as immigrants themselves, like my father, or Old Humility.' He became serious as he looked out onto the town, the fields beyond. 'The people here own this land, Mercia. They think – we think – it is ours. And it is. No fool Duke is going to take it away from us, I can assure you of that.'

The breeze picked up again, drifting through the ensuing silence. 'I saw Sil just now,' she said at last. 'He seemed keen to avoid me.'

'Hmm?' Percy looked round, teased from his thoughts. 'Sil has been distant since Hopewell's death. I do not know why. Perhaps, like the rest, he has become reluctant to involve himself. Standfast, certainly, is saying little beyond prayers for the dead, and he has much influence over his brother. He saved his life once, you know. When they were boys, he fetched him from the river.'

'It is a shame, though.' She winced as a sharp tingling sensation throbbed through the leg she had been pressing on. Stumbling to her feet, she rubbed furiously at her calf.

'Are you well?' said Percy, jumping up beside her.

''Tis merely that tingling sensation. It will pass.'

'I hate that.' He screwed up his face, watching as she shook out her leg. 'Well, I suppose I should be getting back. I will be gone for a couple of days, but when I return I could take you to visit Goffe and Whalley, if you like.'

'You would do that?' The prickly feeling was subsiding. 'Thank you.'

'As long as they agree. But they seemed eager before.' He scooped up his cloak. 'Now, if you are better, shall I accompany you down the hill?'

'That is kind, but no.' Her leg recovered, she looked into the distance, all the way to England, to Halescott. The talk of her father had rekindled painful memories, and she still wanted her time alone. 'I will stay here a while longer and enjoy the view. It is so very calming.'

'Yes.' Percy smiled, his dark eyes fixed on her windswept face. 'It is a beautiful view.'

Chapter Twenty

Done indulging her memories, she walked back into town, a little more enthused than the hour before. She looked for Nathan in the cottage, anxious to tell him of Whalley and Goffe, but she could not find him. Then more gunfire sounded out. Nearer now, the din of it made her jump before she realised it came from the same practice she had witnessed from the hill.

'Still?' she said to herself. 'But I wonder?'

She returned to the street, exiting the palisade through the eastern gate. About twenty men were lined up at the side of a square grassy space marked out with fraying rope, watching Fearing Davison taking a shot at a target not ten-feet distant. The target was a scarecrow of sorts, dressed in furs and topped with an Indian headdress. Fearing fired and missed; most of the onlookers jeered, but Godsgift Brown silenced them with a shout.

'Back in line, Fearing.' He shook his head. 'He's in your company, Vic. If he fires like that when the Indians attack, you're going to lose men.'

Mercia scanned the line. As she had speculated, Nathan was at the far end, clutching a musket and watching the proceedings with interest.

Nicholas was absent, as was Amery, but most of the other townsmen who were not at work were there, even Humility Thomas, despite his age and his corpulence. As they caught sight of her, the men began to mutter to each other, while Nathan raised a tentative arm in greeting. Godsgift turned to the source of their distraction; uttering an expletive, he stormed towards her, brandishing his drawn rapier.

'This is no place for you.' He dragged the tip of his sword through the grass. 'If you could leave, we will continue our practice.'

'You have been practising a long time,' she taunted. 'Do you think your men will miss if a woman is here to watch?'

The men within earshot laughed, causing the constable to redden with annoyance. 'This is not a frivolous enterprise, Mrs Blakewood. This is not Boston, much less London, and we have to be prepared to defend ourselves. It is no dainty woman's task.'

She held her tongue. 'Still, the challenge to your . . . ragbag . . . is there.'

He puffed up his chest, whether deliberate or unknowing she could not say. 'Then let us see what your companion can do. So far he has watched but proved nothing, for all his boasts.' He turned to the line. 'Keyte! Show my ragbag how a soldier shoots.'

'Finally.' Nathan came forward, lazily holding a musket in his right hand. Mercia knew his swagger was to impress the watching men, but the display was justified: he had served in the Cromwellian army and was more than proficient with a gun. He fed the musket with ball and shot, took aim, cocked, and fired. The ball powered through the very centre of the pillow that was serving as the target's chest.

'You see.' Godsgift scorned his men. 'A stranger shoots better than you! Lord help you when the Indians come.'

Sighs and grumblings rose from the men, along with one or two distempered frowns at Nathan. He sauntered across to Mercia, setting the empty musket on the ground.

'Hello,' he said.

'Hello.' She nodded at the gun. 'Enjoying yourself?'

He shrugged. "Tis something to do. This lot need work. Since that mark was brought out, I have watched most of them shoot at it, and six of them clean missed. Four of the others barely grazed the pillow.'

'And the others?'

'Vic Smith and Richard Thorpe. But then as blacksmith and surgeon, you would expect them to have a keen eye. They are also the two captains.'

'Captains?'

"Tis quite the organisation Brown has here. Two companies of men, each headed by a captain, each company divided into three bands of five. All headed by himself, of course. He is very adept, you know.'

She raised an eyebrow. 'The quintessential old soldier.'

He laughed. 'They met at the meeting house and marched out in three lines, their muskets across their fronts. They are well drilled, at least. And to be honest, I think some of them are missing on purpose. Or being deliberately slow.'

Mercia shot him a wry smile. 'Shall I try?'

'Mercia—'

Unheeding his caution, she picked up the musket, holding out her other hand for the pouch at Nathan's belt. He rolled his eyes but handed it over. While the men were still focused on Godsgift's tirade, she dropped a ball into the barrel, shook in some powder, and took aim at the target. The resulting shot made half the men jump.

'Nearly as good as me,' grinned Nathan. 'But not quite.'

She pulled a face, but she was pleased with her attempt. In truth she knew how to wield a gun, if normally a smaller weapon such as a doglock pistol: she had fired one recently during her troubles in New York, and not to her disadvantage.

Godsgift, however, was not so impressed. 'What are you doing, Keyte?' he barked. 'Do not let a woman near a musket! You will have someone killed, most likely herself!'

'She is quite proficient,' said Nathan. 'See for yourself.' He gestured towards the pillow, where a pair of duck feathers were waggling in the wind in a hole in the scarecrow's chest.

'Hmm.' The constable looked at the target. 'Take her out of here. My men have to practise.'

'You are not wrong about that.' Nathan placed his arm around her back as he walked her towards the eastern gate: an action, she assumed, designed to provoke the constable's wrath.

'Not the friendliest welcome,' she said, as they paused inside the palisade.

'He is not so bad. He has a temper—'

'And a murderous streak.'

'That too. But he cares for the town, I think.'

'Enough to kill for it?'

Nathan looked at her. 'You see suspicion everywhere. It is not likely to help your humours.'

Her prior mood vanished. 'I see only what I must, especially when no one else will. Save Nicholas. And maybe now Percy.'

She knew the barb was immature, but it had the desired effect.

'Bloody Nicholas.' Nathan looked skywards. 'So you trust him again, do you?'

'I think so.'

'And Percy?'

She played with the cuff of her bodice. 'We have been talking. He had some news, if you are interested.'

Nathan closed his eyes, tempering his breathing. 'Very well. Let us not argue over nothing. What news does he have?'

'Not here. Come back outside the gate.'

She led him a little way down towards the Hartford road, near the wood. A fallen tree not far from the path provided a suitable spot to rest, a little sodden with the recent rain, but not uncomfortable. When they had finished fidgeting to avoid the roughest bits of bark, she told him about Goffe and Whalley.

'I cannot believe it,' he said, the excited look on his face endearing. 'I never knew Goffe, but I saw Whalley once or twice.' Then he frowned. ''Tis good that he is, but why is Percy trusting you like this? Didn't you say he acted as crazed when he discovered we had helped Dixwell?'

'I think he has a respect for my father. You know how people are. Sometimes they take time to trust.' She paused. 'Can you trust that Remembrance?'

'Mercia.' Nathan laughed, asking the same playful question Clemency had asked in her night-time thoughts. 'Are you jealous?'

The question was not so welcome in real life. 'What has that to do with it?'

He held up his hands. 'Sorry.' His brown eyes sparkled, matching the colour of their makeshift bench. 'But . . . I thought maybe you were jealous.'

'Nathan.'

'She is pretty.'

She stood and folded her arms. 'If you are going to talk like a child, then—'

'Hey.' He stood beside her, lightly grasping her shoulders, a bemused expression on his face. 'What is this? You know how I feel about you. Do not be ridiculous.' He sighed, removing his hands. 'But Mercia, all . . . this.' He extended his arm in the direction of the town. 'It is eating away at you. Away at us. I am . . . concerned.'

She did not know why she said it. Maybe she was tired, or sad, or – yes – ridiculous, but a hard feeling came upon her, an invisible barrier between herself and the world that had been growing ever since Clemency died, and she realised that Nathan, too, was outside that barrier for now.

'There is no us,' she said. 'Not here. There is too much to be done.'

Nathan's face, so calm and eager moments before, seemed to tremble. Her heart ached as he turned away, and again, here, she could have told him what she really felt, but the barrier was still there, sundering her emotions.

'Come,' she said instead. 'We best return inside the town.'

That evening an awkward atmosphere hung low over the cottage as she and Nathan played a silent game of draughts. She looked at him when she thought he was not looking at her, and she wondered: why was she being so defensive? More to the point, why put a dead woman she had barely known before a living man she had known for years? But her father had taught her too well about justice, her sense of it too acute.

She did worry, as she watched him taking a half-hearted move, that the gradual acceptance she could move on from her husband – an acceptance she had thought, in New York, complete – had reversed. The prospect of losing anyone else as she had lost Will, as she had lost Clemency, was unbearable. Right now, she felt she must put her own wants aside, and yet she worried, in that cold room, that she might have put them aside too well.

'Why?' said Clemency, her presence beside her. 'Why do this?'

Mercia studied the board. 'Because I must.'

'Not for me, Mercia.' Clemency shook her head. 'You must think of yourself.'

She jumped three of Nathan's pieces. 'How can I? You invited me here out of kindness. And you remain here still, wandering the streets when you should be safe in heaven. How can I rest until your journey is complete?'

And then a man's voice: 'Well done.'

'What?' She looked up, surprised to see Nathan.

'Well done. Those were my last pieces.'

'Oh.' She stared at the board, two white pieces of shell the only markers left. Dispelling the fog from her mind, she tried a smile, hoping it would help them both. But Nathan's mood remained depressed.

'Perhaps I will take some air,' she said, reaching for her cloak. ''Tis still light. And then early to bed.'

His dulled eyes glanced downwards. 'As you wish.'

'I think I will visit Daniel in the next day or two. Consult with Winthrop about events.'

'He would like that – Daniel, I mean.' He took a sip of beer from a beaker at his side. 'Well, enjoy your walk.'

She threw her cloak around herself, feeling sad he had not offered to join her, or warned her to be safe as he usually would. But then as she was leaving he called out:

'Be safe.'

She wandered a while in the town; as ever the circuit was short, but she kept on circling, moving out towards the woods where the leaves, orange and brown, were now falling more steadily from the trees. As dusk descended she loitered outside the tavern, wanting someone to talk to, suspecting – hoping – Nicholas would be inside. Sure enough, when she made herself enter he was at a high table with two other men, one Lavington's manservant, the other she could not place. As she approached, Nicholas looked up, while his companions frowned, eventually electing to stand.

She stayed the rising men with an outstretched palm. 'I do not want to intrude.'

'You're not,' said Nicholas. 'Do you . . . want to join us?'

The two men looked appalled.

'No,' she declined. 'But perhaps I could speak with you later?'

'We can speak now.' He leapt from his stool, pocketing the few beads of wampum lying on the table. 'Another time, boys.'

'Scared you'll lose it all back?' taunted the unknown man, perhaps travelled from another town, she thought.

'Not if you keep up that twitch of yours.'

219

The man sat back, looking quizzically at Lavington's servant. His expression deadpan, Nicholas followed Mercia outside.

'I bet there is no twitch,' she said.

'Maybe. Maybe not.' He smiled. 'But it doesn't hurt to make them nervous. They're the only two I've been able to find that will play at all.' He looked at her. 'Don't worry, it's very small stakes.'

'Why should I mind?' They walked a short distance, then Nicholas laughed. 'What?'

'I was remembering when we first met.'

The memory brought a smile to her own lips. 'The Anchor.'

'You came looking for me in a tavern then, and you're still looking for me in a tavern now.' He whistled. 'I never thought on that day that I'd sail with you across the ocean.'

A sudden sensation of dislocation and awe came upon her; in that instant, she felt all the trials of the past months, the immensity of all she had witnessed. She staggered a little in the face of such emotion.

Nicholas grabbed her shoulder. 'Are you well?'

She shook her head to clear her thoughts. 'Yes. But what you said, about sailing across the ocean – suddenly it struck me. Everything that has happened.'

'Do you want to sit down?'

'That would be welcome.'

'Come.' He looked at her askance. 'I sense you want to talk.'

They walked in silence through the northern gate, Nicholas grabbing a lit torch from a sconce set into the palisade. Not far from the gate, a sawn-down log served as a bench for workers breaking from their toils in the fields, a smattering of chicken bones and kernels scattered about its base. Nicholas rested the torch in a convenient hole; it seemed man-made, perhaps designed for that very purpose.

They sat for a while in silence. She knew he was waiting for her to speak, but the freshness of the evening air was intoxicating in its fullness, and it was pleasant to be in company without having to say a word. But at length she sighed.

'Do you think I am a fool?'

The question took Nicholas aback. 'Why do you ask that?'

'Nathan seems to.'

'Ah.' He leant forward, entwining his hands. 'I'm sure he doesn't.'

'He thinks we should go back to New York.'

'Has he said so?'

'Not for a day or two, but 'tis quite clear.'

'I think he wants whatever you want. As well as wanting you to be safe.'

'I can look after myself.'

'I know. But you can't blame him for worrying.'

'I wish he wouldn't.'

He looked up at her, sucking in his top lip. 'Can I say something?'

'Of course.'

He hesitated. 'You can be a little . . . difficult . . . at times.'

'So now I'm taking advice from my manservant.' She held up her hands. 'Yes, I know. I did say speak.'

'I'm sorry. All I'm saying is, you can be quite . . .'

'Obsessed?'

'Perhaps.'

'I don't think it's obsessive to want to bring a murderer to justice.'

'No.' He studied the ground. 'And I agree with you. If nobody else is willing to stop this madman then we should.'

She looked at him. 'We?'

He twisted his head towards her. 'We.'

She smiled. In the torchlight she could see his deep green eyes, and there was something comforting in that. She may be paying him as her manservant, but they still shared common bonds, common outlooks. The realisation surprised her, and cheered her at the same time.

'Do you miss her?' she asked. 'Your daughter? 'Tis hard enough leaving

221

Daniel with Winthrop, but I can visit him whenever I want.'

He pulled himself up straight. 'I never knew she was even alive until that day her mother came to my door, handed her over and left. But as soon as I saw her, I could do nothing but love her.' He kicked at the bench with his heels. 'It was a hard decision to agree that my sister should raise her, but it was for the best, and I would visit at least once a week. So not seeing her for months – 'tis difficult. But the money you gave me has made it worth it, and not just that. The voyage itself, getting to know you, working to regain your trust.' He glanced away. 'It sounds absurd, but it has made me a better man.'

'It has had an effect on me too. But Nicholas, you were a kind man to begin with.'

'Hmm.' He grunted. 'I don't know if I want to be called kind. Not very . . . manly.'

She laughed. 'Then what?'

'Oh, I don't know. Adventurous. Virile.'

She arched an eyebrow. 'No doubt there are women in London who would recognise that description.'

He scoffed. 'I wish.'

'Come, you are—' She stopped, unwilling to say any more.

He looked up, fixing her with a smile that agreed better left unsaid. He cleared his throat. 'So – what is happening with you and Nathan?'

'That is none of your business.'

'That's what he told me aboard the *Redemption*. And I'll tell you again what I told you then, whether I'm your manservant or not. Don't let chances slip away when they come along.'

A hollowness burnt in her stomach. 'Bad things seem to happen to people I become close to. I do not think I could face it again.'

A pause. 'Forgive me, but – do you love him?'

It was an impertinent question, but one that needed to be asked, and she was grateful that he had. 'In truth, and do not tell him I told you, I do not know.'

'Why not?'

She shrugged. 'Sometimes I think I do, and others I do not think anything at all.'

'But you never think you don't?'

'No. But I had told myself I would not marry again.'

'Has he asked you?'

'No.'

'And if he does?'

The first image that flashed into her mind was that of her son, warm by a fire in Hartford, and then the picture changed to one she had of him, very early in his young life, sleeping in his father's arms before a similar fire in Halescott, before Will rode off to war and never came back. The memory pierced her forcefully, more so than usual of late.

She looked up at the stars; they were so bright here, so beautiful. 'As I said, he has not asked. And if he does, that will be between me and him.'

Nicholas nodded, shivering slightly as he rubbed at his breeches; it was a cold night, she realised, and he was only wearing a thin shirt. Typical of her to bring him outdoors without noticing.

'Do you want to go back?' she asked.

'In a minute.' He removed his hands from his legs. 'Have you thought any more about those codes? Amery and I were talking about them last night.'

'You two are getting along?'

'I wouldn't say that, as such. But when you have to share quarters, you've got to find a way to make it work.' He scratched his cheek. 'Though I found it easier when I served on the ships. He is a bit – clever.'

She smiled. 'What do you think then?'

'About what?'

'Your question. What do you think about these killings? These codes.'

He widened his eyes. 'You want my opinion?'

'Of course.'

He sat back, clearly pleased. 'Well, I think there is a madman in the town.'

'Or a calculating one. I wish we could determine his motive.'

He nestled his right leg under his left. 'Why does any man kill another? Anger. Hatred. Because he wants to win a fight, steal a coin.'

'I think 'tis more than simple emotion. I think there is a plan at work. Why else would he leave those messages every time? If we solve that, I believe we will be close to solving it all.'

'Maybe. But wouldn't it be better to think about the man, not about what he writes to tease us? The codes might be mere distractions. For example, do you realise they are all thirteen letters long, before the space?'

'I had noticed that.' She inclined her head. 'Well observed. But it might be coincidence.'

'And yet another distraction.'

'Then how else do we solve this?'

'Listen to people. Try to understand how this town works and lives. Think as they do, not as we do back home.'

She looked at him. 'You are a wise man yourself, Nicholas.'

'Just common sense.' He leapt from the bench. 'Now, I'd best get you back, or Nathan will worry some more.'

She laughed, letting him lead her through the gate. Yet she remained perturbed that such conversation was not so straightforward with Nathan, aware of the barrier she had struck up, but having little will to break it down.

As they passed into the town, she thought she heard a rustle in the undergrowth behind, but lost in her thoughts she paid it no heed: there were enough small animals and birds about. Nicholas replaced the torch in its sconce, and she bade him goodnight at the meeting house, refusing his offer to walk her to the cottage. There was no one in the streets, and it was close enough; still, she watched him until he faded out of sight, more worried for his safety than for herself.

She strolled through the dark, enjoying deep gulps of air as she gazed once more at the pristine sky. She remembered some of the constellations from her journey with Winthrop – Pegasus, the mythical horse's body lit by the four points of a great square; Cassiopeia, its five stars marking out a giant letter W twinkling in the sky.

And then she stopped. What if the codes, like Cassiopeia, were hiding a motif in plain sight? A design that could only be seen by combining all its parts?

But then the multitude of stars suddenly blinked out. A rough material was forced over her head, and she was dragged backwards, too dazed to call out.

Chapter Twenty-One

Her assailant did not drag her far, but she was infused with fear, terrified the murderer had chosen his next corpse. She could not see for the – cloak? – could not breathe it was so tight, and all the time a strong grasp was pulling her backwards, making her stumble over the dirt, until she was wrenched off the ground and thrown across her attacker's shoulders. She lashed out a hand, thinking to strike at the man's face, but it connected instead with his chest. She was startled to feel bare flesh, and she flung her hand again at his body, this time connecting with the muscles of his arm, and again, the skin was bare. But there was little time to wonder, little inclination no less; soon she was lowered to the ground, not ungently, the cloak stripped from her head.

'Be quiet,' hissed a woman's voice. 'You are not in danger, but you could be.'

Mercia ceased her struggling, startled to hear a familiar voice. The dark night conspired with her confusion to mask the speaker's identity, but as her eyes adjusted to the gloom the woman came into view, kneeling beside her.

'Sooleawa!' she said, still fearful of the silhouette at the Indian woman's side. 'Why have you done this?'

The hidden man uttered something in the Indians' language. Mercia may not have understood the words, but she could tell the tone, and he sounded agitated.

'I am sorry for this . . . action,' said Sooleawa. 'But the *sachem* wishes to speak with you. I am here to translate if that is needed.'

'The *sachem*?' Mercia swivelled her head, squinting through the darkness to take a look at Sooleawa's companion, but she could make nothing out: there was no torch, no firelight, and the night was as moonless as before. Yet in the faint silhouette she discerned a tall man adorned with feathers, much as the *sachem* had appeared in his grand tent. The *sachem*, also, who had thrown the axe with such precision on the road near New Haven. She decided it would be best to play along – if she tried to run, she did not know whether they would let her escape.

'The *sachem*,' confirmed Sooleawa. 'I suggest you show him the respect he is due.' Standing, she turned to her chief, speaking in their own tongue. As she waited, Mercia sat on the earth, rubbing her aching neck, trying to convince herself there was no call to be afraid. But the night had become much colder.

Sooleawa crouched once more. 'The *sachem* has asked me to explain how things are in our village.' She leant forward on her slippered heels, speaking low. A wolf or some such animal howled in the near distance, and the wind whipped up in the trees, but Mercia's attention was caught. 'The young men of our tribe are demanding retribution. Our *pnieses* – our most feared warriors – are ready to lead them.'

'Because of the farmhand,' said Mercia.

'The boy.' Sooleawa spat out the word, her voice betraying her anger. 'He did not kill Hopewell. It is not possible that any of our people killed him. He was a great friend to us.'

Mercia bowed her head. 'I know.'

'And yet your people seized one of ours in revenge and killed him without question. He had a mother. A sister.'

227

She looked up. 'I abhor what they did to your kinsman, Sooleawa. As I know many others do.'

'Ab – hor?'

'Condemn. Weep for.'

'Ah.' Sooleawa nodded. 'And yet it happened all the same.' She paused, the air laden with the bitterness of her thoughts. 'There is an agreement between our peoples that none shall kill the other without consequence. Yet our scouts have been watching, and they say nothing has been done.'

Feeling a guilt that was not hers, Mercia swallowed. 'Those who repent of what has happened would that something were done.'

'Because they are good people, or through fear of their God?'

'For both reasons.'

'And still they do nothing. As powwow Winthrop did nothing when our own powwow was murdered.'

'I know nothing of that. But I know Governor Winthrop is an honourable man.'

Sooleawa scoffed. 'We have found the Englishman's claims to have honour are often forgotten when it suits him best.'

'That can be true.' She forced herself to stand, the prick of sharp gravel cutting into her palm. 'And not just here, in the wilds. But most English folk are good people, Winthrop foremost among them.'

'Hmm.' Sooleawa stared up at her, unconvinced. 'That has not been my – not been our – experience.' Hastily, she stood. 'The *sachem* wants something done, woman from beyond the seas. He is angry at the deaths of our people and our friends. He knows that you gained Clemency's trust, and that you are arguing to avenge her death. So he will speak with you.'

Mercia rubbed at her throbbing neck. 'Then why did he not simply ask?'

'It is his way.' Sooleawa's voice came proudly through the darkness. 'And he was concerned you would have been afraid to come.'

'Because I am a woman?'

'No.' She stepped to one side. 'Because you are English.'

The *sachem* came forward to fill the space she had left; at close range, the grease on his skin glistened even in the night.

'I am pleased again to meet you,' he said.

The *sachem* was fearsome to look at, especially so in the menace of darkness. She could make out the muscles of his torso, the necklaces of wampum – or bone, she thought – the erect feathers on his head. The man was as utterly strange to her as any she could imagine, yet he still exuded the same need for display she knew well in the English nobility.

'And I you,' she replied. 'Although I wish it had been a more comfortable encounter.'

The *sachem* frowned; at first she panicked she had insulted him, but when Sooleawa translated he merely grunted.

'This is a serious affair, woman of the English. My warriors desire battle. And I think to give it them.'

A nauseous terror filled her soul. She had known war and loss – by God she had known that – but the prospect of an Indian assault on the town, here in the middle of the wilderness, was terrifying. Her irrational mind filled her head with nervous thoughts. What did they do to prisoners? To women? She thought of Daniel, and was glad he was safe with Winthrop in Hartford.

'But my warriors are young,' continued the *sachem*, 'and I am less so. I remember the wars we have had with your people. The deaths. The burnt villages and crops. I will avoid more if I can.' He leant close enough for her to smell the grease on his skin. 'Will you help me?'

She blinked. 'Me?'

'I can hold back my *pnieses* only so long. They wait if they think I act, as I am in speaking with you. But this does not much satisfy, and they soon want more. If we do not get our vengeance I will let them attack.' He threw back his head. 'You try to discover who killed Hopewell and Clemency?'

'Yes, but—'

'Then I want you to discover who killed my powwow also. And tell me who killed the boy. We will have our vengeance on them, not the whole town.'

She turned cold. As much as she hated what Godsgift Brown had done, she could not merely hand him over.

'*Sachem*, I do not know who killed the boy,' she lied, glad of the dark, for it hid her deceit. 'I did not see.'

He grunted. 'Someone made the final blow. That man must give us retribution.'

'With his life?'

The feathers on his head quivered in the wind. 'It is your way also, although you use a . . .' He looked at Sooleawa.

'A noose,' she said.

Mercia shivered. 'And the powwow? That did not happen in Meltwater. Why do you seek my help in that?'

The *sachem* held out his hand. Sooleawa reached to the ground and passed across what looked like a thick sheet of parchment.

'Because of this,' he said, shaking the object in instruction that Mercia take it.

Her fingertips closed around a soft, firm texture, the parchment in fact a leathery scrap of animal hide.

'What is this?'

Sooleawa came forward. 'You have found strange messages on Clemency and Hopewell, have you not?'

'Yes, but how could you—?'

'It does not matter. What matters is that this skin was in the powwow's hand while he was lying dead in the wood for us to find him.' She folded her arms. 'It has markings on it. English ones, like those found on Clemency and Hopewell.'

'What?' Stunned, Mercia brought the hide near her face. She could just make out the scratches on its surface, filled with some sort of ink: sure enough, a series of letters, the individual symbol at the end.

'My God.' Her right leg gave way, but she caught herself from falling. She looked at Sooleawa, then again at the hide. There was no mistake. It was the same kind of pattern as the other three.

'My God,' she repeated, not knowing what else to say.

Not what to say, not what to do: Mercia was in a quandary. It seemed the killer had struck four times now. She sat at the table in the cottage, all four codes copied out on one piece of paper in front of her. Percy, now out of town, had most of the originals, but she did not need them: she knew the codes by heart. With Nathan and Nicholas, she stared at the jumble of letters with aching eyes. The latest – the powwow's – was at the bottom.

RNLENRDFRXSHI O
BNFOWVPSGGJNB .
HDWRVDWMPAQCY †
SXWLLRJLQMLSJ U

'The end symbol is the key,' she said, a headache pounding in her temples. 'But I think they need to be read together, somehow. I thought so last night when there were three codes, and I am all the more certain of it now.'

'But are you certain you are well?' said Nathan. 'If I could get my hands on that *sachem* . . .'

'It does not matter now, Nat. He has done us a favour – I think.'

'Hardly. You said yourself he is using you to bring him answers. People say Clemency and Hopewell were their fiercest supporters.'

'Perhaps. But this is not helping with these.' She blew out her cheeks. 'The last symbol in the latest code is a U. Another letter, like the O from Mason's code.' She tapped her finger on the first inscription. 'Whereas on the other two, the last symbol is a dot, and a cross, not a letter at all.'

'Wait a minute.' Nicholas leant over her shoulder, his unshaved cheek almost grazing her own. 'I can't make much sense of these, but if they form some kind of set, what about – put them in the right order?'

'What do you mean?'

'Order of death. The powwow's first, then the minister's. Then Clemency's and Hopewell's.'

'We have already put them in all possible orders, Nicholas. Nathan and I. Percy and Amery too.'

'Not including that fourth one you haven't.'

'True.' She tore the paper into separate strips, one code on each, setting them in chronological order:

SXWLLRJLQMLSJ U
RNLENRDFRXSHI O
BNFOWVPSGGJNB .
HDWRVDWMPAQCY †

'Better?'

He continued to stare. 'That last symbol, you reckon.' He pulled back his head, rubbing at his chin. Then he gasped.

'What is it?' she said, simultaneously with Nathan.

'Letters are a mess to me at the best of times, but I can see the lines they are made of well enough.' He looked at her, a great excitement in his eyes. 'Where is that book Winthrop gave you? The one on alchemy you had the other day?'

'In my trunk. I have not much bothered to take it out. Do you want it?'

He nodded vigorously and she rushed to get it. Bounding down the stairs she handed over the musty tome.

'Where is that page near the front you showed me?' He leafed through the crinkling book. 'Damn it, where is—ah!' He thrust the book on the table, flattening it at a diagram of the *monas hieroglyphica*, the alchemists' symbol Winthrop had drawn for her in Hartford:

'The *monas*?' She looked at him. 'Why?'

'Look at it! Look what it's made of!'

'I am sorry,' she said, flustered, 'but I cannot—'

'Nathan?' he said, but he too shook his head, seemingly as puzzled as she.

'Look.' Nicholas jabbed his finger at the book. 'This *monas* is made up of different pieces. An upside-down arch. A circle, with a dot in it. A cross. Some – wavy hill things.' He looked at Mercia, begging her to see it. 'An upside-down arch, a circle, dot, and cross!'

She looked between the *monas* and the codes, searching for the connection, and then—

'By God's wounds! You are right!'

Nathan leant over. 'I still cannot—'

'Look,' she said, as agitated now as Nicholas. 'An upside-down arch, a circle, a dot, and a cross!' Then she pointed at the symbols at the end of each code. 'The letter U – 'tis not a letter! 'Tis an upside-down arch! The O – 'tis a circle! The dot – well. And finally the cross. My God!' She stared at him. 'We were reading them wrong.' Then she looked up at Nicholas. 'Very, very well done.'

He beamed. 'I just saw it.'

'But what does it mean, Mercia?' said Nathan. 'If the killer is hiding a *monas* in the codes, is an alchemist behind this, after all? Lavington, perhaps, maybe Amery?'

'Or someone interested in alchemy,' said Nicholas. 'Someone who keeps that interest quiet?'

'Or maybe,' said Nathan, 'someone who wants us to think it's to do with alchemy. Mercia? What say you?'

But Mercia was staring over the opened book, her enthusiasm already vanquished. Her face paled as a sinking feeling descended in her chest.

Nathan frowned. 'What is it?'

She looked at him, and again at the *monas*. Then she closed her eyes.

'I know what it means. But it is not good.' She paused, and in that moment the immensity of the situation once more weighed heavy upon her. 'It means there will be another murder.'

Buoyed and disheartened in equal measure by their breakthrough, the next day she rode to Hartford with Nathan, intending to consult Winthrop and visit Daniel. She left Nicholas in Meltwater with instructions to observe, and to discuss nothing with anyone, but he needed no telling. She wondered if he would be safe there, from the Indians as much as from the killer, but he was young and strong, and forewarned about the possibility of attack. Nevertheless, when she asked him to look after their cottage, she chose not to tell him it was because she wanted him away from Amery, even though she could scarcely believe the waspish schoolmaster could be a killer. But it was better to be safe: perhaps she, too, was growing paranoid of late.

When she arrived, the sight of her son running into her arms filled her with such love that she had to hold him a long time lest she be overwhelmed by his happy face. After a few seconds he began to squirm, but she held him tighter, kissing his forehead until eventually she felt able to release him.

'Mamma,' he scolded. 'Don't squeeze so hard.'

She looked at him, and an image filled her mind of the day she would no longer be able to hold him, when he would be a grown man dressed in finery, and she knew she would be fiercely proud. She thought of the manor house, hoping the King would be good to his word and return it. Then Daniel smiled, and she changed her mind – however old he was, however frail she became, she was still going to squeeze him tight.

'Have you missed me?' she asked.

Daniel nodded. He was dressed smartly in a little black outfit that was remarkably free of dirt. His cheeks were full and healthy: clearly, the Winthrops had been looking after him well.

'I have a friend,' he said.

'Oh yes?'

'Another boy.'

'I guessed that. What's his name?'

'Pen.'

'That's unusual.'

"Tis short for something.' He frowned, trying to think. 'Er . . . Repent. Repentance.'

She looked at Nathan. 'Repentance?' He shrugged his shoulders. 'Not a very nice name for a child.'

'Some of our names are rather strange.' Mercia looked up to see Winthrop standing in the doorway to his house, dressed as usual in sober black. 'Pen is a product of adultery, and Repentance is the name the ministers enforced on him. And yet, like your boy, he is a delightful child.'

'Governor.' Mercia stood. 'Thank you so much for looking after Daniel.'

He smiled. 'It is a pleasure. It is bracing to have a child in the house again.'

'Was the coin I left for you sufficient? I was worried it was not enough, but with crossing the ocean, I could not bring—'

Winthrop waved a dismissive hand. 'Do not concern yourself with that. 'Tis the least I can do to help.' He gave her a thoughtful stare. 'When you have spent time with your son, let us talk.'

'Come, Mamma.' Daniel tugged at her dress. 'I want to show you a bird's nest I found.'

She nodded at the governor. 'Patience, Danny. But yes, let's go and play.'

* * *

Winthrop's usually calm face was askew; he was blinking without cease, his lips parted, looking down at the copies of the codes Mercia had brought with her.

'You are right,' he said. 'There will be another murder. The *monas* is not yet complete.'

'No.' Sitting beside him, her own countenance was grim. 'The wavy semicircles at the bottom are missing, while each of the other elements is present. The circle, the dot, the arch and the cross.'

'But what does it mean? One more murder? Two, for each of the two semicircles? And who will it be?'

'Damn these codes.' Nathan sat opposite at the dining-room table, his chin cupped in his hands. 'Why can't we read them?'

Winthrop shook his head. 'Maybe now we have four, I will be able to decipher the letters. Maybe. But 'tis nothing I recognise offhand. Not like the puzzle I set you, Mercia, no one step forward, two steps back. I do not think it is merely a substitution, either, with each letter always corresponding to an exact other. Not across all four, at least.' He sighed. 'In the powwow's code, the letter L appears multiple times. In a substitution, that could translate to the letter E, the most commonly used letter. But then it does not appear in the third and fourth codes at all.'

'But why are they even left on the bodies?' Mercia bit off a fingernail she had unknowingly been chewing down. 'If the *monas* is involved, do you not think this is to do with alchemy?'

'I cannot think how. Other than, as I told you, we alchemists love to write in code.'

'Could it be Lavington?' asked Nathan. 'Amery Oldfield?'

Winthrop screwed up his aged face. 'I cannot see Lavington as a killer. And it feels' – he scratched at his neck – 'almost a personal attack on me. I know that is selfish to think so, but everyone knows the *monas* is a favourite symbol of mine. I use it frequently in my work, on the orders for equipment I place with my suppliers in London.' He threw himself back in his chair. 'Why would an alchemist do this? Purification, perhaps? But this extreme . . . surely no one of science would sink to such barbaric depths.'

Mercia looked at him. 'Why purification?'

'You recall when I explained how the two goals of alchemy are the philosopher's stone, to turn base metals precious, and the alkahest, to cure all ills?'

'Yes.'

'Well, there are those who think we will only uncover these prizes in a land that is totally pure, untainted by human corruption.' He raised a grey eyebrow. 'A puritan environment, you could say. But Lavington has never subscribed to that tenet in any discussions we have had. As for young Oldfield, I do not much know him.'

'Then perhaps the killer is merely employing a known symbol, aware we will realise its meaning to some end. Or he wants to sow ill feeling for alchemists, as Nathan suggested before.'

'But again, why?' Winthrop was more distressed than Mercia had yet seen. 'Damn these commissioners of the King, roaming New England on their infernal surveys! I should be focusing on these deaths, not on disputes of boundary!'

She reached out a hand. 'Governor, I am there. I will help you solve this.' She looked up. 'Nathan and me.'

Winthrop nodded, wiping a handkerchief across his brow. ''Tis just so maddening, when I have spent my life immersed in alchemy, devising and reading codes.'

'I understand.' She withdrew her hand. 'Nicholas, my manservant, suggests we should think of the killer rather than the ciphers. He thinks they may be left to taunt us rather than as any real message. Perhaps we should concentrate on that.'

'I hope he will be safe,' said Nathan, looking through the window. 'We left him there with a killer.'

Mercia glanced across. 'I did not think you much cared for him.'

'I do not want him killed, Mercia.' He fixed her with a look.

'I am sorry.' She shook her head. 'I worry for him too.'

'I suspect he is in no danger,' said Winthrop, his voice steadier now. 'This sequence started before you even arrived in Connecticut. The powwow was slain many weeks ago. And these codes suggest a methodical mind, someone who enjoys playing games. I think the next . . . victim . . . has been earmarked for death for a long while.'

A cold sense of despair tugged at Mercia's being. 'Then we need to act quickly. What links all these murders?'

'Indians,' said Nathan straightaway.

'That does not feel right. Why the *monas*?'

Winthrop arched his hands. 'Clemency and Hopewell were friends to the Indians, and somewhat free-thinking, I suppose. But then Mason was not.'

'He did have a fancy for an Indian woman,' said Nathan.

'Did he?' Winthrop looked surprised. 'Then maybe your guess is correct after all. Or is somebody judging what they think of as a sin?'

'We had thought of that,' said Mercia. 'But what of the powwow? And why would anyone kill for such minor things?'

'Only God can know that,' he replied. 'Or perhaps it is the Devil spinning his foul tales to a twistable mind. But many people here are totally devout, Mercia. What is minor to you may be heresy to another. Most think the cries of the Indian powwows prove they are allies of Satan.' His head jerked. 'The *monas* is a symbol of perfection, indeed . . . and so if it is broken into its parts, as it is throughout these codes, could that be a judgement on the failure of perfection? That the killer wants to tell me, and Lavington, as alchemists of some standing, what he thinks of the society we preside over?'

Elbows on the table, Mercia rubbed her eyes; to her, that seemed self-indulgent. 'Perhaps,' she said. 'But while we talk, another innocent seems likely to suffer the same fate.'

Winthrop sighed. 'Of course, for the next victim, it may already be too late.'

Chapter Twenty-Two

A sharp sense of dread pervaded Mercia's steps as she wandered Meltwater's streets. Every person she saw could be a callous ender of lives, every person the next to reach their premature end. With Lavington ranged against her, Lavington indeed a suspect, she did not want to broach with him her discovery about the *monas*, and she continued to receive glances of mistrust in the streets. She thought of talking with Vic Smith, one of the few who had helped, but even his marked face, she wondered, could be hiding unknown truths. So she waited, retreating into the familiarity of Nathan and Nicholas, holding out until Percy returned, and all the while terrified the killer would strike first. Nicholas took to sleeping with a knife in his bed, doubting Mercia's concerns for his safety, but acting on them all the same.

And still it gnawed at her they were saying nothing to the town. Surely, she agonised, its people should be told a life was in danger? Overcoming her disdain, she spoke with Godsgift Brown, urging him to prepare for an Indian attack, obscuring her meeting with the *sachem* by simple talk of plausible retaliation. But he scorned her once again, well aware, as he said, that the Indians could come, blustering how the townsmen were ready and would kill every last stinking savage as they poured from the woods.

'But what if the killer becomes frustrated?' she said to Nathan, strolling along the river to the waterfall for some air. 'He placed those codes to be found, and we are hiding them. What if he changes his plan, brings it forward?'

'If he is as methodical as Winthrop says he is, then he will not. Besides, 'tis not just us keeping them quiet. Lavington knows about them, and we can assume the constable does too.'

'I would sooner assume nothing.' She sighed. 'We cannot abnegate responsibility, merely because Lavington is the magistrate and we are not.'

He shook his head. 'Telling the town might be the worst thing we could do, if we can find him before he strikes. And we did all agree at the meeting.'

'But we can't find him, can we? Even with four codes. We cannot decipher them. And we did not know about the *monas* before.' She exhaled deeply. 'Let us see what Percy thinks when he returns.'

Nathan scoffed. 'Never mind what I think.'

'Nat, he knows the townsfolk. Do not be petulant.'

And so they continued to argue, while no progress was made.

By the time Percy rode back, they were no further forward. Life marched on in its uneasy, unsure way, the townsfolk becoming used to Mercia's persistent presence. The Indian farmhand's stare continued to look down on anyone who came through the southern gate, and for Mercia, the message was stark: her failure to uncover the killer could lead to a terrible attack.

'I think Nathan is right,' said Percy, his brown horse trotting amiably alongside Mercia's bay mare as they enjoyed the ride he had suggested they take. 'Godsgift has been aching to impose a form of martial law on us for a long time. He would love this excuse. My father may have his failings, but his resistance to soldierly discipline is not one of them. We are a free society in this land, and should remain so, able to live as we please.'

Mercia stooped to pass under a low-hanging branch. 'That turned into a speech.'

He laughed. 'I suppose it did. But there would be panic if people were told of your discovery about the *monas*. Some of them would call it diabolical magic, with all the superstitious idiocy that would entail.'

'I still worry we may be doing the wrong thing.'

'You are assuming people here are rational.'

'Percy, they are as rational as any people. Perhaps more so.' She looked at the trees around her, the rising piles of russet and yellow leaves building up across the ground. 'What you do here is remarkable, living like this, far from England. Far from anywhere.'

He smiled. 'So you do understand. Perhaps you should stay and live among us.'

'I doubt I would be welcome. Nathan, though – I think he would like it. Do you know he is helping on the Davisons' farmland now?'

'Is he?'

'Since a couple of days ago. He says it gives him something physical to do. You know he is a farmer himself, back home. And he talks often with that Remembrance. He says it is because she takes solace from speaking with him about the loss of her brother, as he lost his daughter. I am sure that is right, and he is good to do so, but—'

'But it makes you a little annoyed with her.'

She reddened. 'Not particularly.'

'Well, you will just have to spend more time with me.' He gripped his horse's reins as they emerged onto a wider path. 'How about we give these horses a real ride?'

Caught off guard, she watched as he urged on his horse and shot away. But she did not hesitate for long.

'Think I cannot keep up?'

She whistled, knocking her knees into the mare's flank through her slit riding dress, spurring the horse on in her turn. For several minutes they charged through the woods, Mercia never quite coming level but keeping Percy always in sight. It was a tricky course, scattered trees obstructing the winding path at irregular intervals, and he knew this land intimately, but she observed him, noting which way he leant, he turned, and she readied herself to copy him in advance. It was exhilarating racing through the woods, and when eventually he reined in his horse and she pulled up beside him, her heart was beating quickly in glad excitement, the thrill of the ride encouraging her to look at him in unbridled enjoyment.

He laughed. 'So you can keep up.'

'I know how to ride a horse.'

'And shoot a weapon too, if Vic is to be believed.'

'He told you about that?' She glanced away, hiding her pleasure. 'Well, Godsgift was being so pompous.'

'The men found it amusing.'

'As did I.' She looked at him, light-headed with the sharpness of the wind that had flown into her cheeks, and she realised she was feeling something other than rage, or melancholy, for the first time in days. He held her softened gaze until his horse pawed at the ground and he bent forward to calm it.

'Now,' he said. 'I want to take you somewhere.'

'Oh?'

'You will like it, I hope.' He winked. 'It has the grace of nowhere finer, not even Halescott.' He faltered as a shadow passed over her face. 'I am sorry. I should not have—'

But her humour was not vanquished. 'Do not worry. My house may not be mine again quite yet, but I am confident it will be.'

He cocked his head. 'So you will go back?'

'Why – yes. I did not think you were being serious.'

'Why not?' He gestured at the autumnal forest. 'Look at this place, how magnificent it is. What need have you of England when you have all this?' He grew animated. 'God has given us this land and we intend to keep it. Surely you have felt this as you have lived with us?'

242

She looked around, at the silver-barked trees, at the patches of blue sky seeping through the canopy above. A small mouse-like creature, a black stripe running the length of its furry back, scurried across the tapestry of fallen leaves beneath the hooves of her silken horse.

'I understand, but you were born here, Percy. This is your home. As England is mine.'

'I will change your mind yet. But come. We have to leave the path now. Our destination is well hidden.'

She raised a hand to her mouth. 'We are not – are we?'

He winked. 'Wait and see.'

Not far into the deeper forest, they tied their horses to a fallen trunk and set out on foot. The light was more elusive here, penetrating the dense trees in stark rays and columns, tiny floating detritus whirling in its invisible grasp. With each step Mercia's expectation grew; she knew where he was taking her, but the confidence he was showing and the thought of meeting men who would have known her father pricked her with excitement.

'You must not tell anyone where this is or who is here,' said Percy, as their boots kicked through the drying leaves. 'Not even Nathan.'

'Percy, the trees all look the same to me. Besides, Nathan would never reveal anything. He is a true Parliamentarian – or what used to be called a Parliamentarian, anyway.'

'That may be, but I have expended a lot of effort into keeping this place safe. The fewer people who know about it the better.'

'Then why bring me?'

He turned his head. 'Because they have asked for you.'

Observing as he curled in a finger each time he made a slight turn, meticulously counting off each section of his route, she soon followed him out to reach a small hollow surrounded on three sides by a series of close-linked rocks. The entrance was wide, while a narrow cleft in the back served as an alternative way out. The sound of water trickled through the gap, signifying the presence of a nearby river, probably the same that cascaded over the waterfall near Meltwater.

'Wait here,' he said at the entrance.

He held his palm towards her, then leapt onto the rocks to make a tour of the hollow's crest, jumping over the cleft with ease. His circuit concluded, he jumped back down, his previous easy demeanour replaced by a serious air. Of a sudden it struck her that she was alone in the woods with a man she did not much know, from a town with an unidentified killer. She stepped subtly back, keeping a reasonable distance between them.

As she followed him into the hollow, she noticed how one of the rocks on the left side stuck out from its neighbours, hiding the area immediately behind: a feature not at all obvious even at the hollow's entrance. Behind the protrusion, a dark space came into view, a low opening just large enough for a person to crawl through.

'I cannot expect you to squeeze into here,' said Percy. 'If you wait, I will fetch them.' He disappeared inside the opening, and she was alone in the wood.

It was the middle of the day, but the light was dim here. This was the true wild, not the forests of Oxfordshire where she could ride in one direction and hope to find a road or a track. If Percy never re-emerged, and she headed the wrong way, she could ride for days and never reach anywhere. Nobody knew how far America stretched westwards. A nervousness took her, the wind in the grasses and trees stoking her unease.

An unseen bird hooted its shrill call, making her jump. A sharp cracking from behind the narrow cleft nearly made her scream. Probably an animal, she thought, but she put her head through to check. There was nothing in sight, and then – another crack, and a deer broke cover and ran away. She let out a sigh of relief. Then a finger tapped her shoulder, and she did scream.

'By God's truth!' Percy stood behind her, his face white. 'I hope nobody is nearby, or they will come running.'

She was back in her skin. 'Don't creep up on people like that!'

For a moment his eyes blazed, but then they softened and he nodded. 'You are right. I should have whispered.' He looked to the cleft. 'What were you looking at?'

'What?'

'Through the gap?'

'Oh.' Her heart was still pumping fast. 'Just a deer. Nothing.'

'All the same, best we wait a short while to be sure.'

She glanced at the dark opening. 'They will not just come out?'

'Not until I give the signal.'

They stood in silence, almost holding their breath. The sounds of the forest seemed amplified, each falling leaf audible as it landed on the deepening mosaic that stretched over the covered earth. After five minutes, Percy relaxed his shoulders. He returned to the hollow's other side, walking four times in front of the cramped opening, scraping his boot on a jagged rock beside it and clearing his throat seven times, using a melody of sorts. Seconds later a scrambling noise emanated from within the cave and a man's head emerged, followed by the rest of his body; stretching his arms skywards, he drew himself upright.

'That call is a little convoluted, Percy,' he said.

Mercia broke into a broad smile. The man's creased face was dirty, his grey hair speckled with a dusty brown film, but she recognised him easily enough. She walked towards him, arms outstretched.

'Colonel Dixwell.' She clapped her hands quietly together. 'I am so pleased to see you again, peculiar setting though this is.'

'Mercia Blakewood.' Dixwell's timbre was no less joyous. 'A peculiar setting indeed, but we do seem to meet in such circumstances.' He grabbed her shoulders, shaking them in gentle affection. 'Now,' he said, releasing his grasp. 'There are two gentlemen here with a great desire to meet you.'

She could not help but beam. 'I cannot think why.'

'Because you are the child of Rowland Goodridge, of course.' He leant in closer. 'But more so because I have told them of your adventures in New Amsterdam and they do love a good story.' He corrected himself. 'Although I suppose I should now say New York.' He barked the last word with a scoff; his antipathy for the Duke was obvious.

Behind him, another figure was emerging from the cave, standing very erect – a man with obvious military heritage. Then another came out, taking a little longer, betraying his more advanced years, but he too stood proudly, dusting the dirt from his worn jacket. The two men looked at Percy; he nodded, and they approached.

'Mrs Blakewood.' The elder of the two bowed. 'I cannot tell you how much pleasure this meeting gives me.'

'Nor I,' said the younger. 'To meet Rowland's daughter at last, albeit in these wilds, is a great honour.' His eyes saddened. 'I am deeply sorry for what befell him last winter.'

'Thank you.' She acknowledged the sympathy with a demure nod. 'It would have given him equal pleasure to know that you are all three still alive.'

'Allow me to introduce you to William Goffe,' said Dixwell, pointing to the younger man. 'And Edward Whalley.' He nodded towards the elder.

'The King-killers,' smiled Goffe. 'Father-in-law and son-in-law both.'

'William.' Whalley frowned a gentle admonishment. 'But in seriousness, Mrs Blakewood, we are happy to meet you.'

'How are you faring?' she asked, looking towards the opening. 'I fear there is not much of comfort in that cave.'

'Indeed not,' said Goffe. 'But the alternative is death, and with God's support we will endure it. 'Tis only for a short time, until we journey elsewhere.' He looked at Percy, who nodded once again. 'We will depart northwards soon.'

'Although there, too, we must remain in hiding.' Dixwell sighed. 'At least, these two must. I have not yet decided what course I should take. I am not sure the safe house will accommodate all three of us.' He raised an eyebrow. 'I am rather an unexpected guest.'

'We will think of something,' said Percy, setting off on another circuit of the surrounding rocks.

'You always do.'

Whalley laughed, his sallow cheeks creasing as though he were any genial old man. And yet his mirth seemed forced, holding little real delight. Mercia looked at the cave mouth, at how small it was, and felt a deep pity. Then Percy jumped past overhead, and her pity turned to shame at the apprehension she had felt when they had arrived at the hollow. He may have been quick to put the killings onto her conscience, but what he did for the regicides was a wholly selfless act. She watched him peering over the edge, ever anxious for his charges, and she realised she was looking on him with a warmth she had not noticed develop.

Whalley followed her gaze. 'He is a good man, Mrs Blakewood, but he will have to calm himself lest his humours grow unbalanced.'

'He is in danger for his life if he is discovered helping you, I fear.'

'Fortunately you are in no such danger, or I would never have agreed to this meeting.' Dixwell brought her attention back to the three men. 'If he did his job correctly, nobody will know you were ever here, and if anyone ever finds its location, we will be long gone.'

She recalled their circuitous route. 'Do not worry. He did his job well.'

Whalley chuckled. 'Shall we sit? We have found this rock here a pleasant seat.' He walked to a light grey recess that did indeed resemble a stony chair.

'Percy,' shouted Goffe. 'Sit with us.'

Percy held a finger to his lips, shaking his head.

'You see?' said Whalley, as Mercia sat beside him, Goffe dropping to

247

the space at her other side. 'But let us talk. John has told us much, but what news from England?'

They lapsed into conversation, talking of England and of New York, of the Atlantic crossings they had all endured, of the hardships, of the loss. But they spoke with good heart, and by the time half an hour had passed, the trees were strumming with the warmth of burgeoning friendship.

'And so Sir William Calde has taken a fancy to you?' said Goffe. 'The preening fool. Still, he is a good man of sorts.'

'I met him in New York, with Mercia,' said Dixwell. 'He . . . helped.'

She smiled at his hesitation. 'He is in New England now, on a survey of the colonies.'

'To ready them for the Duke's dominion, no doubt.' Goffe shook his head. 'But these people will not give in easily. They are not used to interference from England. Many are vehemently disappointed at the restoration of the King.'

'They may not have much choice.'

'Maybe not, but if men like Percy have anything to do with it, they will make it hard for the Duke.' Still standing, Dixwell rested his hands on his hips, looking down at her. 'He has told us what is happening in Meltwater. The deaths. Are you sure 'tis wise for you to remain?'

She stared at a brittle leaf on the ground, tracing the pattern of its intricate veins. 'I will not leave.'

'No.' Dixwell sighed. 'If I learnt anything of you in New Amsterdam, it is you are as stubborn and determined as your father. But if you will take my advice, you will be careful of Godsgift Brown.'

She looked up. 'You know of him?'

'No, but from what Edward says I do not think much of the man.'

Whalley nodded. 'He has visited New Haven many a time. Our host there, whose name I will not divulge, spoke ill of him. There is something in his past, something of violence.'

'There is violence in all of us,' mused Goffe.

Whalley swivelled on the rock, looking at his son-in-law across her head. 'Yes, but this was different, if you remember. This was feared.'

'In what way?' she pressed.

'Our host would not say. Maybe he did not know. But – just be cautious. His reputation is that of a belligerent man.'

She nodded thoughtfully. 'I do not suppose you know aught of the other Meltwater townsfolk? What of Richard Thorpe? Your enemy, it seems.'

'Ah, Mr Thorpe.' Goffe barked a scornful laugh. 'If he knew we were here, he would scour the forests to find us if it took him all year.'

'He works for a man in Springfield,' said Whalley. 'Not far from here, over the border into Massachusetts Bay land. John Pynchon, a town elder, and obsessed with hunting us down. He has agents throughout New England.' He smiled. 'We call them our friends, for the wit of it. Thorpe is one of his men, but an especially ambitious one, particularly since he lost his wife. We are told that when he heard of the Duke's takeover of New York he rode straight there to offer his services.'

Mercia glanced up at Dixwell. 'He caught us on the way from Hartford.'

'John told us.' Goffe's lips curved in smug satisfaction. 'A narrow escape, and he has you to thank for it.'

'Rather, thank Clemency Carter.' She sighed. 'She was part of the group that helped you. Did she ever say anything that might help me uncover her murderer?'

A slight look passed between Whalley and Goffe. She turned from one to the other, trying to read their meaning.

'In truth,' said Goffe, 'we had never heard of her until Percy told us of her death when he brought us here.' His shoulders shrugged a little, as if in embarrassment. 'It is deemed safer that not everyone in the group should know everyone else. Not even us.'

'I understand.' She must have appeared despondent, for Dixwell leant down to squeeze her hand.

'Do not be sorrowful,' he said. 'You will avenge Clemency's death, as you avenged your father's. Justice is in your blood, and it will be served.'

'You are one of us,' smiled Goffe. 'Despite everything, there is a hope that sustains you. Hope is precious, Mercia Blakewood. Be mindful always of that.'

Chapter Twenty-Three

She felt like she was being watched. She knew she was on alert: despite Winthrop's conviction that the murders had been planned beforehand, she could not help but worry that the target might next fall on her. As she looked from the window of the cottage, she felt as though someone was observing from the street, but she could see no peripheral movement, no curious shadows to deepen the dark.

Nathan was out, invited to the tavern by Percy; he had been surprised to be asked, but Mercia was glad, wanting them to get along. Still, he had insisted that Nicholas sit at home with her, and she was glad for his presence, even if he was asleep in a chair by the fireplace, his steady breaths reassuring as he performed an unconscious balancing trick keeping himself upright on the tiny seat.

She listened to the popping of the wood as it burnt, growing drowsy with the headiness of the smoke. There was something about the crackling of a fire, its warmth, that encouraged sleep. She wished she were back in Halescott before a hearty fire, reading a volume of Donne's poetry or some such, a mug of mint whey at her side. But the welcome image vanished as she looked again into the darkness, wondering whether she was losing her mind.

Leaning against the wall, she tried to dispel the image of whatever spectre could be out there, thinking instead of Goffe's words about hope, but the crackling of the fire teased at her weariness, and she felt her eyelids drooping, her body crying out for rest. She jerked herself alert, but mere seconds passed before she slumped again on the wall, the eyelids making their inevitable descent.

She entered that state between consciousness and sleep, neither one nor the other, where reality was dream, and dream reality, and her worry that someone was watching led Clemency to her window, the brown curls of her hair vibrant beneath her red hood, and this Clemency, an accusing Clemency, stood there baleful, demanding to know what Mercia had done, why she still could not find her peace. And guilty, again, Mercia pulled herself round, feeling the roughness of the wall on her cheek, the gentle burn of the fire on her back, and then she gasped, as Clemency morphed into Sooleawa, the Indian woman up against the window looking in.

'Do not worry,' Sooleawa mouthed, a finger to her lips. 'I have come to speak with you.'

Now fully alert, Mercia looked further out to see if Sooleawa were alone, but she remarked no one – not that it much consoled her, for she had not seen Sooleawa until she was right before her eyes. She walked to the door and eased it open; for some maternal reason, she did not want to wake Nicholas.

'May I come in?' asked Sooleawa. 'I do not want anyone to see that I am here.'

She looked over Sooleawa's shoulder into the dim evening light. 'Is anyone with you?'

Sooleawa shook her head. 'Please?'

She hesitated only briefly before standing aside. As Sooleawa entered, she looked at Nicholas sleeping.

'Where is the other man – Nathan?'

'He will be back soon.' Mercia frowned. 'How did you know his name?'

252

'I know most of what goes on in this town. It is not difficult.'

She waited, but Sooleawa merely stood in the middle of the room. 'Forgive me,' she said at last, 'but why are you here?'

Sooleawa glanced again at Nicholas. 'Just you.'

'I do not think I should—'

'It is about Clemency.'

Mercia shuddered, as though the dreamlike apparition of Clemency had taken physical presence in the form of Sooleawa, arrived with news. 'Very well,' she said. 'I will wake him.'

Sooleawa folded her arms. 'He is awake. I can tell from the way he breathes.'

A smile spread over Nicholas's lips as he opened his eyes. 'I have been awake the whole time.'

'I thought you were sleeping?' said Mercia.

'And let Nathan accuse me of negligence? I've been pretending, so you could think.' He stretched his arms and stood. 'I know your habits well enough by now.'

'So it would seem.'

He drew a knife. 'I have been ready to use this the whole time.'

Sooleawa did not seem interested in the blade. 'Would you leave us?'

'Of course not.'

She turned to depart. 'Then I will leave instead.'

'Wait,' said Mercia. 'Nicholas, go upstairs.' She raised a questioning eyebrow at Sooleawa, who nodded her assent.

He hesitated. 'I think it would be better if—'

'There is no danger,' said Sooleawa. 'Why would I wish to harm her?'

'By the Lord, I cannot think.' He jiggled his head. 'Maybe because last time you dragged her into the woods.'

'She was not hurt.'

'Nicholas, go upstairs,' repeated Mercia. 'If I need you I will call.'

He threw Sooleawa a look. 'Make sure you do.'

When the stairs had finished their creaking, Sooleawa seemed to relax.

'Men,' she said. 'They think we women need their protection at all times. As if the world would end otherwise.'

'They have their uses.'

'At times.' She closed her eyes. 'Now I would speak with you. The *sachem* is impatient for news. He knows you visited Hartford this week. Has powwow Winthrop been able to help?'

Mercia indicated the vacated chair. 'Have you been following me?'

Sooleawa remained standing. 'No.'

'Has anyone else?'

She shrugged. 'The *sachem* must be sure you are acting as you promised.'

'I see.' She did not much like the idea. 'Why do you call Winthrop powwow?'

Sooleawa twisted the thick cord of shells adorning her slender neck. 'Because he is a medicine man like our own. His medicines may be different, and he chooses to remain silent and let others apply them rather than invoke the spirits in dance, but a powwow he is, nonetheless.'

Again, she indicated the chair. 'Would you sit?'

This time Sooleawa accepted. 'Thank you. I would welcome the warmth. 'Tis a cold night outside.'

Mercia pulled up a less comfortable stool; its one leg was longer than the rest, but a slight crack in the floor was a useful solution. 'Do you not feel the cold more because of your bare skin?'

Sooleawa leant back into the chair. 'You English are always trying to get us to wear more clothing, but we are plenty warm. We wear grease in place of your wool. Yet for some reason our appearance seems to offend those who are new to us. The markings we paint on our bodies.'

'We are not used to it, that is all.'

'As we are not used to your heavy clothes.'

Mercia smiled. 'They can be cumbersome.' She held up the pleats of her dress, exposing the thin petticoat beneath the slit at the front. A faint aroma of repeated use wafted upwards; she reminded herself to wash what she could tomorrow. 'Try riding a horse in this.'

'I never understood your need to wear wool. It is not healthy, with the lice.'

'That depends.' Mercia let her dress drop, drawing up to the warmth of the fire. 'What do you wish to say about Clemency?'

Sooleawa looked into the flames, very much as Mercia often did herself. 'She was my friend.'

The thoughtful eyes seemed genuine. 'So you have said before.'

'And Hopewell.' She looked directly at her. 'These killings sadden me. They anger me.'

'They anger me also.'

Now it was Sooleawa's turn to study her companion; Mercia felt a tingling as she endured the searching look. When Sooleawa finally spoke, she was succinct.

'I believe they do.'

The flames played out their orange dance across her darkened cheek. For a moment there was silence, as the two women held each other's gaze. And then simultaneously they nodded, as if in approval of the other.

'Was Clemency happy before her end?' Sooleawa asked.

It was an unexpected question. 'She seemed to be.'

'She always was a happy person, with me.' She tugged at the deerskin covering her chest. 'She did not take her own life. But I fear she remains with us. Can you not see her?'

'Yes.' Startled, Mercia leant in. 'I can.'

Sooleawa nodded. 'It is as I thought. You are the last person Clemency was close with. She calls upon you to release her spirit, so she can travel to the south-west.'

'The south-west?'

'The place where we came from, where we return to, is in the south-west. We know nothing of it, other than we will go there once this life is done. And in the meantime we live here, not concerned with what comes next.'

'You do not believe in heaven?'

'The heaven of your God?' Sooleawa edged closer to the fire, her several wampum bracelets jangling against each other. 'There are those of us in this land who believe in that. But not here, despite the efforts of your tribe.'

'I have found there are times when there is much comfort in God.'

Sooleawa shook her head. 'Your God is a warrior, skilled in death and destruction. I do not wish to follow such a God.'

'And yet He is love, and charity. In Him you can find peace.'

'Not for us.' Sooleawa's voice crackled like the logs in the fire. 'When the Englishman first came to live with us, so our elders say, he brought the wrath of his God on us through a terrible disease. A plague, you call it. Thousands of us were killed. And then those who were not slaughtered by this demon were soon killed in war, or else through the greed of your people. We have been forced out of our own lands.' She looked up. 'I tell you, Mercia, there are young men in the tribes who are ready to follow a leader when he comes and says it is time to take it all back.' She was becoming impassioned. 'You are a kind woman. I do not suggest you stay in America. There will be much blood soon.' She narrowed her eyes. 'Some men are already marked.'

The speech had made Mercia uncomfortable. 'Some men here?'

'Those who kill our brothers without reason, who rape our sisters and our mothers, who abandon us when they say they are friend.' Her eyes sparkled in the firelight, as menacing an expression as any Mercia had seen. 'Have you found out yet who killed our powwow, our boy, our friends?'

The expectation weighed heavy. 'I am afraid not yet.'

'Then I have nothing to tell the *sachem*.'

She hesitated. 'There may be another murder.'

'Why do you say that?'

'The hide you gave me. When put with the others, it suggests there is more to come. We hope to catch him before he does this, and then you will know.'

256

A shadow passed Sooleawa's face. 'And in the meantime my tribe grows restless. The *sachem* is counting on you to help him keep peace.'

'Sooleawa, I am doing what I can.'

'I know.' Her proud cheeks taut, Sooleawa's eyes softened as she reached to grasp Mercia's hand, rattling the wampum bracelets. 'But the men will not listen. Not mine, not yours.'

She looked down at her captured wrist, Sooleawa's physical touch birthing an unexpected complicity. 'You speak with such pride, Sooleawa, such conviction. When you talked of brothers just then, of abandonment . . . it sounded like there was something . . . personal.'

Sooleawa looked into her eyes, the same ethereal understanding passing between them. 'Because you have something – personal – too?'

Mercia closed her eyes, breaking the contact, for Sooleawa was right, that her unusually brusque interest stemmed from her own past, from something she never discussed. But here, before the shared fire, with this strange woman – no, just with this woman – she felt able to broach the painful memory, somehow.

'My brother,' she said at last. 'He was killed.'

Sooleawa's face stayed impassive. 'I am sorry for it.'

'My mother could not cope. Now she lives inside her head, in the past. My father – he too was murdered, in the end.'

'Then it is true.' Sooleawa looked through the window, staring into some unknown past. 'We have both known loss.'

Mercia waited for her to say more, but she remained silent, unready to talk further, or unwilling. Yet the complicity did not dim, even as the light outside was fading away.

'You speak as if you already knew these things about me.'

'No. But I can see them in the fervour of your eyes, in your need to find this killer. You think there will be some form of vengeance in it, some form of sense to be made of what has happened in your life.' She tilted her head. 'I understand.'

Mercia looked at her, trying to divine her thoughts. 'I do not know.

But I will see this through until the end. The man who killed Clemency, your powwow – you can tell your *sachem* I will find him.'

Sooleawa released her hand. 'I know you will. And now I must go.' She rose to her feet. 'Thank you for the use of your fire.'

Mercia followed her to the door. 'You have not told me what you wanted to say about Clemency.'

'But I have.' Sooleawa rested her hand on the wood. 'I have told you that Clemency walks with you, giving you strength from the happiness with which she lived this life. You are not alone, woman from across the waters, even though sometimes you must feel it. Clemency is with you. I am sure of it.'

Mercia stood in the cottage garden the next morning, a mug of hot milk in her hand. For all the reassurances, Sooleawa's visit had disturbed her, and she was reflecting with uncertainty on their forthright conversation. Sooleawa's convictions ran deep, her words about heaven unsettling, and she realised, inhaling the steam, how much she needed convictions from her own faith. Perhaps that could sustain her, as much as Goffe's hope. Perhaps, she thought, they were one and the same thing.

It was idyllic where she walked – the river, its drop from the waterfall done, racing through a narrow channel in a tree-bordered glade, turning the wheel of the sawmill that nestled on its bank. The gurgling of the water, the groaning of the wheel, the fresh scent of the nearby pines – all this infused her as she stood outside the mill, breathing in the autumnal air. She knocked once and pushed open the creaking door. Inside, the mill was flooded with sunlight, the sundered rays bursting through the several windows in its wooden walls.

'Hello,' she called, her voice strange in the open space. 'Kit?'

At the far end, the sawyer was leaning over a workbench, whittling away with some sort of tool.

'Hello?' she called louder.

'Come in,' he shouted, not looking up.

258

She ambled to the bench, passing the mechanism of the wheel to her left, carved levers and poles twisting their harmonious dance. A large saw jutted into the mill, the shavings of countless labours piled up on the earth beneath. The teeth were sharp, a fearsome counterpart to the tranquillity of the setting outside.

'Good morning, Kit.' Now upon him, she could see he was working at a table leg with a simple plane. Near at hand, a vast pile of shaved-down lumber sat waiting to be collected; to construct a new house, or new barn, perhaps.

'Good morning, Mrs Blakewood.' His black hair was loose, falling over his shoulders, but the concentration in his eyes was absolute.

'I am sorry to disturb you. I will wait for you to finish.'

She watched as he smoothed down the leg with the plane; to her it seemed perfect already, but he worked a few strokes more before setting down his tool and casting an eye over his handiwork.

'There.' He broke into a smile. 'Done.'

'I have not much seen you smile since I arrived,' said Mercia. 'You must enjoy your work.'

He shook out his hands, wiping away the sawdust, although it fair covered his bare forearms and rolled-up sleeves.

'Very much.' He leant against the bench. 'I was never a sawyer until I came here. A carpenter. But I needed something to do, something with my hands, and the town needed this.' He gestured at the mill. 'So I taught myself, and found the Lord had made me good at it. It eases the labour of the townsmen who would otherwise need to fashion wood for themselves.'

The eager look on his face warmed her. 'Amery said you start early. I hope you do not mind.'

'Not at all.' He took a drink from a beaker at his side. 'I am glad of the interruption.' He held up his cup. 'Would you like some?'

'I am not thirsty, thank you. I was hoping we could talk a little?'

'By all means. About . . . our gathering the other night?'

259

Her smile faded. 'Partly that. Partly to talk. Although I have been wondering – you are recently arrived from England. Perhaps you have a clearer eye on your fellow townsfolk than those who have been here all their lives?'

He looked at her, his gaze intense. 'I am from here now, Mrs Blakewood. I was from England, but that was before.'

She inclined her head. 'Do you not miss it?'

'No. And I do not wish to go back.'

'You do not miss any family?'

He played with the cord around his neck. 'As I say, I do not wish to return. Can we talk of something else?'

'Forgive me.' She studied his neck, wondering what it was that he kept hidden against his chest. But she gave that up for now. 'What do you think, then, of what is happening to Meltwater?' She hesitated. 'You talked at the meeting of trusting to God.'

He shrugged. 'I think either God has some plan, or else His will is being abused in some way. Is it for us to question that?'

She nodded. 'You have a strong faith, Kit.'

He took up the plane, dunking it into a pail of water. 'When I crossed the ocean, I was lost. Used, like this tool.' He swivelled the plane in the water and pulled it out, clean. 'But God saved me and brought me here. If that is faith, then yes, I have it.' He looked at her. 'You do not?'

'I believe in God, as I believe there are things we cannot hope to understand. But I think, perhaps, that He would want us to try to understand what we can. At least that is what my father always taught.'

He rubbed some of the sawdust from his arms. 'And I say we are mortal men here, men and women. It is not our role to understand, not everything, but to have trust in how life will unfold.'

Mercia pondered his words. 'Your friend Amery might disagree, perhaps even the governor. They think as alchemists, that God has merely hidden His secrets, waiting until the time when men are worthy enough to discover them.'

Kit smiled, his chest rising as he folded his arms across his stained shirt. 'But surely, Mrs Blakewood, only those among us who have most faith will ever be worthy enough, and yet those are the same people who do not need these truths.' His face took on an animated sharpness. 'Standfast, Renatus, many of the godly – myself – we believe the Second Coming is near. When Christ returns, He will know who has been most faithful.' He nodded back at the bench. 'I am but a sawyer, a shaper of wood, not a governor or an alchemist. But I serve, as do we all, or as we should.'

'I too pray to God. I ask Him for answers, but on this, none come.' She looked down. 'I think God guides me, but cannot provide all we seek.'

He took up his mug. 'You ask me what I think of these killings. Who has done them.' He sniffed. 'Well, then. If God is truly guiding you, then the answer must be here, in view of all the town. And yet still we do not know.'

'Then what should we do? You have no suspicions? No thoughts yourself?'

He shook his head. 'I wish to assist you, Mrs Blakewood, but on this I am no help.' He opened out his palms. ''Tis my body that is of use, not my mind. As for the man, well. Not even Percy, who has lived here his whole life, seems to know. Clearly there are men here who have the temperament for violence. But murder?'

She thought of the Indian farmhand and felt a sadness. 'Your constable proved his aptitude well enough last week.'

Kit nodded. 'But his hatred of the Indians makes him a simple man, a man of quick passions. He is not a thinker, or a writer of mischievous codes.'

She sighed. 'You are sure you saw nothing before Hopewell's death?' She held up a hand. 'I know I have asked before, but asking seems the only thing I can do.'

He looked on her with indulgence. 'Truly, all I can say is I was here, in the sawmill. When I saw all the torches I came running, and that is all.'

'At least you are talking with me. Most people are keen to avoid any conversation. Not even Percy can encourage them to help.'

'But they do think, Mrs Blakewood. And they have faith, or most of them do, when they are not taken by a moment of weakness.' He rinsed his hands in the pail of water, shaking the drops onto the floor. 'It is said even the weakest can be strong when the moment demands it, but I think the strength of our faith will sustain us best. Surely not even a killer can know for certain why he acts.' He smiled. 'But I know we will find out in the end, because we have faith. It is there at the meeting house every Sunday, guiding us, nurturing us, making the land ready for our Lord. And when we do find out, then shall we understand.' He looked at her. 'Is that not really why you came here today? For guidance from one you know believes, and for whom his belief is enough?'

'Perhaps.' She looked at his ardent face, unsurprised he had seen through her, and knowing what he said was right, just as Sooleawa had been right, in her way. 'I envy you your certainty, Kit. But I shall pray, as I know you shall, and let us ask that this ends soon.'

She prayed in her bedroom that night before bed; she spoke to her father too, or else to his spirit. But answers were still elusive. As she eased herself under the itchy blanket, she thought back on her talks with Sooleawa and Kit. One spoke of a presence that needed release; the other of God and faith, trusting to a greater power. But in the end, neither satisfied Mercia, for all she believed in God herself, for all she saw Clemency walking in the streets. Surely she had the aptitude to work this out. Surely she, a mortal woman, could have that gift.

Her mind drifted from such abstract thought, focusing on events. She found it hard to believe that Sooleawa had come into Meltwater purely to offer encouragement. But life here was strange, and she chose to accept it. It was stranger, she thought, that the *sachem* seemed ready to believe her while John Lavington, her own countryman of a sort, was not. Or was the magistrate, too, playing games?

Laying down her head, she closed her eyes, wondering if Sooleawa was right, that Clemency was trapped, waiting to leave for the south-west. She had seen her face at the cottage window last night, she was sure of it. But now, when she opened her eyes in the tiny room, all she could she was the dark.

Chapter Twenty-Four

Mid October, the leaves a cacophony of colour, the river clogging with the debris of autumn. To the sound of a patchwork band formed of three of the townsfolk – Victory on the pipes, Remembrance on the whistle, Seaborn's wife, Charity, on the fiddle – a procession of villagers was ferrying fresh produce to the field on the west side of town, a thrown-together assemblage of blankets covering a wooden frame, beneath which the pile of bounty steadily grew.

Mercia sat on a green quilt on the lightly damp grass, watching the scene that to her seemed bizarre – bizarre yet understandable, as Nathan said resting alongside, for it was natural that the townsfolk should want normality to prevail. Accordingly, kneeling at her other side, Nicholas passed her an apple; she took a bite, staring at Remembrance whose eyes flitted over at their elm-shaded spot from time to time.

'She keeps looking at you,' she said.

'Who?' said Nathan.

'That Remembrance.'

'I don't think so.' He laid a gentle hand on her shoulder; normally, she might have shrugged it off in public, but in front of this particular band she allowed him to leave it in place. To her right, she noticed Nicholas smile.

'What is the matter with you?' she asked curtly.

'Oh, nothing,' he replied. 'Just – you know – enjoying the weather.'

It was a fine afternoon now, although the light was beginning to dim; the morning had brought a heavy shower, but the clouds had cleared before noon and the lowering New England sun was casting a shimmering yellow glaze over the town. Harvest was earlier this year, so Percy said, the soil producing sooner than normal, and his father had brought forward the festival in an effort to keep the villagers' minds off recent events. Encouraged by Percy, he had even gone further, agreeing to import a festival from England: in two weeks' time the town would celebrate Guy Fawkes Night, hoping to release tension in the most crowd-pleasing way, a festival that attacked the hated Catholics, and by definition the Catholic Duke of York, whose soldiers were now spreading through his new territory to the west.

Looking across at the industry of people, Mercia thought all did look as it should. Nobody seemed overtly worried, or mournful, nobody was shirking their duty, or protesting the futility of the day. And yet beneath it all, she could discern an undercurrent of anxiety: one too many corn slipped from the top of the pile; the band missed one too many notes; one too many children glanced furtively across before their harried parents called them back. The town knew things were not right, that seemed certain, but they were determined to make it appear as if they were.

She had given up trying to unravel the codes. After long days of staring at their confusion, she had begun to concede that Nicholas might be right, that they were deliberately obtuse, designed to throw anyone who should bother to investigate while the murderer prepared for his next kill. A few days after her conversations with Sooleawa and Kit, Winthrop had written that he too was at a loss. Sitting under the tree, she let the music drift over her, thinking how Clemency would have listened the year before, and wondering if she was still here, listening today, until Mercia was able to help her to where she belonged.

Superstitious idiocy. She chided herself for even thinking such things. Her father would have been appalled.

And yet . . .

The band stopped their playing, earning subdued applause. Setting down her fiddle, Remembrance ambled over towards Mercia's group.

Her thin shadow fell on Nathan. 'May I join you?' she asked.

'Of course.' He moved up to make room at the edge of the quilt. 'That was wonderful playing.'

'I'm not so good,' she protested. 'But I try.'

Mercia forced a smile, in little mood for the intrusion. Over the past days, Nathan had been spending more and more time with the young woman, or so it had seemed to her. But then the gentle breeze sweeping over them was interrupted by a yet more unwelcome invader.

'Mrs Blakewood,' said Richard Thorpe, although he was looking at Remembrance, his expression one of glowering disdain. 'I would speak with you.'

Remembrance returned his derisory look. 'Nathan, I think instead I will help with the harvest.' She nodded to Mercia. 'Mrs Blakewood.' With a scowl at Thorpe, she walked away.

'Silly girl.' Thorpe shifted his gaze to Nathan. 'Now you too, and your man.'

Nathan scoffed. 'I am going nowhere.'

He folded his arms, once again in his brown sash. 'As the King's appointed servant here, I have a message for Mrs Blakewood I would like to deliver alone.'

'Do not worry, Nat,' she said. 'I will hear what he has to say.'

Nathan looked him in the eye, but the physician did not flinch. He pulled himself slowly to his feet, jerking his head at Nicholas to follow. As they disappeared across the field, Mercia patted the quilt beside her.

'Would you join me, Mr Thorpe?'

'I prefer to stand.' Thorpe's patronising eyes peered down, their corners creasing, suppressing what emotion she could only guess. Contempt, most like.

She smiled. 'You do not like me.'

'That is beside the point.'

'But it is true.'

He remained impassive. 'I am to deliver you this.'

He reached into his jacket, his forearm catching on the black material just enough that a shining knife was exposed in his belt. He took such time feeling in his pockets that she wondered if he had intended her to see it. Then he withdrew his hand, holding out an envelope for her to take, the folds of his jacket sliding back over the menacing blade.

She turned her attention to the envelope. 'What is this?'

'It is a letter, naturally.' He waggled it gently. 'For you.'

'From whom?'

'If you read it, you will know. A rider brought it this morning, care of myself.'

'You have waited long enough to deliver it, then.' She reached up, but Thorpe held the envelope out of reach. 'If it is for me, Mr Thorpe, I should be obliged if you could pass it down.'

He stayed his hand. 'I know you are helping Percy Lavington.'

'Pardon me?'

'I have seen the two of you together. I have seen you go into the woods.'

'Really, Mr Thorpe. What Percy and I do in the woods is not your affair.'

He bent his face lower. 'You and Keyte are clearly sympathisers. I know why you are here. And know this. I will not allow such corruption in this town. I will root out your friends ere long.'

'I do not know what you mean.'

'Of course not.' He thrust out the envelope. 'Take it. I cannot think why he is writing to you, but I have been asked to deliver it, and so here it is.'

Not taking her eyes from his, she gripped the white envelope between finger and thumb, tugging it from his grasp. She held his stare until he broke off and marched through the palisade gate. Moments later, Nathan reappeared at her side.

'That was quick,' she said.

'I was watching.'

'Close enough to hear?'

'No. But I can tell his words were not welcome. I can feel the annoyance steaming off you.'

She sighed. 'He came to give me this. This, and a warning.'

She looked down at the envelope, the inverse side, sealed with a red lump of wax. Her heart sank as she recognised the crest. She turned it over to read the direction on the front:

For the attention of Mrs Mercia Blakewood, care of Mr Richard Thorpe, Meltwater, Connecticut. To be opened by Mrs Blakewood solely, on strict order of the King's commissioners.

She checked the envelope for tampering, but it appeared to be intact. 'Recognise the handwriting?'

Nathan peered down, studying the cursive script. 'I should say so. It is from our old friend.'

She tore open the envelope to pull out a thick piece of paper. Unfolding the crinkled leaf, she examined the signature. 'Oh yes. It is from him all right.'

'Sir William Calde. What does he want?' He scratched at the scar under his chin. 'I thought he was busy subduing the colonists or some such nonsense.'

She skimmed the large handwriting. 'It seems he wants nothing. He sends his wishes and asks how I am.'

Nathan frowned. 'That is all?'

'Just – he is returning to New York in a month by way of Hartford.'

She glanced at the letterhead. 'This is dated two weeks ago, in Boston, so we can expect him in the area in another two.' She pursed her lips. 'I wonder. Could he be useful here?'

'Sir William? How?'

She considered. 'I do not know.'

'That's helpful. But . . . it could be a goal.'

'What do you mean?'

He crouched, resting a hand on her knee. 'We have been here over a month now, Mercia. Look around you. Life is going on as best it can. We have not found the killer, or deciphered those messages. And it is not really our concern.' He ventured a smile. 'Perhaps it is time to return to New York, try to get the last ship home before winter sets in. As it is, the crossing may be arduous already. We know Sir William does not intend to remain in America. Why not accompany him when he passes through?' He looked at her, a mixture of pleading and kindness in his eyes. 'You have tried very hard, Mercia. There is no shame in letting go. Your manor house is waiting.'

She pulled at a loose thread in the quilt. 'We do not know that.'

'You were as good as told so after the Oxford Section business.' He hesitated. 'Besides, if you do not return soon, then your uncle may do so before you and try to stake a counter claim with the King.'

'He would not dare.'

'You know he would. We do not know how his condition fares. He may have improved sufficiently well to travel. And . . . Daniel needs his mother.'

She twisted harder at the thread. 'I am well aware of what Daniel needs. But he also needs a mother who can show him perseverance and justice. And . . . I see her all the time, Nathan. I see her when I close my eyes, when a woman from the village walks by me. I see her everywhere. I do not think I can find peace until she does.'

Nathan's hand tensed. 'At the expense of your own house? Your own son?'

269

'There is something . . . I cannot just let this go. Can you not understand that?'

'And me?' He got to his feet. 'If I ask you outright to leave?'

'I told you. I cannot.'

His whole body seemed to harden. 'You have to face it, Mercia. This may not be for you to solve. And I can be patient only so long.'

'What does that mean?'

'Nothing. Just that, if we have any chance of a future together, you need to decide what is truly important.'

Her stomach iced over. 'I know what is important. But so is this.'

'It is . . . taking you over. I worry for your soul.'

'My soul?' She scoffed. 'You sound like a preacher.'

He growled, a strange animal sound she did not like. 'Mercia, if you want to talk, come and find me. I am going to help with the festival.'

She watched him walk away. 'If you like it here so much, why do you want to leave?'

He stopped, turning to face her. 'I want you to leave. I want to leave with you. Can you understand that?'

She did not reply, wrenching the troublesome thread clean out of the quilt. She threw it in the air and it caught on the breeze, drifting to the earth as he vanished into the crowd, leaving her sad and alone.

Not alone. By the time the wisps of a cloud in the nonchalant sky had separated and reformed, Nicholas returned to sit beside her. She was glad of his company, their relationship so much more straightforward than hers and Nathan's. When she told him to do something, he did it; when she rejected his advice, he was not angry. She thought of a sudden of that night in New York, when she and Nathan had been trapped in the fort, when she had wondered whether she preferred their relationship the way it had been, the way of friends. She wondered now whether she had been right to be cautious. But then she remembered Nicholas, and she looked at him and forced a smile.

He smiled back, and she knew he had seen her and Nathan argue. She held her breath, waiting for him to suggest in his tentative way that Nathan was worth arguing with. But he did not.

''Tis such a lovely day,' was all he said.

She could have hugged him – by God, she needed the warmth of a friend's touch right now – but she did not.

'It is.' She took a deep breath, shaking her head to brush away her angst. She knew Nathan was probably right, but she could not let herself admit it. Not yet.

'Look what Thorpe brought me,' she said, tapping the letter beside her.

He listened as she related its contents. 'So Sir William's coming back. I suppose he's not a bad man, for one of them.'

'I just wish he did not—'

'Want to ravish you?' Nicholas looked skywards. 'Sorry. That was uncouth.'

She let out a startled laugh. 'You said that to shock me from my thoughts.'

'Did I?' His stubbled cheeks twitched, radiating the afternoon's warmth. 'Well, then. What now?'

'You are so . . . vexing.' She shook her head, suppressing her own smile. 'In honesty, I do not know. Perhaps there will come a time when—'

She trailed off as she caught sight of Percy running in their direction, leaping Fearing Davison who was hunched over an immense sack of some vegetable or other, dragging the heavy produce across the ground as though it were merely a bunch of flowers.

'There you are,' Percy cried, arresting his speed with an outstretched hand against the elm tree. In his other he was holding a black-rimmed parchment. In contrast his face was ashen white.

She felt a foreboding fear. 'What is it?'

'This.' He cast down the parchment. 'I just found this.'

She looked at it and gasped. A sharp pain overcame her, so intense she felt as if her whole body were being clawed at by demons:

PWKTZWKAOCMEV ∩∩

'No,' she said. 'Please – no.' A tear of panic came to her eye.

Nicholas snatched up the parchment. 'Hell's teeth.'

'Another code,' stammered Percy. 'A new one.'

Mercia stared listlessly forward. 'Someone has been murdered.' The festival, the people, all faded. Death stalked the meadow, taunting her failure.

'Perhaps not. I only found this, not a body.'

She closed her eyes in prayer. 'Lord, please let no one else have died.'

Nicholas scrambled to his feet. 'We have to search the town.'

His assertive words roused her from her depression. 'You are right. We have to account for everybody.' She pulled herself up. 'Percy, where did you find it?'

'Outside my house, in amongst a heap of corn I was to bring to the festival.' He looked about him as if in a daze. 'It was meant for me to find. No one else could have – my God! He is marking me!'

Nicholas stood in front of him, scanning the area for threats. Mercia placed herself at his other side, thinking quickly.

'If it is you, we will keep you safe. But he may just have wanted you to be the one to find it.' She looked over at the milling crowd, searching for Nathan, but he was not among them; she noticed there was no sign of Remembrance either. She turned back to Percy. 'We have to get the entire town out. You will be safe in their number. And we have to tell them they are in danger. The time for secrecy is over.'

Percy nodded.

'I cannot do that. They will not listen to me. But they will to you. We will call them out to the festival, and you can speak to them.' She gestured to Nicholas. 'Go with him. Make sure he is safe. I will look for Nathan.'

'Get Amery to help,' said Percy, collecting himself. 'He will be in the schoolhouse.'

She nodded, watching Nicholas lead Percy towards the crowd in the field before setting off herself, the need for action spurring her on. Now she had overcome her momentary gloom, her head felt clear and sharp for the first time in days. She hurried through the gate, her senses alert, telling everyone she passed that something was about to start at the festival, hoping that at least some of them would follow her advice.

She rounded the meeting house, pulling up short. John Lavington was chiding his manservant, wagging his finger even as he surveyed the activities of the townspeople carrying still more produce to the meadow.

'Please,' she urged, Lavington's man looking grateful for the interruption. 'You need to go to the festival. Percy has important news he wishes to tell you all.'

Lavington sighed, but she gave him no time to respond, and she continued north towards the nearby schoolhouse. Outside the low stone building, Amery was pulling shut the door, an overflowing satchel thrown across his shoulder.

He turned around and jumped. 'Oh.' He laughed, a hand on his chest. 'You startled me, Mrs Blakewood. Are you not at the festival?'

Quickly, she explained what had happened, how Percy had sent her to enlist his help. As she spoke, his eyes began to blink, his fingers gripping the cut of his bag.

'I knew this would happen,' he murmured. Then he looked up. 'But you are right. It is time to speak. We should have done so already.'

'Forget all that.' She beckoned him follow her from the schoolhouse. 'Let us act now.'

Now she had Amery at her side, it was easier to cajole people to the festival field, and the streets soon grew deserted. They made a final sweep of the four roads, finishing again at the meeting house, Lavington now disappeared from view.

'Still no sign of the constable,' she mused as they returned to the western gate, the sight of Clemency's cottage for once drawing no emotion. 'Or Standfast, for that matter. But perhaps they have gone to the field by now.'

'Standfast?' Amery stroked the wrinkling tops of the parchments stuffed into his satchel. 'He passed the schoolhouse earlier. I have not seen him since.'

Mercia paused outside the gate, looking across at the field where the multitude was now milling in groups, each absorbed in its own discussions. At the far end of the field, Percy was staring at the ground, Nicholas behind him, as if composing himself. In the midst of all, Lavington was talking with Thorpe and Humility, the grand cut of his cloak standing out against the simplicity of the townsfolk's general attire.

'No, I cannot see Standfast,' she said. 'Or Nathan. We should find them.'

They ducked back inside the palisade, separating at the meeting house where Mercia headed south and Amery north. Moments later she heard running behind her and her heartbeat quickened. She turned her head, ready to leap inside the smithy to snatch a heavy tool, but it was only Amery come back.

'I just saw Nathan, standing in the northern gate,' he said. 'You go that way and I will look down here.'

She nodded, returning past the meeting house to catch sight of Nathan, now framed in the gate, but he was not alone. Remembrance was leaning against the palisade beside him, laughing at something he had said. She could have sworn she had seen her in the festival field, but with everyone in front of each other it was difficult to be sure who was who.

She tapped Nathan's arm. 'You have to come. Percy has found another code.'

274

The smile on his lips vanished. 'By the Lord. Who?'

'Nobody. At least, nobody yet.'

His eyes widened. 'Then he could still strike?'

She looked through the gate; at the meadow's edge, a deer darted from the trees, disturbing a flock of birds that took umbrageous flight. 'I fear so.'

'Jesus, Mercia.' Nathan's hand reached down to his side. 'I will make sure you are safe. Both of you.'

'Never mind that. Have you seen Standfast or the constable? We cannot find them anywhere.'

'I have,' answered Remembrance, turned as white as Percy. 'I saw Standfast on that fallen tree by the wood. Only five minutes ago. I was walking round the palisade to fetch some balls of twine. He seemed restless, fiddling with his hands all the time.'

'Restless?' Her eyes darted about. 'Nat, everyone is gathering at the field. We had better walk Remembrance there and then go after him, fast.'

He nodded, gesturing to Remembrance to walk ahead. Once she was safely through the western gate, they doubled back to the other side of town. They were now quite alone in the abandoned streets.

'I am sorry,' he said, matching her speed. 'I should not have left you.'

She quickened her pace. 'Nathan, what about Standfast? If he is acting strangely, and Percy has found a new code . . .'

'By God's truth!' He looked at her. 'You don't think . . . ?'

She halted at the eastern gate. Sure enough, Standfast was near the fallen trunk, but he was no longer seated. He was standing at the edge of the forest, his hand covering the mole on his neck, pacing up and down as though thinking.

'What is he doing?' she whispered.

'I don't know, but—what is that?'

'What?'

He pointed to Standfast's left. 'That movement, there.'

Seemingly oblivious, Standfast stopped his pacing, before making up his mind and disappearing into the forest.

And then a second figure emerged from an unseen hiding place, following him into the wood.

Chapter Twenty-Five

Mercia put her hand to her mouth. Even at a distance, she could tell the figure following Standfast was not much clothed.

'That was Sooleawa! I thought she would have shunned the festival. What is she doing here?'

Her whirling mind assembled the fractured pieces within its jumble, trying to make sense of all the component parts. Then a realisation grabbed her, the Indian woman's talk of vengeance bursting through the rest. Was that why Sooleawa had come to see her that night – as a form of confession?

'By our Lord!' She tugged on Nathan's arm. 'We have to go after her! Standfast could be in danger.'

'Standfast?' A moment, and then – 'Hell's teeth, you think the Indians are behind all this? That he is their next target?'

'I have no idea. Sooleawa seemed sincere when she claimed to be Clemency's friend, but . . . she is strong enough, and determined.'

'But the codes, Mercia? And their powwow? He was one of the victims, it seems.'

She danced on the spot in agitation. 'All I know is that right now, someone may be in danger. Whatever the reason, we have to follow.'

He frowned, clearly unconvinced. 'Perhaps, but—'

She gave him no time to finish. She sped towards the forest, pausing at its edge to survey the territory ahead. In the shadow of the deep trees, she could make out two figures nearby, Standfast and Sooleawa, in earnest discussion. But instead of nervous shouts or defensive gestures, they were standing close together, apparently at ease. Then Standfast pressed his hand against Sooleawa's back and the two disappeared further into the wood.

'Surely not,' she muttered, as Nathan fell in beside her.

'Surely what?'

'No matter. We have to be sure.' Breathing hard, she turned to him. 'I don't suppose you have a weapon?'

He pulled back his jacket to reveal a doglock pistol tucked into the top of his breeches. She arched an eyebrow. 'Since when did you carry a gun?'

'Since we came here. Which way did they go?'

She pointed in the direction Standfast had vanished. 'That way.'

'Right. Now stay behind me.'

It was dark in the wood, and close; maintaining pace with Nathan was tricky, especially in her heavy dress. She began to slow, her boots dragging in the twisted undergrowth. But she kept up as best she could, tracking his stealthy progress through the trees, her ears alert for warning sounds behind. Then she saw him slow up, coming to a halt behind a distended birch, its twin trunks splitting the one from the other at its gnarled base. Quietly, she fell in to crouch beside him.

'Why have you stopped?'

He raised a cautious finger. 'Look.'

In front of them, Sooleawa and Standfast were standing in a large clearing, its blackened earth testament to a scorching in the past. Standfast turned to his companion, holding up his hands as if in question. In response, she reached to the knife at her side. Nathan tensed to rush forward, but Sooleawa merely patted the sheath.

'What do you think?' said Mercia. 'Should we walk in?'

Nathan shifted his head left and right, his searching eyes sharp. He opened his mouth to respond but then a loud crack in the forest drew their swift attention, and another figure emerged from the trees. A shining rapier swung low against his jerkin.

'Godsgift Brown!' she whispered. 'What is going on?'

'Why am I here?' called Godsgift, his voice strong in the quiet wood. 'You said you wanted to see me, Standfast. But why have you brought . . . that?' He flicked a wrist towards Sooleawa, not looking her in the eye, and spat on the earth.

'Constable.' Standfast's tone was scathing, devoid of any respect. 'How pleased I am that you have come.'

'What do you want, Standfast?' Godsgift folded his arms. 'There is a commotion in town. You said you had something to tell me about these murders, but if you do not, I shall have to go back.'

'Murders?' said Mercia, nearly losing her footing. 'But I thought he didn't believe—' She clutched Nathan's arm. 'By the Lord, what is Standfast doing?'

In the clearing, Standfast had pulled out a gun. His eyes pulsating with hatred, he raised the barrel, pointing the weapon at Godsgift's chest.

'What is this?' barked the constable. 'I have no time for your ridiculous games.'

Standfast laughed. 'This is no game, Constable. This is revenge.'

'Jesus,' swore Nathan.

Godsgift was standing very still, showing no sign of fear. 'So it is you, is it? Killing all these people? I should never have thought you so capable.'

Standfast narrowed his eyes. 'Of course not. And it is not me you should be worried about.' He stepped aside, allowing Sooleawa to approach. 'It is her.'

Sooleawa came forward, an arrow pulled taut in her bow. Swapping places with Standfast, she raised her aim as he lowered his own.

'I knew you were too weak.' Even now, Godsgift did not seem afraid.

'You employed this . . . filth . . . to carry out your vile work for you.'

'Are you listening, old man?' Sooleawa's bow was perfectly steady. 'This is nothing to do with Standfast, or the murders. Nor even my tribe. It is my revenge I will have. Mine alone.'

Godsgift scoffed. 'What new confusion is this?'

'She means,' said Standfast, 'that your secret is revealed. And God will judge you for it.'

'You realise I will have you punished for this insolence. You have no hope of becoming minister now.'

Standfast jangled his gun. 'That decision is not yours to make.'

'Besides, you will not be telling the town a thing.' Sooleawa stalked still closer. 'You will be dead. I have searched a long time for you, Matthew Brown. It is time to pay for what you did.'

Finally, Godsgift turned his head. 'Your words are hollow, savage. I have no idea what they mean.'

'Do you not? You may have changed your name since but I know who you are.' She pulled back on the bow, the muscle in her bicep beginning to tighten.

'Now, Nathan!' said Mercia.

Without waiting, she broke cover and called out. The sudden action was enough to surprise Sooleawa into breaking her focus from Godsgift: an instant only, but sufficient for him to seize his chance and jump towards the cover of the woods. But not enough to evade Standfast. The young preacher raised his loaded gun and fired. The ball flew through Godsgift's leg, sending him tumbling to the ground.

'What are you doing?' seethed Sooleawa, even as she swung her attention, and her bow, back on Godsgift. 'This is not your concern.'

'So people keep saying.' Nathan raised his own weapon towards her heart. 'I suggest you point that thing away. And you, Edwards. Reload that gun and I will shoot you likewise.'

Sooleawa creased her face into a contortion of disgust. 'Shoot me if you like. You English are all the same. You claim to have friendship with

280

us and yet you choose your own each time. But I thought you might be different, Mercia.'

'I know your people want vengeance for the friends you have lost.' Mercia took a tentative step forward. 'I understand. But I cannot let you kill anyone, not even for that.'

'You understand nothing.' Sooleawa tautened her bow; to her right, Nathan's finger pawed the trigger of his gun. 'And you listen even less. Were you here when the English burnt our lands, killed our families? When we welcomed men like this and received deceit in return?'

Mercia dared to walk closer. 'You know I was not. Tell me of it.'

'In the war,' she hissed. 'Do you recall that, Matthew Brown? The war against my mother's tribe, the Pequot people. It was twenty-seven years ago, and its memory burns yet, in the spirits of all those you murdered.'

Godsgift was writhing on the ground, clutching at his leg. 'Take that bow from her, Keyte!'

'Wait.' Mercia held up a staying hand. 'I want to hear what she has to say.'

'There is little to say.' Sooleawa's eyes were fixed on Godsgift. 'This man was a warrior in his youth. When the enemies of my tribe persuaded the English to join them in attacking us, he was one of the most ready. He fooled a young woman into thinking he was kind and he betrayed her, burning her village and murdering her tribe, forty men and women killed as they woke. But some escaped, including me. I was just a babe-in-arms then, so of course I did not remember. But last year, the woman's sister was released from a vow she had made her, and she confessed to me the truth. And I swore then that I would find the demon who had done this to my birth tribe and I would slay him for us all. So you see, you will have to kill me, if you want to stop me from killing him.'

Slowly, Mercia faced Godsgift. 'Is this true?'

'It was war.' The constable burnt with contempt. 'A real war. Not muskets and castles, not roundheads and cavaliers as in England. It was survival. It was us against them, it was Christian against heathen, it was the blessed of heaven against the Devil's own brood.' He spat, gripping his leg to staunch the flow of blood. 'They are savages. They are nothing. And in war, there are things men do to the nothingness of their enemies to make them suffer for their slaughter and their insolence. I do not expect you to understand. Not even you, Keyte.' His eyes dropped. 'But if this woman she speaks of is the woman I knew, then pretending that I fooled her proves the justice of my acts.'

'The tales of your past do not lie,' said Sooleawa. 'They are scattered everywhere you have walked, telling their truths of the man that you are, fouling the woods with your deceit.'

'Sooleawa,' said Mercia. 'If this man has killed innocents, he will be held to account. But please. Not in this way.'

'It is my way.'

'He can be brought to trial and—'

Sooleawa laughed. 'No, he will not. You do not know this place at all, do you? Your kind never pay for what you have done. Not even for a crime committed yesterday, so there is no chance he will be made to answer for this.'

Godsgift growled. 'The only one who will answer is her.'

She thrust back her head. 'As Keme answered?'

'Keme?' said Nathan.

'The farmhand. The boy. Whose name you clearly never took time to learn.' She narrowed her eyes. 'I do not know it was this man who killed him, for Standfast has never said. He is just like the rest of you. But I can guess.'

'Sooleawa!' Standfast's face clouded in pain. 'You cannot think I am like him.'

'Why not? You are all alike.'

'But I thought—'

'That I wanted you? Then you are a fool. But I am not, for I could tell it was never love that you desired.'

'Sooleawa, I—'

282

'Be quiet, Standfast, and live up to your name. So few of you do.' She lowered her bow. 'But maybe you are right, woman from over the waters. Maybe I should not kill this evil spirit here, in the privacy of the forest. Maybe I should wait to do it in front of everyone, and then all will know my birth tribe is avenged, and that it was I who did it, and they can go to the south-west in peace. But you will not deny me one shot.'

Before Nathan could stop her, she lifted her bow and fired. The arrow pierced Godsgift's other leg, and he cried out in pain, turning speedily white.

'Beware, old man.' Sooleawa backed towards the wood. 'I will come for you yet. These people stand witness.'

She vanished into the trees. Godsgift slumped on the ground, finally unconscious.

'I thought she loved me.' Standfast was blabbering to one side, his voice growing higher as he spoke. 'She said she loved me.'

'If she did, she was using you to get to him,' said Nathan. 'I am sorry.'

'Pick him up,' said Mercia. 'I do not much care, but he will die if his bleeding is not staunched.'

'You do not mean that.'

'I damn well should do. I had no idea he was so – murderous.'

Nathan stooped to the ground. 'Men do things in war, Mercia, things they would never think of at any other time. And he is right, we do not know what it was like.'

'Are you trying to excuse a massacre?' She stared at him. 'Do you say the same about all those farms, those villages, razed in our own war back home?'

'No.' Nathan put his arms around Godsgift's chest. 'But this is not the time for such a debate.' He heaved him up. 'By the Lord, he is heavy.'

She glanced down. ''Tis that armour he always wears.'

'It may not have done much had she fired at his chest.'

283

She looked towards the forest. 'Why do you suppose she called him Matthew?'

'I have no idea.' He fell back. 'Standfast! I need your help.'

Standfast walked across in a daze. 'She said she loved me. I cannot believe—'

'We can deal with your heart later,' said Nathan. 'For now, we must get him back to the town.'

Mercia watched as Standfast bent to assist. 'Standfast, how did she know he was the man she wanted?'

Aiding Nathan was helping Standfast collect himself. 'She did not at first. She merely knew a man from the Pequot war was living in Meltwater, and that he had changed his name since.'

'Why?'

'We don't know. But she knew he was called Matthew, and of course Matthew means gift of God, so once she . . . confided in me this summer . . . I was able to help her find the truth. She thought to confront him today in the wood, while everyone was at the festival.'

'But we intervened.' She shook her head. 'When you drew your gun, we feared you could have been the murderer, and the constable your next target.'

He frowned. 'Mr Lavington says there have been no murders.'

'Oh come, Standfast!' She was in no mood for this. 'If you opened your eyes, maybe you would not have been deluded by Sooleawa either.' She sighed. 'I am sorry. That was not a pleasant thing to say.'

'But it is the truth.' While Nathan lifted Godsgift's torso, Standfast shuffled to drag him up by the legs. 'Ow, he is heavy. Can we carry him all that way?'

'I hope so.' Nathan turned them sideways, shifting his arms to bear the load. 'We are not far into the wood.'

They set off, struggling under the weight of the unconscious man. Mercia tried to support him in the middle, but the bulkiness of her dress made such assistance impractical, so she walked on ahead, thinking to get help.

She was not far out of the wood when a huge explosion resounded from outside the southern part of town. Chunks of wood rocketed into the sky, multiple clumps of grass powering upwards in their wake. She stopped, amazed, uncertain how to react. And then another explosion followed the first, shaking the ground.

'Mercia!' Nathan called. 'What was that?'

She blinked, looking towards the smoke rising straight ahead. 'It came from over there. Stay with Godsgift while I go and look.'

She ran south around the palisade, aware of someone sprinting behind. She looked back to see Standfast in pursuit, Godsgift now laid out on the ground. Nathan was leaning over his prostrate frame, ripping at his shirt, presumably improvising a tourniquet.

The southern gate came into sight. In the field outside it, a black steaming hole had appeared in the earth. It was surrounded by fragments of wood and other detritus, the shattered leaves of a vaporised barrel strewn across the grass. Black smoke was diffusing everywhere, the smell of gunpowder filling the burning air.

She began to choke, waving the smoke from her face. As she searched the area, a crowd descended on the field; the entire village, it seemed, come from the festival gathering place. A confusion of voices mingled with the smoke, the field thronging with the clamour of agitation.

And then someone screamed – a woman, she could not tell who – pointing at an object on the ground. Mercia hurried towards the incessant cry, the same phrase repeated over and over:

'An arm! An arm! An arm!'

And sure enough, on the earth at her feet, a human arm lay blackened in the smoke.

Another scream. A man. This time: 'A leg! Oh God, a leg!'

So it went, as the villagers discovered more and more of the macabre finds, until Standfast, not far behind her, let out an agonised cry.

'This bracelet . . . I know this bracelet . . .'

He was staring at the arm the woman had found, in a total daze.

She did not remember much of the next minute. She recalled Nicholas rushing to steer her away, but it was the next sight that made her memory block out much of the rest. For as he gently pushed her towards the gate, away from the carnage, she made the mistake of looking up. And there, on the gate, in place of the head of the Indian farmhand, a new atrocity had taken its place: another head, congealed blood clogging the neck, nailed to the fearsome spike. Behind her, she remembered hearing Standfast scream, dropping to his knees with a piercing cry. Perhaps it was the sympathy for his pain that made her truly forget those moments, for of all the townsfolk, it was he who must grieve the most. If Standfast could not live up to his name, then his brother Silence surely now embodied his. He could talk no more: the severed head was his.

Chapter Twenty-Six

There was no keeping secrets from the townsfolk any more, and nor could the deniers continue to pretend: a savage killer was on the loose in Meltwater, and it was beholden on them all to uncover him. Mercia took no consolation from the urgency of this change. The terrible death of Silence Edwards disgusted her, almost as much as Clemency's had, for as with his use of indecipherable codes, the methods of their murderer were callous and perverse.

Standfast had collapsed on seeing his brother's head nailed to the gate. He had clasped his hands together in incoherent prayer, wailing and calling out for mercy; when Vic had tried to help him up it had proven impossible to get him to rise, and he had to be carried senseless to his cottage, where Remembrance had finally managed to coax his hands loose. Now the morning after, Standfast was continuing to babble pleadings to heaven. Nobody knew how to handle his torment, but Renatus Fox stayed with him, praying and watching his soul, as he said.

After the explosions, the horrified townspeople had wavered uncertain in the meadow, angry, crying, distraught, until Percy had roused his father into bringing order. He had been speaking about his discovery of the codes when the first explosion had shaken the ground, swaying the tent where the harvest festival had been due to take place, the assembled beans and corn falling from their piles. And then the townsfolk ran, not deterred by the second explosion, needing to know what was happening, surely never expecting what they found.

'How did he do it?' said Nathan. 'How could he?' Curt, he was still shaken by the spectacle of Silence's death. Mercia knew he was not squeamish, but he had a high sense of honour. The abomination of the murder would have appalled him.

'Kit says his keenest saw has been taken from his mill.' Standing beside him, Percy's words were as emotionless as Nathan's were not. 'Nobody can find it. And gunpowder is missing from Godsgift's supply. It is locked from the Indians, but he never thought one of our own would take it.' He swallowed. 'From what we can deduce, it seems Silence was killed before he was . . . cut up with the saw and his . . . pieces . . . hidden in a barrel for the festival. It was blown up for effect, and the head—' He clutched his neck. 'The head, you know. The Indian boy's was lying on the ground.'

'Bastard.' Nathan curled his fist. 'This bastard, who dares to nail a head – a damn head – to the gate, in broad daylight, when anyone could have seen!'

Mercia rose from her chair to look out the window. 'I think not. Everyone was at the festival, waiting for Percy to talk.'

'But how would he have known that would happen?'

'Perhaps he didn't,' said Percy. 'Perhaps he took the opportunity, thinking to mount a still more fearsome display.'

'And that code.' Nathan's tone overflowed with disgust. 'As indecipherable as the others. He is playing with us. He is a coward.'

'A clever one, at least. Calculating and obsessive.' Mercia turned round. 'But regardless of the codes, we now have a different message. A real one. I have been thinking about it all night.'

288

'Which is?' Nathan folded his arms.

'The killer's methods. They can be no mere coincidence.' She looked at the two men, sure they would have realised, but Percy merely frowned in puzzlement.

'The last three murders.' Once again, she was surprised at her own detachment. 'Forget the old minister's death for now.'

Nathan pondered. 'Clemency was hanged. Hopewell had his stomach slashed. And Silence . . . Silence was blown apart.'

'Precisely.' She injected no drama, no pause for effect into her words. 'One hanged. One drawn. One effectively quartered. Especially if he was sawn apart.'

'My God.' Percy stared at Nathan. 'I had not considered it in the day's horror, but . . . those are the three elements of a traitor's death.'

She gave the slightest nod. 'And in the correct order. I cannot say why Mason was not part of the sequence, other than there could be only three. Or the Indians' powwow.'

'Perhaps the killer views those particular three as traitors,' said Nathan. 'Or he only came to the idea of this method, as you call it, later on.'

'Why not a more straightforward view of treason?' said Percy. 'We are the godly here – Puritans as they call us. Is someone passing judgement that we are all traitors to the Crown?'

'Again we come back to Thorpe.' She creased her forehead. 'Percy, you don't think he knows the regicides are harboured near here, do you, that the town – that you – are hiding them? After all, Clemency was in your group.'

He hesitated. 'As was Sil.'

'Silence?'

'He . . . did not know much, but he wanted to help. Stored things at his house when I asked, simple tasks like that. Hardly anything. But he was linked with us.' He scratched at his neck. 'We were discussing it when you met us at the waterfall that time.'

'I see. And Hopewell?'

'Not unless Clemency sought his help without telling me, and I doubt that she would.'

'Then – Mason?'

'Again, no. And the powwow was not with us, clearly.'

'At least now the *monas* sequence is complete,' said Nathan. 'Now all five components are used, perhaps we can unravel the code. If that is the end of it.' He looked at Mercia, the anger in his eyes morphing to concern.

She looked down at her hands. 'I tried last night. I was distressed, of course, but even so – it was as nonsensical as before.'

A shuffling in the hall passage made them look across. Kit was standing on the threshold, the outside light falling through the front door swinging open behind him. Mercia glanced at Percy, wondering how long he had been waiting to interrupt. She had not heard him come in.

He removed his hat. 'I've just been with Godsgift. I thought you'd want to know he is somewhat recovered.' He looked at Nathan. 'Remy says he has you to thank. Your bandage staunched the bleeding.'

Some of the tension seemed to leave Nathan's face. 'He will live?'

'She thinks so. He is weak, and it will take some days . . . but yes.'

'Has he . . . said anything?' said Mercia.

'About what?'

'About anything.' About what happened in the woods, she thought. About how Standfast shot him, about Sooleawa's accusations.

'As ever he talks little. He is in God's hands now. We must pray for him.'

'Then pray God allows him to come back to strength,' said Percy. 'He may be difficult, but he is the best militia leader we have.'

'I saw Mr Lavington on the way here,' said Kit. 'He asked me to say he would like to speak with you.'

It took a moment before Mercia realised he was talking to her. With a surprised point of her finger at her chest, and a confirmatory nod from Kit, she shrugged her shoulders and sidled past, leaving the men to their discussion.

She found Lavington in his laboratory, rearranging a series of empty glass vials in a futile attempt at tidying. She loitered in the doorway, observing his hurried behaviour, remarking the pallor of his cheeks. Then she cleared her throat and entered, but he continued to bustle. Finally, his energy seemed to fade; his back still turned, he laid out his palms to flatten a curling piece of yellowing parchment on the edge of his desk.

'So,' he said. 'You have come.'

'You asked for me.'

He remained hunched over his parchments. 'I suppose I did.' Still he did not turn round. 'I was wondering. What happened to Godsgift?'

She gave herself an ironic smile. 'Is that why you wish to see me?'

'Partly.' As though a demon was resting on his shoulders, his back drooped beneath his fine jacket; at last, he dragged up his stooped frame to face her. 'Is it to do with the—' He closed his eyes. 'The murders?'

'So Silence's death has finally convinced you.' She took no satisfaction from his acknowledgment. 'I take it you have spoken with Percy. Although he said nothing just now.'

'Percy and I have . . . had words.' The magistrate drew himself up, regaining his proper height. 'I asked him to say nothing until I was ready. In any case, it is nothing to do with him.' He jutted out his chin. 'I always knew.'

'What?' The poise she had tried to foster slipped.

'We both knew. Godsgift and me.' He teased flecks of old parchment from his fingertips. 'He has been trying to uncover the truth since George Mason died. If unsuccessfully, as ever.'

She let out an exasperated gasp. 'Then why have you been preventing me from acting? Why have you been obstructive, refusing to heed me? Heed your own son?'

291

He waved a dismissive hand. 'I wanted to protect Percy. As for you, Mrs Blakewood, you are a stranger. And let me be blunt. You brought two men with you. Two strong men, both of them capable.' He snorted, his familiar arrogance reasserting its dominance. 'You, too, if you are working with them.'

'You do not mean—?' She felt her lips part open in a mixture of shock and incredulity. 'You have thought we could be behind this?'

He folded his arms, his diamond-patterned doublet creasing at the sleeves. 'Would you not find it suspicious, that three strangers appear as your fellow townsfolk continue to die?'

'I suppose . . . you are right. But Clemency invited us here. We would not have come otherwise.'

'And yet you stayed once she had died.' He pulled a cloth from his pocket and wiped his hands. 'Would you not think that peculiar? Why would I be honest with you, speak with you at all?'

'Perhaps not,' she conceded. 'And now? Do we remain suspects?'

'Everyone is a suspect. That is why I have pretended to the town that nothing is amiss. Why I decided to humour Percy and allow you to stay, so I could better keep an eye on you.' He fixed her with a harsh glare. 'But Amery told me your story. A remarkable tale, sailing the ocean in search of the King's lost paintings. Godsgift investigated it further.' He raised a wry eyebrow. 'I hear the *patroon* of Haarlem is still mighty aggrieved.'

She inclined her head. 'On this point, your constable is thorough.'

'Even when the Dutch controlled New York we had friends there, by necessity as well as by choice. It is not hard to verify events. And . . . Percy seems to trust you, which is unusual for him. Nor can I think why you would come here from England to kill folk. But mostly, I do not want more deaths. I would like to propose a truce.'

She studied his face, wondering whether he was truly being sincere. 'I think we would all benefit from cooperation. And I see now what Godsgift meant in the forest. He talked of the murders, as if he believed in them. Now I see that he did.'

'So we come back to that affair.' Unconsciously, he twisted his left earlobe. 'I have a very taciturn constable, Mrs Blakewood. What did happen in the wood?'

She considered her response. Despite Lavington's newfound claim that he wished to collaborate, most likely he still did not trust her, and she was certainly not about to reveal all that she knew to him. She decided to play with the truth.

'Nathan and I were helping Percy fetch everyone to the festival – you saw me yourself, if you recall. Then there was a cry, from the eaves of the forest. By the time we got there we found Godsgift had been shot. We saw an Indian running away. I doubt it was to do with the murders.'

He frowned. 'An Indian?'

'I fear they are unsettled because of the death of the farmhand.' As she spoke, the *sachem*'s threats of retribution rang out clear. 'Magistrate, I think it would be wise to prepare for further retaliation.'

His eyes darted about, and for a moment she thought he was ignoring her plea, but then he looked straight at her.

'Then we had best hope Godsgift recovers quickly. In the meantime, Percy talked of the murders yesterday before I could stop him. Of those . . . codes. Now the whole town thinks one of their own is a killer. Order is already breaking down.'

She had seen it herself on her way to the house, angry murmurings filling the disturbed streets. 'Perhaps. But you can hardly hope to keep things quiet now.'

'It seems I never could. Percy tells me Vic copied down the code he found on Clemency, even though I had asked him to stay silent.'

'He did stay silent. There is no call to reproach him. He talked to me and me alone.'

'And you talked to Percy.' He sighed. 'But little matter now. The whole town is aware.'

'Until yesterday, Percy agreed with your wish for silence.' She took a calming breath. 'But enough of this. I take it you cannot unravel the meaning of those messages, otherwise I hope you would have said.'

Darkness washed over his face. 'Neither – I take it – can you. Although as an alchemist, there is one thing I have been able to deduce.'

'Yes,' she said. 'The use of the *monas*. Nicholas saw that some days ago.'

'Your manservant?' His cheek twitched.

'And there is something else. How many codes are you aware of, Magistrate?'

'You refer to the missing symbol, I suppose, the semicircle that represents the moon?'

'Ah.' As she had wondered, it seemed he did not know about the code found on the powwow. 'Then I fear I must bring you further confusion.'

'So he was investigating the murders all along.' Back in her cottage, Nicholas shook his head. 'The wily dog.'

Waiting in the open door, she watched Nathan come up to the gate. 'And yet he still acts strangely. When I told him of the powwow, he seemed more concerned that the missing piece of his puzzle had been found than that someone else had been killed. Not that he could read the codes – or would tell me that he could.'

Nicholas stretched his booted legs onto a three-legged stool. 'Well, we know he hides things. No reason to think he won't continue to do so.'

'No.' She stood aside to allow Nathan in. 'How is he? Standfast?'

Nathan threw his hat onto the wall hook; it bounced off the dulled point, but he left it on the floor.

'Not well. Learning Sooleawa did not really care for him, and then seeing his brother . . . like that . . . it has destroyed the balance of his humours. Thorpe was there, as physician, doing more harm than good, but I think Remy fared better. She is calming him with warm draughts and trying to make him eat.'

'It was good that you went.' She rubbed her eyes, a wave of tiredness sweeping over her. 'He has told nobody of what happened in the forest?'

'Unless he has been raving to Remy. I doubt he would want to otherwise.' He blew out his cheeks. 'After all, he is supposed to be godly.'

'Hardly new with that sort.' Nicholas smirked. 'He probably preaches to make up for his sin.'

'A man of deep feelings, perhaps.' Nathan shot him a glance. 'I will ask Remy if he has said anything more later. I . . . said I would call in.' He cleared his throat. 'Godsgift is saying nothing, unsurprisingly. I tried to see him, but his servant says he will not speak to a soul. So we can keep Standfast's part secret, if you think best.'

She bent to pick up his hat. 'I see no reason why not.'

'And you?' He pulled out a chair and collapsed into it. 'What did Lavington want?'

'To talk.' Placing the hat on the hook, she recapped her discussion.

'Hmm.' He scratched at his chin. 'I think you are right not to be too trusting. I have been talking with some of the townsmen.' He laid his head on the top of his chair. 'You should see them. After days of turned-away looks, they suddenly want to stop me in the street, tell me all sorts of tales. Eager to blame.' He closed his eyes. 'Just like in the war, when we were younger. Everyone worried for themselves, panicking about their neighbours, desperate to seem loyal and innocent all at once.'

'Same where I grew up.' Nicholas took a bite from the apple he was eating. 'In London. At least, for those who cared about it.'

'How could you know?' said Mercia, lowering herself into a chair of her own. 'You were just a child during the wars.'

'Childhood didn't last long round Cow Cross. But you're right. Round us, it was more about how to make a coin – sometimes a lot of coin – from what was happening.'

'Noble as ever,' said Nathan.

'Trying to stay alive usually isn't.' He twisted to face him. 'And I'll tell you something else. If the townspeople here are now scared for their lives, they're not about to be very noble either.'

'No.' Mercia tugged out a caught fold of her dress to make herself more comfortable. 'So is any of what they have told you useful, Nat?'

'Well.' Nathan copied Nicholas in stretching out his legs; he looked as weary as she felt. 'Something about everyone, it seems. Amery got up to no good in Boston when he was younger, disobeying the rules, like most kids. Godsgift isn't the only one to change his name. Kit West did too, when he came to America. Apparently his real name is Roger, not Christ-carry.'

She could not prevent a small smile. 'His new awakening?'

'I suppose. And there is a lot of finger pointing at Thorpe.' He pushed off the back of his seat, leaning his elbows on his thighs. 'People seem very ready to give him the blame. All sorts of ridiculous tales. Humility's wife Sarah told me he was once seen talking to a goat, like that meant something. And a group of lads – Obedience, is it? – said they see him skulking around the forest at night, that he did for his own wife, but I think they just don't like him.' He hesitated. 'And that he was seen outside Clemency's cottage the night of her murder.'

'What?' She rounded on him. 'You left this until last?'

'Those lads were playing about, Mercia, spreading rumours, prittle-prattle. You know the sort.'

'Even so, sometimes there is truth in rumour.'

'That's right. And so just in case, I went to Fearing's farm and talked to some of the men there. I thought as I've been helping them, they might be more ready with the truth.' He held up a hand before she could interrupt. 'One of them did tell me something that supported what the boys said, claiming Godsgift had been overheard talking with Lavington about someone he had seen on his rounds that night. But when anyone asked about it, Godsgift merely ignored them.'

'Nat, we cannot dismiss anything. Did the man on the farm think it was Thorpe?'

'No. But he did make another guess.' He shuffled his chair closer to hers. 'And this is one story I think you should hear.'

Chapter Twenty-Seven

'I know what he said, but I still want to see him.'

Mercia stood in the tiny hall of Godsgift Brown's cottage, the same she had marched from the day she had found Clemency dead, and still the constable was proving obstructive. Or at least his indentured servant was, her hand on the wall blocking Mercia's way.

'And I told you, Mrs Blakewood, he needs his rest.' The gaunt woman's mouth was turned down. 'He has two grave wounds in his legs.'

'Yes, Rose.' Mercia tried a conciliatory tone. 'I was there. I just want to wish him well.'

'Even so, he does not want—'

She lost her patience. 'You have been in the streets, Rose? Heard tell of these murders everyone now seems to believe?'

Rose pulled her hand from the wall, fiddling with the cuff of her black dress. 'It is God's judgement, Mrs Blakewood. God's punishment.'

'Maybe so. But you want to stop them, don't you? Protect your town?'

Her eyes widened. 'You don't think . . . there could be more?'

'I do not know.' She softened her harsh timbre. 'But I do know the constable is the man who can help us.' She smiled in reassurance. 'Please. Let me in.'

Rose wavered, looking through the open front door. In the street, Seaborn Adams was gesturing wildly at Humility Thomas, the tavern keeper shaking his head.

'Well . . . if he doesn't ask you to leave. Go up, on the left. He is decent.'

Mouthing a thank you, Mercia edged past and climbed the stairs, knocking two forceful raps before entering the room. The constable was lying on his bed, his wounded legs both bandaged. His face was a terrible white, and he was sprawled on the covers with none of his usual decorum. A book at his side lay unopened, his fingers curled on the bound cover as though that were as far as he could manage.

His closed eyes flicked open. Despite his condition, he still managed to look aggrieved.

'I told that woman not to let anyone up,' he croaked. 'I would not long speak to Lavington and I will certainly not speak to you.'

She pushed shut the door and came in. '"That woman" is concerned for you.'

'Then she should not be.' He winced in pain, reaching towards his right thigh. She looked at it; the bandage was well applied, but red had still seeped through.

'Has the arrow been removed?'

'Thorpe cut it out.' He fell back on his pillow. 'Whatever else he is, he is very good at that.'

'I am glad.' She looked over his face, his unkempt hair. At the side of his bed, his rapier lay discarded on the floor. 'In spite of what Sooleawa said you did to her tribe.'

He coughed: a pitiful attempt. 'I might have known you would side with *that*, over me.'

'Constable, we can discuss your past when you are better. For now I merely need you to confirm something I have learnt, and I will leave you to your book.' She tilted her head to examine its fine cover. 'To your Bible.'

'It is hard to read.' He leant up on his elbows, or he tried to, for he quickly dropped back on the quilt. 'Mrs Blakewood, I am not going to explain what I have done in my life to protect others. If you have a question to ask, do so and leave.'

She nodded, her attention briefly caught by a blood-splattered doublet hanging from the wall, presumably what he had been wearing under his armour in the wood.

'It is about the murders. If only you and Lavington had confided in me sooner, in Percy, then perhaps we could have worked together to prevent Silence's death.'

'Percy could have confided in us.' Godsgift sucked in air through his teeth as his left leg twitched. 'He is so very secretive, that one. He thinks I do not know what he does, when most everyone here applauds him for it.'

'Applauds him for . . . ?'

'I know he has talked of it with you, so do not pretend.' He made another attempt to pull himself up. 'Those men he helps are heroes. Good soldiers, fighting their fight, as I do.' The effort became too great and he sank again into the sheets. 'Now speak.'

She coughed, recovering herself. 'It is about the night of Clemency's death.'

The lightest of frowns caused the strongest of winces. 'What about it?'

'Nathan has heard a curious allegation I need you to explain.' She opened the door a crack to check Rose was not listening and then shut it again, lowering her voice. 'And this time, Constable, when I ask what you saw that night, I hope you will decide to speak true.'

Beads of sweat dripped down her back as she sidled further from the roaring forge, waiting for Vic Smith to hammer his fourth horseshoe into shape. He had been working the first when she had arrived in his yard, but she had not wanted to risk his leaving before they could talk, and so she waited, sipping ale, turning red in her too-heavy dress, pondering how she would phrase what she wanted to ask when he finally finished his work. For safety, Nicholas was stationed in the street, but she hoped she would not need to call on his physical talents. Nathan had gone to check on Remembrance: Mercia had seen no reason to wait for his return, notwithstanding the assurance she had given that she would.

She broke from her musings as the ringing ceased. Despite the force of each hammer strike, Vic did not seem out of breath. He pulled a torn cloth from a nail on a post, wiping his torso of sweat and grime, then threw a woollen shirt over his head, letting the material slide down before freeing his tied-back hair, shaking the black strands into place. Taking his own swig of ale, he fixed her with a steady glance and traversed the dusty yard.

'Now you should be able to make a shoe as well as I can.'

She put on a smile. 'You are very proficient.'

'I try.' He took another swig from his cup. 'So what do you want?'

She took a deep breath, inhaling a profound smell of smoke. 'Nathan told me an interesting story earlier.'

'Oh?'

'He heard it in the town. People are beginning to talk.'

'After all this? Can't say I'm surprised.'

Another breath. *Courage, Mercia.*

'This story is about you. More to the point, about you and Clemency.' She ignored the chill in her stomach as she reached inside her pocket. 'I found these in her cottage.'

'Pieces of paper?' His fingers twitched on his cup.

'Letters.'

She extended her arm. Setting the cup on a low wall, he took the proffered sheets, quickly scanning the first leaf and reading to the end. Then his eyes raked over the other sheets. She watched his expression, but it was unfathomable.

'Well.' He ran a tongue around his cheek. 'These are interesting.'

'Interesting? If certain people were to read them, they would say the writer was immoral.'

Still no reaction. 'I try not to judge folk.'

'But many do.' She nodded at the letters now dangling in his fingertips. 'Careful. They may drift into your forge.'

'Then nobody would be offended by them, at least.' He glanced again at the sheets of paper. 'Is this all of them?'

'You should know.'

A slight frown. 'I thought you wanted to talk about Clemency.'

'We are. Those letters are addressed to her.'

'I can see that.'

'As I can see you wrote them.'

Slowly, he raised his head. 'Why do you say that?'

'I dislike rumour, Vic.' She sighed for effect, and straightaway wished she had not. 'But here is a rumour that fits the facts. And . . . you are not denying it.'

He folded his arms, the letters crumpling against his chest. 'You dislike rumour, you say. Well, I dislike lies. I ask again, why do you say I wrote these?'

'I would be careful, Vic. People are starting to accuse each other. Accusing you.'

'Who is?'

'That does not matter.'

'Who?'

She waved a hand, as much to steady herself as anything. 'One of those people we dislike, Vic, who likes pouring blame on others. Someone overheard amidst a group of tattlers.'

His face was as rigid as one of his iron tools. 'Then no doubt their claim is baseless.' He wedged the letters beneath his cup. 'We may be close out here, Mrs Blakewood, but we still have the same enmities you do.'

301

'That is becoming clearer every day.' An uncomfortable heat was creeping up her body, not entirely from her warm surroundings. 'And talking of close, it seems you and Clemency were close once. The sort of close that gets mischievous people talking.' She hesitated, but she had come this far. 'It seems you laughed it off, but some people noticed the long looks. Even so, nobody gave it much credence – until now, when they are forced to accept she was killed. Now, they are ready to believe anything, so long as it turns the blame from them.'

He looked away, just briefly, but she was watching. 'I'm disappointed, Mrs Blakewood. I did not think you so ready to place credence in clattermouths.'

'But you did write those letters, Vic. Stop pretending.'

He took a step forward, but she held her ground. And then he seemed to deflate, his shoulders losing their tautness: a chink in his guard, perhaps? He turned away, rubbing the back of his head.

'Do you . . . intend to tell the town?'

A chink indeed. 'That depends.'

'I could deny it if you do.'

'What happened to disliking lies?'

A long pause. A long sigh. Unlike her earlier pretence, his seemed genuine. 'She told me she had destroyed them.'

A gaping crack. 'I found them in her house.'

'It does not do to rifle through other people's belongings, Mrs Blakewood.'

'I do not think Clemency would have minded, in the end.' She bore his accusing gaze. 'You seem remarkably calm, Vic. Even with this . . . revelation. With all that happened yesterday, the rest of the town has fallen into panic.'

'You know full well I always thought these were murders. I gave you that cloth, didn't I? And you don't seem so bothered yourself.'

'Believe me, I am.'

He yanked at the letters, sending his cup crashing to the ground. 'Then what do you mean threatening me with these?'

'They are a motive for murder, would you not say?' Inside, the heat burnt stronger.

'You don't think I—' He laughed. 'Have you read these? I was in love with Clemency. Why in heaven would I have wanted her dead?'

A chasm at last. 'An individual sort of love, Vic. Those letters speak of some uncommon tastes.'

His face darkened. 'Who have you shown these to?'

'I hope I need not show them to anyone. I am not interested in marking people out for unjust condemnation. But there are others still hidden away. I would not retaliate too strongly.'

His eyes flicked to the doorway, and for a moment she thought she had pressed him too far. Even with Nicholas's reflexes she could be in danger were Vic to make any sudden move. But he merely tensed on the spot.

'What do you want?'

'Just your help.'

'If it's to do with the murders, I've already done that.'

'And you are afraid that if you do more, then whatever hold Lavington has on you will be used to hound you out of town? But that will not happen. Lavington is as keen to solve these murders as I am. He has confessed he has thought so all along.'

'Perhaps you are just saying that. And Lavington has the same hold on me that you now have.'

She nodded; ever since Nathan had related the farmer's tale, she had suspected as much. 'Yet I think you do want to help.' She glanced again at the letters in his hand. 'I have read those several times while trying to work all this out. I had hoped they might lead me to the killer, and they yet may, but less directly than I had thought.'

'You read much into simple words, Mrs Blakewood.'

'Maybe. And there may be some perversities in those words, some proposals I do not wish to dwell upon, but in spite of that, one thing is quite clear.'

'And what is that?'

'That you did love her, Vic.' She paused, observing his face. 'You loved her when you wrote those letters, and you loved her when she died. You still do, I think.' She stepped closer. 'That is why you gave me the code. Because you loved her and you wanted her killer found.'

He bowed his head. 'Please. I have a wife. A son.'

'Yet you were obsessed with Clemency. You kept it as quiet as you could, yes, but you made enough people wonder. And so I think it was you she talked of the day she died, when she spoke of matters she had to conclude. I thought she meant correspondence, or her medicines, but now I think she meant you.'

He shook his head. 'I never harmed her.' His whole body seemed to shrink. 'I would never have harmed her.'

'But you made her uncomfortable.'

His red face paled. 'I didn't kill her. I swear it. Neither her, nor Silence.'

'And yet still there are those letters. Others might not be so ready to believe you in this newfound climate of mistrust.' She pressed home, making herself hard for Clemency's sake. 'Godsgift has admitted he saw you near her house that night, in the shadows. That he believed you were sincere when you said the day after you had not killed her. But I know about the letters, Vic, and Godsgift did not.' She twisted her blade still deeper. 'I will not tell anyone, as long as you help me in exchange. All I want to know is what you saw that night. You were there for some time, it seems. If you truly are innocent, I need you to speak.'

He swallowed. 'I . . . I don't know.'

'Even now, Vic? What is more important? Your unfounded fear I might tell your wife, or your loyalty to the woman you claim to have loved?'

The strong man had become a miserable boy, fallen against the wall for support. She felt sick she had done this to him, but if he did know anything, she needed to know it too.

'Vic? Lavington will not harm you now. There is no need to keep silent.'

He could not look at her. 'I was there a long time, 'tis true.' His voice was shaking. 'I-I often was. I had to see her, don't you see? It was a sickness. And Godsgift knew, although I had learnt in time how to hide from his patrols. He threatened to tell my wife if I did not stop, but all I did was make sure to be careful.' He took a deep breath. 'Then that night, Clemency called me to her house, and she told me to leave her be. So I was upset, confused, and this time Godsgift saw me. I promised to go home, but my sickness lured me back, and when I heard the footsteps . . .' He swallowed. 'But I didn't think it mattered. Not like giving you the cloth.' His jaw shook. 'Or her bodice.'

'My God.' She stared in disbelief. 'That was you?'

He nodded sadly. 'When she was changed, before her burial, I offered to burn the clothes she was . . . killed in. I took them to my forge, but I kept the bodice. I wanted something of hers, to cherish still.' A tear dropped to the dry earth. 'But I knew I could not keep it. If my wife found out . . . if God found out . . .'

'As so you gave it to me?'

'I was not thinking. I thought perhaps you . . . you would want it. Straightaway I realised it would only upset you. Giving you the code was supposed to help make that right.'

'Oh, Vic.' She looked on him with great pity. 'Then help me again. Tell me what you saw that night. Those footsteps.'

'Yes.' He sniffed, wiping his pockmarked cheek. She leant forward, waiting for him to continue. 'I was hidden. Too distant to see clear.' He looked up, and his eyes were as red as his forge. 'But . . . it wasn't a man.'

'What?' She jerked back her head.

'Not one man alone. It was two.' By now his voice was regaining its strength. 'Two men, wearing hooded cloaks. One of them . . . one of them holding a rope.'

'God's death,' swore Nicholas. 'What did he think they were going to do in there?'

She scuffed her boot on a stone as they walked. 'He says that when he saw them, he thought they were after her medical help. It seems people often sought her assistance because she knew herbs and remedies.' She set her face. 'They only ever dared come after dark, of course, too ashamed to be seen wanting help.'

'The secrecies of village life! But two men with a rope . . . and he never said anything later?'

'He was scared his wife would learn of his visit. Of his mania.'

'A big man like Vic Smith?'

'Even so.'

He shook his head. 'I'm not convinced.'

'Then he was putting on a good show.' A sorry guilt came over her. 'He seemed terrified after I accused him of being in love with her. May the Lord forgive me for treating him like that.'

'You are not one to appeal to heaven.' Nicholas looked at her askance. 'You have some useful information now. Why not use your wits?'

They passed the meeting house steps. 'I would if I could. After all that, all we know is there were two of them at Clemency's cottage, not which two.'

'But that doesn't mean there were always two of them at each of the killings.' He turned in the street, walking backwards as he continued to talk. 'For the other murders, one of them could have played lookout while the other . . . carried it out. One could have nailed Silence's head to that spike while the other made sure no one came near.'

She screwed up her face at the awful image. 'You are right,' she said.

'Or perhaps they are alternating.' She grabbed his arm, bringing them to a halt. 'Making sure one of them is seen elsewhere while the other is . . . and then swapping roles for the next. A different man for different murders, while we have always assumed it was one killer present at each.'

'Maybe.' Nicholas scratched at his neck. 'Maybe not. But 'tis a thought.'

Chapter Twenty-Eight

That more than one person was involved in the murders was only part of the worry Mercia was feeling. Sooleawa had vanished, the Indians fallen quiet. Panic and paranoia were besieging the town. All the discipline of Godsgift's drills threatened to become undone, the tight-knit community of pioneers at risk of degenerating into a squabbling of individual families, terrified by their self-induced fear.

Percy, the veteran of Cromwell's government, was doing his best to rally the people, but his father seemed at a loss in the face of the disorder, ill-equipped to handle a group of rowdy disparates. But although some listened, within a short time they had found new ways of distrusting their neighbours, new tales from years past resurrecting from the grave. And so the bird of rumour returned, flitting from rooftop to picket fence, hay bale to palisade, cawing its portent of ruin around the hitherto prosperous town.

Yet there was one other leader at hand. One fine morning, Renatus Fox stood on the steps of the meeting house, calling to the people to join him in prayer. His words drifted through the streets, fighting the screeching of the bird of rumour, beseeching the townsfolk he would make his flock to seek God's deliverance from their trials. Little by little the number around him grew, adding their voices to his own, until a merging of their pleas rang out, willing heaven to reply to their faith. And for those who had come, for that moment, the comfort of that unity was enough.

She watched them at a distance, surveying the nervous faces, wondering if the murderers stooped among them, affecting a pretence, or if they had stayed away, not all the town so easily reposed. Close to Renatus, some of the younger town members had been among the first to join: Amery, bowing his head; Remembrance, doubtless praying for her brother's soul; Kit, adding his own prayers, his hands clasped tight on his chest.

Then another joined the praying crowd, the outliers shuffling aside to let Nathan in. She was not surprised, all told, for she knew his sympathies lay with the Puritan cause, but she realised that it saddened her, although she knew it should not, as though he was choosing to be with them instead of with her. But did it truly matter, when she had a call of her own, the ceaseless pull of more earthbound justice? She was her father's daughter, as John Dixwell had observed. Of that, she had little doubt.

She wandered into the fields, walking to the waterfall, listening to its babbling flow. She touched the trees as though drawing inspiration from their roughness, the long-lived witnesses of all they surveyed. Unlike the communal prayers, she wanted to be alone, the scent of the grasses infiltrating her soul. Inhaling deep, fresh air, she closed her eyes, imagining for a moment this tranquillity could last. But she could not keep her eyes shut forever. After a time she climbed back down the path, and she left the forest, hoping to speak with Nathan.

The meeting house steps were empty, the prayer session over. She went back to the cottage, but he was not inside. She sought out Nicholas instead, finding him near the eastern gate with Amery.

'He went for a stroll too,' he said, feigning an innocent expression she saw right through.

'So why the strange look?'

He sighed. 'He's with Remembrance. They've been an hour or so. I'm sure 'tis nothing, but I know you don't like her, and—'

'Nicholas, I have no feelings about it at all.'

She continued her walk, ambling clockwise around the palisade with Nicholas now at her side, but neither said much to the other. Caught up in her thoughts, the northern gate had only just come into view when a man – Seaborn Adams – peered through the open gap. He craned his neck forward, looking out towards the forest.

'I can see them,' he shouted back. 'Coming this way. I think it is – yes, Remy and the Englishman – Keyte. But I still can't see why they're running so fast.'

Now at the gate, Mercia turned to face north herself. True enough, Nathan and Remembrance were running towards the town. She frowned, looking at Nicholas, but when she turned back to the field, the determined steel in Nathan's fast-approaching face scared her.

'Ready the defences!' he shouted as he drew near. 'The Indians have massed in the woods!'

A sharp combination of terror and failure pierced her. 'My God, Nicholas,' she said. 'The *sachem* has lost patience. He has sent his warriors to take his revenge.'

As Seaborn dashed back through the gate, Nathan skidded to a halt. 'Mercia,' he said. 'Thank God. You have to get out of here.' He looked at Nicholas. 'Will you take her? I have to stay to help.'

She shook her head. 'No, I should help too. It is my fault they are—'

He grabbed her shoulders, cutting her off. 'Damn it, Mercia, there is no time for this. They are armed, and not just with bows and axes. They have muskets, guns.' He stared into her eyes with unshakable conviction. 'It is not your fault if they choose to attack. It is not your fault that some unholy bastard is killing their friends.' He glanced to her side. 'Nicholas, if I need you once it is now. Get her away from this place. Do you hear?'

He reached for her arm. 'Of course.'

'And quickly. Take Remy with her.'

As he disappeared into the town, the shrill sounds of the alarm bell ringing out, Remembrance ran up to join them. She leant forward on her thighs, the hems of her dress splattered in mud. When she looked up, the terror in her eyes was absolute.

'Mrs Blakewood!' she panted. 'You must leave now!'

Mercia took in her fearful expression, but then she started into the meadow, ignoring the shouts of warning to come back. Behind, in the town, she could hear the cries of uncertainty start up, voices cut through with fright. In truth she shared their fear, but she needed to see for herself. For if the Indians were coming, whatever Nathan argued she would blame herself, her failure to assuage the *sachem* the clear reason for the assault. Or so her irrational mind would say, and she was in no temper to dispute it.

Not far from the gate, she paused. The sun was behind her, but the day was bright, and she raised her right hand to her forehead, shielding her eyes so as better to see. Squinting towards the forest, at first she could make nothing out. But then yes, a slight tremor to the left, a long, dark pole sticking from the undergrowth. She took another step forward, and yes, the pole became a musket. Then a shaking of bushes quivered to the right, and a party of young men leapt out, still a way off, but even from here she could tell their faces and chests were covered in red paint. They began a shrill cry that carried across the open field, and as more Indians broke cover, the massing warriors began a violent dance, as if taunting the townsfolk with their brazen display.

A hand on her shoulder made her jump, but it was only Nicholas come to fetch her back.

'Humility says there is a plan for taking the women and children to a safe place. He – I – think you should go with them.'

'And you, Nicholas? Will you run also?'

'Of course not. This is not my town, but I will not let men die if I can fight.'

311

'But still. I should not want you to suffer here, not like that.'
A sudden panic took her, her chest heaving with shallow breaths, a
hollow twinge of guilt. Nicholas and Nathan were only in Meltwater
because of her need to find Clemency's killer. If they were to die, to
be hurt . . .

'Come.' He placed his arm around her back, steering her inside the
palisade. 'Humility told me where the women are being taken.'

In a daze, she allowed him to shepherd her through the town and
the southern gate until they merged into a procession of women and
children, all making their way to the half-finished fort atop the low hill.
The worry on the faces of the women was obvious, but they stepped aside
to allow her to join their line, staring in suspicion at Nicholas until he
gave her a grim nod and ran back towards the town, at which the women
gave a satisfied nod of their own. Mercia arched her neck to watch him
disappear through the gate, then carried forward with the rest of the
women into the wooden fort.

There was one man come with the nervous group, and unlike with
Nicholas they did not find his presence unwelcome, for he was in charge
of the solitary mortar, the larger cannon beside it too unwieldy for one
gunner alone. Fearing Davison, his daughter at his side, stood looking
over the town towards the northern meadow. Mercia paused beside him,
straining to get a glimpse, but the far view was inadequate. With the
attack coming from the opposite side of town, the mortar would be more
or less worthless.

'What will happen?' she said. 'How will the town resist?'

Fearing was chewing on a blade of grass, seemingly unafraid. 'They
will fight them, and they will fall back here if they must, do battle from
the fort. If they do, I am to fire this to scare the bastards away.'

She looked at the small mortar. 'With that alone?'

He spat out the grass. 'This fort was meant to defend against the
Dutch, if ever it was needed. We were due to get more of these guns, but
they never came. Now we must use whatever we have.'

312

One of the women behind them was pacing up and down. 'Why are they attacking now?' she fretted. 'Why?'

'Because of that Indian boy, why do you think?' snapped another. 'Because of Godsgift.'

Unwilling to join the fractious crowd, Mercia stayed with Fearing. 'Are the men organised? In the town?'

'Well . . .' His eyes dropped.

'Mr Davison?'

Remembrance looked up. 'With the constable in bed, there is nobody to lead them. Mr Lavington is not a soldier, and Thorpe . . . he may be one of the captains, but the men will never follow him. Vic too is no real proxy. This attack is well timed. The Indians must have known.'

Sooleawa, thought Mercia. She must have told the *sachem* what happened in the woods.

'You want to know the truth, Mrs Blakewood?' Fearing narrowed his eyes. 'You who wish to know all truths?' He lowered his voice so the others could not hear. 'We are in trouble. The men have no strong leader when they need one most. A saviour from heaven.'

Mercia looked over the town, the anxious shouts of men drifting up from the palisade. 'He is not from heaven, perhaps, but Nathan was a soldier once. He has led men into battle. But these men are so terrified, they need a general to—' She gasped. 'Think, Mercia, damn you!' She turned back to Fearing. 'Is Percy still in the town?'

'He will be with the other men, but he is no—hey! Where are you going?'

She was already through the unfinished fort gate. Sliding on the grass, she began to descend the hill, weaving her way around the straggling flow of women and children, their pale faces finding pause to stare as she dodged them, heading the wrong way.

At the bottom of the hill she jarred her ankle as she misjudged the last bit of slope; she tripped over a stone in her haste, but she managed to keep herself upright, squeezing sideways past Humility Thomas just

313

outside the southern gate. The innkeeper was calling the final women through, herding them towards the fort, although his corpulent frame was more hindrance than help. He frowned as she ran by, but then she swivelled on her boot heel and stopped.

'Where is Percy?' she demanded. Humility stared, his face pure bewilderment. 'Where is he?'

'Probably at the practice ground,' he mumbled.

'And Godsgift?'

'Still abed. When we need him most he is—'

She set off for the eastern gate. Despite the exodus, the streets were full of noise, men darting in and out of houses, grabbing muskets and axes, any weapons they could find. Some were milling around, looking uncertain what to do, even when more coherent minds shouted out instructions. One or two cursed when they saw her, ordering her to leave with the other women, but most just ignored her, or looked up only briefly. The fear in their eyes made her stomach cold, but she had an idea.

Coming out onto the practice area an assemblage of men was lined up, muskets at their sides. On the edge of the field a mound of closer-contact weapons was forming, the dulled points of worn swords protruding from the violent mass. At the front of the line, Percy was standing with Nathan, both attempting to inject order, but their task was hopeless: some of the men were clearly panicking, not listening to Percy but staring at the Indians' position.

'What now?' he shouted at Kit, the sawyer climbed halfway up a tree.

'They are still dancing,' he called back.

'Perhaps that is all they will do.' Amery was shaking, barely able to hold his gun.

'No,' said Percy, more controlled. 'This time I fear they will attack. But the dance could take hours. We must stay ready for when they come.'

His eyes roved the field, studying the haphazard preparations until he caught sight of Mercia. Nudging Nathan, he nodded in her direction. Nathan looked up and with an expletive marched across.

'What in God's name are you doing here?' He glared at the line of men. 'Nicholas! What did I tell you?'

Nicholas had been facing the other way, but at Nathan's angry words he walked across.

'I took her to the hill,' he said. 'But we both know how she can't resist trouble.'

She ignored them. 'I need to speak to Percy.' Nathan grabbed her by the elbow, but she shook him off. 'It is important.'

He fell in beside her as she strode across the field. 'Why can you not once, just once, do as I ask? Do you not understand how dangerous this is?'

She maintained her pace. 'Which is why I need Percy.'

'And me? Do you not need me any more?'

'Nathan, this is not the time.'

'It never seems to be.'

She shook her head, but by now they had crossed the field. She got straight to the point.

'Percy, the men need a leader. With Godsgift injured, they are a mess.' She lowered her voice. 'And I think we both know who.'

He looked at her with a quizzical stare somewhere between surprise and admiration. And then he laughed.

'Mercia, you are astounding. I should have known you would reach the same conclusion I have.'

Nathan frowned. 'What conclusion?'

Percy's smile dropped. 'You see how the men vacillate, Nathan, how they yearn for the constable.' He drew them both aside, away from the townsfolk. 'The longer the Indians delay, the more the men think about the attack, and the more they panic. I have already heard muttering about abandoning the town, but then the Indians will burn everything and we will be nothing more than cowards. We have to defend ourselves.'

Mercia nodded. 'You need someone used to dealing with such

wavering. Someone used to war, who can hold troops together, body and mind. Someone the men know of, and who they trust.'

Nathan's eyes lit up. 'Of course!'

'I did not want this to happen.' Percy's face had turned sombre. 'But people could die. And not just the men, but the women in the fort. The children.' Rhythmically, his chest rose and fell. 'I shall have to ride to them. In spite of all my secrecy, damn it!'

'They can judge the risks,' said Mercia. 'It seems folly not to ask for their help. But you should stay. You said yourself the men are panicking. They will need your reassurance in the meantime.' She looked him in the eye. 'No, I will go. I will fetch Whalley and Goffe.'

Chapter Twenty-Nine

She rode quickly; it was fortunate the sun was bright, for if the Indians had arrived at nightfall she would easily have become lost in the darkness. She strayed from Percy's directions several times as it was, missing the pile of rocks here, the cleaved branch there. For the fourth time she reined in her horse, retracing her steps until she once more picked up the path using the instructions he had hastily scrawled. For all his agreement, she knew how this course must dismay him, for if the regicides agreed to help it would mean revealing they were near, notwithstanding Godsgift's words of support for Percy's actions. But he was to move them on again soon, and perhaps that was what had swayed him. That, and the massed Indian ranks in view.

The last time she had come this way, she had not much noticed the landmarks Percy used to find his path, but with the instructions they seemed obvious. The final marker was the hardest, a wide trunk with a black heart-shaped carving where the sound of the river was most prominent. She leant forward on her horse to check every tree, hearing plentiful water, but not seeing what she needed. And then she found it, an easy matter from thereon in to turn right at the heart-shaped marker and so arrive at a convenient stabling post, a large, lichen-free branch.

She jumped quietly from the horse. She was near now, and she wondered whether the regicides had set a watch, or worse, traps. She kept her eyes trained on the ground as she crept towards their hollow, but it was strewn with fallen leaves, and her going was slow. When she arrived at the hollow's entrance she paused, a quiet sigh of relief shuffling her forward towards the cave.

She was less nervous now than last time, but when a twig snapped behind her, just as before she jumped, laying an alarmed hand on her chest. She pressed against the enclosing rocks, and although nobody was there, she waited several minutes before she dared proceed, hearing no further sounds save the close-by river and the rustling of the last few leaves hanging on their branches.

She reached the cave, easily missed even when nearly upon it: Percy had chosen his hideout well. She put her head into the opening, wondering whether to stoop and enter or to call into the black. Then her mind was made up as a hand reached out and grabbed her wrist. The action was unexpected; in the tense environment, she screamed.

'Shh!' whispered a man's voice. 'Is Percy with you?'

'You scared me.' Her heart was beating hard. 'No. I am alone.'

'You are sure?'

Involuntarily, she looked behind her. 'Nothing there.'

The hand released her wrist and a head of grey hair emerged, the man bending to fit through the low gap. He took his time to stand up straight, and although he smiled, his piercing eyes were full of question.

'Welcome back, Mercia.' He looked over her shoulder. ''Tis a pleasure to see you again.'

'And you, Colonel Dixwell.' Focused, she returned no smile of her own. 'Are the others inside?'

'Indeed they are.' He inclined his head. 'But I sense you are not here for conversation.'

'No.' Even the short word caught her breathless; she realised she was somehow panting, although she had ridden most of the way. 'Indian warriors have gathered on the edge of Meltwater. We need your help.'

'God save them.' Whalley dragged himself from the cave, his son-in-law Goffe close behind. 'You need our help how?'

She looked at the veteran general. 'The people need a leader, sir. They are in trouble. They need your valour to help them defend their homes.'

It was a magnificent, almost holy sight. As Lavington was dithering; as his son was striving to rally the men; as the women and children looked down from the half-finished fort, a strange figure appeared, riding on horseback from the forest. The sun glinted off his tarnished breastplate, as though approved by heaven, his head hidden by a well-worn helmet from years gone by. As though an angel he circled the palisade, reining in his horse where the men had gathered, and the breeze picked up in the leaves as they turned to stare at this soldier, dressed for battle, come into their midst.

The newcomer sat up straight on his horse – Mercia's horse – looking at the men now encircling him. One of the men – the magistrate's son – took a step forward and saluted, holding open his arms in a gesture of submission and welcome. Still the horseman uttered no word, and in his stead, the magistrate's son turned to his fellows and declared that here was their saviour, come to win their victory and their lives. The men stood still, uncertain, until one – the sawyer – looked to the skies and cried out thanks. Then the English yeoman stepped forward, and the schoolmaster, and the smith, and the farmers, the tanners, the everyone, and all yelled a great cheer of deliverance. Although distant, the women in the fort took up their cry, as amazed by this apparition as their menfolk, but they accepted it, believed in it, for whether human or no, it was certainly sent from God.

And then the old general dismounted his horse, and he spoke, and the men listened, and they learnt, and they did as they were bade. Muskets were taken up, swords buckled, a purpose firing in their hearts where before there had dwelt fear, the men ready to follow this hero from England, who had sought the sanctuary of his American brothers when he needed their help and who now, here in Meltwater, had come to repay them that salvation, the old general into battle once more.

From the edge of the field, Mercia watched as Colonel Whalley inspired the men, wondering at his words, his skill, and feeling a great pride at what he did, at what her father must have done in situations before, and she knew, though the Indians were concluding their dance, that the town would be safe, that this saviour would lead them to victory. Not a savage victory, for she had told him how the Indians had reason to be angry, but a victory of defence, of preservation, and soon, with the anger abated, the hope for reconciliation. But that, she knew, would be the hardest-fought victory of all.

The regicides had not spent long in discussing Mercia's request, knowing there was only one answer: that they would agree to help. They chose Whalley to be the man the people needed, for one leader was what was required, not three, and if aught went wrong, and Whalley was reported, there was no sense in giving up the other two as well. So he went into the cave and he fetched his old armour, carried across the ocean all this way.

And now the town was abuzz with preparation. Even Lavington deferred to Whalley's leadership, and Godsgift Brown, infirm as he was, took strength from the Englishman's presence, allowing himself to be carried to the practice ground to look upon his amassed militia. The men, fired up, gave him a welcoming cheer, and the constable, usually so gruff, permitted himself a smile. Mercia found she could not tear herself away from the animated scene, so different to the moroseness of earlier, but finally Nathan came over and insisted that she leave; she supposed he was right, in the end, that she should return to the fort and await the outcome of the day. Yet before she had been frightened; now, if still uneasy, at least she felt uplifted, tingling with the thrill her husband must have felt every time he was encouraged by the words of a respected general.

It was hard to tell looking down from the fort how the defence went, for the fight was swift and frenzied. As Whalley lined up the men, she saw an Indian scout running back from his hiding place near the town. Reaching his fellows, the red-painted warriors ceased their war dance and looked towards the palisade, perhaps made aware of the change of mood. But whatever the scout reported they were undaunted, and she felt the cold shiver of fear anew as they picked up their muskets and ran for the town with a resonant cry.

She held her breath, willing casualties to be light, hoping Nathan and Nicholas would be unharmed. When the first shot rang out, the ring of women around her gasped, an odd, aspirant sound that seemed louder than any gun. Those women with children held them close, shielding their young senses from the fear and the onslaught. Those who did not drew comfort from each other, and Mercia was glad her own son was safe in Winthrop's care.

Gunshots resounded, arrows twanged, the high-pitched calls of the Indian men filled the air with rage and bloodlust. As the two groups clashed, she turned her face from the low-fenced wall of the fort, but she made herself look back: if she was unable to fight, the least she could do was listen and watch. It was not like this was the first time she had known the anguish of battle.

And now two Indians appeared from the left side of town, circling the palisade fast. Distracted by the women's clamour, they looked up at the fort, but then they put down their heads and raced on, hoping no doubt to surprise the townsmen from the rear. Some of the women screamed out, some of the children cried, most everyone called on Fearing to let loose his mortar, but the farmer refused, and Mercia was glad: the sound would have deafened them while missing their swift-running target.

'Why will you not fire?' shouted Sarah Thomas. 'They will come up behind the men! Poor Humility!'

Fearing stood firm. 'I will fire this if they run up the hill, not otherwise. It will scare them and make them run back.'

I doubt that, thought Mercia, but she smiled at Sarah all the same. Then two musket shots rang out, and she looked down the hill to see the Indian men, not yet disappeared around the right side of the palisade, both fallen: Whalley, the veteran, had made certain his flanks were secure.

So the battle – more a fight – continued. At first caught against the palisade, soon the townsmen succeeded in pushing the Indians back, until the clashing of blades and the bellowing of muskets could be seen from the fort above the town. Seen indeed, for the smoking guns and the shining swords hammered into the women's eyes.

The colonists formed into a line, forcing splits in the Indian ranks as they resisted their attempts to break forward. At the same time, three men atop the palisade brought down their enemy with a precise firing of their muskets. All the while, his armour gleaming in the setting sun, Whalley strode amidst all, rallying his men; Mercia could feel the strength of his presence even from the fort. With his firm encouragement, there seemed a purpose to the defence, a hope, and so it prevailed. Unable to breach the townsmen's resistance, when two more Indians were felled the warriors turned and ran, the *pniese* who had led Mercia to Hopewell firing off a parting shot as the last to leave the field. The Puritans raised their own guns, ready to fire at the retreat, but Whalley roared a command, holding up a restraining arm, and the muskets were lowered, allowing the Indians to return to their homes unscathed.

A great cheer of victory from the town; a great cheer in response from the fort. Fearing slumped against the mortar, his hand on his chest, breathing deeply out. But the day was not yet over. Whalley ordered the men to stay watching the forest, but when the Indians did not return, he dismissed the majority, detailing a small group to remain on guard. Some of the rest made straight for the fort, their children running to meet them. Mercia walked down more gently, feeling uneasy relief that the attack was over, but guilt that she could have prevented it all.

Nearer the town, the mood became sober, for the victory had not been bought without cost. A limp body was being carried inside the palisade: Seaborn Adams, his chest shot through with a musket ball, his days on Earth over. Yet Whalley's leadership had ensured not only the town's survival, but that of all the other men too. Still, the pleasure of victory soon vanished, for Seaborn's death reminded them all of the real tragedy gripping the town.

As for Whalley, there was no sign. When Mercia looked for him, the old general had gone, vanished back into the air from where he seemed to have come.

'Have you seen Thorpe?' Percy's face was riddled with worry. 'I haven't seen him. Have you?'

Thinking of Seaborn as she sat on the meeting-house steps, Mercia looked up. 'No. Was he with the men in the fight?'

Percy's eyes darted about. 'Behind the rest of us, but yes. He should be thankful Whalley posted those sentries at the side, for he may now be dead if he had not. But that will count for naught with him. He saw Whalley, and he knows full well who he is.'

She bit her lip. 'Did Whalley go back to the cave? I gave him your directions.'

He sat beside her, lowering his voice. 'If he has any sense. I will have to go there myself when things have calmed down here.'

'Do you think Thorpe followed him?'

'I hope not. If he did, I trust Whalley will have lost him on the way. But they will have to move tomorrow. I will have to take them to their next hiding place earlier than I had hoped.'

'He saved the town, Percy. He would think his revealing himself worth the risk.'

'I know.' Percy sighed. 'I have not thanked you for bringing him here today.'

'You are welcome. But now – we have to end this. Somehow or other, before the Indians come again. If you are to move them, next time they will not be here for the townsfolk.'

'Did you see? God sent us an angel!' A large crowd was making its way down the northern street, Kit West walking backwards at its head. He turned as they reached the meeting house, a joyful smile on his freckled face. 'Percy! The angel came, just as I said would happen.'

Percy glanced at Mercia and stood. 'That you did, my friend.'

Kit turned back to the crowd, the small gathering hanging on his words. 'You see! The Devil used his minions to pierce Godsgift through, but God indeed gave us a better gift, for He would not allow us to perish, and He sent us His own messenger for our salvation!'

'The Devil indeed! Except the Devil was what was sent!'

A familiar voice boomed out from their right. Mercia rose to her feet, gripping Percy's arm.

'Thorpe!'

Wearing his broad sash, Thorpe stood directly in front of Kit, the intrigued crowd formed up behind the sawyer. Thorpe towered a good foot over the younger man, but Kit was broader, the outline of the muscles in his arms much more defined. Mercia knew who she would bet on in a fight, if one took place.

'You dare say that?' bridled Kit. 'It was an angel sent from God. It came when we needed and then it left.'

'An angel, hah! Something much more earthly-bound.' Thorpe narrowed his eyes. 'A traitor.'

The growing crowd murmured, shaking many heads. Clearly they did not like what Thorpe was saying.

'Take care, physician.' Kit pulled at the cord around his neck, yanking a locket from under his shirt. 'That angel now walks with my brother.'

'He does indeed?' Thorpe's lips twitched. 'Then they are two traitors together.'

Kit clenched his fist. 'My brother was no traitor.'

'Your brother rose up against the King. I should say that was treason. The hangman's noose certainly thought so.'

Kit's eyes blazed. He swung his fist, punching Thorpe to the ground. Rubbing his sore hand he leant over the fallen man. 'Never talk of my brother again. Do you hear?'

Thorpe staggered to his feet. 'I will talk of whom I wish.' He wiped at the side of his mouth, a lazy stream of blood flowing from the corner. Then he glared at the crowd. 'Look at you all, encouraging him. And not one of you loyal to the King. Well, friends, mark this: the King's men are near, in New York, and they will no longer allow you to keep your precious colonies untouched. And you.' He turned to Percy. 'We all know what you do, who you hide. You think me a fool? 'Tis obvious who your so-called angel was.' He licked at his bloody lip. 'And one day soon, it will not be me who is scorned here, but you, and I will be the magistrate and you will be where you belong: on a gallows in England, for helping the traitors to the King.'

The crowd snarled. Lavington had appeared at the back, looking for all the world amused. Then a stone flew over the heads of those at the front, but it landed to Thorpe's left, bouncing on the dusty street.

'You will see,' he said, standing his ground. Despite his words, Mercia admired him for that, but then he shattered that respect when he turned to her. 'Ask this woman what the King does to traitors. Her father should know.'

'Get out of here, Thorpe,' shouted Vic, in the crowd. 'What do you think your Joanna would have said to hear you speak so uncivilly with strangers?'

Thorpe glowered, wiping again at his cheek, but then Nicholas burst through, and the certainty in his eyes faded. He strode away, yet holding his head up high.

'Pity,' said Nicholas, joining Mercia at the steps. 'I should have liked to bring him down some more.'

'No doubt.' She looked at the now dispersing crowd, their lingering anger unsatisfied; at their edge, Kit was standing alone, the melancholy in his eyes a contrast to his previous ecstasy. She walked up to him, feeling an affinity from his words about his brother.

'Kit, I hope you do not mind, but . . . I am sure what he said must have hurt.'

Kit rounded on her. 'What business is it of yours?' She stepped back, for his eyes were once more aflame. 'I know my brother will have begged God to send us the angel, but I suppose you do not believe that either.' He shook his head. 'Heathen folk, all of you!' Then he too walked away.

'You will have to forgive him,' said Percy as she retreated to the steps. 'His brother is a difficult memory.'

'Is that the suffering from his past we have discussed?' She raised an eyebrow; Kit's unexpected reaction had displaced any decorum.

He hesitated a moment. 'Well, we are better acquainted now . . . so yes. He has a drawing of his brother in that locket of his. His brother . . . who was with the Fifth Monarchists.'

She widened her eyes. 'Surely not?'

'Kit wanted to join them. But when they were broken and his brother was taken, he sailed to America instead. I met him in Boston, and later he came here.'

'I've heard of the Fifth Monarchists,' said Nicholas. 'But I don't know much about them. Other than they ended up dead.'

Mercia nodded. 'They believed the country needed reform,' she explained, 'and that this would herald the Second Coming of Christ. But when the King regained his throne, some of them thought that a threat. They assembled in a tavern in London, hoping to unite the people against him.'

''Tis always in London you get the buffle-heads.' Nicholas smirked. 'But I know what happened next. They took to the streets, nobody joined them, and they were executed.'

'Kit's brother among them,' said Percy. 'His family locked Kit in his room to prevent him from joining the revolt. A providential act, for it saved his life.'

'And yet he came here,' she mused.

'He never forgave them. On the ship across the ocean, he had ample time to reflect. His faith grew strong, and now it upholds him.'

'It assuredly did today. And what of Thorpe? Why does he remain here when everyone mistrusts him?'

'To keep watch on us.' Percy shrugged. 'And because he loved his wife, who rests now in our cemetery, God protect her. But mostly to keep watch, and not just since he returned with that pompous commission. There is a network of the King's supporters throughout New England. In each town, at least one man or woman passes information back. We tolerate them, because we can pass false news that way. But it will be difficult to do so this time, when Whalley has been seen by so many. And speaking of that, I must . . . see to business when I can.' Giving her a smile, he put his thumbs in the top of his breeches and sauntered away.

She turned back to Nicholas, but he was looking at her, his head cocked.

'What?' she said.

'I know that walk. That look.'

'What look?'

'Percy's, just now. That . . . smile.'

She flushed. 'Do not be absurd. I think he has just . . . softened since first we met.' She changed the subject. 'Nicholas, that was brave, what you did today, fighting with the townsmen. But poor Seaborn Adams dead.' She clasped his arm. 'Where is Nathan? I was told he is safe, but I have yet to find him.'

'I was wondering when you would ask.' He grinned. 'He is part of the guard Whalley left to watch the forest. He volunteered, in truth. During the attack, he fought as though he was one of the local men.'

'Yes.' She looked towards the palisade, the same strange sadness returning that she had felt before. 'He is becoming more as one of them every day.'

Chapter Thirty

Thorpe had done something, she was sure of it. After his altercation with the town, he had become too withdrawn, and not merely because he was worried for himself: no, he was too proud for that, she thought. Was it connected with the regicides? With the murders, even? She was unsure if that were so, but she was watching him, waiting for him to make a mistake, if such a man ever could.

Nathan came into the kitchen area where she was half-heartedly perusing her old volume of the Anglo-Saxon kingdoms, distracted by her thoughts as she stirred a pot over the fire. He smiled, but there was little warmth in the gesture, more a saddened resignation.

'Hello,' she said, setting down the well-thumbed book, a family keepsake she had brought with her from England. 'Where are you going?'

'Oh, just out.'

'You are going to the Davisons' farm again, I suppose?'

He sighed. 'Mercia, I have told you. I am helping while we wait to leave. It gives me something to do.' He looked at her. 'You remember our conversation?'

'That depends which one.'

'About Sir William returning to the area. About that being the point when we decide to return home.'

She looked down at the pot; it was beginning to bubble. 'Yes, I recall it.'

'Well, it cannot be long now.'

'Which means?'

'It means we are out of time. Sometimes, Mercia, there are matters we cannot resolve. Even Whalley knows that.'

She watched the bubbles multiply, boiling faster and faster. 'What of your anger about Silence?'

'It is still there, Mercia, still deep. But I will bear it, if it means I can keep you safe, get you home.'

Wisps of steam began to rise. 'I have told you before, I do not need keeping safe.'

'No.' He snatched his jacket from a wall hook. 'It seems you need me for little these days. But I will not give up on you so easily. On us.' He paused in the doorway. 'Percy Lavington is back, if you are interested.'

She raised her head. 'Has he—are they safe?'

'I have not had chance to ask. But I thought you might want to.' He opened the door to the street. 'I will see you later, then.'

'Goodbye,' she murmured, as he eased shut the door.

The mood in the cottage had been oppressive; now the mood was brighter. After finishing her scant meal she was back outside, on horseback with Percy in the rapidly baring forest. Being outdoors always seemed to lighten her humours, even when, as now, she could feel the light haze of dampness on her cheeks as a light drizzle twirled in the air.

'I think we're on our own now,' said Percy.

She turned to look behind them. 'Yes, there is no one around.'

'Out here there usually isn't.' He took a deep breath, closing his eyes as he inhaled, held his breath, and released again. 'In spite of everything that is happening, I love it here.' He laughed. 'It is absurd. Here we are, surrounded by Indians and death and men who would have me arrested, and yet I would not change being here, being born here for anything.'

'I think I understand. There is something about this place that is above all that. But would you not have stayed in England, had Cromwell lived, or his son held onto power?'

Percy scratched at his ear. 'I always intended to come back one day. But yes, right then, I wanted to be in London, at the heart of it all. My father encouraged me. I wanted to learn from it and bring the lessons back to America, to help my people make their own way.' His face glowed as he looked across from his saddle. 'It still could be like that, you know.'

She smiled at his enthusiasm. 'Like what?'

'A land free of kings, free of arbitrary rule. A land of opportunity, of wealth.' He reined in his horse and gestured around him. 'Look at how much space there is here, how much land, and the best thing is we have no idea, none at all, how far west these lands stretch. It could be hundreds of miles. With such wonders at our disposal, what need we of kings then – of England, even?'

She raised an eyebrow. ''Tis well we are alone, speaking such words.'

'So what do you think, daughter of Rowland Goodridge? Do you agree with me?'

'It matters little what I think. And you have forgotten the Duke of York now owns a huge swathe of land directly to that westward direction of yours.'

'Oh, I could never forget that.' He scoffed. 'If the mighty Duke knew what I was doing with Whalley and the others . . . Thorpe is right. I would most likely be taken as a traitor.'

'But the people here would protect you, would they not?' She thought of Godsgift. 'They support what you do?'

'Those who know. They do not care for kings and dukes, that is certain.'

'And our three friends – you were away four days. Are they safe?'

'Secret and safe. To the north, in the attic of a man of complete trustworthiness. But I pity them.' His knuckles whitened on his reins. 'They should be leading us, as Whalley did here, but they are forced to hide in cramped conditions, hoping that one day they may be forgiven. In the meantime they are denied the chance to see their wives and their children.' He shook his head. 'Whalley and Goffe, at least. Dixwell is not known around here: it was a surprise when he arrived. I am not sure the King's men know he is in America at all.'

She hesitated. 'One of them does. He is coming here soon.'

He stared at her, aghast. 'What have you—to Meltwater?'

'To Hartford. But do not worry. He will say nothing. At least that is what he promised Dixwell in New York.'

'Mercia, I do not trust these men at all. Who is he?'

'His name is Sir William Calde.'

'Ah.' His hands loosened their tight grip on the reins. 'I know him. His position under Cromwell was somewhat ambiguous. But even so.'

'He was of help in New York. In any case, it matters not. Dixwell and the others are safe. But Percy, Nathan wants to leave when Sir William comes through. I am running out of time.'

His lips seemed to quiver. 'But I . . . you are leaving already?'

'Did you think we would stay for ever?' She smiled. 'I have told you before, England is home, as much as this is home to you.'

'I just . . . did not think it would be so soon.'

'We have been here a while, in truth.' She looked at him. 'Percy?'

'I'm sorry.' He turned his head. 'I was thinking. 'Tis only that . . . I have been enjoying spending time with you.'

There was something in his tone, something warm. She felt her cheeks reddening, but in the drizzle she hoped he would not notice. 'And I with you. I just wish it could have been at a less harrowing time.'

'You are right about that.' He tugged down the brim of his hat.

'Perhaps, then, if I cannot convince you to stay, you will agree to spend some more time with me tomorrow?'

'Perhaps.' She sighed. 'The strangest thing is, although Nathan says he wants to leave, I see him looking at the town, talking with its people, and I can tell he feels almost as you do about the work there, the life you lead. But I know he wants to protect me.'

Percy looked at her askance. 'You and he have not been getting along.'

'You could say that.'

'Well then . . . I will have to see if I cannot find some way to keep you by me.' He laughed. 'It might not be proper to invite you to my house to enjoy a good dinner, but you can help me clear the cave if you like, remove all the belongings they have not had chance to take.'

She rolled her eyes. 'Such an attractive offer.'

He grew serious, looking at her with a deep intensity. 'Mercia, since you came here I . . .' He trailed off. 'No, never mind.'

'Never mind what?'

He shook his head. 'It does not matter. Come. Why not try to beat me back to the town?'

They raced across the damp fields, startling Nathan as they hurtled past the Davisons' farm, hoe in hand as he looked up from his work. Nearing the palisade, Mercia spurred on her horse and flew past Percy's slowing mount, but when he reined in at the gate beside her she gave him a wry glance.

'You slowed down on purpose.'

He grinned. 'Why would I do that?'

'To let me win. Next time, no favours.'

'So there will be a next time?'

She jiggled her head. 'Perhaps.'

'Welcome back,' called a voice from the gate. 'I have been waiting for you for an hour.'

'Amery.' Percy danced his horse around the speaker. 'Waiting why?'

'On your father's orders, that's why. He has had me waiting since not long after you rode out.'

'Again, why?'

'How should I know?' His face darkened. 'I am merely the schoolmaster.'

'You know how he is. Spoilt one of his experiments, did you?'

Amery scowled. 'You as well, Mrs Blakewood.'

'Me?' She frowned. 'Why?'

'Always "why"! Go and find out. I have matters to attend to.'

Percy watched him stride arms folded through the gate. 'Poor fellow. I cannot blame him for being terse.' He cleared his throat. 'Best see what my father wants.'

Tying up their horses, they walked to the magistrate's house, a lightness in Mercia's gait she had not experienced for some time. Lavington's servant Stephen opened the door of the grand house to let them in. He led them directly to the parlour, but his master was not alone.

'Forgive me, Father.' His back to Mercia in the doorway, Percy's tone was terse. 'I did not realise you would have company.'

'Stay, Percy,' said Lavington. 'Richard's presence is why I have asked you here.'

Mercia followed him into the green-walled room; seated beside Lavington, Richard Thorpe barely acknowledged her presence.

'And me?' she enquired.

'That would be my fault.' A commanding voice boomed from the corner, where a finely dressed man was rising from Lavington's satin armchair. 'But it seems I have come at an interesting time, nonetheless.'

Startled, Mercia dipped her head. 'Sir William? I did not expect to see you so soon, and not in Meltwater.'

'Oh?' Sir William Calde, Mercia's noble admirer, sniffed. 'But your . . . friend. Keyte. He wrote a letter by way of Winthrop advising me you wished an escort to New York. I spoke to him just this morning about it, at the southern gate.'

She stared at him. 'Nathan has—what?'

'I would have come for you as soon as I arrived, but I had tedious matters to address with the magistrate.' He smiled. 'I must say, I am delighted to be asked.'

Percy swallowed as he looked at her. 'But you just said . . . I thought . . .'

'A slight misunderstanding.' She spoke through gritted teeth. 'One which I shall clear up forthwith.'

'So, Mrs Blakewood,' said Lavington. 'It seems you will be leaving us, after all.'

She glanced at him. 'Not quite yet.'

'No, we have a few days.' Sir William was fair beaming. 'Governor Nicolls is not expecting my report in New York until next week, although I have sent my retinue on ahead. Lavington has been good enough to offer me the use of his guest room.' His cheerful eyes grew mired with concern. 'But from what I hear of events, 'tis nigh time you were leaving. As for now, you will doubtless want to listen to what Thorpe here has to say.'

Lavington frowned. 'I do not think Mrs Blakewood would—'

Sir William turned his head, the smallest amount. 'I, on the other hand, do think she would like to hear.'

Her interest sparked despite her annoyance. 'Hear what?'

Thorpe was gazing at Sir William with the look of a fawning courtier in the presence of the King himself. He cleared his throat. 'With your permission, Sir William.'

The great man swept his hand across the room as though he owned it. 'By all means.'

'Well, then.' Thorpe's sash strained as he took a long breath. ''Tis this. I know who is responsible for the murders.'

'What?' Percy spoke over Mercia as she uttered the same exclamation. He looked at his father, but Lavington's face was impassive.

''Tis obvious, when you consider it.' Thorpe was shaking, whether because of Sir William's presence or for another reason Mercia could not say. 'Although with your interest, Percy, it seems likely you could never see the truth.'

Percy folded his arms. 'Do not speak in riddles, Richard. If you have an accusation to make, make it.'

'Then I shall.' He glanced at Sir William, who nodded for him to continue. 'What I mean, Percy, is that the killers . . .' His face flashed with sudden zeal. 'Is that the killers are your own friends. The killers are the regicides, Whalley and Goffe.'

Percy began to laugh. 'Oh yes. No matter that they have not been seen in many a year.'

'We all know you have been hiding them. The whole town does.' Thorpe looked up. 'Even your father.'

Percy's expression did not change. 'You should be careful what you insinuate, Richard.'

'Come now.' Thorpe's shaking had gone, colour bursting across his cheeks. 'Your father is no fool, and neither am I. He may dispute it, but I can see where there is no conviction.' He scoffed. 'How was it Whalley appeared the other day? A miracle? You see, Sir William, the regicides are nearby, and this is the man who has been protecting them.'

'As you said before he arrived.' Sir William toyed with the ostrich feathers that adorned his substantial hat. 'Whalley, Goffe, even John Dixwell somehow, too.' He shot Mercia a barely perceptible glance over Thorpe's head: a warning? A sign of complicity? 'But his father denies it.'

'As he tried to before, when we talked alone.' His head was lightly bowed as he looked on the great man. 'But I have considered it well since. The magistrate is in a difficult position. After all, Percy is his son, and he would not want the presence of the regicides so near his town to be widely known.' He cleared his throat. 'But it is beholden on us all, is it not, that we take every measure we can to apprehend those men, regardless of personal feeling?'

336

Percy narrowed his eyes. 'If you are so sure that was Whalley, why did you not arrest him at the time?'

'The whole town was against me, if you had not noticed.'

'Mr Thorpe,' interjected Mercia, striving to hold her voice neutral. 'Why do you claim those men are the killers we seek?'

'He has said so to the whole town, from what I hear,' said Sir William. 'Is that not right, Lavington?'

Lavington had been staring forward, but now he stirred himself to speech. 'He has been somewhat free with his tongue.'

'You have made this preposterous accusation in front of others?' Percy took a step forward. 'I cannot believe this, even from you.'

'It is the truth,' pursued Thorpe. 'And you will hide it no longer. As for you, Mrs Blakewood, I saw you ride out of town just before Whalley appeared. What say you to that?'

She held his keen gaze. 'I say you are searching for explanations that do not hold true. I was advised to leave before the Indians attacked, but I did not get far before I realised I could not abandon my friends.'

'A merry explanation. I shall find you out, Mrs Blakewood. We all know how your father served Cromwell.'

'Enough, Thorpe,' growled Sir William. 'You will speak civilly to women who are in America on the King's own business.'

Thorpe blinked madly as he turned his head, his mouth fallen half open in surprise. Clearly nobody had ever told him the reason Mercia was in America at all, and indeed why should they have?

'The . . . the King's business?'

Sir William inclined his head. 'And no, it is not for you to know on what business precisely, so do not ask.'

Mercia looked at Sir William, feeling a strange appreciation for his words. 'On which basis,' she said to Thorpe, 'you who claim to be loyal to the King, answer my question.'

'Very well.' Thorpe looked at her with darting eyes. 'First, they have been seen in this area. Deny it or no, I think we all know the truth of that. And second, there is motive, that they want to stay hidden. They hope to cover their tracks by killing those with whom they have had most contact.'

'Then why not kill me, Thorpe, I who am supposed to have harboured them?' Percy shook his head. 'Oh, that is right. Because they are not even here.'

Thorpe ignored the taunt. 'People may not like talking with me, but they talk with each other, and I hear what they say. And they say that George Mason visited Goffe and Whalley in New Haven, where he preached for them; that Clemency Carter gave them medicines when they were sick; that Hopewell Quayle supplied them with food and drink he traded from the Indians; that Silence Edwards talked with them when they were in want of company. And now all four are dead, the very four who had the most knowledge of their whereabouts. Except you, of course. I cannot explain that.' He jutted out his chin. 'Unless, of course, you have been aiding them.'

'That is too far, Richard,' said Lavington. 'You cross a line when you accuse my son of that.'

Mercia glanced from the one to the other. 'Besides, it is still not proof. It is supposition.'

'Refute it all you like. But the matter is slipping out of your hands.' Thorpe nodded, as if to reassure himself. 'I have made my accusations, and when I find where they are hiding, I will show you real proof you can no longer ignore.'

'This is an insult,' said Percy. 'If that is all, Father, then I can stand this malice no longer. I will be outside, taking some air.'

'Take as much air as you like,' said Thorpe. 'But think hard on what I have said, as others in the town are beginning to. Then perhaps you will see that the answer has been in front of you this whole time, and that turning over those men is the best course of action you can take.'

* * *

By the time Mercia had finished speaking with Sir William, Percy had vanished. Deep in thought, she walked slowly back towards her cottage. Under normal circumstances she would have dismissed Thorpe's contentions as fanciful, the accusations of an aspirant bent on rooting out his enemies to prove his loyalty to the King's men recently arrived on his shores. And yet, there was something in the force of his words, something that gnawed at her. Whalley and Goffe, Dixwell too, these were men who were wanted for treason, who would be executed if they were discovered. Was it not just possible that such men, forced to hide for so long in cramped quarters, was it not just possible that they could turn to savage acts to preserve their hounded lives? Like Godsgift Brown, she thought, they were versed well enough in war, to the atrocities of battle and the deaths of friends.

She turned the corner at the meeting house, eyes to the ground. She knew Dixwell, a little, and had reason to trust him, but she did not know the other two, the father-in-law and son-in-law. Was that familial connection strong enough that they might work together on such desperate crimes? Whalley had come to the aid of the town during the Indian attack, true, and that did not chime with Thorpe's accusation. And what of the methods of killing, the hanging, drawing and quartering? With a sickening lurch, as she approached the cottage gate, she realised it could be a comment on the fate that awaited the regicides themselves if ever they were captured. Perhaps . . . a kind of message to those who would investigate . . . to those believers like Percy, she thought, who would never betray them, not even then, who knew the intricacies of their lives and where they hid away. She had heard how such killers sometimes needed to confess.

And then, one hand on the gate, she stopped. The codes that had been left on the bodies. What if they too, as she had speculated, had been placed to confess? And if they were such a confession . . . if they were . . . would there not also exist, left somewhere secret, the means for those trusted friends to decipher them?

She turned back. The guilt that rose up was immense, but in the face of Thorpe's assertions she had to find out, if only to eliminate the doubt. Thorpe may not know where to start looking for the proof he so badly sought, but she did, and she would fetch Nicholas, and she would go looking herself now.

Chapter Thirty-One

'Are you sure about this?'

Nicholas was feeling his way through the trees by the light of a diminishing torch, the greys and purples of dusk obscured to black by the encroaching woods. Foregoing horses because of the darkness, they were making slow progress.

'Not at all.' She reached up to stop a gnarled branch swinging into her face as he pushed past it in front. 'But I feel guilty enough as it is. I need to do this while I am still able.'

A sigh came from up ahead as he stopped. 'This is hopeless. See, we should have brought Percy. He knows the path.'

'I told you, I did not want him to come. I am sure nothing will be there, but . . . he is too involved.'

'It won't matter if we can't find the cave at all.'

'Just keep going. I found it last time.'

'Yes, in the middle of the day.'

She blew out her cheeks. 'Look. There should be a cloven stump soon. I think. Then all we need do is head in the direction of the long root at its base.'

It was near impossible to see what lay in front, the hems of her dress dragging in the leaves and the dirt. Nicholas was continuously swearing: she knew he thought this madness, but he had come even so. Nathan would have too, she supposed, but she was furious that he had written to Sir William, even more that he hidden from her the nobleman's arrival. It was an argument she would happily delay until she returned to the town. If she returned, that was, for out here in the wilderness, the sounds of the forest growing ever louder as darkness enveloped them, her fantasies taunted her that she could be lost out here for ever, and that Daniel would never see his vanished mother again.

Calm yourself, she ordered. Trusting to Nicholas and his torch, and to her hands, reaching out to find safe ways around branches and scrub, she forced herself to press on. Then there it was, the cloven stump, and they followed the root, listening for the sound of the river to grow until they arrived at the heart-shaped carving, and finally the hollow itself. Passing once more into the walled-in space, the darkness fell stronger still, but Nicholas raised his torch and the flames bounced from the rocks, drawing light into its hidden realm.

He called from within his halo. 'Where is the cave?'

'Here. The far corner.'

He lowered his torch, swinging the flickering light left and right until he found the opening. 'What – that? How on earth did they live in there?'

How indeed, she thought. Still, she bent to go in, pulling in her dress, stooping to fit her topknot under the stony passage roof.

Nicholas had other ideas. 'Wait. I'll go first and let you know if there's room.'

'There has to be. Three men were living here for a number of days. Besides, I do not want to stand out here on my own. Foolish, I know, but still.'

'Very well, but I'll lead. Grab hold of my shirt and follow me in.'

Holding the torch before him, he crouched to slip through the narrow opening. She caught up a fold in his shirt back and, the chill ever growing, allowed him to pull her through. She banged her head twice as they passed through the passage, squeezing sideways to come into the cave proper, envying Nicholas his man's shirt and breeches as she watched him glide in. Once inside the cave they straightened up, but she felt the bumpy roof on her topknot before she could stand fully upright. The lit, open space was larger than would be supposed, the further reaches of the cavern still shrouded in darkness.

'I wonder how he discovered it,' she mused, looking at the shadows on the walls and ceiling.

'How does anyone? When you need somewhere to hide, you find it.' Nicholas inched deeper into the cave, swinging the torch. The already weakening light flickered.

'Take care,' she said. 'We will be in trouble if that goes out.'

'Don't worry. Hold it a moment, would you?'

He passed her the torch and bent down to pick up a long, branch-like object from the floor. 'Look. Here's another one.'

'Still, not much use if this burns out first.'

'Then let's be quick. If that starts to go down, we'll light this one.' He looked around. 'What are you searching for?'

'Hopefully nothing. But I have to be certain. Can you take back the torch while I look?'

Although low-roofed, the cave was deep, and many discarded items littered the earthen floor. In one corner loomed clear evidence that someone had stayed here: seeds and bones, the remnants of meals. As Nicholas passed the torch around the space, different sections became illuminated, others tumbling into blackness. The effect was eerie, giving the constant impression that the cave was shrinking and being reformed.

'Wait.' She held up a hand Nicholas could not have seen. 'What is that over there?'

'Over where?'

'Just behind you. That – rectangular shape. I think . . . is it a chest of some sort?'

'I don't know. Let me—'

A loud crack resounded through the cave. Nicholas cried out, slumping to the floor and dropping the torch. As it bounced on the hard surface, a cloth appeared as if from nowhere, cast across the light. Within moments, the cave had plunged into total darkness.

'Nicholas,' she called out, her voice echoing. 'Nicholas!'

A low moaning came from in front. She edged forwards, blind, but she stepped too far and she fell over his outstretched leg. Falling over headfirst, she put out her hands in involuntary reflex; they smashed into the hard ground, the force of her rigid arms vibrating through her chest in agony, but she managed to roll over into a crouching stance. Her sight gone, her other senses combined with the tension coursing through her blood to set her on high alert.

'Who is there?' she called. 'That cloth did not throw itself.'

Try as she might, she could not keep the trembling from her voice. Not being able to see was terrifying. She was aware of a damp smell all around her, and the steady dripping of water through rock from somewhere to her right. And then – a shuffle of feet on the other side of Nicholas, near where she had seen the supposed chest. The sound of breathing, as unsteady as her own. A dull thud as something struck at Nicholas, causing his moans to cease.

She backed away but could not retreat far: the rough sharpness of the stony cave wall soon pressed into her back. Then the shuffling became a scuffle, heading right for her. A feeling of terror flooded her soul, a snatching of absolute, total panic. She opened her mouth to plead for mercy, but found she could no longer speak.

Whoever was in the cave paused right in front of her, and still she could not see, the darkness was so acute. But her heightened senses heard the irregular breaths, smelt the fresh leather of a jacket or coat.

'Please,' she stammered, her instinct for survival releasing her voice. 'Please don't.'

For a moment the presence lingered. The image of her father on the scaffold flew uncalled into her mind. Was this what he had felt before his end? She raised her arms, readying for the attack. She would not die without resisting, not here in this dark cave, far from home. Now almost upon her, the presence paused, and she heard herself whining, a terrified, unhuman sound. But then it seemed to back away, the oppressiveness lifting. And then Nicholas groaned anew, regaining his wits.

She heard him pull himself up. 'Mercia,' he croaked. 'Where are you?'

'Nicholas, there is someone with us!'

She waited for the presence to strike, not daring to move. But then she realised the breathing had gone, and she could no longer smell leather. Instinctively she felt out with her arms, but – there was nothing.

'Is he still here? Nicholas, can you tell?'

A hand brushed against her own. She screamed out, the cry reverberating round the cave.

''Tis just me,' said Nicholas, his voice close. He clutched at her forearm. 'Just me.'

'Where is he?' She reached out once more. 'He was here. Right in front.'

For an anxiety of moments they felt round the cave, crawling in the dirt, keeping a hand always touching. But of their ghostly companion they encountered no trace.

She breathed out in pure relief. The presence had gone.

Nicholas winced as she dabbed at a wound on his temple, splashing a piece of cloth she had ripped from his shirt with water from the stream near the hollow. Back in the open air, her heart was still pounding, her senses on edge, but at least she could now see, to a point.

'I don't know what's worse,' he said. 'The stinging from that water or the pain in our eyes when we came out of the cave. I never knew night could be so bright.'

'Anything is bright compared to in there.' She wrung out the cloth. 'Stop moving your head.'

'I'm thankful I've a head left to move. Then again, I don't think he meant to kill me, just put me out. He didn't hit me hard enough for that.'

She paused with the cloth in her hand. 'I was sure he was going to kill me. When he came forwards.' Renewed terror fluttered down her spine. 'But before you came round, he halted, as though he was looking at me, even though he could not see. And then he left.'

'You think it was the murderer? One of them, at least?'

'I think it could have been.'

'Perhaps it was Percy, come to do the same we have.'

She shook her head. 'Whoever it was, he knew it was me. I called your name. Percy would have revealed himself.'

'Thorpe, then?'

'Perhaps.' She sighed. 'Do you think he could be a murderer, Nicholas? I am not sure. Why make up such a story about the regicides if he were?'

He shrugged. 'To pass blame onto them, away from himself? To sow doubts to bring them into the open, while punishing those who helped them hide?' She dabbed again at his wound; this time he bore the sting. 'But it sounds a little extreme.'

'Not to me, not any more. We have seen enough fanatics in our time to believe the same could be happening in America. And Thorpe is adamant about tracking those men down. Whatever else he is, he has threatened to find them out. Maybe he followed us here.'

'Maybe he followed at some point in the past, or maybe someone else did, but not tonight. That man was in there before we arrived. He only attacked when we got close.'

She straightened up. 'Well, if he was not looking for the regicides themselves, then perhaps he was looking for something else. We may have surprised him before he could finish his task.' She walked a few yards along the river, carefully setting down one foot before raising the other, until she stooped to paw at the earth. 'Come, Nicholas. Put some of those old sailors' skills to use.'

He lurched upright. 'How so?'

She began to amass a pile of twigs, calling him across. Between tending to his injury and talking she seemed to have vanquished her former fear.

'You can start a fire, can you not, to relight our torch? Relight both torches, indeed. That other we saw must have been his, dropped as he heard us enter.' She reached for more twigs. 'So when we go back in, that should make the task quicker, thank God.'

It took longer than she had hoped for Nicholas to light the fire, but he managed it, using a sharp stone he found at the side of the stream. Once the fire was going he disappeared into the cave, emerging soon after with one of the torches, which he lit before returning for the other.

'Thank you,' she said as he handed the second torch across. She reached down to light it. 'Now we had best extinguish this fire.' She stamped on the ground, putting the flames out with her boots. 'Are you ready?'

He grinned. 'Always.'

The warmth of the gesture encouraged her, in spite of the renewed dread she was feeling, and she knew he had done it on purpose.

'Then let us go in quickly in case he decides to return.'

They squeezed back inside, checking again for signs of an intruder, but this time there was nobody there. Hasty all the same, they swept their torches over each part of the cave, circling the walls before coming to the middle. As she had thought, there was a small chest to one side, composed of two drawers; a pen and inkstand sat atop.

Nicholas was beginning to cough. 'There is too much smoke from these torches,' he said. 'How did they live in here? It must have been dark most of the time.'

She leant down to the chest. 'I suppose they slept when it was night, one of them probably on watch, and when it was light, they came into the hollow.'

She tugged at the handle of the top drawer, but it was locked. The bottom drawer pulled open, but there was nothing inside.

She looked at Nicholas. 'Whoever that man was, he may have emptied this already. But the top drawer is secure. Have you found a key?'

'No. But let me see.'

She stood aside so he could examine the drawer. He took one look, drew a knife from his belt, and stabbed into the puny lock.

'Shame I could not use this earlier, when that bastard was here.' He twisted the tip of the blade. 'There. It should open now.' He tugged at the handle and the drawer flew from the chest, scattering its contents as it tumbled to the ground.

Mercia crouched down. 'Watch the entrance, will you?'

As he moved off, she rummaged through the objects that had fallen from the drawer: a chain of some sort; a buckle, perhaps broken from a belt; a Bible; a whole sheaf of papers now littered about. She leafed through them.

'Oh.' She smiled. 'A letter Goffe has started to his wife. I will have to leave this for Percy so he can take it for him to finish.' She continued to peer through the pages. 'More correspondence. And what is this? Drawings, to pass the time no doubt.' She cast her eye across the small pictures covering the entirety of one of the sheets. Then she turned cold. 'Hell's teeth!'

'Have you found something?' Nicholas called.

She ignored him, her attention captured by the series of drawings on the page. It was a number of impressions of the *monas*, some complete, some split into its parts. A series of drawings of the alchemists' symbol that had been divided among the murderous codes.

'Christ.' Nicholas's shout startled her. ''Tis so dark in here we missed this!'

Her mind in turmoil, she turned to look. In one hand he was gripping his torch, while in the other, he held out a saw for her to see. She did not need to examine it to know it would be the same Kit claimed to have lost. Near Nicholas's feet, his light was illuminating a large knife.

'It is speckled with dried blood,' he said.

'Is it?' she replied. 'Is it?'

She turned back to the papers, leafing swiftly through, and then a shiver passed her soul as she found what she had never thought to discover, not in this cave, at least.

Nicholas peered over her shoulder. 'What is it?'

It was a series of ten leaves of paper, designed to be used in pairs: the first set of five sheets numbered one through to five, and the second set the same, numbered one through to five. On the first set, the letters of the alphabet were scattered over the page, each time jumbled in a different order. Tiny windows were cut into each sheet of the second set, twenty-six square holes with a cursive letter alongside. When the matching pairs were placed together, the windowed page on top, corresponding letters were revealed on the jumbled sheet beneath.

'It is a key.' She closed her eyes. 'A key, Nicholas. Indeed five of them.'

He took a shallow breath. 'To go with five codes.'

Holding the papers in one hand, she reached with the other for the unfinished letter to Goffe's wife; her heart sank as she saw the writing matched. Then she pulled from her pockets the by now tattered parchment on which she had scrawled all five codes.

'Here, take this.' She passed him the parchment, and then assembled the first pair of papers, the windowed sheet on top of the jumbled alphabet. 'And read me the letters from the first code, the powwow's. My mind is too affected to recall them precisely.'

'I'll try.' He peered at the code. 'S. I think.'

She looked at the key. The window labelled 'S' showed a 'T' underneath.

'And then the second is – X,' he said. 'That's easy. Everyone I know signs their name with X.'

'X is the letter . . . O.' She looked up. 'T, followed by O. To?'

'Makes sense. The next is W.'

'Which is K.'

'Now, L.'

'E, then.'

349

'Another L.'

'Another E.' She shook her head. 'As Winthrop thought. If only we had tried harder.'

'You tried as hard as you could. You couldn't know each code would have a different key.' He looked back down. 'The next is R.'

'Which is . . . P.' She considered a moment. 'T-O-K-E-E-P . . . tokeep – to keep! To keep what?'

'Let's continue. The next is I – no, J. There's a curl at the bottom.'

'You are sure?'

'Yes. J.'

'J corresponds to . . . S.' She frowned. 'Isn't there a J at the end of that code too?'

He paused. 'Yes. Yes there is.'

'So another S, at the end.'

'Seems that way. But going in order, the next letter is L.' He coughed. 'Damn this smoke. E again, correct?'

'Correct.'

'Then there is Q, and M.'

'Which are . . . C . . . and R.' She stared down at the papers. 'To keep . . . S-E-C-R. . .' She closed her eyes. 'The next will show E and T, I think.'

'Well, the final three letters are . . . L again . . . S . . . and that J.'

She read from the key to be sure. 'E . . . then T . . . and S. So yes. This code reads, *To keep secrets.*' A melancholy washed over her, a cold sense of betrayal and despair. 'A motive, perhaps. We should move onto the next.'

And so it went, Mercia descending through ever more layers of hurt. The second code, from George Mason: *To protect many.* The third, the worst, from Clemency: *We must kill few.* The fourth, from Hopewell: *Lord forgive us.* The fifth, from Silence, a repetition of the fourth, an emphasis perhaps of the anguished plea. Now all five meanings were revealed.

To keep secrets
To protect many
We must kill few
Lord forgive us
Lord forgive us

She slumped in the cave, the message ringing through her heart. A motive indeed. And a confession no less.

Chapter Thirty-Two

She talked with Percy. He could not believe it: indeed, partisan as he was, he refused to believe it, dismissing the idea out of hand. Understanding his point of view, and yet unwilling to be so inflexible herself, she rode to Hartford to talk with Winthrop. The calm and rational governor could not believe it either. How could such noble men be guilty of such crimes, went his argument? And yet there, in that cave, she had found the key to the codes, apparently written in William Goffe's hand.

But to her doubting mind, her confusions dipping and rising much like the ruts in the Meltwater road, it seemed wrong. That the regicides had left the incriminating key, and more so the saw, seemed too careless, the killings far too callous. She decided there was only one thing to do: confront the men herself and demand the truth. In a rage, Percy had snapped that they were safe in a town called Hadley, some hours to the north, and so to Hadley she would ride, even if Percy refused to go with her to show her the way.

As she returned to Meltwater from Hartford, the inaugural Guy Fawkes festivities scheduled for that night were underway. It had been two weeks since Silence's murder, and the townsfolk were still on edge, understandable, so she thought, but they were pouring their energies into this new distraction, hoping the burning of the guy would help burn away some of their fear. In the western field, Humility Thomas was overseeing two boys as they stacked frayed pieces of wood in a haphazard pile, the macabre guy discarded in a small cart beside them, its long black hair and stern expression an uncanny surrogate for the Duke of York.

She passed inside the palisade, finding Nicholas sitting with Amery on the meeting-house steps. Rising, the schoolmaster greeted her with little enthusiasm before sauntering towards the schoolhouse to leave them alone. She was shocked to learn from Nicholas that the whole town was humming with the news that the regicides had moved on from killing Kings to killing ordinary people too.

'Percy,' he explained. 'He was so angry he took it on himself to rubbish the claims before anyone could spread them. Now Thorpe is demanding to know what really happened, and the town is full of wild tales.'

She bit her lip. 'Do they believe it?'

'After Whalley's appearance against the Indians?' Nicholas shrugged. 'Not many, but I sense a few just want to accuse someone and be done with it. 'Tis easier that way, perhaps.'

'But not just.'

'No.' He hesitated. 'Sir William was asking where you were. He seemed upset you'd gone to Hartford for a couple of days.'

She sucked in her cheek. 'He can be as upset as he wants. What says he of all this?'

'Oh, come now, you don't expect him to talk to the likes of me, do you?'

'I suppose not.' She took a deep breath; the air still seemed fresh, even now. 'Have you seen Nathan? Daniel was asking after him.'

'How is he? Daniel?'

'Growing restless now. Eager for home.' She sighed. 'So 'tis past time we concluded this. I am going to Hadley. Will you come?'

'Hadley?' His eyes flicked down. 'What about Nathan?'

'What of him? He seems more interested in farming nowadays.'

'I wouldn't—' He broke off as he saw her face. 'Look, since the attack, none of the Indian farmhands have dared come back to work. He likes to help.' He looked at her askance. 'I take it you haven't spoken with him yet?'

'Not yet.'

'Don't you . . . think you should?'

She frowned. 'Is there something you are not telling me?'

'Just . . . speak to him.'

She shook her head. 'I will, after I have wet my face. That Hartford road feels very long.' She fixed him a stare as she walked away. 'But we ride tomorrow. At first light.'

Despite her persisting rancour at Nathan for having written to Sir William, she did as Nicholas suggested and rode out to the Davisons' farm. Walking through the town to collect her horse, she heard people talking in the streets, gossiping in closed huddles.

'I said it all along,' one man was saying. 'Richard was right. We should have listened.'

'Don't be ridiculous,' replied his companion. ''Tis as Percy says. Something doesn't feel right.'

'Tell that to Standfast. He is raving still with despair.'

Outside the palisade, she mounted her horse and rode the short distance to the farm. She found Nathan bent over in the corner of a half-harvested field, nailing together a shaky fence. She paused for a moment to look at him, dressed in clothes he must have borrowed – rough farmworkers' attire designed to get dirty. He seemed quite at ease working in the fields, even more than when she had watched him supervising his own farm back in England. Strange, she thought. The soldier, a man who had killed men, become a farmer, tending the earth to grow food to feed them. The circle of life, and on, and on.

She reined in her horse. 'Hello.'

'Hello.' He looked up and smiled. 'So you are talking to me.'

'For now.'

'I told you why I wrote to him.'

She focused on the nearly finished fence. 'You seem quite happy here.'

'That is beside the point.' He laid his tools on the dry earth. 'How is Daniel?'

Her lips twitched into an aborted smile. 'He is well, thank you.'

'Was he asking after me?'

'Of course.'

'I wager he wants to return home too.'

She jiggled her head. 'Maybe.'

'Come, Mercia.' He patted the horse's neck. 'There is no sense in our falling out.'

She looked across the meadow, into the distance. 'We do not seem to have done much more of late.'

'No. Under the windmill in New York, it seemed like such a good idea to come here. Now . . . maybe not.'

The breeze whipped up around them, teasing the horse's mane. 'But Clemency would still be dead, and there would be nobody to avenge her.'

He glanced up. 'Avenge?'

'Avenge, help her find peace, what does it matter?' She jerked at the reins. 'I came to say I am going . . . somewhere again.'

'Yes. To see Whalley and the others. I thought you might.' He rotated his neck as though creasing out the stiffness of his labour. 'But there is no need. I have gone for you.'

She looked down aghast. 'When?'

'While you were in Hartford. I wanted to do something to help you. Can you understand that?'

'But . . . Nicholas said nothing.'

'So you have spoken to him already.' He sighed. 'There was a time when you would have come to me as soon as you returned. Well. I suppose he wanted you to hear this from me, as he should.'

Agitated, she jumped from her horse. 'Wait a moment. Let me tie her up.' That done, she turned to face him, lowering her voice. 'Now speak.'

He leant against the newly sturdy fence, talking quietly. 'As soon as you had gone, I went to see Percy, but he refused to ride with me to see them. His mind, you see, cannot accept they could be guilty.'

'And you? What do you think?'

'I think any man can commit atrocities when he fears for his life. I have seen as much.'

She nodded, waiting for him to continue.

'I spoke to Nicholas. I rebuked him for letting you travel to Hartford alone and then I got him to tell me more about what happened in the cave. You never told me he had been attacked.' His face seemed to fall. 'You trust him now, it seems. You took him to search for answers instead of me.'

'Nathan, I did not want you to worry. And I was angry with you. To speak true, I still am.' Some of the hurt she had buried inside burst up, breaking through the wall she had built. 'Why the hell did you have to write to Sir William without telling me?'

'You know why.' He did not turn away. 'I think you are suffering here, and I want to take you and Daniel home.'

'That is for me to decide, not you. But . . . carry on with your account.'

He looked at her a moment as though trying to read her thoughts, but she held her face impassive. He shook his head.

'I rode to Hadley. 'Tis two days' journey, by rights, but I managed it in one. I wanted to be back by the time you returned.'

'Did no one question where you were going?'

'I said I had changed my mind about accompanying you to Hartford. Then when I returned first, I said you had stayed a little longer with the governor's wife.' He scratched at his old scar, sticking up from under his loose shirt. 'I got into some trouble for letting you ride on your own.'

'I was on my own the whole way.' Impatient, she bade him continue. 'What happened in Hadley?'

A wistfulness came into his eyes. ''Tis a beautiful village, smaller than

Meltwater, and just as remote. It is a remarkable life they lead here, you know.'

'Is it?'

His lips curled into a sorry smile. 'When I got there, I made a fuss in the street, shouting I was come from here. It did not take long for their minister to approach me. He took me to Dixwell, and I explained what had happened. Needless to say he was outraged. He spoke with Goffe and Whalley right away, although I was not allowed to see their hiding place.'

She leant towards him. 'So what did they say?'

'That they were innocent. That Goffe never wrote that code, not even that letter to his wife. And that they could not possibly have committed the murders, for he and Whalley were in New Haven when they all happened, other than the last.'

'I had thought that would be so. But could not one of them, pushing hard, have ridden to Meltwater to carry out the killings while the other feigned his innocence?' Even as she said it, she knew how far-fetched it sounded. She longed for Nathan to give her something to tear the weak argument apart.

'Then who would have been the second person Vic saw?' He bounced on his heels. 'No, Mercia. Their host in New Haven can vouch for them, as can Dixwell since they came here, as can a number of people all around – people who supposedly know nothing about them, but who would come forward if their lives were at stake.' He looked her full in the face. 'They never left their attic that whole time. Mercia, it is not possible that they committed the murders. I do not know why, but someone is playing a heartless game with both them and the town.'

She stared at the ground. 'You are sure of this?'

'It would be very simple to speak with the people whom they say can prove they were miles away. So why should they lie? And why should they leave those codes as admission of guilt if they did not want to be found out?'

'This is incredible.' She felt a powerful mixture of relief and guilt. 'Have you told Percy?'

'I was waiting for you.'

She managed a smile. 'You have saved me a long ride. Thank you.'

'You are welcome. 'Tis what friends – supposedly good ones – are for.'

From farm to town, the distance was not far, the Davisons' land the closest plot to the palisade: a fatal choice of employer, then, for the innocent farmhand caught so close to the scene of Hopewell's murder. But she pushed her horse nonetheless, leaning far over its withers, so when the face appeared at the edge of the forest, it was only the horse's momentum that held her upright as she lost her grip on the reins.

'That was Sooleawa!' she shouted as she recovered her wits, continuing without pause.

'I'm not surprised,' called Nathan. 'Remy says she has been watching the town ever since the Indians attacked.'

'I cannot hear,' she yelled. 'Talk to me when we get back to the town.'

For the rest of the short ride they kept their silence, but when Mercia looked round, she could see Sooleawa looking straight at her from just outside the forest. Bow in hand, she made no move to follow or even react, and then she vanished back into the wood. Once in Meltwater, Mercia secured her horse and turned to Nathan.

He shrugged. 'Many of the townsfolk have seen her. Vic and Kit rode out to chase her away, but she seems not to want to leave.'

'Is she alone?'

'No one else has been spotted, at least.' He looked at her. 'I think we both know why she is here.'

'She is still after Godsgift.' She set off towards the bonfire site. 'But I thought . . . did she not say she wanted to kill him in front of everyone?'

'Maybe that's the thing. With this celebration, everyone will be gathered outside, Godsgift too. Perhaps she intends to strike then.'

'Is he well enough to come outdoors?'

'Not really, but he—hey, steady!' A pair of girls rushed past, the taller crashing into his legs. He smiled and they continued on their heedless way. 'He insists,' he finished. 'He says he won't let any such . . . Indian . . . stop him from joining in.'

'I suspect he did not use quite that word.'

'No. And nobody else but Standfast knows she is after him, so nobody else knows why she is watching. I think some of them worry she is scouting for another assault, but apparently it happens all the time.'

They came into view of the ever-enlarging pile of wood. 'An assault?'

'An Indian stationed nearby, just watching.'

'I suppose. Vic suggested as much before.' She sighed. 'But we have no time to worry about Sooleawa. We need to find Percy and tell him what you have learnt.'

It took more than an hour to seek him out. Wobbling on a stool beside the bonfire, Humility grudgingly broke from his ale to admit Percy had been helping there earlier, but when one of the boys had repeatedly asked about the regicides he had stormed into the woods in fury. By the time the light was fading and the townsfolk were gathering for the procession of the guy, he was still missing. But they persevered with their search, until nearing the low hill the sound of frenzied banging finally drew their attention. Climbing to check, they found Percy hard at work, tying up logs to strengthen the forlorn barricade of the half-finished fort.

'I need something to do,' he said, not looking up. 'Something away from other people. They are making me angry.'

Mercia glanced at Nathan. 'I fear we are not come to assuage that angst.'

He paused in his work. 'Oh?'

She told him about the regicides, about how they could not have been the killers. He listened impassively, scarcely seeming to pay attention, but when she had finished he picked up the axe at his feet and thundered the sharp head into the side of the fort.

'I know all that. I know they cannot be the killers. The question you should be considering is who would make them out to be so?'

Nathan folded his arms. 'Mercia has gone to Hartford. I have ridden to Hadley. You do not seem to be doing much to disprove the notion yourself.'

Percy glared at him. 'Do you never listen? I said I have been too angry.' Mercia jerked back her head, for there was a fervour in his eyes stronger than she had seen, in those instances when he talked of his charges, of his duty. 'But I have been thinking. And I am tired of playing his games.' He wrenched the axe from the barricade. 'You want me to do something?' He looked down toward the town. 'And you? All of you?' He pushed past Nathan, causing him to sway despite his bulk. 'Follow me. Let us settle this for good and all.'

He marched down the hill as a man with a purpose, heading straight for the site of the bonfire. In the field, a murmuring of people was now surrounding the finished edifice: Lavington, Kit, Amery; Remembrance, Humility, Vic; Fearing, Thorpe, Godsgift, the blanketed constable in a chair in the midst of all, his faithful servant Rose at his side. Mercia hurried in Percy's wake, worried to know what he had in mind, Nathan keeping up the pace as avidly as she.

Reaching the bonfire, she lingered at the edge of the field, watching as Percy leapt onto a large outcrop of rock a few yards from the huge pile of wood. Brandishing the axe, he thrust the tool skywards and bellowed for silence.

As one, the town turned towards him. On the rock, in the trickery of dusk, he seemed taller than usual: he was raised above them all, of course, but it was more than that, Mercia thought, more . . . menacing. His axe held high, he appeared more aggressive, more focused, and all the townspeople could sense it. His father raised his head in the semi-light, and nearer to Mercia, the constable shifted in his chair, a determined expression of – approval? – on his pale visage. Next to Lavington, Humility had been bending to set a torch to start the fire, but he left the wood uncaught, heaving himself upright to listen.

'People of Meltwater!' Percy began. 'We are deceived!'

A feeling of doom settled on Mercia. She brought her hand to her mouth and looked at the people close by, Nicholas not far down among them, arms folded beside Vic and Kit. Further off, Richard Thorpe was standing with his head held back, Sir William Calde at his side, the great man looking vaguely bemused. Yet the power in Percy's voice was enrapturing: Cromwell's man come through at last.

'Our friends,' he cried, his strong words piercing the air. 'Those brave men.' He surveyed his audience. 'You know who I mean. Our friends, who have been guests in our country these past years. Our friends, who have come to escape the tyranny of England, where they were rejected through malice and spite. Our friends, dear to us as fellows, who have been accused now of crimes their noble morality would never allow them even to contemplate.'

'Very stirring,' muttered Nathan. 'What is he hoping to achieve?'

'I am not sure,' she whispered. 'But if he is prepared to break his usual silence, I do not think it can be good.'

'In England,' pursued Percy, 'they call these friends traitors.' He thrust out his axe towards Thorpe. 'And there are those among us who share this view. But it is not they who are traitors. No! It is those who would call them such.'

A grumble of agreement shot through the crowd, the enthusiasm of shared opinion taking hold. Despite his injury, Godsgift crossed his legs, nodding with satisfaction.

'And now, as these noble men, these great . . . patriots – as they stand accused of the terrible murders that have fallen on this town, the Duke of York himself has sent an army to subdue us!' He swept the axe towards the guy lying listless in the cart. 'Behold, there, the image of the tyrant itself! And there!' He stabbed the axe to the back of the crowd. 'His henchman, the great Sir William Calde, peer of the realm of England, and would-be ruler of this!'

'What is he talking about?' said Mercia, all eyes turning to Sir William, the nobleman shifting uneasily on his feet. 'He is getting carried away.'

'We all know how the King craves the men he calls the regicides, but whom we call kin. But we did not know the lengths he would go to in order to seize them!'

Nathan shook his head. 'Carried away to the executioner's noose if he keeps this up.'

'Notes were found in their hiding place.' Percy lowered the axe, reaching into his pocket to pull out the sheets of paper Mercia had since given him. 'But they are fake, left there by the King's own men to implicate them.' He looked around the crowd. 'And you know what I think? About who has killed all our friends, our own blood?'

The sound of the breeze stirring the branches, and then, 'Tell us!' shouted Amery and Fearing across each other, the one apprehensive, the other more brash. There was a tension in the crowd, a holding back, as if a coil that was primed and ready for release.

Percy's eyes blazed as surely as any bonfire could. 'Who hanged Clemency Carter? Who cut open Hopewell Quayle? Who dared saw apart Silence Edwards and scatter his remains across our hard-won land?'

'Who?' Speaking as one, the crowd was fast growing hysterical.

'Then it is this! It was the King's own men responsible for these murders! The King's own men, in a perverse attempt to scare us into handing over our friends, Whalley and Goffe!' He gripped his axe and shook it. 'For such runs the spite of the King's ill will!'

'Yes!' The grumblings became shouts, the unfulfilled tension finding its release in one fulsome leap. 'You are right!'

'And there,' he concluded, holding the axe out again at Thorpe, 'is the demon who has plotted this appalling deed!'

'He is mad!' said Thorpe, backing away. Near at hand, John Lavington looked between his son and Sir William with frantic eyes. 'We all know he harbours them. He would say anything to make them look innocent!'

'What I say is the truth!' cried Percy. 'But there is no need to take my word. Let us go to his house and find out!'

He leapt from the rock, pushing through the crowd, making eye contact with no one. As he passed Godsgift, the constable reached up to grab him by the wrist, and for a moment Mercia thought he was trying to stop him pursuing his foolishness. But he merely nodded in support, releasing Percy's wrist to allow him on. The crowd noticed the gesture, even those who were uneasy, and for them it was enough.

They fell in behind Percy, marching on their own town.

Chapter Thirty-Three

Sir William, no longer bemused, edged backwards with Thorpe. But the great man's coat was long, and he stumbled on its hems, the action distracting the crowd from their singular purpose. Within an instant he and Thorpe were surrounded.

'Percy!' Scuttling forward with tentative steps, Lavington tugged at his son's sleeve. 'Percy, stop!' He strained his neck to peer over his shoulder. 'This is not my doing, Sir William, I implore you!'

Fearing Davison looked on him with unbridled glee. 'So you're with them, are you? Years of service . . . and not an ounce of respect.'

Before he could react, Lavington was grabbed by the mob and spun through its ranks. He fell against Thorpe, the pallor of the physician's face a contrast to his usual fiery temperament.

'I am your magistrate!' cried Lavington. 'End this madness!'

But the crowd, his manservant, his son; nobody was in any mood to listen. While some held back to guard the captives, Percy led the rest to Thorpe's house, Mercia following in the mob's wake. For a moment he waited, gripping the gate with his left hand as his shoulders rose and fell in time with his steady breaths, but then he pivoted to face his audience.

'This does not need all of us!' He searched the faces in the crowd. 'Who will oblige?'

A pause, and then Amery stepped forward, staring up at Percy with – what was that? Admiration? Then Vic pushed through to join him, his own face grim.

'I will help,' he said. 'For Clemency, and for the others.'

Nathan and Nicholas were flanking Mercia at the back; she lowered her voice, not that it much mattered in the tumult.

'One of you go with them, if you can.'

Nathan made to move off, but Nicholas was ahead of him. The crowd was edging left and right, weeks of repressed worry finally finding an outlet, but he wove a quick path to the front, leaping the cottage gate before Percy could prevent him. He disappeared into the house behind Amery and Vic.

'Tell us more,' shouted a lone woman as the crowd waited. But Percy shook his head. An impatient muttering descended, an angry, unsatisfied need for action after the terrible weeks of pain. Not far from the restless group, the three prisoners could be heard protesting loudly, while the occasional dull thud emanated from the house as some heavy object was wrenched from its place, or a groan as another door was opened.

Then silence. The sudden quiet was frightening. It would almost have been better, Mercia thought, if Percy had allowed the mob to ransack the house, for the dearth of noise loomed more ominous. The whole gathering quivered and swayed, eager to dispel its energy and yet wanting to stay in place. Then a first-floor window was flung outward and Amery's head appeared.

'You were right.' His shrill voice penetrated the night as he thrust his arm through the gap, waving a piece of paper. 'This proves it.'

Face twitching, Percy lifted his eyes. 'What does it say?'

'They are orders from the Duke of York. Shall I read them?'

The crowd roared its consent.

'The relevant bits, then.' He cleared his throat. 'To Richard Thorpe, by command of His Royal Majesty Charles the Second, King of England . . . and so on. I thank you for your unwavering loyalty . . . hereby order you to take any means necessary to discover the whereabouts of those barbarous traitors Goffe and Whalley' – he paused, and the town growled its rage – 'through scaring the people into panic for their lives, whereat they will surely be persuaded to renounce their cause . . . and I further order that you make efforts to foment alliance with the Indians of that country, by which means we shall take the territory most easily into the lands of my brother the Duke. It is signed Sir Bernard Dittering, whoever he is, for the King and the Duke of York.'

The crowd went wild. No longer content to wait for instruction, they turned as one, sweeping past Mercia and clawing for Thorpe. The story was shared with those guarding the prisoners, and the two groups merged, seizing Thorpe and Sir William, dragging them towards the field, leaving Lavington behind to stare after the whipped-up mob. Percy followed, allowing Vic and Amery time to catch him as Nicholas halted at Mercia's side.

'Is it true?' she said. 'Did you see that note?'

He nodded. 'He found it in a desk. It has the seal of the Duke, if I remember it rightly from the ship we arrived on.'

She stared at the back of the vanishing crowd. 'What is going on here?' She turned to Nathan. 'Does that letter not seem too . . . convenient? And the Duke, he may be dislikeable, but I cannot see him sanctioning Thorpe to foster an Indian revolt.'

'Then what?' he said.

'I am not sure, but—Lavington!' The magistrate was the only townsman left with them inside the palisade. 'Mr Lavington, can you not control them? Percy is so incensed with the accusations against the regicides he could encourage the people to anything.'

Lavington turned his head, a glib whiteness in his eyes. 'They have become crazed,' he said, matter-of-fact. 'What can I do until they calm themselves?'

She shook her head. 'Come.' She set off for the field. 'He is no use when he is needed.'

Abandoning the magistrate, the three hurried through the western gate. Back in the field she halted, gripping Nathan's arm as she took in the scene before them. The bonfire was now lit, flames springing to life throughout the hungry mound as it began its fearsome burn. The guy had been flung face down in the dirt, and in its place in the cart, Thorpe and Sir William were being wheeled around the meadow, the gloating crowd chanting its malice.

'By the Lord!' she cried.

A small section of the townsfolk was clapping a slow rhythm, a fiendish monotone to urge on the boys pushing the captured men, their young faces ecstatic with vulgar pleasure as they jarred the ramshackle cart over every bump and rut. The steady beat lured the people even further into their trance, and as Mercia looked on, they began to hurl stones and abuse at their terrified victims. Then the boys overturned the cart, dumping their captives to the ground. A musket was produced, and at gunpoint the men were forced towards the woodpile, screaming yet unable to resist.

The crowd was no longer under any kind of control. Like the flames licking the base of the bonfire, the people were uncontainable, returned to the savagery of the wilds in which they lived. Yet on the side, looking on, Percy stood with Amery, observing in silent contemplation as his friend tried to talk. Remembrance, too, seemed immune to the town's spell, shouting from the side for them to stop, but a rough arm shoved her aside. By now Mercia had seen enough. While Nathan and Nicholas joined with Remembrance, she circled the field's edge to reach Percy.

Amery watched her come up. 'That is enough, isn't it?' He tapped Percy's arm. 'You've scared them enough? After all, those are men, whatever they have done.'

'He is right,' said Mercia as she joined them. 'Do neither of you sense something odd about this whole affair?'

'Odd?' Percy's attention was trained on the mob. 'I should say 'tis clear. Thorpe is the murderer, as we always thought. Purely to root out Whalley and Goffe.' His voice began to shake. 'He gambled that the only way to make the town give them up was to make them guilty of such crimes that the people would turn against them. It is . . . astonishing, Mercia. But he should have known, too, that I would unmask him. No, 'tis the hangman's noose for him, so he may as well have his judgement passed now.'

'Whose judgement?' She stepped round to face him. 'Yours? Percy, I know you are incensed, but I am still not convinced it is him. Your reasoning is too . . . straightforward.' She searched his face for any sign of compassion. 'And what of the right to a fair trial? Or does that not exist in your noble America?'

His gaze drifted once more, following a wisp of ash as it floated into the sky. 'Was he fair with his victims? With Clemency?'

She did not rise to the bait. 'What good will I do Clemency if the wrong man is accused? Percy, I need to be sure.' She grabbed his chin and yanked it towards her. 'Do not allow this madness. Think of Sir William! He is not involved, that is certain.'

He wrenched himself from her grip. 'There were two men went into Clemency's house, so you said. Strange that he happens to be in town at just this time.'

'That is preposterous. He is here because of me, as you well know. Besides, he has only just arrived.'

'So he says.'

'That is exactly what was said of your charges, and you disputed it strongly enough then.' She shook her head in frustration. 'Very well. Stand by and do nothing if you wish. But I cannot simply watch those men die, even if it means diving into the crowd and ending on the fire for it myself.'

She held his gaze, daring him to let the chaos continue, knowing there was little influence she could work on the mob herself. But she counted on his seeing reason. He was intelligent, after all. Rational.

Wasn't he?

She waited. The fire began to crackle, the mob's chants taking on ever more menacing tones. And then he surprised her.

'No.'

She blinked. 'What?'

'I will not act. They chose their path, and it is at odds with ours. If the people want them to burn, let them.'

She stared, unbelieving what she heard. Behind her, a cry for help rang out, Sir William's usually deep voice shrill with fright.

'Tell me you are not serious.'

'Why not? Enough of his kind executed – murdered – good people who only wished for peace.' He folded his arms. 'Hanging up men and slicing their stomachs, cutting them down and wrenching them in four? That punishment was approved of by men like him, and he did naught to stop it. So what if he burns? Is that not just recompense?'

Amery grabbed his sleeve. 'Listen to her, Perseverance. What of your ideals? Your plans for a fairer world, a rebirthing of freedom and hope? I know you are angry, but this is too—'

Percy shrugged off his hand. 'You say that to me now? You, who call yourself friend?'

'And me?' said Mercia. 'Am I not your friend?' She looked back at the bonfire, witnessing the mob as it slithered and curled to wind its coils around its prey, refusing Nathan's appeals to cease its inhuman dance. Then a rock flew from its midst, striking him on the temple. He staggered, dazed, while Nicholas swore at the townsfolk, reaching down to pull him out of harm's way.

'Damn this,' she said. She took a deep breath, the smoke of the fire seeping inside her lungs. 'Will you save Sir William or not?'

Slowly, Percy shook his head. 'And betray all those men – those good, good men! – who died fighting against his kind, against the King? No, he is part of the whole stinking edifice, and in Cromwell's name I will see it brought down!'

His years of fury had proven too much. 'And so you stoke the fire in the people as surely as they stoke that real flame. But I will not stay to look.'

'Mercia, I—'

She refused to meet his eye. Dragging her dress hems over her boots, he made no move to stop her as she fled his presence to find Nathan's group. Once there she laid her hand on Nicholas's shoulder, taking reassurance in his familiar touch.

'How is he?' She looked down at Nathan; now sat on the ground, he was clutching his forehead.

'Bleeding, but not much harmed. Though that rock hit him hard.' Nicholas frowned. 'What is it?'

She shook her head. 'Is it safe to leave him?'

'Leave?' Nathan looked up, the slight action making him wince. 'Where are you going?'

'You will see.' She huddled close to Nicholas. 'In a moment, I want you to come with me. I want you to pretend to be escorting me away.' She glanced again at Nathan. 'You are sure you are well?'

'Mercia, I am not a child.'

'Then gather your strength and make ready. When the crowd turn away, go in and rescue Sir William. Thorpe too, if you can. We cannot let them burn.'

Before he could press further, she laid her head in her hands, affecting a distress it was not difficult to feign, and she fled the viperous crowd. Seconds later, Nicholas ran past, then swivelled to walk backwards, bending to check her face.

'To pretend I'm seeing if you're upset.'

'Very good,' she said through closed fingertips. 'Now look behind me and see if anyone is watching.'

Keeping his head still, he flicked up his eyes. 'Just Percy. Amery is trying to speak to him, and the rest are . . . engrossed in their work.' He paused. 'Are you going to tell me what's going on?'

She kept her face covered. 'Not now, Nicholas.' She shivered. 'How do people become like that? We so easily descend into brutality.'

'You know how. Fear. Mistrust. The need to stay alive. Mostly because they are scared, as they were scared the night of Hopewell's death. And now their fear has found its release.'

'That may be.' She set down her hands. 'But I will be damned if I let anyone else die for it tonight.'

Fading into the low light of dusk, she hurried around the palisade to reach the southern gate, grabbing one of the torches from its sconce and speeding on towards the hill. In the penumbra, the unfinished fort at its summit took on an unnatural aspect, unseen forces darkening its barricade, but such ethereal spectres were meaningless to her as she led Nicholas into its dim embrace, not stopping to catch her breath. Once inside the open structure she made straight for the mortar, laying a hand on its cold metal, the crest of the old King hard beneath her purposeful hand.

'Nicholas,' she said, 'you have to fire this.'

'What?' He let out a nervous laugh. 'My, you are serious.'

'If we fire the mortar, it will draw the attention of the townsfolk, and then maybe Nathan will be able to get Sir William away.' She looked at the squat weapon, its maw gaping like a ravenous creature desperate to make its kill. 'When I was here during the Indian attack, Fearing loaded it ready to use. So take that rammer over there and set it off. You were on the ships. You must have seen cannons being fired.'

'Well yes, but I never manned—'

'Can you do it?'

He stared at the gun, stifling a grin. 'Hell's teeth, I will give it a try.'

She held the torch in front so he could see. In its light, he quickly found the wooden rammer, thrust it inside the mortar and pushed down hard.

'Right,' he said. 'Give me the torch.' She handed it over and took a step back. 'Further than that.'

She took another two. 'Hurry!'

Standing back himself, he set the torch to the taper that led into the mortar. The short fuse took hold, burning fast. Then he leapt back.

'Cover your ears!'

She did as he bade her, and just in time. With a loud bang the mortar recoiled, firing its load into the sky. The shot flew out of sight, falling to earth with a series of hard thuds.

'Wo-ah!' cried Nicholas. 'That should get their attention!'

She looked towards the now fierce bonfire, its flames engaged in their mesmerising whirl. Before the orange mass two figures stood slightly apart from the rest, their arms behind their backs, but as she watched, a number of people broke from the massed crowd and started towards the hill.

'Christ,' said Nicholas. 'We better get out of here.'

Taking back the torch, she scurried from the fort, pausing to look down the slope of the hill as another figure pushed through the remaining crowd to reach the bound men. Yet another silhouette, in a dress she thought, placed herself in front of the few townsfolk who turned towards him, giving him time to release one of the prisoners, but the other was still bound when the crowd dodged past her outstretched hands. The dark couple sprinted with the freed man into the darkness of the forest, leaving the unfortunate second victim behind. While some of the townsfolk stayed to prevent his escape, others plunged after them into the woods.

By now the shouts of the group approaching the hill were growing louder. Nicholas grabbed Mercia's arm and pulled her along.

'Drop that torch!' he cried.

Throwing down her light, she followed him down the back of the hill, slipping on damp patches until with a garble of a cry she stumbled, shocking her ankle. But her boot was strong, and the pain not great;

Nicholas helped her up and they carried on. Behind them, the mob was now at the fort, lifting their torches to survey the landscape. One of the townsfolk – Lavington's man Stephen, she thought – cried out '*There!*' and the pursuers emptied the fort in swift pursuit.

'Into the wood,' cried Nicholas. 'It will be harder to spy us.'

She raced amongst the trees. It was pitch-dark, and she had to slow down lest she fall on a stray root, or collide with an unseen trunk. She had caught her ankle more severely than she had thought, and up ahead, she could tell Nicholas was racing away, the rustling of the leaves under his boots growing steadily quieter. She tried to keep up the pace but before long she had lost him to the gloom. She could not call out: behind, her pursuers made no effort to disguise their own movement.

She pressed on, left around one tree, right around another, aiming back towards the town to find her bearings. Then a man's shout startled a deer into flight not far off, and to her left a twig snapped. Turning cold, she stopped still as the leaves crackled beside her feet, and a black silhouette appeared in the corner of her eye. She inched away but the silhouette reached out a hand and grabbed her. Yet it was a loose grip, and she was able to snatch herself free.

'Mercia, is that you?' he whispered.

'Amery!'

'I knew it was you fired that shot.' He brought his face close to hers. 'Percy sent me with this group to protect you. One of them said she thought she saw you, but I sent them in a different direction while I came to look.'

'Thank you.' She realised she was panting, out of breath. 'Have you seen Nicholas? I heard a cry.'

'That was me.' Amery swallowed. 'I tripped. I hoped Nicholas was with you?'

'We became separated. I shall have to find him, and quickly.' She looked about her, but the calls of pursuit were trailing off and it was too dark to see far into the forest. 'Did you manage to talk sense into Percy?'

He laughed: odd for the circumstances, she thought. 'He may share the people's anger at what you have done, but he does not want to see you harmed. Maybe it would be best if you hide for a time, until things have calmed. The . . . clearing at the top of the waterfall, perhaps.' The leaves under his feet rustled. 'One of us will fetch you when we can.'

She looked at him, as well as she could in the blackness. 'I had to stop them, Amery. I could not let them kill Sir William, not even Thorpe.'

'No. But you understand Percy's fury with men like those. 'Tis misplaced, on this occasion, but you understand it.'

'Do I?' Something in his tone gave her cause to hesitate, something . . . pleading? She creased her forehead as an indefinable concern crept into her chest, as if the chill air itself had seeped into her consciousness. 'Whom did Nathan free?' she asked, tearing her mind from its unwelcome paths. 'I saw one of them was left at the bonfire.'

'He freed Sir William.' Amery's voice resounded more strongly now. 'I do not know where they have gone.'

'Sir William.' She bit her lip. 'Amery, what do you think about Thorpe?'

He hesitated. 'I think . . . he must be the killer. Percy says the letter we found proves it.'

'And what say you?'

The outline of his head turned this way and that, the creasing of his shirt collar more audible in the dark.

'I think Percy is usually right.'

'But not always. And not in this case. Either he is too maddened to see what should be obvious to him otherwise, or else he—'

The woods fell utterly silent. The wind, the night birds, the creaking of the trees vanished.

Surely not? Oh Lord God, surely not that?

'Or else he what?'

Did someone speak? She turned her eyes upwards to see Amery, closer now than a moment before. An intense ray of fear shot through her soul.

There were two of them, Vic had said.

She began to back away.

'Where are you going?' he asked, taking one step forwards for every pace she took back.

She tried to steady her voice. 'I think it best . . . if I go to the waterfall now.'

'Oh, I don't think you're in any trouble here. Everyone has gone.'

'Still—'

'And I wouldn't keep walking backwards, if I were you.' Of a sudden he lunged towards her, stopping her retreat with an outstretched arm. She felt his hand against the back of her dress, holding her in place.

'What are you doing?' she said.

He grabbed her by the shoulders, turning her to face the other way.

'Helping, I hope. You almost fell on that root behind you.' He eased away his fingertips. 'If you walk in this direction, you will come out near the town. The light of the bonfire should guide you. From there you know how to reach the waterfall, I think.' He pushed her lightly forward. 'That way, then.'

Feigning composure, she walked quickly away, almost a run. Alone amongst the trees, she hurried on, the pines and the elms beginning to thin as her back crawled with the anxiety that a bullet or an arrow could strike. But none came. She fled ever faster until soon the trees ended and the palisade loomed into view, its dark mass of pointed staves a menacing witness to her attempts at stealth. But then she looked back, and she saw a man creeping from tree to tree on the forest's perimeter, peering in and out.

Her stomach turned ever colder, but she waited, observing, until the man whispered loud enough to hear, searching for his lost companion. A relief as intense as her dread took hold as she realised who it was, and she strode out towards Nicholas, causing him to tense until he recognised her in his turn. She said nothing of her encounter with Amery, refusing to give in to her paranoid thoughts. But her mind was as frantic as the leaves now whipping in the wind at her feet, leading her to a conclusion she did not want to reach.

Go to the waterfall, Amery had said. Go to the waterfall, where one of us will fetch you.

And so there was no other choice. She knew there could be danger, but she had to go. Had to learn if she was right.

For Clemency. And for herself.

Chapter Thirty-Four

They walked to the waterfall in silence. Nicholas tried to talk, but she was not in the mood. She was reflecting on what she was going to say; what she was going to do if events turned sour. She toyed with the idea of returning the other way, to see if they could help free Thorpe, but she knew where the real answers lay. Nor was she concerned for Sir William, trusting Nathan and Remembrance to hide him somewhere safe. And so up the narrow path she clambered, ducking encroaching branches and stepping over sharp-pointed rocks.

The water's descent seemed to run louder at night: unsurprising, perhaps, with the tension coursing through her veins. Nearing the clearing at the top of the falls, Nicholas put out an arm to stop her advance. Placing a finger on his lips he crept forward, peeking into the open space from behind a rotting trunk. She waited several moments, listening through the chirping of the insects and the murmuring of the trees, watching for any sign. But he remained immobile. For all she could tell, they were alone up here.

'Nobody there,' he confirmed as she slipped alongside. 'What now?'

'We wait, out of sight, in silence.'

They waited a long time it felt, but that too might have been the nerves, the wish to bring an end to the weeks of grief. To steel herself, she thought of Clemency, how all this had been for her, and how soon, she hoped, her friend would find her justice. And then she thought of Nathan, how their relationship had diminished; and of Daniel, waiting motherless in Hartford, of how she would make it up to him as soon as all was over. And also she thought of the risk she was taking, how her son might not have a mother at all. But persistence was her only choice; she cast that heady thought from her mind.

A thump nearby. Another. The heavy plod of boots on their way to the meeting place. She stopped breathing altogether as two dark figures, illuminated by a torch, seemed to glide up the path towards them. Passing them unnoticed, they emerged as if tall imps onto the plateau atop the gurgling falls. She inched forwards with Nicholas, as quietly as they could, straining to glimpse the new arrivals. Then a rustle from behind made her stop dead and look back. For a moment she thought she could see another shape, crouched, but only for a moment. Now there was nothing, just a bush. She signalled to Nicholas, pointing back, but he too shook his head. She returned her attention to the duo before her, spectral as they seemed in the night.

One nodded to the other. 'Mercia,' the second called, sweeping his torch. 'Mercia, did you come?'

'Amery,' she heard Nicholas mutter, too quietly for the pair to remark. 'Can you see who the other is? Amery is in the way.'

'No. He is hooded.' She lowered her eyes: pointless in the darkness. 'But I know who it will be. These two . . . are the two behind everything.' Even now she could barely say it. 'The murderers.'

A long pause, and she knew what he was thinking. 'Amery?' Another pause. 'But I . . . I shared his lodging. You are certain?'

She touched his forearm. 'They have deluded us all. I should have seen this, not you.' She took back her hand. 'Stay hidden for now. If I need you, I will make a sign.'

'No, Mercia.' Even in a whisper, his worry was clear. 'If what you say is true, you should not go out alone.'

'Mrs Blakewood?' called Amery.

'I have to. I think 'tis better.'

A quiet resignation. 'What sign then?'

'I will . . . put my hands on my hips. If I am in trouble, use your judgement, but do not put yourself at risk.'

She got to her feet, brushing loose stones from her dress, dismissing his silent objections by striking into the open. Now exposed, she made no attempt to hide her approach. The two men turned towards her, Amery bareheaded, the other in a well-fitting cloak.

'Amery,' she acknowledged. Then she turned to the other. 'And you.' Her voice rolled deep with bitterness. 'I know who you are. You can show your sorry face.'

As the man did as she bade, she closed her eyes, overrun by sadness and pain. For her supposition had been right, and worse, she had been betrayed.

Percy cast off his hood. And smiled.

'Welcome, Mercia. I knew you would come.' He inclined his head, looking at her with a great curiosity. 'Tell me, when did you realise the truth?'

'Only tonight.' Her expression was as sterile as his was animate. 'I should have listened to myself sooner, instead of to your lies.'

'I never lied, Mercia. As I never miss a thing. I regret this, but— Amery?'

He nodded at the schoolmaster. From under his cloak, Amery retrieved a doglock pistol and aimed it at the undergrowth behind her.

'Another gun,' she said. 'How you men do like your toys.'

'This is not a toy, Mercia. Nor is this a game.' Percy looked towards the wood. 'If you do not come out, we will shoot.'

'Damn you.' A rustling told her Nicholas had broken cover.

379

'Hands in the air,' said Percy. 'Except . . . lift up your shirt.'

'Why? Fancy a look?'

'Just do it.'

Stepping into view, Nicholas pulled his shirt above his breeches, revealing the knife in his belt.

'As I thought. You can throw that over here.' Percy watched as Nicholas sent the knife thudding between his feet. 'Now sit down and stay quiet while I talk to your mistress.'

Not breaking from his gaze, Nicholas lowered himself deliberately to the ground. Amery exhaled, loosening his hold on his gun.

Nicholas spat. 'A nice pair of murderers and cowards, both of you.' He looked up at Amery, disgust across his face. 'But you. I expected much better of you.'

'Whereas I expect nothing from you, Wildmoor, at all.' Percy shook his head. 'Exactly the type I saw every day in London. Thieving ne'er-do-wells who care naught for anything save themselves and the coin in their pockets, even when there is a cause to fight for that would see their lives improved.' He scoffed. 'Or perhaps, the coin in other people's pockets.'

'Do not speak to my manservant that way,' bristled Mercia. 'There is more in him than in either of you.' Of a sudden she was taken by a violent nausea, a powerful rage swelling inside. 'You bastards! You killed Clemency! You talk of people who care for naught, and yet you slaughter an innocent woman who cared only for helping others!'

Without thinking, she started forwards, the intensity of her feeling forcing her to acts her rational mind would never have countenanced. She brought up her hands, and for that savage instant she wanted to wrap her fingers around Percy's throat, to make him suffer as Clemency had suffered in the rope. But then she heard a voice, Nicholas calling from the ground.

'No,' he cried. 'You don't want to end it, not like this.'

His urgent words were enough to break the enchantment, and she stopped her advance, subdued. She had only covered three paces, but the horror of what she had hoped to do caught her short. She swallowed and stepped back.

'I am sorry, Nicholas. I do not know what happened.'

'I do.' His green eyes stared up at her. 'Believe me, I do.'

She looked around. Amery was lowering his gun, but she could see his hands were shaking, the flames of the torch in his left hand as unsteady as his pistol in his right. Percy had paled, seemingly taken aback, but then he smiled and held up his palms.

'No matter, Mercia, I know you are upset.' His taut shoulders relaxed. 'To speak true, I had hoped you would not find out the truth, that you would join me in ignorance as the rest of the town joins us now. But you are the daughter of Sir Rowland Goodridge. When I explain, you will understand me, I know.'

'How?' A heavy sadness descended on the clearing, replacing her vanquished fury; even the rush of the water away to her side could not penetrate its gloom. 'I thought you were my friend, Percy. But – Hell's teeth!' She looked away, striving to master her angst. 'No reason can explain what you have done!'

He waited for her to look back at him, a puzzled frown marring his forehead.

'I am your friend. And you are mine. You said so at the bonfire.' He pulled at the seam of his cloak. 'Shall we set a fire here? At least we can have comfort as we talk.'

Her mind numb, she waited as Percy gathered kindling and wood, taking Amery's torch to light the tiny pile: a pitiful comparison to the bonfire at the palisade, its wavering flames were nonetheless more illuminating than the torch. Close by, Amery kept his gun trained on Nicholas, his knuckles white as he gripped the well-fashioned handle. To Mercia it seemed an age since she had last sat amongst these rocks, when Silence had still been alive. The memory smelt as sour as the burgeoning smoke.

'I know how you like it here,' Percy said at last. Shedding his cloak, he rose to his feet. 'I know how it calms you, makes you able to think.'

'Tonight has made it somewhat tainted. Like your ideals.' Disdaining his attempts to set her at ease, she turned to his companion. 'A fairer world of freedom and hope, Amery, was that how you described it before? I see little of fairness here.'

'Fairness?' Amery stared, his eyes as wild as the woods around them. 'This is all about fairness. It is about leaving tyranny behind and forging a fair life for us all.'

'Very grand.' Nicholas laughed. 'Is that what you told the people you killed?'

His pistol slipped at his side. 'I realise some of our methods are not—'

'Amery,' said Percy. 'Keep that pointed at him. He cannot understand us, that is certain.' He peered down at Nicholas. 'I told you to stay quiet.'

'Yes.' Amery steadied his gun. 'Yes, of course.'

Mercia looked from the one to the other. There was a definite anxiety permeating Amery, his eyes looking this way and that.

'Is this your idea of a fair life?' she ventured. She glanced at Nicholas, nodding imperceptibly as a signal to obey Percy's instruction. 'Being told what to do by this man?'

'There must be an order, Mercia. A hierarchy of sorts.' The uncertainty in Amery's gaze morphed into shimmering enthusiasm; endearing in other circumstances, tonight it was out of place. ''Tis only when the shackles of tyranny are cast down that we will find those prizes that elude us. The philosopher's stone, the alkahest . . . the ultimate elixir, you remember? When we uncover its glory, nobody will die again. But I have learnt that unless the land is made pure through hardship, its splendour will forever be denied us.'

'Did Percy tell you that?' She shook her head. 'I doubt alchemy is what he has in mind. Sedition seems more to his taste.'

'So be it,' said Percy. 'If sedition will allow me to throw off the Royalist chains that stifle us.' He took a step towards her. 'I speak of the future,

382

Mercia. A new future, in which I offer you a choice. Either stay and join us.' He looked at her keenly. 'Join me.'

'Or?'

'Or . . .' He smiled. 'But that will not happen. You must see what I do here is for the common good.'

She had to fight to control herself. 'I found Clemency hanging from her bedroom eaves. Hopewell carrying his stomach across the fields. And Silence – cut into four, his head nailed to the gate?' The memories made her sick. 'How is that for the common good?'

Percy lowered himself onto the same flat rock she had enjoyed with Clemency those few weeks before. 'Have you tried to rouse the people, Mercia? Do you know what it takes?' He drew up his leg, folding it underneath his other. 'But then, I know you do. Your father certainly did.'

She narrowed her eyes. 'My father would be appalled by what has happened here.'

'Perhaps. But perhaps he would also say, that the means are justified if they achieve the desired end. Do you think he was bloodless in the war?'

'He commanded men. He had to make decisions that led to lives being lost, I know that. But killing for a game, no. That is beneath anyone like him.'

'It is the reality of life.' He straightened a crease in his breeches. 'War and death, panic and fear . . . they are what stir the people. Scare them and they will follow. Try to persuade them by rational argument and you are doomed to fail.'

'And so this is your explanation? That you killed all those people to scare the rest into obeying your will? Sowing panic besides, through scattering those monstrous codes?' A faintness passed over her. 'You are sick, Percy.'

'No. But my country is, and I am the doctor who can cure it. By country I mean here, of course. America. I have tried to tell you so often enough.'

'It is a beautiful place. It must feel sorrow at such pointless death.'

'It will be free.' He looked into the flames of the fire. 'I went to England once, you know that. I served Cromwell, a minor part only, but I knew with industry and hard work I would rise to his council, and I would help England and America become the power they should be.' He jumped up, staring over the edge of the falls. 'How powerful could England be with all this land at its disposal? But I will not let England have it if England is to be ruled by kings and the enemies of we Elect.' He swivelled to face her. 'No, God has shown us this land, and He means it for us. It was our forefathers who arrived on the first ships, stepping onto that shore to found Plymouth. And now we, their children, will break from the motherland, and we will free the people to live as they should, by our own laws and morals. Any who do not wish it can return to England where they belong.'

'A high cause indeed.' Her voice was emotionless; it would have been impossible to divine her thoughts. 'With murder its sordid call to arms.'

'It was necessary.' For a moment he seemed to falter, but he quickly composed himself. 'Nothing else worked. All the times I spoke of our freedom, they counted for naught. Even in Boston my speeches largely went unheeded.' Sorrow played down his cheeks. 'And I understood. Life is hard here. People were too concerned with their own lives, with their families and their farms, to be able to care. But I did care, deeply, and I realised it would take sterner persuasion to make the people see where their future truly must lie.'

'The people will be free, Mercia,' said Amery. 'Pure. God will grant us the wisdom of His secrets so we can live as in Eden. Heaven, here on Earth.'

A light spray from the falls settled on her brow. 'A fine marriage of alchemy and power,' she scorned. 'And yet I think, Amery, an unequal partnership. There is more of one than the other in this scheme.'

Amery blinked, looking sideways at Percy, but he merely continued unheeding.

'The invasion fleet you arrived on was the catalyst. Ever since the King reclaimed his throne, we all knew it would come. And so a fear was already there, dormant in the people. If I could but harness that fear, make them panic their own lives could be forfeit, then I knew they would yearn for a reasoning voice to tell them what needed to be done.'

She would have laughed, if she could. 'A voice such as yours?'

He nodded, seemingly oblivious. 'The murders were no mere whim, Mercia. They had a purpose. To make the people listen, I had to convince them that my enemy . . . that our enemy, was prepared to commit any act. That the King would do anything in pursuit of his relentless task.'

'His task to find the men who killed his father,' she said. 'The regicides.'

'Indeed!' Percy's fingers clenched and relaxed in his excitement. 'Finally, the people are outraged! Discovering that the King's men – that Thorpe – were responsible for killing their fellows, solely to scare them into renouncing Whalley and the others, their very heroes?' He cast down his gaze. 'It pained me I had to feign their guilt through the codes. But the key in their hiding place was so obvious a fake, the loose means I needed to convince the people they were innocent.'

She frowned. 'But to do that the key had to be found. How did you know I would search for it?'

'I didn't. I intended Thorpe to find the key. I planned to lead him unawares to the cave once I had been able to leave it. But you got there first.' He sighed. 'I was saddened, Mercia. That you would suspect those men in that way.'

She sucked in his disappointment through her teeth. 'That was you in the cave.'

'I went straight after the discussion with my father. But I should have known you would ponder Thorpe's words and come yourself.' Once again, his eyes flicked away. 'I never wanted to use you as a pawn, Mercia, for you to be the one to bring the key to Meltwater. But you put yourself in that position through your diligence.' His cheeks reddened. 'Then this evening you came to me with the truth I already knew. You are a clever woman, Mercia, an . . . equal, I hope. But I have always been a little ahead. By the time you found me, I was already about to set things in motion.'

'With a note smuggled into Thorpe's house to prove your claims, no less.'

'But the *monas*, Percy?' Still standing over Nicholas, Amery's brow had been steadily furrowing. 'We put that in the codes as a confession of our own, I thought? A symbol of alchemy to explain to God our intent?'

'Oh, come, Amery.' Percy waved a dismissive hand. 'That fool's pursuit is as nothing compared to our true purpose.'

'See what he thinks of your alkahest, Amery?' She folded her arms. 'He used the *monas* to make the people afraid, that is all. They worry it is a symbol of devilish magic. All he wanted was to scare them into handing him power.'

'This is not about power.' A brief shadow crossed Percy's face. 'Or about me. I have been . . . the match that sets flame to the cannon, no more. I have kindled the anger that was already there, made certain the uprising has begun.' His darkness erupted into rapture. 'What happens in Meltwater tonight, we take to Hartford tomorrow, then to Springfield, New Haven, and Boston itself. There is little love in America for the King. We will expel his rule and we will prevail.'

'Percy, how can you hope to?' She laid her head in her hands. 'There is an army of the King's soldiers just landed in New York. You think they will sit back and let you revolt?'

'This is our home, Mercia. We number in the thousands. We will fight for it to the last drop of blood.' His eyes gleamed in the firelight. 'Despite your firing the mortar, Richard is still captive. He will confess, or he will die. Either way I have my murderer, and the people will rise.'

'And yet Sir William is free.'

'Hardly troubling. We both know his presence here is an unforeseen occurrence.'

She looked at him. He was breathing fast, his face aglow. His mouth was upturned into a childlike smile. In contrast Amery was staring towards the falls, his face set, his hold on his gun slackening by the minute. She dared a glance at Nicholas, and she could see he was watching more carefully than she had thought. He met her gaze, and his right eye fashioned an almost imperceptible wink. Quickly, she turned her attention back.

'I do not doubt your ardour, Percy.' She meant, madness. 'Maybe I could agree with your aims of a life free from oppression. But you cannot kill the innocent to achieve it.' She took a step forward, but Amery found the wits to shake his gun. 'Why Clemency, Percy? Why a kind woman who helped you hide those men you claim to cherish?'

Her words cut through his trance. 'For that reason, Mercia. Because she knew of them, and they have to be safe. And because she was friends with the Indians, as Hopewell was. To give them reason to attack when it was needed.'

Startled, she threw back her head. 'Do not tell me you planned that assault?'

'Father may have tried to destroy the codes, but I was always in control. I knew that if I waited to talk of them all at once, to reveal their strange nature, then the town would be consumed with fear. An Indian attack could only inflame that.' He shrugged, but his haughty eyes betrayed his arrogance. 'And of course, at least one of Whalley or Goffe had to reveal himself, so the people – so that Thorpe – could know for certain they were near. Only such a threat would persuade them out of hiding.'

Her mouth was open in shock. 'But Whalley only came because Godsgift was injured. How could you possibly have foreseen that?'

Did he roll his eyes? 'Because I do see things, Mercia. I knew Standfast and the Indian woman were searching for Godsgift, and I helped them. I encouraged Standfast to lure him to the wood. To say true, I thought she would kill him. But incapacitating him was enough.'

She barked an incredulous laugh. 'And Silence?' To her right, Nicholas set his palms on the ground. 'George Mason, the minister?'

'Mason would have rallied the town if he were alive, as the powwow would have counselled his tribe towards peace.' He waggled a finger. 'I was not sure what the Indians would think of the code we left on him. But they are not foolish, whatever some of my fellow townsmen like to pretend. Once they learnt of the rest, I knew they would share it. As for Silence, well. He was on the edge of my group, and – somebody had to be quartered. Else why bother with the hanging and the drawing?'

'Why bother?' In the corner of her eye, Nicholas gave her a gentle nod. 'Percy, you are truly crazed. You have used me, as you have used everyone else. But perhaps . . . you are not so much in control as you think.'

Of a sudden Nicholas pounced, straight into the path of Amery's loaded gun.

Chapter Thirty-Five

'Nicholas!' she cried. 'No!'

She need not have worried. Amery dithered, allowing Nicholas to draw close before he could pull the trigger. With a harsh cry he knocked the pistol from Amery's hand. It tumbled towards the fire, and Nicholas sprang fast, sending them both careering to the ground. But then somehow Nicholas was off him, rolling on the earth alone, as Amery struggled to his feet, picking up the pistol before Mercia had chance to run in and grab it. Aiming at her chest, he watched, anxiety on his face, as Percy pulled Nicholas round, striking him with a powerful blow she would never have thought he could muster. Although Nicholas was the stronger, Percy's unexpected attack caught him off guard. Blood trickled from his mouth, and he fell backwards, insensible.

Shaking out his fist, Percy stood. 'You will have to keep him in check, Mercia. I do not want to hurt him again.'

'You killed all the others. Why not him too?' She looked at Nicholas and felt a deep resentment. On the borders of unconsciousness, his chest was nonetheless rising steadily. 'Why not me?'

'Because I—' He looked away. 'Do you think I devised this for pleasure?'

'I do not know.' She was seething, Nicholas's failed attempt the outlet for her rage to find its release. 'But I do know your aims are not so noble as you espouse.' She glanced at Amery. His eyes were wide, repeatedly flitting to Nicholas lying prostrate on the earth. 'Naught to do with purity.'

Percy's face twitched. 'What do you mean?'

'We both know what this is truly about. It is about a young man.' As she spoke, a heat flooded her cheeks, but she found the indignation to continue. 'A young man who went to England to seek power, but who had his hopes torn asunder at Cromwell's death. A young man, who longed to surpass his father, but who was forced to return with his dreams unfulfilled. A young man burning with injustice, with stopped ambition, who plotted and planned and addled his mind to try to achieve power here in its place.' She bored into his eyes. 'But you are wrong, Percy, and there is no way I could ever join you or condone you.'

'No!' He pounded his right hand into his left and winced. 'You are the daughter of a great man of Parliament! You must understand me!'

'A young man,' she pursued, 'who played on his friend's alchemical ideals, but who enslaved his own thoughts to his deepening vanity. Whalley, Goffe, Dixwell? My father, Cromwell . . . me? You think any of us could approve this?' She stepped forward, unafraid, bringing her face close into his. 'How did it feel to put the rope around Clemency? How did it feel to watch her life slip away?'

'Enough!' Percy growled as he turned from her, facing the falls. 'Know this, Mercia. I am not so terrible as you suppose. I did not kill Clemency. Nor any of them.'

'What?' The unexpected declaration brought her up short. 'Then . . . who? Surely not Amery. He is too terrified. Merely your shadow. Too cowardly.'

'Stop it!' Amery's shaking voice rang through the night. 'Both of you! Percy, 'tis obvious she will not join us. But I will not let you kill her. I should have stopped you before.' He jangled his hand, his arm quaking as surely as his gun had shook ever since they had arrived. ''Tis all over, isn't it? I should never have believed you! And now I have to make you let her go, and she will tell the governor, and we will all be hanged.' He looked at her, wild-eyed. 'I killed nobody! I didn't even help them plan those deaths! But Percy told me this was the only way to find the alkahest, that sacrifices were needed to prove our devotion, just as Abraham was prepared to sacrifice Isaac!' His face trembled. 'But he lied, and it will never happen, never, and we have to let her go!'

He was raving, snatching for breath, but his panic was not mere desperation. His repentance seemed real. Mercia seized on the chance.

'Amery, if you want me to live, point that gun at Percy and do not let him move. I will fetch help, and I will come back for you and for Nicholas, and all will be well. Do you hear? If you confess your part, all will be well.'

She nodded in encouragement, hoping he was too confused to realise she was lying. In response he raised his gun, for a moment at her, but then he swung the barrel towards Percy.

'She is right,' he said. 'We must let her go.'

'Come.' Percy took a bold step towards him. 'These melancholies of yours, we always overcome them. Think of those marvels you seek. Will you give them up now?'

He shook his head. 'It is too late. It is over!'

Another step, and another, until he had covered half the distance. 'You will not kill me.'

'I will if I must!' By now his whole body was shivering. 'I will not hang!'

Mercia looked at Nicholas on the ground. She could try to run while the other two were arguing, but if she did, he would still be trapped.

'Amery,' she called. 'Do not let him get any closer. He knows now I can never join him. And so he must kill me, and Nicholas too.'

Amery glanced down: barely half a second, but his doubt was evident. 'Nicholas?'

391

'You have become friends of sorts, have you not, sharing your house? He is a good man, Amery, a father too. He must have told you. Would you let his daughter lose him?'

'Do not listen,' said Percy. 'I know you are with us, even if she claims she is not.' His eyes flicked towards the forest. 'You see, Mercia, you do not understand me as you think.' He took another large step. It was one too many. Of a sudden, Amery's fear vanished into the wind, and he held his gun steady at Percy's heart.

'You are wrong, Percy,' he said. 'And I think you mean to have me killed too now I have wavered.' He cocked the pistol. 'So I will be saving myself as well as these others.'

Percy inched forwards. 'Amery, I—'

A gunshot rang out. Birds fled from the trees behind.

On the ground, the noise made Nicholas stir.

Percy stared at Amery, clutching his chest. But then he looked down, and breathed steadily out, for he could see there was no shower of blood streaming from his doublet.

Mercia watched horrified as not Percy but Amery fell to his knees, the pistol falling from his grasp. With one last, lingering look at his friend, he slumped to the ground, and was still.

She wheeled round. On the edge of the wood, scarcely ten feet from where she was standing, a figure was holding his raised pistol towards the spot where Amery had fallen, the black space above thickening with the smell of gunpowder.

'You let him talk too much,' said the newcomer. 'I always knew he was the weak one among us.'

Percy looked across, visibly upset. 'He would not have fired. Why did you do that?'

'You trust too easily, Percy. You trusted Amery and you trust this woman. Neither would give you what you need.' He lowered his gun. 'But now, it matters not. The evening is at hand.'

Kit West strode into the firelight. Nonchalant, he reached into a pouch at his side, drawing out a ball and powder to reload his gun. 'For the Lord will judge and find those unworthy wanting.'

'Kit,' Percy sighed. 'This is not the time.'

'It is always the time.' He peered down at Amery. 'Tonight especially. And you, Mercia. Over there with Nicholas where I can see you both.' Without looking, he pointed the gun in her direction; more nervous of Kit than of Percy, she complied.

'So, Percy,' she said. 'This is your murderer.'

Kit scarcely glanced across. 'Rather, a protector of souls. All those I killed were troubled.'

Her bile rose afresh. 'It is not for you to judge what is troubled.'

'No, it is for God to judge.' He held up his head. 'Now they have the chance to explain themselves. If He accepts their penitence, they will enter into heaven.'

Percy let out an unsure laugh. 'What is this, Kit? Some kind of pretence?'

'Not at all.' His eyes searched the area. 'Sit down beside her. And do not try to reach Amery's gun.'

He nudged the dropped pistol out of reach. Face aghast, Percy did as he was bade.

Mercia turned from him. 'You, Amery, now Kit.' She felt sick. 'That meeting we all had, it was merely a ruse.' He made to reply, but she shook her head. Now near Nicholas, she slipped the toe of her boot under his side and pushed, hoping to stir him awake. 'But if you have been acting together, why is he talking like this?'

'Because,' Kit answered, 'I have never been acting for him. He thought to command me, as he thinks to command everyone else. But his lust for power is irrelevant.'

'Stop this, Kit,' Percy spoke clearly, but there was a faint tremor in his voice. 'You have had your jest, as is your wont.' He looked at Amery lying dead on the ground. 'Yet hardly a jest.'

Kit shook his head. 'Do you think the Lord is interested in your delusions? You seek to establish your petty government, while I work to reveal the throne of Christ itself.'

'Kit.' The moon shone its white light on Mercia's uneasy face. 'What is going on?'

Kit looked to the sky, his aim never straying from his captives. 'I had a different name once, did you know that? Like many in this place. But unlike any other, my purpose is sacred.' He turned to face her, reaching into his shirt with his free hand to withdraw his beloved locket. 'Roger Alvechurch, that was me. And I had a brother. Mark.' He opened the clasp to show her an image of a young man's face, although in the gloom she could barely see. 'He was with the Fifth Monarchists, or what you would call as such. To me he was simply my brother.'

'I too had a brother,' she tried, but Kit ignored her. He closed the locket, leaving it hanging over his shirt.

'I came to realise that what he said was right, that the King was the Devil himself. But all would come right, for Christ would soon rise again to herald the Millennium of peace. And so he and his friends defied the King, but the Devil spewed his poison and they were slaughtered.' His piercing eyes saddened. 'I should have died with them, but my mother had locked me away. I did not know why, but later I understood. God had saved me to continue Mark's calling. But not in England, where the corruption was too great. Instead He told me to come to America, where the land is untouched. For here in this wilderness will be the Second Coming.'

As Kit spoke, Mercia rammed her boot more firmly under Nicholas's belly. His eyes eased half open, but if Kit had noticed, it did not distract him from his speech.

'I changed my name on the crossing. To Christ-carry West, because that was my mission. In Boston I met Amery, who talked of the secrets of the earth, of knowledge he believed God would reveal if he was worthy.' He gazed at his corpse. 'But he never was. Through him I met Percy, who saw a devout man in me and thought to sway me to his cause, encouraging me to kill through the lie that I might cleanse the land of sin. But I could tell his real intentions, for they were weak, of temporal power. And so his false reasons became my truth.' He bounded onto a wide pillar of rock. 'And now I have purged this land, tonight the town sheds its unholy skin of pain and beseeches the Lord's deliverance. The signs are revealed, the glory of Eden shall descend!' He looked up at the stars. 'Come Lord, for I have made all ready!'

Mercia looked skywards herself, half expecting some answer. But the night continued untouched. Kit twisted his neck, the glow of the fanatic in his eyes.

'He will come, Percy. It is prophesised.'

'Stop this foolishness,' Percy said. 'We need to return to our tasks in the town.'

Kit laughed. 'Your blindness is persistent, unbeliever. Your days are over. As are your father's, Winthrop's, the King's . . . any mortal man's who has shunned the Lord's true teachings.' He grasped his locket and held it high. 'Brother, come now! Lead the angels from heaven as I know is your duty, and unite with me once more!'

'I don't know what he is doing.' Agitated, Percy turned to Mercia. 'I have heard none of this before.'

'Of course you have not. He is as crazed as you have been, and you could not see it.' She shifted still closer to Nicholas. 'You see, you cannot control men's minds as you think. And once tonight is over, those townsfolk you have roused, they will feel the relief of knowing the killer is found and they will go back to their lives, King or no. But our lives are forfeit if we do not work together now. Kit must be stopped.'

She kicked again at Nicholas. Percy hesitated, then followed suit. This time Nicholas groaned. Mercia leant forward to cover his mouth, whispering in his ear.

'What are you doing?' said Kit.

'Checking to see if he lives.'

'No matter. He lives or dies through God's will.' He held up his hands. 'The gates to Eden stand open!'

Nicholas was now awake, but Mercia held him still. 'Stay silent,' she whispered. 'I need you to run to Nathan and get help.'

Clearly groggy, he nonetheless tried to lift himself up, gazing blindly about him. Over to the right, the leaves of a bush seemed to tremble.

'I will not leave you,' he managed.

'You must. Nathan can—'

'You!' A terrible cry came from the woods, a guttural shrieking of unnaturally high pitch. Startled by its violence, Mercia looked up to be surprised by Sooleawa, the Indian woman advancing through the darkness, her bow pulled tightly back.

'Why are you here?' rasped Kit. 'This is no savage's concern!'

'You!' she repeated, a deranged look in her eyes. 'I came tonight to take my vengeance on your constable, but some madness has taken you all, and he is protected by your great fire.' She glanced at Mercia. 'I saw her climb to the fort, and loose the big gun, and I heard her words. I have followed her through the woods, and I have watched this madness grow, seen you shoot this man down.' Slowly, she walked ever forwards. 'I have not understood all you have said, but one thing I know. You are the man who has killed my friends.'

'Go, heathen.' Kit looked on Sooleawa with the conceit of his zeal. 'The Lord will allow no intrusion tonight.'

'Your warrior Lord?' Her eyes burnt as fiercely as his. 'I do not think He will deny me my revenge!'

'Sooleawa,' called Mercia, but she refused to hear.

'You killed our powwow!' she cried, releasing her arrow into Kit's left arm. The sawyer tumbled from the pillar, dropping his gun as he landed close to the edge of the falls. 'You killed Clemency!' She took another step, strung her bow, and fired a second arrow, this time into his neck. 'You killed Hopewell!' She took another pace and loosed a third arrow, penetrating his stomach. With none remaining, she reached for a dagger at her side. 'And now I will have my vengeance, if not on Godsgift then on you!'

In unexpected silence, she rushed forward. Crawling on the ground in agony, Kit still managed to look up in surprise, long enough for Nicholas to stagger to his feet and for Mercia to crawl backwards with Percy. But the blow to Nicholas's head had been too much, and he nearly fell, catching his breath.

Sooleawa had no such impediment. As if the air itself, she roared towards Kit and crashed into him, stabbing her knife through his shirt. But she did not stop' there, for her motion carried her onwards, and with a terrible cry she toppled them both from the waterfall's height, plummeting over the cascades to the river below.

Mercia ran to the edge, looking over. She thought she could see a figure pull itself from the shallow water, another left for dead at its side, but it was too dark to be sure. Then she heard someone running behind her, and she turned, but there was no time to recover. With Nicholas dazed, Percy had snatched up Kit's gun and was aiming at her chest.

She circled away from the waterfall. 'Percy. You do not need to do this.'

'I do.' His jaw was shaking, the panic he had sought to foster in others now taking hold in himself. 'Whatever Kit said, this is not over. I can rule here still. It is my right!' His words came fast. 'I had hoped . . . I wanted you to stay, to be together. To forge this new world together, you and me. But now I have to put aside those feelings and . . .' He raised the gun. 'If you will not join with me, you shall have to join with Clemency instead.'

She closed her eyes, thinking only of Daniel. But then she felt disturbed air, and her eyes sprang open as Percy swivelled his gun towards Nicholas, the two beginning a fight for dominance. For a moment Nicholas pressed his attack, but he was weak with his wound. Cracking the gun barrel over his skull, Percy forced him down, the intensity of the blow careering the pistol in her direction. Percy hauled Nicholas up by his shoulders, pushing him to his feet near the waterfall's edge.

'I will do it,' he said. 'I will push him if I must.'

Calm, in contrast, Mercia reached for the gun. She looked at the trigger, at Percy, at the mourning ring she wore still. She cocked the gun and lifted it.

'Let him go, Percy. It is over.'

'No!' He took another step, taking them to the edge. 'I will not lose!'

'You killed Clemency as surely as Kit did. Even so, I do not want to do this.' She held the gun steady. 'Damn you, Percy! Let him go.'

His cheeks trembled. 'I cannot.'

For an instant, she hesitated. Then Nicholas roared again to life, thrusting his elbows into Percy's stomach. With a cry, his arms fell away, but for Nicholas the effort was too great. He collapsed at Percy's feet.

Percy snatched up a rock. 'I will strike him with it. Lower your gun, or I will!'

'He will do it anyway,' slurred Nicholas. 'You know he can let neither of us live.'

She knew, but the knowledge did not soothe her. Percy stared, the madness filling his wide eyes. He raised his arms higher, and she knew the instant she dropped the gun he would dash the rock against Nicholas and then he would come for her.

She prayed that God and her son would forgive her.

His fingers tightened on the rock.

She fired.

Chapter Thirty-Six

She laid the flowers at Clemency's grave, saying a prayer for the woman she had called friend. She paused a moment in tranquil solitude, remembering the happy evening in the illicit Hartford tavern, the horse rides in the woods, the joyful, smiling face. Tears welled up, and now all was over, she allowed them to flow, crying out the hurt and the pain, the sorrow at needless loss, the remorse that she was alive, while her friend was not. Half an hour later she dried her eyes, calming her breathing. She said another prayer, to add to the innumerable she had already uttered, and then she left, stroking the hard gravestone, reading anew the expression the townspeople had allowed her to write: *Here lies Clemency Carter, vibrant of mind and of spirit.*

The small graveyard had multiplied of late, the fatal triumvirate of Amery, Kit and Percy now lying in hallowed ground, gone to their eternal rest. John Lavington was broken at the news of his son's death, and for him she felt a deep pity. Enough tragedy had befallen this beautiful corner of America of late. Surely, she hoped, that was enough.

Governor Winthrop had come from Hartford, bringing Daniel

with him, and it was perhaps only the comfort of her son that kept Mercia alive through those dark days. Over and again she saw the moment in her mind, the recoil of the gun, the shock on Percy's face, how he tumbled backwards over the waterfall's edge to join his false accomplice in his grave. There had been no choice, she knew, Nicholas knew, Nathan knew, the whole town in its guilt and its grief knew, but for herself, she would say that there had been a choice, that she could have saved him if she had realised sooner, and she felt a deep and painful guilt that would not go away. She would see Percy's startled face for a long time in her dreams, waking and asleep, of that she was certain. Never again, she told herself that day, would she allow herself to become close to anyone, for she always lost them, she always blamed herself, right or wrong, and she would not allow that to go on.

So when Nathan came to comfort her, she brushed him away. She knew deep down how she loved him, desperately and without hope, for she could never let herself show it, even though he loved her, desperately and with hope, and she longed for the life where they could share his farm and her manor house, raising Daniel together, perhaps with a sister or brother, but she tore that from her mind because she knew, there in Meltwater, that it must never be.

Nicholas saw her pain and read her thoughts; he argued with her, tried to convince her she was wrong, that the barriers she had thrown up were barriers of the mind that she could overcome as surely as she overcame the tragedies of real life. But she shook her head, begging him to desist from his words. She could be honest with him, because he was but her manservant, and perhaps, one day, her friend, but never anything more, and so as she turned from Nathan, because she loved him so much, she drew closer to Nicholas, because he was a man with whom love would never be.

Nathan tried, so very hard, to get close. He talked with her, he waited beside her when she did not want to speak, he held out his hand to touch her with the comfort of his warmth, but she edged away, no emotion on her face, knowing she could never give him what he wanted – what she wanted – because she would lose him as surely as she had lost everyone else: her father, her brother, her friends.

He saw her sorrow, but he could not understand it. He wanted to help, but she would not let him in. Then one morning, a beautiful day in a pine-scented meadow under the bluest of skies, he came to her while she was sitting beneath a tree, watching Daniel playing in the dew-filled field.

He sat beside her, and he made her hold his hands.

'Mercia,' he began. 'You know I love you.'

She closed her eyes.

'And I know, I hope, that you love me too. And I know you are sad, and in a deep melancholy. I know you want to shut out the world and live in your head.'

An involuntary tear dropped to her cheek. He reached across to brush it away.

'I think, perhaps, you are scared of the feelings inside you, but I hope, my beautiful Mercia, that you can let me in.'

Her chest began to heave, and the tears began to flow.

'All I ask is that you let me help, because I love you.' He squeezed her hands tight. 'Mercia, I love you with all my life. Please, Mercia, open your eyes and look at me?'

She did as he asked, although she did not want to.

'That's better.' He smiled. 'I know you think you will feel this way forever, but I promise that you will not. Not everyone has left you. Nobody ever really did. They are all still there, in your heart.' A tear fell down his own cheek. 'But I am here now.' He gripped her hands harder. 'Feel me, Mercia. Feel the life and the warmth, here, right now. I know it will be hard, but I can help. I want so much to help.'

The tears dropped from her cheeks onto her dress.

'Mercia, will you marry me?'

The tears stopped. She looked at Nathan and she saw the kindness and the hope in his eyes. She looked inside herself and she saw the fear and the worry for the future. Yes, she told herself, yes, I do want to marry you. But I love you too much to put you at risk. And so I know what the answer must be.

'I cannot,' she said.

His jaw shook. 'Mercia. Please. Remember the happy days we have spent together, and think of the happy days that could lie ahead.'

But she looked at him one more time, suppressing the anguish she felt, and she lightly shook her head.

'I am sorry, Nathan. Too much has happened.' She lowered her head as his grip on her hands loosened. 'Please, do not ask again. I could not bear it.'

He waited a moment, and then he stood, and he nodded, his face trembling as much as hers did not.

'Then I have to go now. Mercia, I want to help, you know how much, but if you will not let me, then I cannot stay with you. You must understand it is too painful.' He took a deep breath. 'And that is why I decided that if you said no, I would not travel back to England with you. It would hurt too much.' His lip shook. 'I want you to know I am going to stay here, in America, unless you change your mind. And if you don't, well, maybe one day we can meet again, and things will be different.' He laughed, an awful, sorry sound. 'The ocean is not that far across. For now, please do something for me. Let yourself live, and let yourself hope, and let my love into your heart, however far away it is, and you will be protected and safe. For I love you, Mercia, and I will never stop.'

And he walked away.

'Today,' she mumbled as he went. For she had listened to his words and a tiny ray of love had nestled in her heart. 'Oh, my love. Today. I cannot marry you today.'

And then she cried, and her son ran to her to find out her troubles, and she held him, feeling an overwhelming love, and she wept out her sorrow until she steeled herself to face whatever would come next.

Nicholas had packed all their things in a cart they would share with Sir William, the great man saved from the mob's wrath by Nathan and Remembrance, hiding him at the Davisons' farmhouse while they waited for the crowd to calm. It would be too late now to gain passage home from New York before winter, but she preferred to wait out the cold in the new possession of the English than in the Puritan town tainted by death. She planned to slip away without much fuss, but when she left Hopewell's cottage for the last time, turning the corner at the meeting house to walk south past the smithy and Lavington's grand house, she passed through the gate, unadorned by any head, to be received by a line of well-wishers, keen to say goodbye.

The town had descended into reproachful silence after the events of that night, ashamed as individuals and as a whole by their actions. When she had returned to the bonfire with Nicholas, in her angst she had collapsed, raving about Percy; and Godsgift Brown, more composed, had ordered Fearing and Vic to the waterfall in response to Nicholas's adamant pleas. They had returned with a body, Amery, leaving Kit for the moment with Percy at the base of the falls, and Renatus, constant, had stood on the rock in the field, comforting the people as Percy had inflamed them. Since that day, Richard Thorpe had already left, saved from the fire by the townsfolk's hesitation, as they waited for orders that would never come. Too bruised to remain, he had finally found reason to leave his wife's grave, gone to the east to make a new home.

Now, the morning of her departure, Vic walked up, a horseshoe he had made in his hand, and he bowed his head as he passed it across, a present, he said, for her time among them. But his words, and the faces of the others who mumbled farewell or nodded goodbye, were tinged with shame and with sadness, and in truth she wondered whether the town could endure in the face of its loss. But if any folk could do it, it would be these pioneers who had braved so much already to live as they wished in the American wilds.

She reached the end of the line, unsure if she hoped to see Nathan, but then as she was turning to clamber onto her horse, Nicholas tapped her shoulder, and she looked back to see him running across the field, skidding to a halt as he reached her. Her heart leapt, and she wondered if he would change his mind and come with her, but she pushed the hope down, not wanting it. Not yet.

His face feigned brightness, but she could tell it hid his grief.

'I could not let you leave without saying goodbye. I had thought it might be easier not to, but I had to see you.' He looked at her and pulled her close. 'Had to hold you once again.' He breathed in deeply, squeezing her tight. 'I love you, Mercia Blakewood. I always will. Don't ever forget it. If you need me, I will find you. I swear.'

And then he released her, and she looked at his handsome face, and she managed a small smile.

'I know.'

Daniel pushed forward. 'I wish you were coming with us. Mamma, why is he staying behind?'

She looked at him, his face full of innocence, but not even for that could she change her mind.

'One day I will tell you, and then you will understand. Now, say goodbye.'

'We will see each other again,' said Nathan, ruffling Daniel's hair. Then he turned away, easing Daniel towards his mother, and she knew he could not look because he was too upset to see. So sparing him more sorrow, she swung her son onto her horse, and while Nathan beckoned to Nicholas for a final word, she joined him in the saddle. And so they set off south, leaving Meltwater and her heart behind.

At least, that was, for today.

* * *

They rode through the woods, Mercia trying desperately not to think about Nathan. It was the right thing, she knew, to refuse him. And it was his choice to stay if he wished. In time, he would learn to live without her, and maybe Remembrance Davison would make him a good wife. But still . . .

Up ahead, a woman stepped out onto the path. Sir William cried out, startled, but Mercia recognised her well enough. Her right arm was covered in bruises, her face with healing cuts, but she was whole, and she was alive.

'Sooleawa,' she said. 'I did not think to see you again.'

The Indian woman approached. 'We heard you were leaving. The *sachem* wanted me to come and say goodbye. And to thank you.'

'The *sachem*?'

Sooleawa smiled. 'And me also. I am sorry events came between us. But I am not sorry for what I did. The honour of my tribe is satisfied. As is the young woman's from many years ago.' She paused. 'My mother.'

Mercia steadied her anxious horse. 'Is it true what you said about Godsgift?'

'It is. The young woman . . . my mother – she loved him. She fell pregnant with his child, but he abandoned her. Or so my aunt said, after my brother – his son – fell last year in battle, and she was freed from the promise she had made to hide the truth. But now I have seen the lies that can divide a people apart, I do not know. Perhaps there is more to find out. He changed his name to forget about his past. I wonder why.'

'I hope 'tis for a better reason than Kit did. And I hope you can find peace, Sooleawa. I think you saved our lives at the waterfall. Thank you.'

She stroked the horse's mane. 'There has been too much death of late. It is time to let the spirits go to the south-west and be satisfied.'

'So Godsgift is safe?'

She smiled, the feathered arrows in the quiver across her back shaking in the breeze.

'Perhaps.'

And then she plunged into the woods, returning the way she had come.

As they continued, Nicholas fell in alongside her.

'That was good of her,' he said. 'A brave woman, all told.'

'That she is,' said Mercia. 'As we must be now.'

He looked at her askance. 'What of Dixwell and the rest? Whalley and Goffe?'

'I do not know. The reverend who is hiding them will be in charge now, and they have other friends. Winthrop, too, will help them. But they will be distraught to learn the truth.'

'Did you not want to see them again?'

'I cannot. Not with Sir William riding with us. No, 'tis better if I stay away. At least I can see Winthrop once more before we return to New York.'

They rode a short while in silence, until she asked the question she had been hoping to resist.

'What did he say?'

'Who?'

She looked at him.

He sighed. 'I know you have told me to stop asking, but I don't know why this is happening.'

'Because it must. Because I will lose him, as much as I have lost everyone else.'

'But Mercia, you have lost him already if you let him stay.'

'Just tell me what he said.'

He raised an eyebrow. 'That I had better take damn good care of you, or he would find me out and hunt me for the rest of my days.'

She smiled. 'Anything else?'

'That he hoped I would find someone I could love as much as he loves you.'

She reined in the horse, drawing to a sudden halt.

Nicholas lingered up ahead, waiting for her to decide what to do.

Then she looked at her son, and she thought of her house and his future: the reason she had come to America at all. Kicking her horse's flanks, she started up again.

'Come then, *nétop*. Let us go back. Let us begin our long journey back home.'

Historical Note

Throughout *Puritan*, I have used the term 'Indian', among other such references, to reflect terms the colonists themselves would have known. In the modern day, 'American Indian' or 'Native American' are commonly used, but neither is universally accepted. Regardless of terminology, it is important to note that the multiple American Indian Nations have never been a homogenous entity, each enjoying distinct identities, traditions and dialects of their own.

I have been filled with immense awe in writing of the colonists of seventeenth-century New England. That these pioneers had the courage to travel the ocean to start a new life is bravery enough; that they remained in their new home in the face of disease, hardship and conflict, astounds and humbles me. That so many tried to coexist peacefully with their American Indian neighbours is a shining mark on their humanity; that so many did not, a terrible blot.

In 1664, when this novel is set, the land we know today as the United States of America was almost a total unknown to the Europeans spreading into its embrace. When Percy asserts he has no idea what lies westwards, he is speaking truly. And yet just forty-four years after the landing of the *Mayflower*, five separate colonies had emerged in New England: Connecticut, where *Puritan* is based; Massachusetts Bay; New Haven; Rhode Island; and Plymouth. Representatives from four of these (but not the heretical Rhode Island!) were convening at a pan-New England council to consider issues of common interest. Although separate, Virginia further south was an older territory still, and the royal conquest of New York was assimilating land previously held by the Dutch. As New Haven was subsumed into Connecticut, so Plymouth would some years later merge with Massachusetts. The political geography of the modern eastern seaboard was fast being shaped.

Already by the 1660s, a great number of towns spanned the New England wilderness. Unlike the Roanoke failure of the previous century, these settlers were here to stay. Many made homes on cleared American Indian land that the native population thought to loan or share, rather than sell for good. Communities founded on Puritan zeal centred around their meeting house, a simple, communal structure used for religious worship and town hall debate. Farmers worked the land, artisans crafted goods, preachers carried the Gospel within and beyond the town. I may have stretched the limits of authenticity at times, such as in relaxing the strict rules governing taverns, but the fictional Meltwater is infused with the spirit of these women and men. Their unusual names are reflected in those of the townsfolk, the much earlier trend for Latinised names (Renatus) long since given way to plain English traits (Clemency, Perseverance), attitudes to God and morality (Fearing, Remembrance), hopes for the future (Victory) or recognitions of the past (Seaborn), mixed in with more traditional names such as Richard and John.

One of five historical figures in this book, John Winthrop Jr, was a hugely respected figure across New England and beyond. The alchemy he practised was anything but fantasy, taken utterly seriously by those learned men who immersed themselves in its promise. To them, alchemy

410

was nothing short of the means of liberating humankind to a more fruitful existence. That they truly believed in the philosopher's stone and the alkahest may sound remarkable now, but real advances stemmed from Winthrop's research: his wife Elizabeth is not boasting when she talks of his achievements, for he treated many grateful patients with the minerals he refined. His membership of the Royal Society, the newly founded organisation of science and learning, speaks for itself. Yet as to most things, there was a flip side. Many self-styled alchemists were solely motivated by profit, and in general alchemical work was mistrusted by the population. The *monas hieroglyphica*, devised by John Dee in the sixteenth century to reflect the cosmos and the earth, was as much a sign of promise to Winthrop and his like as it was a sign of suspicion to those who feared it could be the harbinger of unnatural magic.

Besides Winthrop and his wife, *Puritan's* other real-life characters are the three regicides Dixwell, Whalley and Goffe. That these men were used by Percy to frame the Royalists and inflame the people is a political fiction for this book, but that they were in the area is anything but. When Charles II was restored to the throne in 1660, he issued orders for the arrest of the several men who had signed his father's death warrant. Those who were not imprisoned or executed had to lie low or flee, often overseas. It is not surprising that Whalley and Goffe, both Puritans themselves, chose to sail to New England. As Percy says, they were initially greeted with open arms, mingling openly with the colonists for whom they were Puritan heroes. But when the King's demands arrived in Boston, they were forced into hiding.

These demands were soon reinforced by the arrival in America of a royal fleet, whose mission was, as readers of *Birthright* know, to seize New Amsterdam from the Dutch and thereby found New York. But the fleet was also instructed to seek out Whalley and Goffe, and so in October 1664, precisely when this novel is set, the two men left their hideout in coastal New Haven to travel north to Hadley, Massachusetts – a route taking them through the vicinity of the fictional Meltwater. John Dixwell is not recorded as journeying with them, but there is a reference to his visiting Hadley the following year. More recently (and more discreetly) arrived than his fellows, Dixwell was, in time, able to live openly in New Haven under his pseudonym of James Davids, indeed marrying and having children. Not so fortunate, Goffe and Whalley were to remain in hiding for the rest of their lives, except for one day in 1675, maybe 1676 (the sources are not clear), when legend tells of a man who appeared from nowhere to lead Hadley's defence against an Indian attack . . . the Angel of Hadley, supposedly – on this occasion – William Goffe.

Evidently, religion was a matter of utmost importance to the Puritans (not, incidentally, a term they would have preferred for themselves). The persecution of their beliefs was the factor that drove them to the New World in the first place. While migration to America slowed over the Cromwell years, the restoration of Charles II gave rise back in Britain to a heightened political nervousness and worries for renewed civil war. Many people, regardless of denomination, were ever more certain the Second Coming of Christ was near. A millennial fervour had been developing through the century, a conviction that Christ would descend from heaven to cast out the unworthy and herald a thousand years of peace. Groups like the Fifth Monarchists, to which Kit's brother belonged, took instruction from the prophesies in the Books of Daniel and Revelation, believing the recent civil wars to be a foretold necessity for the so-called Rule of the Saints. The Restoration shook that belief, and they rose up against the new King. Yet few were prepared to turn words into deeds, and they were slaughtered as they made their stand. In New England, the religious ardour of the first immigrants was dimming in the next generation, but passions could still be firmly aroused. Until the 1660s, only the children of those believers who could claim a genuine conversion experience were permitted baptism. The Half-Way Covenant easing this restriction was the fierce religious question of their day.

Colonial–Indian relations were yet more fraught. Fuelled by suspicion and misunderstanding, intolerant attitudes like Godsgift Brown's were all too commonplace. By the time of this novel, it is estimated that possibly ninety per cent of the pre-Columbian population of America had died of diseases against which they had no natural immunity. The diminished groups that survived were often harried from their lands and treated with contempt. At times, skirmishes and arguments descended into full-scale conflict: the Pequot War, from which stems the story of Sooleawa's quest for vengeance, is an early, bloodstained example. Eleven years after the events of this book, the long and violent King Philip's War was to be the defining conflict of the American seventeenth century, when the Nations united in a failed attempt to take back all they had lost, a struggle Sooleawa predicts before the fire of Hopewell's cottage.

And yet others took a more compassionate view. Where I have used American Indian words, as in chapters one or twelve, I have consulted a captivating book of the period: Roger Williams's *A Key into the Language of America*, a detailed phrase book embellished by the author's descriptions of everyday living and manners; an author, besides, who urges harmony over war and who made great efforts to live peaceably alongside his neighbours. His religious platitudes aside, Williams's book is a remarkable document full of observation and wonder. And for me, it is a beautiful notion indeed that I can have the same book on my writing desk as Mercia carried in her saddlebag when she braved the American wilderness three and a half centuries ago.